BOOKS BY STANLEY WOLPERT

Fiction

ABOARD THE FLYING SWAN

NINE HOURS TO RAMA

THE EXPEDITION

Nonfiction

TILAK AND GOKHALE

INDIA

MORLEY AND INDIA, 1906–1910

THE
EXPEDITION

THE EXPEDITION

a novel by

Stanley Wolpert

Little, Brown and Company · Boston · Toronto

Published simultaneously in Canada
by Little, Brown & Company (Canada) Limited

PRINTED IN THE UNITED STATES OF AMERICA

to
the memory of
Allen Guberman
who led a great expedition

THE
EXPEDITION

CHAPTER 1

HODGE raced up the front steps of the Georgian mansion two at a stride. He had never felt better, more elated. All of London shone with a brilliance and clarity that September morning, which seemed cosmically to reflect his personal state of mind. He had walked to the Club from the Savoy without once breaking his pace. Even the traffic signals appeared to understand that nothing could stop Roger McNeill today. The expedition he had conceived of four years ago, and worked on with painstaking devotion and unflagging energy ever since, was about to be launched. He felt like a thoroughbred who had just taken his last hurdle, and was galloping in the clear toward the finish tape. He passed through the open outer door, and crossed the foyer, without bothering to greet the butler. But the inner door was locked. With his hand frozen on the unyielding knob, Hodge was brought to a disturbingly sudden halt.

"What name, sir?"

"McNeill," Hodge snapped, but seeing that his name evoked no glimmer of recognition in the servant, he was obliged to add, "Sir Charles Baker is expecting me for lunch."

"Oh, yes. Of course, sir. Please go right in, Mr. McNeill." The butler smiled with the sweet civility of a well-trained mastiff, and finally pressed the buzzer, which released the locked door.

Entering the rogues' gallery of the Club's carpeted hallway, Hodge became uncomfortably conscious of his past. For that moment he felt almost like a peddler, an interloper, a medieval serf graciously granted permission to step into the drawing room of the manor. It was the sort of déclassé sensation he never felt in more elegant places like the Savoy or Claridge's, for, however imposing their éclat, it was for sale, after all, part of the open marketplace, available by reservation in advance. Yet if he lived to be a hundred, Hodge knew, he could never become a member of this Club. You were born to that, or you died without it. There was nothing more disturbing to Hodge than the idea of exclusion by birth.

He glanced irately at the smug faces of the deceased members, whose portraits hung like weapons in a castle corridor, tilting forward as though ready to topple on the head of any intruder. In less than six months their heirs would be flattered to shake his hand! They might even offer to amend their idiot rules to invite him to join their fraternity. He would have no part of it. The shabby gentility of this atmosphere oppressed Hodge. The faded velvet on the high-backed chairs along the wall was as threadbare as the Persian carpet beneath his feet. In the four years since last he'd been here for lunch, nothing had changed. It would be like living in a roped-off room of a museum, he decided.

To the left of the palatial stairway at the far end of the hall was the library drawing room, where members received their guests. A blazing fire gave a warm glow to the dull crimson silk that covered the windowless walls of the drawing room. There were oval rugs scattered upon the carpet before deep leather chairs, on each of which was a fur blanket for rheumatoid knees. A room to die in, Hodge thought.

"Ah, here you are, McNeill! Splendid," wheezed Sir Charles, pushing himself out of a corner chair, leaving his lap rug to fall, leaning heavily on his gnarled cane as he hobbled forward.

"It's good of you to see me on such short notice, Sir Charles."

"Nonsense, lad. I'm delighted to learn of your good fortune." He loomed over Hodge like the cornice of some great glacier, precariously poised, yet defying the elements of time and gravity by the remarkable solidity of his substance. His full beard was glacially white, and the top of his head shone as smoothly as translucent ice. His handshake was as strong as Hodge remembered it, like the clasp of a crampon.

"So you've got your backing, have you?"

"Yessir, and the permit too! That came with this morning's mail." Hodge said it with all the exuberance of a schoolboy informing his parents that he'd just skipped a grade. It was the way he'd felt when he won his pilot's wings, twenty years ago. Surprisingly enough, Hodge realized that in all the forty-five years of his life this virtual stranger was really the first person he'd ever been able to rush to with good news. His foster parents came to mind and he remembered how his "father" would warn, "Don't blow your own horn, boy! You gotta learn t'be more humble."

"The permit too, eh? Well, lad, you have made progress since our little chat last year — "

"That was four years ago, Sir Charles."

"Was it four? Ah, but it doesn't seem that long since I've addressed the Society," he mused, staring vacantly over Hodge's head.

"Almost four and a half years, in fact. I'll never forget that day, sir — May seventeenth, the most important date of my life." He'd stopped over in London for a week then on his way back to India to explore the prospects of oil refining in Bengal, and accepted the invitation of an old R.A.F. friend to attend a meeting of the Asiatic Society at which Sir Charles Baker was to talk about the subject he knew best, Nepalese natural life. The lecture sounded as dull at first as the topic, but Hodge had gone to make new "India-hand" contacts, and resigned himself to sitting patiently. Baker began discussing the Yeti, and by the time he stopped talking, Hodge had found a new purpose in life.

"And it's all thanks to you, Sir Charles," he said, feeling magnanimous in his good fortune and in the realization of the fame he would reap before another year elapsed.

"No, I can't take credit for what you've done, McNeill. Must have been fifty others heard me say what you did that night, but none of them has tried finding him. They still think he's a myth, I expect, the figment of primitive superstition or inflamed imagination. Others dismiss him as an inconsequential ape."

Hodge knew all too well what most people thought of the Yeti. Despite his own fascination at the challenge of capturing this unconquered Snowman of the Himalayas, even after his first luncheon conversation with Sir Charles, he'd remained skeptical for almost a year. There had been no time for him to do research into Yeti lore until after his oil-prospecting venture collapsed. Only during his return visit to London could he pore over the literature. It was then that he studied reports of the *Daily Mail*'s expedition, the books of Shipton, Izzard, and Sanderson, the journals of Schaefer, and accounts left by Bury, Newman, Visser. He read every line of print he could find containing the slightest reference to an Abominable Snowman, Meh-Teh, Yeh-Teh, or Yeti. He had even traced literary references to the "Red-Haired One" as far back as the Old Testament, troubling biblical scholars with questions they could not answer about Jacob and Esau. He peered at every photograph of the tracks preserved at the British Museum, and talked with naturalists, zoologists, and anthropologists at a dozen universities. He corresponded with scientists and explorers around the world before embarking full time on the job of planning his expedition, compiling his lists of possible backers, potential teammates, and provisions. But it was the financial support he needed that had almost forced Hodge to abandon his dream For twenty-eight months he struggled to convince private philanthropists, and the directors or employees of foundations, government agencies, and scientific societies throughout the world that Yetis were worth risking a million dollars to find.

"I've learned there's no prejudice on earth, Sir Charles, that's stronger than confirmed ignorance."

"I expect it's more fear than ignorance, lad. The fear of probing too deep into the origin of our species, don't you think? Of finding ourselves too nakedly revealed, eh? Perhaps it's more comforting not to believe that there is someone closer to ourselves than any beast, wandering up there, alone —" his voice trailed off. He seemed remote suddenly, and sadder than Hodge had ever seen him. Then stirring his craggy frame, he muttered, "Come along, we'd best get on to the dining room."

Light flooded the high windows of the spacious room. Only two of the many round mahogany tables were occupied, by aged members eating alone. The waiter greeted Sir Charles with that easy admixture of familiarity and solicitude, which distinguished the service at the best of clubs as well as restaurants, escorting them to his table under the portrait of George III.

"Tomato soup this afternoon, Sir Charles — your favorite. Shall I bring you the bowl?"

"No, I couldn't manage the bowl. He will. He's a young man,

you see. Bring him the bowl — a cup will do nicely for me. Now then, McNeill," he said, tucking his napkin biblike under his beard, "you haven't told me about your teammates."

"I don't actually have a team at the moment. My backer has just confirmed his support, and —"

"Who is he?"

"Tony Judson — Judson Foundation. You've probably never heard of him. Runs a chain of western American enterprises. The foundation was only set up two years ago."

"Never mind. As long as he has the money, eh? But surely you've thought of some names for your team?"

"Oh, I've done more than that," Hodge replied. For it was true that he had compiled dossiers on some thirty climber-explorers from five nations. He knew them all personally. The list had shrunk somewhat during the past two years, of course. Several of his first choices died in falls, others were committed to expeditions elsewhere. Nonetheless, his list remained far larger than the team he could afford. Hodge merely waited for official permission from the government of Nepal to hunt for Yeti before sending his cables. "This morning I wired the four men who have top priority on my list. I should hear very soon . . ."

"But that's only five with yourself, lad! No, that's not enough."

"It's spare," Hodge admitted, "but I want to keep our weight down so that we can fly to Kathmandu from Delhi, and even just the five of us will need over a ton of provisions."

"Yes. Well, of course, when I was in Kathmandu they walked in, you know. I watched them all, lad. Watched them come, and saw them go. Over thirty years I was there. Many a brave man has tried it before you, McNeill. They all failed. Wouldn't want that to happen to you."

"It won't. If I can get the team I've sent for today, I think the five of us will be as strong —" he felt like saying stronger "— experiencewise in climbing and hunting, as any ten man team."

Feeling as good as he did today, the slightest insinuation of doubt concerning the viability of his plan angered Hodge intensely. Not that he'd ever been tolerant of disagreement. "I suppose a hundred men would stand even a better chance of finding him, or a thousand, for that matter! The economics of the thing *is* a factor,

Sir Charles, and I'm more concerned about the quality of my men than numbers. I expect I could find him alone right now, but I'd need help bringing him back."

"Oh, no, lad! Don't tackle him alone."

He sounded so alarmed that Hodge could not resist asking, "Weren't you ever tempted to try him yourself, Sir Charles?"

"Of course I was tempted." His milky eyes stared anxiously toward the ceiling. "It's the one thing I really wanted — that I never could do."

"Why not, sir? You were there."

"Too many commitments. Too many crises, you see! Too many cables from Simla and London. For years I was our only man in Nepal, and . . ."

He became so agitated that his hands trembled. As he paused, groping for other excuses, Hodge quickly injected, "I understand perfectly what you mean, Sir Charles. I'm sure you were much too busy."

"No, it wasn't that. It was none of those reasons." He looked down at his gnarled fingers, all but frozen with age. "It was cowardice, McNeill. I kept postponing it — one year because of weather, the next because I couldn't assemble enough men, you see." His smile was gentle, ineffably sad. "I lacked your courage, lad. I was afraid of the curse."

He referred, Hodge knew, to the Sherpa superstition that anyone who saw a Yeti close enough to look into his eyes would die almost instantly. It was so clearly absurd a myth of the unarmed and uneducated that Hodge was amazed to hear this confession of credulity from a man of Baker's scientific renown and worldly experience.

"You don't believe it anymore, do you, sir?"

"No, certainly not. I'd almost believed it of Everest too once, you see. Living among those people so long, seeing so many of the Sherpas who actually died shortly after reporting they'd seen him, you know. They would fall into a sort of delirium. We'd call it madness, of course, but somehow while I was still there in Kathmandu —" He shook his head wearily, and sighed. "Oh, it wouldn't stop me now. It's one thing growing old has taught me: to regret what I haven't done."

"But you've done so much." Hodge recalled how impressed he had been four years ago when he looked up Baker in *The International Who's Who* and found a long paragraph in small type, listing his titles, honors, clubs, and positions in the Empire.

"No, it's what we haven't done that we remember with age. You're right, lad, never mind the size of your team. Go to it!"

"Thank you, sir." Hodge felt buoyed again by the wave of triumphant self-assurance which had carried him here.

"And if there's anything I can do to help . . . ?"

It was the one question Hodge had hoped this meeting with Baker would evoke. He tried not to answer it too eagerly, saying, "You've done so much already . . . but I really don't know anyone in Kathmandu. If you could possibly suggest someone I might call upon there to help me find a good sirdar and porters . . ."

"Mmm, yes." Sir Charles toyed with his beard. "Let's see. Most of the people I knew are gone now, unfortunately . . ." He pondered it silently.

"Excuse me, sir," interrupted the waiter. "You did want the lamb?" He held the prepared plate suspended in front of Sir Charles, distracting him just when Hodge sensed he was about to come up with a name or two.

"What? Yes — that's lovely. Give him some of that, too. And let my young friend have a glass of red wine. He'll enjoy that."

Hodge was so annoyed by the waiter's inopportune interruption, that he felt like saying he would prefer being permitted to order for himself. He simmered silently, wondering if Sir Charles would remember his request, or if he would have to repeat it at the risk of sounding too eager.

"Now tell me about your battle plan, lad," Sir Charles said, digging into his meat. "Where will you establish your base camp, eh?"

"I've thought of Namche —"

"Not high enough. Best push up to Tyangboche. You'll be nearer his stomping grounds there."

It was useful advice, but Hodge needed the names of people in Nepal, not places.

"And there's a monastery at Pangboche —"

"Where they have a Yeti scalp," Hodge injected. He became restless as well as resentful at what might turn out to be nothing more than a waste of his valuable time in exchanging pleasantries and platitudes with this rambling relic. Provisions were still to be ordered, travel arrangements completed. He could not afford to expend another hour in idle conversation.

"Yes, that's where they keep the scalp. You must have a look at it. Ask the abbot. He was quite young, and most cooperative when I knew him — Father Nyima. Tell him Dawa Sahib sent you. I first arrived at the monastery on a Monday, you see, so they called me Dawa Sahib. It's the only name I'm known by there at Pangboche. Curious, but I've often thought about that . . ." He sounded almost incoherent as he reflected upon the relativity of identity, the illusory nature of life. Then Hodge heard him say ". . . and I suppose I should give you a letter of introduction to Mandeva, shouldn't I?"

"*General* Mandeva?" Hodge was jolted to attention by that name. "Did you know him, sir?" He had hardly raised his sights to Mandeva's eminence when he thought of calling on Baker today.

"I've known him since he was a boy, you see. Knew his father also. Interesting chap, Mandeva. Brightest man in Nepal I should say, most capable at any rate, but terribly ambitious. Rather enjoys his power. Strange fascination power seems to have for bright people, wouldn't you agree, McNeill?"

Hodge had the uncomfortable suspicion that Baker was toying with him as though he were catnip. He felt that those milky eyes peered past the bland and genial polish of his clean-cut all-American boyish features, past his smooth suntan and the slick crew-cut hair bristling with gray at his temples, probing to the innermost convolutions of his brain, to the almost feverish ambition to accomplish what no man in history had. He was going to find the most elusive human on earth, and bring him back, dead or alive, in the flesh or on film, for all mankind to study and see. He would do what no scientific genius, no hunter, no explorer, no soldier of fortune had ever done. His earlier dreams paled by comparison with this one; the inventions he never completed, the schemes never brought quite fully to fruition, the fortune that had always somehow eluded his grasp. It no longer bothered Hodge that he hadn't been considered good enough for outer-space flight. He saw that rejection of five years ago now as the luckiest washout of his life.

The sky was full of anonymous jerks in orbit! He was going to achieve something unique. The name McNeill would be added to the list that began with Columbus and went up through Lindbergh to Hillary. The bastard from Nebraska, whose parents didn't think him worth keeping, would become a household hero throughout America, an inspiration to generations of boys unborn.

Hodge returned Baker's stare without flinching, without wavering. He was not ashamed to let Sir Charles see how he felt, to admit to him or anyone that fame and power, insatiable ambition, hunger of every sort, motivated him as much as any abstract desire to further the cause of science, or deepen the roots of man's understanding of himself. His idealism was as practical as his dream was now fully realizable.

"I'd be most grateful, Sir Charles, if you would give me a letter to Mandeva."

"Yes, of course I will, but come let's finish our meal. You'll enjoy the raspberry tarts. They're a special formula of our club."

They returned to the drawing room for coffee, and Sir Charles wrote his letter at the antique desk. His hand was halting, Hodge noticed, but discretion kept him at the distance of the fireplace, from which he could not read the introduction. Nor did Baker offer to show Hodge what he had written before sealing the envelope.

"Here you are, lad. Good luck."

Sir Charles held his hand in the crampon grip for a long moment of silence.

"Be careful, McNeill," he added at last.

Then he let go.

CHAPTER 2

SETH Goodman climbed above the timberline, reaching a plateau of stone just as the sun's slanting rays cut through the cloud bank to burnish the barren rocks about him. The air was cool, sweet as the nectar of the sugar cane he had cut below and crunched in his teeth as he climbed. His world seemed golden as he stood surveying horizons pure as the dawn of creation. Exhilarated, he stared at the setting sun, feeling almost as light as a bird who had flown to this eagle's perch, almost capable now of flying out across the jungled valley. He wanted to shout, "I am free!"

The peremptory buzz, signaling closing time, rang through the reading room of the British Museum, jolting Seth from his semi-somnolence, dragging him in distressing haste back to the weighty periodical volumes stacked mausoleumlike on his desk. He blinked at the clock. A quarter of five! Another day buried! Returning his books, he tucked his briefcase under one arm, buttoned his jacket, and hurried in unprofessorial haste from the room.

On the pillared portico of the museum, bright rectangles of sky beckoned beyond the fluted columns of soot-blackened stone, like doorways through a prison wall. The freshness of London's September breeze welcomed him, and Seth felt less morbid. If only the visas would come, he could take Stella and Ethan to the airport tonight. By morning they would all be in India! He could get on to his fieldwork in Orissa then, pursuing the project he'd planned for his sabbatical, instead of killing more time dredging through dry literary sources in London libraries. If a hippopotamus had wings he'd be a pelican! His momentary euphoria departed.

An exhaust-belching bus parked in front of the museum steps, leaving its motor running, as a phalanx of camera-armed tourists marched toward him, grimly prepared for their pilgrimage to the Elgin Marbles. A class of blue-capped schoolboys raced bare-kneed from the lobby, pushing past Seth as he started across the yard toward the traffic streaming along Great Russell Street. He should have known better than to believe the Indian attaché in Washington, who assured him the visas would be waiting here by the time they reached London. He knew enough about faith in reincarnation to understand the casual Indian attitude toward time.

Or was it just that?

The fear, which lurked unacknowledged in his mind, like a malignant growth, suspected but ignored, roiled with paralyzing swiftness to the surface of Seth's consciousness, making him stop before he reached the sidewalk gate. What if the visas never came?

Distractedly, his fingers fumbled about in the baggy pockets of his jacket, removing a crushed pack of cigarettes, hastily lighting one. It wasn't possible — was it? He was an anthropologist, after all, not a political scientist. He'd never given a damn about politics. He inwardly cringed at the memory of those beefy-handed politicians who invaded his father's store in Brooklyn before each election. *Ganefs,* his father called them. Surely the Indian government wouldn't blackball me, he thought. Yet four years ago, on his last trip to India, he'd received the visa months before he left home. Then, in Assam, it was renewed for a second year without delay. He'd been almost as friendly with Indian officials as he had with the village peasants, among whom he lived. He'd gone home to write his study on *Social Change in the North Eastern Frontier Provinces — Acculturation or Extermination?* which the University Press had published last year. Anyone who read the book knew it was just a scholarly monograph, not an attack against the Indian government. Hell, they can't blackball me for that, he thought.

The visor-capped guard at the front gate eyed him suspiciously as he approached.

"So long," Seth said, smiling in his melancholy way, half raising his arm in a gesture of salutation. Passing the same man every day for three weeks it seemed only human to offer at least this minimal recognition, but the guard remained stoically silent as usual, nodding his head as if his neck were sprained, and staring suspiciously at Seth's briefcase. All the warmth of civilized society in that face, he thought, hunching his shoulders as he trudged along the sidewalk beside the museum's wall. He felt more weary now than after ten hours on the trail with a forty pound pack. He could walk for weeks over country as rugged as the Shillong Plateau, climb for days on rock piles as barren as the moon, and never feel this sort of strain, or fatigue. The first summer he lived on his uncle's farm in the Berkshires, he walked down along the mill brook, past the pine grove, on over a pasture of clover, across rolling meadows, till it was sundown, and he couldn't remember the way back. He just lay on moist grass then, and counted stars till he fell asleep. It was a sleep of peace, of calm contentment with nature. It had never occurred to him to be afraid, till he heard the hounds barking and saw his uncle standing over him with a flashlight, the rusty pitchfork firm in his hands.

The blare of a taxi horn!

Seth jumped back onto the curb as a cortege of funereally black cabs rolled over the asphalt on which he'd stood a second earlier. He kept forgetting to look right when he crossed London streets. Life was far less dangerous among the "headhunters" of Assam. Essentially what he'd concluded in his monograph; that the villagers were better off before urban industrialization came to destroy the balance of traditional self-sufficiency, before government with its "help" came to sap the wellsprings of local communal life. The tribals and peasants among whom he'd lived were dying off at an alarmingly high rate wherever modernization intruded to civilize their lives. Not from disease or lack of food, since there was less of the former, and more of the latter. They seemed simply to lose attachment to life. He'd only reported what he observed. Surely they wouldn't deny him another visa for that?

Yet the more he thought about it, the less sanguine Seth became of his prospects of returning to India. When he had applied for his research grant and sabbatical leave, rented his house, purchased his plane tickets, brought his family to London, he had done it on the assumption that the government of India would welcome him back. The possibility of not being permitted to return to the tribes and villages, where he felt more at home than he did on his own campus, was too terrifying to contemplate. His fieldwork had become the only meaningful portion of life. The rest of his time was the fallow between plantings, the intermission between acts. As teacher and scholar he repaid society for these hours of freedom. That was his personal bargain with life, the compromise contract he managed to negotiate after thirty-seven years of attrition and frustration. Once he had sworn eternal battle against compromise of any sort, but time eroded him. Or as Stella put it, he'd "matured."

Seth opened the front door of the shabby "bed and breakfast" building off Russell Square. Entering the musty hallway, he shuddered at the prospect of finding himself trapped here. The stairs groaned under the weariness of his weight.

Coming up to the third-floor landing, he heard a soprano voice: "Bang, bang! You're dead!"

"Ugh, they got me," he whispered, clutching his briefcase against his stomach and collapsing onto the stairway.

"Not *really*, Dad! It's me," Ethan called.

"Ah, that's a relief," he said, rising and smiling at his son, who stood waiting with six-shooters drawn, the red cowboy hat pushed off his forelock of golden hair. He was tall and slim, looking at least six, rather than four.

"Hi, Ethan," Seth said, bending to kiss his son's cheek.

"Hi, Dad. Didja bring anything for me?"

"Just myself."

"I missed you, Dad. Can you take me for a boat ride tomorrow?"

"We'll see. Where's Mom?"

"Reading."

As usual, Seth thought. He held Ethan's hand, and walked more slowly toward their room at the end of the top floor. The door was open a crack, and entering the suitcase-cluttered bed–sitting room, they found Stella propped against the pillows on the high, heavily quilted bed, reading a paperback.

"Hi, Stell. Tired?"

"Sort of," she replied, still distracted by the book, which she turned face down on the quilt, reluctant it seemed to abandon her reading simply to welcome her husband home. "Get a lot done today?"

"Not much," he said, sounding as listless as she did, falling with alarming ease into the lethargic pattern of their habitual meaningless exchange, which of later comprised the bulk of their daily dialogue. It had taken ten years of marriage to reach this state of vapid conversation yet it was not hard to recall those early years when Stella would often engage him in a duel of wits. She once wanted to hear about every detail of his day's activity, what he'd read, whom he saw, the things he'd thought about. She had really seemed to care about things he often found trivial or dull, but how dimly distant that time seemed now.

"Where'd you and Ethan go today?" he asked, trying to sound exuberant.

"Trafalgar Square," she muttered. It was where they had gone yesterday and the day before. She stared vacantly at the dirt-stained window that faced a row of rooftops crowded with narrow chimney pipes, rising like gun muzzles from the block of houses across the court. Since the miscarriage eight months ago she had stopped bothering about her appearance. Her hair lay lank, carelessly tucked behind her ears. She used no makeup or perfume, and looked much older than twenty-eight. Seth hoped this trip might rejuvenate her spirits. He still felt guilty about not having been able to take her the last time, when she had remained at home for two years with Ethan.

"I thought you were planning to try one of those boat rides down the Thames," he said, going to sit beside her on the bed, taking her hand between his own.

"Ethan likes to feed the pigeons," she replied.

"Aw, I wish we could go for a boat ride!"

"Don't whine," she snapped.

"But — gosh, Dad says —"

"And don't you talk to me in that fresh tone of voice, young man. Now go and play in the hall. Your father's too tired to listen to your impertinence!"

"I don't mind . . ." Seth began.

"Well I do! Ever since you left us this morning he's nagged, nagged, nagged at me, and I've got a splitting headache."

Seth locked his jaw, avoiding Ethan's eyes as his son sulked out of the room.

"We better look for a bigger apartment," Seth said.

"I thought we're going to India any day now?"

"So did I, but until those visas come —"

"And how long is *that* going to take?"

"Let me get you some aspirin," he said, using it as an excuse to let go of her hand, to move away from her.

"I just took some."

"Well, maybe I'd better turn on the heat."

"I don't care."

Dropping to his haunches to light the gas burner, he was tempted to ask what she did care about. Other than paperback detective stories. But he no longer challenged Stella with questions. She had carried the child for six months, and when she then miscarried they'd been obliged to perform a hysterectomy "to save her life," as the doctor put it. Seth stared at the fingertips of orange-blue gas slowly spreading a golden glow to the metal grillwork fastened into the old coal fireplace's small opening.

"Professor Goodman, you in there, luv?" called the shrill-voiced landlady, tapping at the door. She peered in before he could answer, oblivious after decades of running a rooming house to all laws of privacy. "Sorry t'bother yer, but they just brought this telegram, and I'm always quick deliverin' telegrams, ya know, since the Blitz an' all. Was yer expectin' somethin' urgent?"

"Yes, we were," he said, taking the telegram eagerly, thanking her as he opened it. "This must be — what the devil — ?"

"Is it trouble, luv?"

"What? Oh, no. It's . . . but don't let us detain you. Sorry you had to trouble about coming up."

"Naw, I does it for all my guests, luv. Service of the 'ouse. Cheerio."

Ethan returned asking, "What is it, Dad?"

"Who's it from?" Stella inquired. "You look as though you've seen a ghost."

He felt like saying it was a ghost. "Hodge McNeill, my old buddy from the Air Force."

"Oh, I remember. The one who does all those fascinating things." She sounded suddenly animated.

"Do I know him, Dad?"

No one knows Hodge, he thought.

"Well, what does he say, Seth? Honestly! Aren't you going to read it to me?"

"What? Oh, yes — sorry. He says: ORGANIZING EXPEDITION NEPAL STOP WANT TO JOIN QUESTION CALL ME ANY HOUR SAVOY HOTEL STOP CHEERS HODGE THE MAC."

"What's a mac, Dad?"

"It's just a nickname I used to call him by. He was Hodge the Mac, and I was Seth the Man. You know," he added lamely, because it sounded so foolish now. But Ethan seemed to like the idea, laughing appreciatively.

"What's an exhibition, Dad?"

"Expedition. It, well it could be most anything, but it's usually when a number of people go off — looking for something."

"Like hide-and-seek?"

"Go back to the hall and play till we're ready for dinner," Stella ordered, "and not another word out of you." She got off the bed so menacingly that Ethan left the room crying.

"Aren't you riding him a bit hard these days, Stell?"

"Yes, darling, but we know what a wicked mother I am," she said, taking the telegram and reading it to herself. "Fascinating! What do you suppose he's up to?"

"No good, if I know Hodge," he snapped, unable to meet the challenge of her sarcasm head on, knowing too well that all arguments over Ethan ended with her trump card — "But I was good enough to care for him all alone for two years, wasn't I?"

"Why do you say that? Didn't you tell me that he thought of sailing a raft across the Pacific before *Kon-tiki?* And wasn't he the one who built that bathysphere out of spare airplane parts? I seem to recall that you once spoke of him as a genius, or was that someone else?"

"No, that was Hodge." He must have spoken of him more than he realized during their first few years of marriage. Which was hardly surprising. Hodge had been his pilot and best friend for almost three years.

"Well, aren't you anxious to find out? Don't you want to call him? Will you please *say* something, Seth?"

"I really haven't got time now to get involved in any of Hodge's crazy schemes."

"How do you know it's crazy? Anyway, I thought all we have plenty of is time! Why are you afraid to call him?"

"What the hell are you talking about? I'm not *afraid* of Hodge."

Yet even as he said it Seth knew there was something of fear to his reticence, less of Hodge perhaps than of all his memory evoked, a world as remote and different from that to which Seth had become accustomed over the past decade, as Orissa was from London. He could no more return to that world than he could turn back the clock to his own twenty-first birthday, which he and Hodge had celebrated in a Calcutta brothel. No more than he wanted to return to the hangover that had followed their orgy. For Hodge, he suspected, that life remained the routine of his peacetime existence, as it had been the wartime interlude of Seth's. Their chance meeting at Calcutta's main station three years ago had convinced Seth of that. Hodge had looked not a day older, and was surrounded by a coterie of admiring Indian rajahs and jeweled women in silk saris. Hodge had pressed him then to join his group for a week on the beach at Puri, whispering something about "a top-secret deal" and "top-drawer women," but Seth managed to escape after one convivial drink, pleading an urgent appointment, asking for a rain check. Still, he wondered how Hodge had found him here, and what sort of expedition he planned to launch.

"Look Stell, if I let Hodge talk me into this — whatever the hell it may be — I might as well forget about accomplishing anything on this year's leave."

"What is he, a hypnotist? A phone call won't commit you to anything, will it?"

"Oh, for Christ's sake, will you lay off?"

"Well, don't do it for me, darling! I'm just so bored in this dreary horrid room that it would seem to me anything on earth would be preferable to what we're doing right now."

"I've got the message," he whispered, gnawing off a strip of thumbnail and spitting it into the glowing grate. "Come on, let's eat. I'll phone Hodge from the restaurant."

CHAPTER 3

PETER Partridge converted his last hundred-franc note into plastic chips, as smooth, round, and treacherous as any woman he had known, and returned to the crowded felt-covered table of fate in the Palais de la Méditerranée, feeling, he suspected, much like Napoleon did when he launched his last cavalry reserves at Waterloo. All or nothing, you blackguards, he thought, kissing each of his first two beauties before placing them neatly on the single numbers about which he had dreamed last night, five and fourteen. This was his fifth visit to the Palais in as many days in Nice. It was the fifth day of the week. His room at the Westminster was on the fifth floor. He had been in love five times. And though he'd started playing five at three o'clock, it was now precisely five. For fourteen he could find no numerological logic (other than the doubling of lucky seven), but fourteen he felt in his guts today. Fourteen was him — it was Peter Partridge as sure as his birthplace was Partridge Green!

Having committed his chips to destiny's ride, Peter pretended to lose interest in them. He turned his back to the table now, a calm and casual observer of the passing parade. The blonde, whose naked left shoulder had arrested his eye the moment he'd entered the casino, was still engrossed in baccarat on the other side of the palatial room. He wasn't sure as yet whether her escort was the portly bald man or the swarthy tall one, who flanked her chair at the table. If the latter, he would probably have to lower his sights to the redhead at his own table. Her limpid eye had more than once focused upon him with that look of unmistakable interest, which used to perplex Peter twenty years ago, but which he understood now too well. Several women said it was his bristling mustache that initially attracted them. Others blamed it on the English cut of his hair, which left the front so long that a few strands kept falling across his eyebrows. Still others defined his charm as the eyebrows themselves, sensuously bushy, provocatively mobile. Whatever it was, he had it. He suspected that there was more to life and love, but at the formidable age of forty, Peter hadn't as yet found it. Except for roulette.

"*Rien ne va plus,*" ordered the croupier, and above the din of small talk rose the sweet whirling song of the wheel with its pellet of fortune spinning smoothly in the opposite direction. The musical hum was broken by the pellet's staccato clatter as it danced over the metal strips between number slots, like a whore racing down a corridor of open-doored bedrooms, unable to decide which one to enter. Peter sucked in his gut till his barrel chest nearly popped the golden buttons off his blazer.

"*Dix-sept — noir — impair,*" the croupier announced the victors. Cold-blooded bastard, Peter thought, staring hatefully at the table captain.

"*M'sieurs, 'dames, faites les jeux.*"

Okay, let's play the game, Peter decided, fingering his small stack of chips like a mandarin caressing jade. Thirty-six numbers and zero; the odds hardly seemed all that high. Yet in two hours neither five nor fourteen had taken a single turn.

"*Fait les jeux*," repeated the croupiers, neatly arranging their colorful stacks, making change, dealing chips onto the board like *rangoli* artists fingering colored sand onto carefully smoothed ground at an Indian wedding. The thought of India reminded him of Maya, and frowning in annoyance at that intrusion, he reached forward to set two chips onto five, and another two on fourteen. The redhead stared at him again, and using her private pusher, deliberately mated his bet with chips of her own. He elevated one eyebrow and appraised her more carefully. Her face was expertly powdered, concealing many wrinkles of age. She was older than she looked. Thirty-eight, perhaps. She wore no ring, and her hands were bonier than he liked. Her shoulders were bony too. Given the hair color, upturned nose, and Kelly green of her costume, he decided she was Irish American, a schoolteacher or office girl with one weekend left to her grand tour. Good God, old boy, not another one of *those*, he decided, backing off now for the lucky spin.

The blonde was infinitely more enticing, and at least a decade younger. French or German. Remarkably rich. He watched her rise from the card table, smoothly balanced as a roulette wheel. She moved as though weightless, and he forgot the game entirely, ready to head after her if by some miracle she was unescorted. Then, not one, but both of the men rose to escort her toward the restaurant. They wouldn't have deterred him ten years ago, but Peter still had painfully vivid memories of the last time he'd tackled a similar trio, in Montmartre. He'd been lucky to escape the bloody nightclub alive. Not that life was more precious to him now. Age had simply dampened his ardor. He contented himself with a long, pleasurable look.

"*Dix — noir — pair — manque —*" droned the traitor at the wheel.

And he'd played the ten all of last night! He'd never had a streak of luck as bad as this one. If it didn't change fast he would have to go back to London tomorrow to look for work. He hadn't been reduced to so humiliating an alternative to living in years. As a young man he had actually worked for ten months in a Sussex branch of Barclay's Bank, the institution to which his father had voluntarily sentenced himself for half a century. Dutifully, Peter had reported each morning in his bowler hat and with black umbrella. He sat through each day, fine or foggy, adding numbers and names to the massive ledger, whose clasp the manager, Mr. Pinch, unlocked for him with a key kept in the vest pocket nearest his heart. "Mind your pence, Peter," Pinch always told him, "and the pounds will take care of themselves!" He quit the day after his father confided to him that Pinch was pleased with his progress. ". . . says, now it mustn't get back to him that I've told you this, mind, says you have the makings of a branch manager in you!"

"Save me, you lovelies," he whispered, kissing his final four passports to easy fortune, and setting them with bulldog British tenacity, two by two, on five and fourteen. Now I lay me down to bet, he prayed.

"Zee-ro!"

"Blast!" Half the table looked around at him. "It's a bloody fix," he shouted, burying his fists in his empty pockets.

"Is anyzing zee matter, sir?" softly inquired a tuxedo-clad figure, who looked as if he had just stepped from behind a submachine gun in an old American movie about the Chicago underworld.

"Not a thing, old boy," he said airily. "It's simply that I've lost my last ruddy chip, and at my school our motto used to be 'it's not how you play the bleeding game that counts, but whether you win or lose.' *Comprenez?* No, I can see you have little sympathy for so uncouth a philosophy of sport, but don't let it ruin your evening. Keep your pecker up."

He left the bouncer to work that one out by himself, and hurried to the door.

Now what? he wondered, somewhat sobered by the bright, empty silence of the spacious corridor. This was how he usually felt after leaving the cinema, all the magic and dreams were on the far side of those leather-padded doors. The real problem, Partridge, Peter decided, pacing the plush corridor, is that you're not suited to any job you find, and you can't find a job for which you are suited. There were any number of the latter, of course. A peerage would do nicely. The dukedom of Norfolk, even an earldom in Scotland. He could spend the rest of his days crossing moors and bagging

grouse. Why in Christ's name hadn't his an[...]
for that sort of thing?

The padded doors opened again, and seeing[...]
looked around as she emerged, he realized that[...]
have run to cash in her chips, following him ou[...]
swiftly as possible. He'd entirely forgotten abou[...]
smiled warmly as she caught sight of him and hal[...]
face turned the shimmering red of her hair. She fum[...]
her handbag searching for her coat check, and the[...]
stride, as though it were her original and sole destinati[...]
the checkroom. Good God, what a bitch, he thought, foll[...]
and noticing to his pleasant surprise that her legs were as [...]
trim as any fashion model's. Perhaps she was a model.

"May I help you into that?" he offered, reaching her just [...]
had taken her light coat on her arm and finished paying the c[...]
girl.

"No thank you!" As typically an American female's tone of [...]
dependence as he'd ever encountered. She hurried past him withou[...]
blinking a heavily mascaraed eyelash his way, and pressed the elevator button. He barely managed to keep from laughing. *M'sieurs-
dames, fait les jeux,* he felt like saying, but he knew enough about
this game to censor levity from his speech at so early a stage. The
most desperate female-hunter viewed the chase as seriously as the
stodgiest bank manager viewed his accounts' ledger. The elevator
doors slid open, displaying a golden cubicle devoid of patrons.

"Do you mind if I accompany you down?" he asked in his most
formal and gallant tone.

"It's a public elevator," she said in that blunt manner he found
most repulsive about American women.

He was in fact tempted to leave her to languish through what
would probably be her last night in Nice. Yet he couldn't help being just the least bit curious about how long it would take before
she abandoned her pseudo-respectability and started panting like a
vampire at his jugular vein. He left her to simmer, without making
another pass, till they reached the lobby.

"Are you English, by any chance?" he asked, as they stepped
from the elevator.

"No. American."

Really? I should have sworn you were English, you know."

Oh, I've spent loads of time in England."

"Ah, well that's it! You don't sound a *bit* American."

"Thank you. If I should take that as a compliment?" she added ingenuously.

"Oh, by all means *do*. I certainly meant it as one. What Englishman *wouldn't?*" He flashed his most charming smile and winked intimately, drawing the color back to her cheeks. "But look here, do you know what *really* prompted me to think you were English?" It was a rhetorical question, of course, since Peter's second law of the chase was to keep talking once the bitch was in earshot, to give her that relaxed opportunity of more closely observing her stalker without making her unduly apprehensive about his ultimate intentions. But she seemed to think all questions demanded answers, innocently asking, "What?"

"Well now this *is* a coincidence, and since you've never met me before you might think it's purest fabrication —" He punctuated his speech with vigorous shakes of his head, brushing the hair away from his eyes each time it fell forward, using his mobile eyebrows to their best advantage, and gesturing grandly at choice intervals with his powerful and expressive hands.

"I promise not to doubt your probity," she injected, starting to laugh, caught up in the spirit of his animation, politely covering her parted lips with her fingertips.

". . . most amazing resemblance, honestly, you *could* be the twin of the Duchess of Kent's younger niece! Good God, your name isn't Agatha, I hope?"

"My name is Jane Tylor," she said, looking and sounding much younger than she had upstairs.

"Now there *is* a coincidence for you! Jane was my great-aunt's middle name, and *I* always liked it much better than her first name — Henrietta. Isn't that an abomination? And you know, now that I think of it, I expect it's why she never married, poor woman, though she lived to be ninety-four! And if you promise not to repeat this, I'll tell you an old family secret, shall I?" He glanced about as though making sure they weren't being overheard, then moved a bit closer to her, lowering his voice in a tone of singularly attractive intimacy. "Our local parson was absolutely *mad* for her,

and every Sunday Aunt Henrietta regaled herself in black lace, and simply bathed in perfume. I have vivid memories of these orgiastic preludes to prayer as a boy, when she couldn't have been a day under eighty! Remarkable woman, but don't you breathe a word of this or I shall be excommunicated from the family and cut off without a farthing."

That did it. She was laughing quite freely, promising by the bones of all her own spinster great-aunts never to betray his confidence. Poor old saintly Henrietta. He often wondered if her charitable soul would ever forgive him for defaming her this way.

"But look here, why in heaven's name are we *standing*, obstructing traffic in this marble monstrosity? There must be at least one fairly respectable café outside where we can sit down and sip some champagne mixed with the night air of Nice. Or were you off to a previous engagement?"

"Goodness, no! I hadn't planned a thing! I mean, it's my last night on the Riviera, and —" she blushed again, and was suddenly tongue-tied. "I'd love to have a drink with you."

"Let me help you into your wrap; it may be a bit chilly."

"Oh, thank you very much."

It had taken ten minutes! Perhaps he should approach the Chamber of Commerce of the Côte d'Azur, and offer his services as an official escort for American ladies on their last night in Nice . . .

"Tell me, which part of America are you from, Jane?"

"I live in Santa Barbara," she said, "but I was born in Moylan, that's near Philadelphia."

"Oh, I've been to Philadelphia," he said. "You keep an old bell with a crack in it there, commemorating some silly incident or other, don't you?"

"Now you're being snide, or is it typically English? I should warn you that I'm *very* patriotic and sentimental about American history, even though my mother was born in England. Daddy worked in Washington most of his life, and two of my brothers are there now, and gracious, I don't know your name . . . !"

"Peter Partridge, though I doubt if my original progenitor was a bird. Probably just the gamekeeper of Partridge Green, where we've always lived, seven miles from Steyning."

"From which?"

"Well, it's not too far from Brighton."

"Oh, I've been to Brighton," she said, sounding more at home with him again. "And I adore Beachy Head, though whenever I stand too close to that cliff I feel a horrible compulsion to jump!"

"Yes, I've done it several times."

"*Jumped!*"

"God no — been *tempted!*"

"How stupid of me." She abandoned herself to laughter as they started down the pink marble stairs, with the fragrance of a Mediterranean breeze wafting toward them from the arc of the sea, regally blue and calm as the cloudless evening. The Promenade des Anglais glowed like a double necklace of pearls and rubies strung over the pebbled fabric of the beach. There was an air of opulence and leisure about the promenading couples on the café-lined street below that helped Peter relegate all anxiety over his future to that closet of consciousness where he'd learned to stuff most of life's "serious" problems from the day he chucked the bank, and headed off for London with five pounds ten in his pocket.

"Have you brothers or sisters, Peter?"

"Bags full! Counting halves, of course. My father was married twice before he met mother. There were three girls from the first lot, three boys from the second, and *four* of us — purebred, but a mixed litter. I'm the youngest."

"How wonderful," she exclaimed. "Huge familes are great fun."

"Smashing," he said, eyeing the lovely blondes at the sidewalk cafés, trying to think of some effective shock treatment to send this ingenuous young woman packing, wondering why in God's good name he'd ever bothered to bag her to begin with. "I'm afraid my brothers turned out a bad lot though. Jack, he's the oldest, embezzled funds from the old boy's bank, and they had to put him away. Harry was always a bit daft, joined the Royal Navy when he was underage. Washed overboard on his first bloody hitch in the North Sea; helluva howler they said and poor Harry in the crow's nest with more than his quota of rum in his gut. Michael was caught in the wood with Sir Andrew's daughter, and I do believe they've still got the hounds after him somewhere in Scotland. What are you laughing at, woman? Did I say something funny?"

"Everything! You're the most delightful raconteur I've ever met, Peter."

"But it's all true, you know!"

"Oh, I believe every word. Cross my heart!" She actually did.

"Let's have a drink," he said, stopping at the tables set out in front of his hotel. He'd left traveler's checks for his bill plus an estimated five pounds in his room, knowing how easily he would have been tempted to bet his last shilling had he taken it. He would buy her one for the road and kiss her farewell.

"Good evening, sir. Scotch and soda, as usual?" asked the waiter, which made her look up in surprise.

"I'm staying here," he explained. "I expect you'll want champagne?"

"No, I'd love scotch and soda, thank you."

"I always thought you Americans drank champagne in France, and bourbon at home."

"But I'm not 'you Americans,' Peter Partridge, and I wish you wouldn't treat me as a stereotype from the last grade-B film you saw. I'm Jane Tylor, and I do as I please wherever I am, which happens to include drinking scotch and soda!"

"No offense meant." He liked the way her eyes flashed when she got angry. He even liked the sound of her voice then. It had more timbre to it.

"Sorry. I just hate being patronized."

"Look here, why don't you tell me about yourself. What sort of life do you lead when you're not on holiday in Nice?"

"I paint," she said. "And I haven't been 'on holiday.' I came here to work a few months ago. I rented a small place at Saint-Jean —"

"Really? I love the Cape. But didn't you say your home was Santa Barbara?"

"It is." She had taken out a cigarette and lit it before he could find his matches. "I've kept my home there, but I had to get away." She snuffed the cigarette after one puff, and her voice sounded thinner, strained. "I was going to be married in June. He was killed in an auto accident two days before the wedding."

"Good God," he whispered. The waiter brought their drinks.

"I don't know what ever made me tell you. I haven't been able to speak of it till now." All color had gone from her face. Her eyes were unmoving, wide open, nakedly revealing their pain. She held her chin slightly higher than before, and he could see the full curve of her neck, gracefully long. He reached nervously for his glass.

"Cheers," she said, lifting her glass.

"Cheers." They touched glasses. He drained most of his drink at the first gulp. He was tempted to tell her about Maya, how he'd never proposed marriage before, how they'd planned to elope, because her guardians didn't think he was good enough for the girl they'd reared as the "Divine One," Queen of the Sacred Cult of Shri. And how the morning he came to pick her up for their wedding trip, the gates were locked. It had taken him four days to hear her voice again on the phone. "I don't love you, Peter," she said. "Leave me alone."

"Excuse me, sir," interrupted the waiter. "You are Mr. Partridge, sir? The desk clerk gave me this cable for you."

Peter opened the envelope, and reading the message, exclaimed, "Good God, he's got the money!"

"Who?"

"McNeill! He's got the bloody money! Here, look at it, old girl! You read it to me, will you! I may just be imagining it!" His hand shook as he handed her the paper.

"MONEY ASSURED STOP," she read. "COME IMMEDIATELY SAVOY HOTEL BED WAITING STOP CHEERS MAC." She too appeared pleased, saying, "I'm going to the Savoy myself tomorrow. Our paths must be destined to cross. But what does this message mean, Peter? Is this man giving you a job?"

"Good God, no. He's saving me from one! Who said my luck's run out, eh? Let's see that lovely piece of paper. Look at those numbers at the top, will you! Five and fourteen! Both on the same line. I knew it! Blast the bloody casino! I'll be rich enough to buy that table in less than a year!"

"What's the money for, Peter? Are you buying a business?"

"Business? Do I look the business type, old girl?"

"I don't type people as easily as you do, Peter Partridge. You're the most unusual man I've ever met."

She said it so naïvely, he could not help but avert his eyes, feeling the blood rising in his neck.

28

"Shall I tell you what we're up to, Mac and I? We're going after the Yeti."

"Are you really? How exciting! So *that's* what the money's for — a hunt! How did you ever get the idea?"

"Oh, *I* didn't! I haven't had an idea since the day I quit Barclay's."

"I don't believe that for one moment!"

"Not this one anyway — it's McNeill's baby. I don't think I ever gave a thought to the Yeti till I met Mac in India three years ago. We were together on a hunt in the Punjab Hills when he told me about his plan to capture one. Good God, what a week that was! McNeill's the best blasted shot I know. There's nothing that blackguard *can't* do, actually . . ."

"I'm more interested in Mr. Partridge," Jane said, smiling. "Why don't you tell me about him, Peter?"

"That's rather a dull story, you know."

"I wouldn't find it dull."

She sounded so intense, it made him nervous.

"Look here, Jane, I have to wire Mac now, and . . ."

"Of course," she whispered. "I mustn't detain you." She pushed her chair back from the table. Her voice was thin as she said, "Thanks for the drink."

"Wait," he called. "You could come up to my room while I cable, if you like, and then we could go somewhere for dinner?" He blurted it out impulsively. Once he'd said it, he really hoped she would decline the invitation. Her hesitation made him think she was going to do so.

"That sounds lovely, Peter," she said at last.

CHAPTER 4

BRUNO Jaeger clenched a fistful of stubby grass and flattened his body against the slope, glancing down at the gorge far below. Halfway up the shortcut to Riffelhorn he sensed that the angle was steeper than his eye had estimated, and looking back now he felt a bit light-headed, so for the moment he did not move. The stone supporting his left foot eased away, sliding back with an almost inaudible sigh of loose silt.

"Darling, do you need me?" Charlotte called from the path below. She had decided to remain on the path; since the clouds were so low today they had not even bothered with spiked boots or rope, merely going for a stroll before dinner.

"Just enjoying the view," he answered. It was after all too preposterous for Bruno to admit he was in any sort of trouble within the timber zone. He had conquered the Matterhorn, Castor and Pollux, Monte Rosa. With ice axe and rope he had gone to the top of every major peak in the Swiss Alps, and wandered in the Himalayas as well; how could he possibly need help here?

"Don't enjoy it too long," she warned, "or I beat you, my over-confident *Herr!*"

"Yah, you try," he taunted, jolting himself from the effort of having to shout at her, feeling the grass coming loose in his hand, obliged suddenly to bury bare fingertips into the crusty soil. The air was cool, his scarred face had begun to sweat. How idiotic, he thought. He was experienced enough to know that in mountain climbing brashness was always dangerous, stupidity often fatal. He knew better than to start on such a slope without spikes. What had made him so impulsively leave Charlotte's side to clamber like an infantile monkey in this direction, shouting "I'll beat you to the next level!" As if beating her was to take the Matterhorn from its northern face! You know why, he answered himself, and like a sedative it soothed him. Gently he felt himself easing back, staring down at the feather wisps of smoke trailing from toy chimneys in the valley, like ragged pennants of the superhuman army defeated by snow, ice, and starvation, by just such impulsive stupidity and self-destructive arrogance.

He stared at the ribbon of silver water, gun-barrel silver-gray in the cloud-filtered sun, into which he would fall, the scar tissue of his cheek and neck torn away by the ragged edges of stone, the bright blood washed away by the fast-moving stream, his bones left gristle white by the hawks now circling patiently.

"Bruno!"

Do it *now,* he thought, closing his eyes as sweat blurred his vision, clenching his bared teeth till he felt the vibrating pressure of his jawbone pounding painfully against his skull. Push away *hard* now, and in two moments it will all be over!

"Bruno, why don't you answer me?" she shouted. "Darling, is anything wrong?"

Is anything wrong? It was so incredible a question he could not keep himself from laughing. Poor, naïve idiot that she was, Charlotte had broken the spell, dragging him back from the abyss as firmly as any stout rope with the innocence of her tone.

"No, don't worry," he answered, digging in with his knees, hugging the mountain like a cat on a tree trunk, virtually clawing at the pebbly earth with his teeth, finding another cluster of sod, a half-exposed root, a tiny rock shelf for his shoe, a knee hole, an elbow niche, using the surface of the almost vertical slope the way a fly clutched at a painted wall. He did not peer back again. The grass was thicker along the ridge of the path above. He gripped it, and chinned himself up, springing onto the flat shelf well ahead of her, briskly brushing the dirt from his khaki shirtfront and trouser legs, chiding, "Why so slow, my dear?"

"You mustn't make fun of me today, Bruno," she insisted, pouting slightly and shaking her rich ponytail of ashen blonde hair like the pampered only child of a wealthy and powerful burghermeister, which despite all the misery of the war years and occupation, she still was. Her equipoise and resilience often amazed him, as did the timeless character of her beauty. Thirteen years of marriage had not added a line to her face as he remembered it at twenty when she became his bride. By then his own face had been half-destroyed by the scars of war, the gift of ugliness he bore from his long night on the Russian front. Why she wanted him, looking as he did, was a mystery he could not fathom.

"So? Why mustn't I make fun of you today, Frau Jaeger?"

"You should never make fun of your wife," she said, coyly, her pale blue eyes glittering with mischief.

"Ah, I see! This is our lesson in democratic behavior for today?"

She took hold of both his hands as she came up to him, leaning back at arm's length and tilting her head to one side as if she were riding a merry-go-round.

"Do you find me still beautiful, Bruno?" She pressed her body against him.

"Of course. But here on the trail, Lotte . . ." he moved back.

"Why do you draw so away from me, Bruno, whenever —"

"Ach, do not start this stupid argument again!"

"I'm sorry," she whispered, lowering her eyes. She had hoped that here in the mountains, he would feel less tortured, less remote from her.

"Lotte, you know how I try now to compose again, and how difficult it is to . . ."

"Darling, I know it is not easy for you. It is just that sometimes, I am frightened that perhaps you have lost interest in your Lotte."

He touched her arm lightly, brushing his lips against her ear. "You know there has never been another woman in my life." That was no lie at least. He stared at the thickening clouds. Tomorrow would be no better for climbing.

Winter comes early this year, he thought bitterly. In a few days they would have to leave. And then? Back to Frankfurt? He hated returning to the Conservatory to teach idiots how to play music he himself had not written. Three years of such slavery was enough for anyone. But what alternatives were there? America perhaps. If her father could convince his American general "beer buddy" to vouch for his democratic character. Maybe South Africa? Australia? Not many places still welcomed white settlers of the Nordic race!

"Shall I tell you now?" she asked softly.

"What?"

"Bruno darling, we're going to have a child."

He was too stunned to speak, staring at her face to see if he could detect any sign of levity? Surely she could not be serious! She would not play such a trick on him, be so stupid as to have left herself unprotected?

"Isn't it wonderful, darling?"

"You are quite certain?"

"Yes, yes." She still looked like a child herself. "Aren't you pleased, Bruno?"

"What? Yah, of course I am. Very pleased."

32

She stroked his flaxen hair with her soft fingers. "You are, aren't you? I am. It's what I've always wanted. Since I've known you. Since the very first time I saw you. Do you remember it? When you came to dine at our house with General von Bittern? How beautiful you looked, Bruno, like a Norse god! Our son will look like that. And now that you are so well established at the Conservatory . . ."

"We better start back," he said, abruptly.

"But you wanted to reach the glacier."

"It will strain you."

She laughed heartily. "It's only the second month, darling! You needn't worry. It weighs nothing as yet."

Then get rid of it now, he thought, wanting to say it out loud. No. He would wait a bit longer. Often during the first months such things took care of themselves. There was still time. He could afford to indulge her for a while; he knew an excellent doctor in Frankfurt.

"Let's keep walking," she said, taking his hand. "I'm not a bit tired."

"I am. Anyway, tonight maybe the clouds break, and we can try the Matterhorn early in the morning. It's after five. We start back."

"Whatever you say, Bruno."

So now it is whatever *you* say, Bruno! She was the same as every other woman in the world, after all. Promises, flattery, deception. Suddenly she acts as if she never imagined how he felt about children, as if he had not bemoaned a thousand times the wretched fate of couples they knew who were shackled to the monsters for the best years of their lives! As if . . . His ulcer shot needles of paralyzing pain through his shell-torn stomach — it was futile to think about. He had to stand still a moment.

"What is it?"

"Look, there. Can you see the sheep?"

"Yes, lovely."

"And there is the herder. Can you make out his lederhosen?"

"Bruno, why don't you want to talk about it, to plan?"

"Plan what?"

"Everything," she said, smiling at him with such apparent innocence that, had he not known better now, he might have believed her to be the most guileless creature on earth. "Our future, darling. And *his* future. Oh, Bruno, aren't you excited?"

"So what do we plan, Lotte?" he asked, walking on down the trail. "I have decided I do not go back to the Conservatory."

"But why? When? We have not discussed . . ."

"What I do is my own decision, just as the child is yours!"

"So that is your *true* feeling." She stopped, turning away from him, staring at the mountain. No, her eyes were closed. She looks inside, he thought.

"Have I said something wrong?" he asked impatiently.

"Never mind."

"I don't! But I see you do, so why not say what you think, yah?"

She shook her head. He kicked a stone over the cliff and watched it catapult down. Why hadn't he been strong enough to do it to himself half an hour ago? Bump, bounce, crash — kaput! No more arguments, no more pain, no more plans. Nothing. As a child his nurse had filled his head with nonsensical tales of heaven and hell. The war taught him that both were part of terrestrial reality. His year in Berlin with the S.S. was heaven, the Russian front hell. Fear of death's aftermath did not deter him. Only stupidity. By whatever name you chose to call it, hope, cowardice, love, pity, ambition. To Bruno they all sounded the same now, watching the toy houses of Zermatt below, the toy trails for toy dolls to traverse aimlessly, on the stupid road from yesterday to tomorrow.

"It's getting cold," she said.

They walked back to the Monte Rosa without exchanging another word. Before, their silences had been a bond, a communion through nature, a source of tranquillity. How else could you truly walk or climb, but in silence? The mountains were eloquent enough. Not this time. Seeing her now before him, so surefooted, so perfectly independent, so remotely withdrawn from himself, he felt more distant from her than he had on the wasteland of Russian snow. And he remembered the terror of loneliness he had felt then, the sudden longing for a human sound, the craving for one note of laughter; his body had ached with desire for a single bar of music then, any music. Anything but the eternal bombardment, and the death rattle of children he led into slaughter.

They crossed the bridge with its frothy white hurricane streaming beneath. The church bell tolled six. Farm boys herded their lumbering cows home.

"Lotte," he called, as they headed up the hill street leading to the hotel. "I didn't mean to hurt you. I . . . I don't know what I meant . . ."

She stopped, still as the grave markers in the churchyard across the street. A horse-drawn cart clattered over the old cobblestone road.

"Forgive me what I said before," he whispered.

"Oh, Bruno!" She turned to embrace him, speaking with her head pressed to his body. "You must know how much I want a baby, and now that we can afford him, why should we wait any longer? Soon I would be too old."

She lifted her face to his. He saw the tear lines on her cheeks, like shadow-darkened ski trails on an otherwise glowing hillside. "You will never be old," he said. Taking hands, they walked briskly into the hotel.

"*Guten Abend,* Herr Jaeger," said the desk clerk, giving him his room key, and a cable. He was expecting a cable from Professor Schneller of the Conservatory asking how soon he intended to return. He stuffed it unopened into his shirt pocket. The pine-paneled lobby was crowded with vacationers, discussing the prospects of brighter weather, impatiently waiting for the dinner gong. A roving fiddler, dressed in Swiss costume, entertained guests drinking in the open lounge.

"What did the desk clerk give you, darling?"

"The key," he said, holding it up as they reached the door.

"Bruno, I saw him hand you a cable. Why don't you open it? Maybe it is from father?"

So what better reason not to open it? Each time they escaped for two weeks in the mountains, her father cabled every other day. Always the most important of messages. WHAT IS THE WEATHER LIKE? HOW IS CHARLOTTE FEELING? WE ARE ALL FINE, BUT MISS YOU BOTH!

He removed the crumpled envelope from his pocket, handing it to her, and starting to undress for his shower.

"It is from the American we met here last week," she said, sounding disappointed.

"Ah — Roger! Yes, yes, let me see."

"I thought you are not interested in reading now," she said coquettishly, keeping the cable behind her back.

"Lotte, please let me have the cable."

"You will have to reach around me for it," she said, pressing against him.

"I want the cable," he insisted.

"Very well — if you prefer your American friend to your wife!" She tossed it at him, and walked angrily to the bathroom, slamming the door.

He smoothed out the slip of yellow paper. EXPEDITION WE DISCUSSED READY FOR LAUNCHING STOP CAN YOU JOIN US IMMEDIATELY STOP WIRE ME COLLECT AT SAVOY HOTEL STOP AUFWIEDERSEHEN ROGER MCNEILL

He trembled with excitement as he read it again and still again. There could be no error in his translation of those words. There was no ambiguity of meaning. He felt the blood pounding through his limbs. "Lotte, did you read it?" he shouted . . . I must cable him back immediately!"

"And what will you tell him?" she asked, standing in the bathroom doorway.

"What do you mean *what*? I tell him I come at once! This is for me what I wait now five years to do, the chance to go back to Khumbu, to see *him* again! Only this time he does not escape from Bruno! You will see, Lotte, this time I capture him!"

"Unless he captures you first, you mean!"

"It is easier to catch the Yeti than your Bruno, my dear! So this is why you look so worried? You are the only one could capture me, Lotte. Maybe because you are the only one who ever tried?"

His laugh sent a chill through her spine. "Stop making fun of yourself, Bruno! I don't like you to talk so. Five years ago with the Swiss team was different. Then you went only for mapping the route to Everest. That was dangerous enough, but you promised me then it would be the last time."

His lips tightened and he crumpled the cable in one fist as she spoke, tossing the paper onto the floor.

36

"Bruno, I did not mean to say that! Forgive me."

"What you say is true. I promise I do not leave you again for such adventure. So it is finished."

"Please, Bruno."

"Please, Bruno," he mimicked, grimacing hideously. "Do, Bruno! Don't, Bruno! Good, Bruno; bad, Bruno! This is how you sound to me now, Lotte! The trainer commands her animal. What more do you like me to do?"

She was crying bitterly, her back turned to him. She did not often cry before him. It only infuriated him, she knew.

She should have been born a Jew, he thought, lying back on his bed, covering his eyes with his forearm. And I should not have been born at all. He felt sometimes like a species extinct, the atrophied remnant of some era long past, some preglacial age of Norse myth. His kinsmen were all dead, fossilized jawbones, fragments of skull alone survived of his brothers — the Hunters, the Warriors, the Bards of the Black Forest. Perhaps that was why he felt so eager to find the Yeti, whose plaintive call he had heard so clearly five years ago, and whose lonely lumbering form he had glimpsed in the wasteland world of blinding ice. No one believed him, not even his comrades on the expedition. They listened politely, and said he needed rest. They thought him mad. Then last week this remarkable American had come here just to seek him out, to question him about the account he had read in an obscure German journal of wildlife! And now this cable comes. So, of course, she must prevent him from going!

"Could I come with you, Bruno?"

"What?"

She had stopped crying, and sat down beside him. "At least part of the way — let me come, so we will not be separated again for so long?"

"But you are . . ."

"No, I won't let that interfere with our plans! I know you think I have tricked you by becoming pregnant, but it is not so, Bruno. I have sworn it will not inhibit us! I would rather remove it."

"What do you say, *Liebchen?*"

"Only what I mean, Bruno. I am such a coward to be separated from you. Please let me come this time."

"You could wait for me in Delhi. There are so many excellent hotels and doctors. You would be safe there like at home. Yah! Lotte, do you mean this? I will have to cable Schneller. He will not give me again this job at the Conservatory!" He sprang off the bed.

"Bruno, I love you," she whispered, but he was already at the phone.

CHAPTER 5

NIELS Larsen drained his beer, viewing the familiar scene of Kongens Nytorv traffic grotesquely twisted through the distorting lens of his foam-blistered glass. Cars were bent and crushed, faces flattened, bodies elongated like Gothic statues, sunlight filtered through a veil of bubble-fringed moisture. He set down his goblet. The waiter looked his way, and Niels signaled for another. How many would it take tonight? Yesterday he had lost count, yet somehow he managed to reach home. This morning he woke to find himself on the living-room floor fully dressed.

The closely packed tables at the narrow sidewalk café were starting to fill. Women in soft-brimmed hats and kid gloves, bearing shopping bundles from Stroget, paused for a drink before returning to dine with their families. Touring couples with cameras strung like ammunition belts across their chests, clutching maps of Copenhagen, guide books, and postcards, stopped for a beer before rushing off toward the opera house. Men like himself on their way home from work. The daily cycle of life continued as usual. Almost as usual.

The waiter set down his frothy medicine, and Niels blew lightly at the foam before sipping his drink. The way Ulla used to, trying to avoid the bubble mustache, which clung to her upper lip, grinning shyly as she surreptitiously dabbed at it with her napkin. Always sensitive about her appearance. What hadn't she been sensitive about? Color, voice tone, dress, manners, the texture of stone, the mystery of motion, the miracle of music, a walk along the canal.

38

But now she is gone, he told himself. And you must make your peace with that. He had always prided himself on his calmly realistic approach to life, his maturity of outlook. He rarely raised his voice, he never panicked, and irascibility was foreign to his nature. His sister said he was simply born with less blood than most people, but he was thankful for his equanimity which had served him well. He had been interned in a Nazi prison camp for the better part of the war, where he watched others destroy themselves by one passionate outburst of anger, one desperate dash toward freedom. He had waited patiently, never so desperate as to give his captors cause for killing him. Also, in his work coolness was an asset. What competitors called his genius, Niels recognized mostly as the product of patience, and swift untrembling action. Niels treated photography as he did game hunting. Often the two were interchangeable for him. He could wait at his blind all day without moving a muscle till tiger, panther, or rhino passed within range of his lens, or his gun. His pictures of big game had made his name famous among cognoscenti on two continents. At his studio he applied the same formula to portrait and fashion photography. He never rushed with his camera, and never missed the fleeting moment of perfection, the ineffable smile of Ulla, or sunlight piercing evanescently through a cover of cloud to cast the perfect shadow on a model. His reflexes were trigger perfect. You're no man, his sister often chided. You are a machine, Niels! He had accepted her reprimand in good nature, considering it something of a compliment. Until this month he had almost believed it.

He continued to think of himself as a machine even after falling in love with Ulla the first time she sat for her portrait. He loved her as an object of beauty, an aesthetic phenomenon, a creature of many moods and passions, each to be captured by his camera. He thought himself impervious to any emotional attachment. Even after they married he viewed her somehow as an adjunct to his art. Often when watching and listening to her, even in one of her worst moods, he found himself wishing he had his camera set, thinking, "That would make a good shot."

Niels finished his drink, left a ten kroner note under his coasters, and made his way slowly past the tables to the street. He could not sit at one place very long anymore. He had not put in a full day at his studio since it happened, almost a month ago. Yet surely work was the only solution! He told himself that each morning, but by midday he could barely focus his camera. The life had gone out of his photos. They were all as dead as Ulla.

She is dead, he thought, entering the mainstream of humanity rushing around the square. This I must accept. She is dead, and death is part of life. It was a simple enough catechism. It had worked for him often before. When his parents died, and his elder brother. When his best friend was shot in front of his eyes during the war. He did not run forward, or shout, but thought only, he is dead. At first it worked with Ulla too. The night he returned home to find her body hanging from the light fixture in their bedroom, he had cut the rope and exhausted himself to no purpose with artificial resuscitation, had calmly called the police, the hospital, their doctor, and then waited without tears, telling himself, This you must accept, Niels. She is dead.

He crossed the street to the island of green in the center of the busy square. How many times had they strolled together through this park on their way to the opera or ballet? She always gripped his arm with both hands as they walked, tugging hard as though testing his strength, his ability to support her slight weight. She was thin and small, yet remarkably strong. You will break my arm one day, he would caution her, smiling. But you will enjoy the pain if I inflict it, she replied, laughing her strangely secretive laugh. Anyway, you are big and strong enough to hold me. Oh, look at how lovely those flowers are! Then letting go of him she would dash impulsively to a rhododendron bush or a cluster of carnations, merging her face and loose-flowing flaxen hair with the flowers, rushing back to him without a word of comment, holding even tighter to his arm. His arm felt unused now.

A thin girl, hands buried in the pockets of her black sealskin coat, stared boldly at him as they approached each other on the park path. She slowed her pace, waiting he saw for some overture. He looked aside and walked on. *You have no competitors, Ulla,* he had sworn one night from the cold darkness of their bed, and it was true. *Then why?* she asked. *Niels, what's wrong with me?*

He took a deep breath, yet could not seem to fill his lungs. He tried harder, opening his mouth wide, but his body craved more air.

He felt himself choking. His vision blurred. He decided to sit down on the nearest bench. Storm clouds were rolling in from the north. The wind had freshened. Twilight descended swiftly. He lit his pipe and breathed somewhat easier. The dome of the opera house loomed above the trees and high bush wall. Perhaps I should go, he thought, but decided against it.

Instead, he hailed a taxi and directed the driver to take him to the Strand.

"Which number?" asked the driver, as they reached the waterfront.

"This will do," Niels said, getting out opposite Thorvalden's Museum. The murky water of the canal shimmered with a cool purplish glow. Chains of churning cyclists, bent low with the pressure of peddling, raced home from the castle island over bridges vibrant with traffic life. The fishwives and fruitmongers were covering their carts for the night with tarpaulins tough as the weather-worn faces of seamen loitering by their barges below. Niels leaned on the rail overlooking the canal, and gazed at two old-timers, solid as walrus out of water in their shiny leather jackets and dark knitted caps pulled snug against their ears. Though he could not see their faces he knew them well. He could have talked to them more easily than to any of the well-dressed young men from the *Borsen* or the *Rigsdag,* whose visage, manner, and education more closely reflected his own. They would not have been so glib with words of sympathy or advice, with standard formulas or false comfort.

"Gotta cigarette, handsome?" a waterfront prostitute asked, her low-cut dress revealing the black straps and lace of her undergarments.

"No. Excuse me." Hurrying out of range of her toilet-water fumes, he crossed the street to the old Fish House, which had been Ulla's favorite.

"Ah, Mr. Larsen, good evening," called the owner, coming over to escort him. "A table for two upstairs?"

"I am alone. Yes, thank you, upstairs."

"Certainly, Mr. Larsen." He led the way up the staircase decorated with life preservers and rope to simulate a ship's gangway. Fish nets bearing oyster shells were draped from the ceiling, and the windows were portholes with rims of glittering brass. Kerosene lanterns flickered on the white cloths, and the oak beams of the floor were sprinkled with sawdust, like the deck of a ship in high water. I love the atmosphere of a ship, Ulla used to whisper as they came up, once rebuking him: You are mean never to take me on a ship, darling! Why don't you? He had been on enough ships, he replied, though now . . .

"White wine, Mr. Larsen?"

"Beer, and brandy." The beer alone was taking too long. He lit his pipe, but the smoke only made it more difficult for him to breathe.

"Anything wrong, sir?" the waiter asked, setting down a goblet of ice water.

"No, no." Sipping the water, he turned aside. *Why do you sit so far away from me?* she would ask, moving her chair closer to his, brushing her ankle against his lower leg, her eyes glowing with warmth and life. *You have fire in your eyes,* he told her. *You kindled it,* she replied.

Now she is dead. He swallowed the brandy at one gulp, using the beer as a chaser. He ordered a plate of shrimp, lobster, another brandy. The second brandy came with the shrimp, but Niels had lost his appetite. He finished his drink and asked for the bill.

"Is anything wrong with the shrimp, Mr. Larsen?" The owner returned anxiously to his table.

"No. I just remembered an appointment. I must leave."

"Yes, of course. I do not charge you for the lobster."

"It doesn't matter," he said, removing several bills from his wallet.

He must have run from the restaurant, for he suddenly felt the blood throbbing against his collar, and realized he was panting, his palms wet, his heart racing at an alarming rate. People glanced at him knowingly and hurried on. Another Dane with too much to drink! Another ship's officer on leave! He loosened his tie, opened his shirt collar. Then he saw his dishevelled reflection in the windowpane of a rope-and-tackle store, and was sobered somewhat by that unsteady negative. His hair looked like a terrified porcupine's back. His eyes were strangely distended. He remade his tie and combed his hair.

Steady, he thought, concentrating on his walk. His elder brother killed himself with drink. He remembered all the symptoms, the step-by-step descent into that sewer of self-destruction. How many times had he sworn that no matter what happened he would never lose control of himself the way Eric had? *I must forget her*, he told himself.

Yet each street of Copenhagen was redolent with her voice, indelibly stamped with her step, her smile, or a song that burst impetuously from her lips. She often sang when they walked. *Why shouldn't I? Birds sing in the street!*

A mistlike rain started to fall, helping to sober him as he walked. It soothed his face, all but washing her memory from his consciousness. Was life but a dream in a dream? Perhaps now if he went home, he would find her there waiting, playing the piano. His pace quickened. He did not stop again till he reached the huge modern apartment house, opening the double glass doors of the frescoed lobby, running along the corridor.

"Ulla!"

He entered the dark living room, drapes drawn closed as they had been all month, empty tumblers cluttering the carpeted floor, newspapers scattered about in the same disarray he had fled from this morning. What was that sound? The telephone!

"Hello. Yes? This is he."

The operator's voice sounded like Ulla's. "We have a cablegram for you, Mr. Larsen. May I read it to you now? We'll send it over in the morning."

"If you like."

"Pardon me, what was that?"

"Yes, read it," he said louder.

"Thank you. It's addressed to you, from London. The message reads: EXPEDITION WE DISCUSSED LAST YEAR READY FOR LAUNCHING STOP ARE YOU STILL INTERESTED IN JOINING STOP WIRE ME COLLECT SAVOY HOTEL IMMEDIATELY STOP SKOAL HODGE MCNEILL." She paused a moment, then asked, "Shall I read it again, Mr. Larsen?"

"Please."

She read it again, and asked if he wished to send his reply.

"Yes," he said, touching the velvet polish of the rosewood table she had made for the phone. She could make anything with her deceptively slight ingenious hands, play anything. There could be no escaping her here.

"Go ahead, Mr. Larsen, I've addressed it to Mr. McNeill at the Savoy Hotel. What will the message be?"

"Yes," he said.

"Hello, sir. I'm waiting for your message."

"That's it," he said. "Yes. And my name — Niels Larsen."

"Yes stop," she read back, "Niels Larsen. Is that the complete message?"

It was, he said, hanging up.

Yes, stop, Niels Larsen, he thought, but kneeling to the floor he covered his face with his hands and could not keep from starting to cry.

CHAPTER 6

HODGE filled his glass with bourbon, and touched it against his wardrobe mirror. "To you, Mac! Not a bad day's work!" He winked at his reflection, smiling broadly.

It was less than seven hours since he'd sent his cables. Now three affirmative answers were in his pocket, and he had spoken to Seth who sounded negative, but promised to stop by for a drink, which was as far as he could have hoped the Professor would commit himself before sleeping on any proposition. He had wired responses to Peter, Bruno, and Niels, calling his team together for their first meeting here at the hotel tomorrow at four. After leaving Sir Charles he had stopped at Benson & Moore, where he spent most of the afternoon looking at provisions. They promised to send men over in the morning with samples of the equipment they hadn't had time to demonstrate for him today. He then confirmed the flight reservations to Delhi, and took tea with Das at the High Commissioner's office.

It's too simple, he thought, sipping his drink, and sinking into a chair. Forty-five years of failure, of near misses, not quite, also-ran, almost-made-it ventures of daring ingenuity and careful planning had conditioned Hodge to expect the worst. Just when things looked brightest the thunderclap usually came; he arrived at the patent office a day after his invention had been processed, read of a competitor who planned the same expedition the day before his money was promised, as though some jealous demon had been appointed by God solely to frustrate the glorious dreams of Roger McNeill. He was troubled most when his plans appeared to be going most smoothly. What had he forgotten about this time? He closed his eyes. He hadn't realized how tired he was. The mere idea of getting into his tux to go out with Tony tonight exhausted him.

"It's open, Tony, come in," he called in response to the knock at his door.

"Hi, boy! Hey, ain't you dressed yet?" Tony Judson entered with a convivial wave of one arm. His tuxedo was several sizes too small for his bulging neckline and waist. The bald, freckled dome of his head blistered with perspiration. "Come on, Hodge, let's get us some grub."

"Let me fix you a drink, Tony. You look great."

"Thanks, boy. Heck, I don't look too bad at that, do I?" He glanced at his profile in the mirror, but quickly turned away. "Bet you'd never guess I bought this monkey suit thirty years ago, huh?"

"Nope. You don't look a day over forty-five."

"I was pretty damn good at forty-five. Married Miss Wyomin' that year. Christ, what a build on that girl. Solid as A. Tel. & Tel. More damn bounce in them buttocks than any broncho I've ever seen busted. Damned near killed me, that woman!"

"To you, Tony," Hodge said, handing him a drink.

"To us, boy. Here's good hunting! Come on, we're gonna celebrate tonight. Let's go to the Troc for some'a that rare roast beef, and then . . ." He clicked his tongue and winked.

Hodge winced inwardly at the thought of sitting through another dinner at Trocadero's, while Tony talked endlessly of Judson Enterprises and the Judson Foundation.

"I'd love to join you, Tony, but I'd better stay at my desk tonight. Too many things to be done before our first confab tomorrow."

"Hell, boy, you've gotta eat."

"I'll have them send up something later."

"Now you're beginnin' t'sound like I used ta, Hodge! Well, I like t'see that, but don't overdo it. Did I ever tellya what happened t'my brother Ed?"

"Yes."

"Oh, I did? Well, that's been a lesson t'me, boy. No damn point becomin' the richest man in the graveyard, that's what old Matt Tombstone used t'say. But you're still young enough t'be ambitious. More power t'ya. At my age a man's gotta relax now'n then. Say, you wouldn't know any other bottle clubs like that place we went to last night?"

"I do in fact. It's a bit nicer even, called the Golden Key, in Soho, just ask the taxi driver."

"Maybe I will! Just for the helluv it. Can't do much more than look nowadays."

"You did some pretty fancy dancing last night, Tony."

"That was a cute little blonde there last night, y'know. Man like me could make a damned fool of himself over a girl like that, boy! Fact is, of course, I have, four times! Yessir, Hodge, you're lookin' at the only four-time loser who's never been behind bars in his life!" Tony slapped his knee and enjoyed a raucous laugh. "That reminds me, I've been meanin' t'ask how a young buck like you has kept loose all this time?"

"I was married once. It lasted almost a year," he said softly.

"Oh, well that's about par for me too. Ten months of T.J. and they've had it!" He laughed even louder. "Hell, I better get a move on or there won't be no bronchos left t'bust at that Golden Key! See ya in the mornin'."

"Have fun," Hodge said, closing the door after him. He rarely thought about Margie anymore. She was one of those pages in his memory he had torn out and thrown away. Only the ragged edges remained, sharp as the glasslike quality of her laughter — *You'll never make it, Hodge. You were born to be second-rate!*

He refilled his glass, and paused to look at his face in the mirror. It was the sort of handsome face, at once so familiar and easily forgotten, that adorned many advertisements for men's wear, or automobiles, cigarettes, and whiskey. He'd tried modeling for a while, before the war, but soon tired of that. He'd tried acting too, but wasn't quite photogenic enough to star, nor strange enough for supporting roles. He'd tried most things.

But this time it was going to work! He would push this one across no matter what, no matter who tried to stop him. It was a giddy feeling of greatness, a premonition of victory that had never before come to Hodge with such certainty. I'm going to make it Margie, he thought, and when you call to beg me to take you back (once he was famous enough she would beg all right) I'm going to invite you to the biggest celebration in my honor. He would ask her to sit at his side on the podium . . .

"Ladies and gentlemen," he rose and extended his hand. "I want you to meet the little woman who deserves most of the credit for my achievement. My former wife, Margie! Stand up, and let the crowd see you, baby! Here she is, folks, the loveliest whore in America, but for whose insatiable hunger for sex with man, woman, and beast, I might never have had the time to organize this expedition!"

He started to laugh, but the sour taste of smoke and liquor fumes rising from his empty stomach, made him grimace. The room seemed oppressively close, disconcertingly empty. Hodge went to his desk and reread the telegrams he'd received. The comfort of their messages was as coldly impersonal as the furnishings of his room. He opened his attaché case and removed the carbon copy of his master list of provisions, ten pages of onionskin including everything from aspirin to watertight tents. It was like reading an abridgment of the Sears catalogue without illustrations. Sears Roebuck and the Bible, the two volumes in his foster-parents' library. Many the winter night Hodge had fallen asleep studying that catalogue, and dreaming of the day when he would be rich enough to order whatever he wanted from its glossy pages. Now he'd compiled a catalogue of his own, and tomorrow he would order treasure enough to fill this room. He felt cold. He wondered if Margie had ever remarried. It was almost ten years since he'd heard from her. He pushed his provisions list aside, and went back for his glass. Now he felt too hungry for another drink. The idea of eating alone seemed suddenly uninviting, almost terrifying. Hastily, he put on his jacket, and rushed from the empty room.

The lobby was crowded with couples in evening attire. For a

moment Hodge thought he saw T.J. standing and studying the stock market tape. He hurried outside, past the door captain, whose top hat and full-length gray coat always made Hodge smile. Several people were waiting for cabs. He walked up the alley, and out along the Strand toward the City. He loved walking in London, especially after dark. The strange variety of costume and color in the crowd that surrounded him was soothing. His identity made no difference here. Place of birth, social status, ethnic origin, did not matter in this sea of Swahilis and Swedes, of Bantus and Belgians, of Beatle-maniacs and horseguards-on-holiday. Even sex was uncertain in this center of transvestism and modern coiffures. He relished such anonymity almost as much as he longed for fame. His taste went to extremes, the polar opposites attracted him, not the middle ground between. *When are you goin t'grow up, boy?* his foster-father always shouted. *Never the way you mean it!* was his silent answer.

He hailed a taxi. The crowd had thinned.

"Dean Street," he ordered, sitting back and closing his eyes. He'd begun to feel a slight throb behind them, a dull ache that often plagued him when he was overworked, too tense or tired. He would have to slow down, pace himself carefully from now on. The long haul was still ahead. He felt like a boxer in training for the championship bout; only he was boxer and manager both.

"Any partic'lar number, gov'nor?"

"This'll do," he replied, paying and jumping out into the mainstream of Soho's bustling brightness. He entered a restaurant, but the maitre d' told him that every table was booked until ten. He should have known better than to come without calling. In two hours his head would be splitting. He decided to settle for the closest coffee shop.

It was a bright espresso place with small terrazzo tables set along the window walls, and satellite-shaped chandeliers suspended at varying heights. There weren't many customers as yet, the tourists still at the real restaurants, the locals in their pubs. A sandwich and coffee would hold him nicely now. He could order a steak back at the hotel.

Hodge took the table farthest from the door. The fat mustached owner behind the multi-handled espresso-maker smiled an unctuous greeting. Hodge lit a cigarette and tapped his fingers impatiently on the glazed surface of the bare table. He never liked to be kept waiting. Then he saw her.

She was bending over a table close to his, leaning on her order pad, licking the point of a pencil. She did not notice him at once, for she seemed thoroughly preoccupied with her customer's order. Her hair was lustrous, black and long; her face pale and round, peering furtively from its soft curtain, the face of an infant glimpsed beneath the upraised hood of a passing pram. Her eyes were widely alert, innocently probing, like those of a child gazing out at the wonders of life for the first time. Yet her lips were a woman's, full and strong, slightly parted, brazen almost, as was the bold line of her jaw, the jaw of Miss Liberty, he thought, for it looked French, the symbol to Hodge of French femininity, at once seductively alluring yet defiantly aggressive. Come, take me, it said, if you have the courage to try. There was something quite wild about her look, not fierce or foreboding, but untamed, untrammeled. Yet for all of that she seemed helpless. Her naked arms were reeds beside the loose-fleshed limbs of the heavy woman who wanted to be very sure there would be sufficient whipped cream on her coffee. Her waist looked small enough, Hodge thought, to encircle with his hands, but her breasts were full, firmly outlined against the red of her flimsy cotton dress, and her legs were perfectly shaped, surprisingly long for so short a girl.

He was still staring, when she caught his eye, and for an instant she looked puzzled, tensely alert and frozen as a stalked animal arrested by the sound of a snapping twig. But he made no effort to disguise how he felt, and instantly she seemed to understand, for her complexion deepened and she nervously lowered her eyes, straightening up, trying to sound very waitresslike and efficient as she called out to him, "I will take your order in one moment, sir."

"Take your time," he responded, surprised to hear himself, thinking, I could wait all night for you, baby. He watched her walk to the chromed machine at the counter. She moved timidly, as though approaching a stormy surf from the beach. Her steps were short, delicate as those of a kimono-wrapped geisha. There was a quality of natural grace about her, he thought, feeling so strangely tender, so intensely interested in her slightest gesture, that he wondered if it might not be wiser for him to eat elsewhere. It was hardly an opportune time, after all, for an adventure of this particular sort.

Yet merely thinking that, Hodge almost laughed aloud. He had managed to escape the allure of prettier faces, and shapelier legs, since arriving in London. No woman would interfere with his plans at this point. He would enjoy the diversion of watching her while he ate. Nothing more.

"It is not right to make you wait so long," she apologized, coming over to his table and extracting the pad and pencil from her belt. It was a strange accent.

"Tell me, what do you like to have?"

"You —" he said, watching her closely as he paused to place a cigarette between his lips. Her eyes widened with astonishment, then anger. They became so large that they seemed to cover her entire face, like the glowing eyes of a tigress peering through a fringe of tall grass. Her parted lips closed to a thin line. Her face flushed, and just as she appeared ready to sputter irately at him, he added, "— haven't give me a menu yet."

"Oh! I'm sorry," she gasped, sounding relieved, smiling warmly as she handed the glossy card to him.

"What do you recommend?" he asked.

"How should I know what you like?" She shrugged, biting her thumbnail, distractedly gazing out the window. She was suddenly far away, withdrawn from her work. She had a mysterious manner, a look of remoteness which fascinated Hodge. Despite his earlier resolution, he felt the compulsion to know all about her now.

"Order whatever you think I would like," he said, never once glancing at the menu, never taking his eyes off her.

"B-but I don't know you," she said, staring at him with ferretlike curiosity, noticing his clothes now as well as his face.

"Then we'll see how good a judge of strange appetites you are."

She inclined her head ever so slightly, contemplating him at a new angle, lightly tapping her pencil against her pad. She turned on her heel without saying another word, and watching her walk again, he thought, she's either a virgin or a whore. Everything about her was as mysterious to Hodge as her accent, which wasn't French, he'd decided.

She returned with coffee and Viennese chocolate cake.

"Do I look underweight?" he asked, as she set the rich fare before him.

"I'll take it back," she said angrily.

"Better not try," he warned, smiling. "It's just what I wanted!"

"Good. Anything else?"

"What's your name?"

"Why do you ask?" she snapped.

"I couldn't help thinking that you looked somehow out of place here, and I wondered if you might be interested in working as my secretary."

It was a long shot, a crazy hunch, perhaps, but T.J. did say a secretary was needed, and Hodge, riding high now on his good luck, spoke without reservation.

"Are you joking?"

"I never joke."

"B-but I . . . I have never been secretary to anyone."

"Good. I'll train you properly then." He took a card from his wallet, writing the hotel and room number on it. "Be there tomorrow morning at ten. I'll explain the job to you." He handed her the card.

"You are Mr. McNeill?"

"Hodge."

"*Hodge?*" She said it her own way, as no one ever had before. "Hodge? Is it right, how I pronounce your name?"

"Perfect," he told her.

"Hodge," she repeated, like a child testing a new toy, while continually turning the card over as if expecting to find something written on the reverse side, mysteriously self-absorbed again. He thought she had forgotten his earlier question. She looked quite carefully into his eyes, and moved her lips tensely as though debating with herself. She is not the most beautiful woman I have ever seen, he thought, yet she is more than beautiful.

"My name is Rena, Rena Gold," she said.

CHAPTER 7

Twice Rena walked the full length of the alley, almost to the front door of the Savoy, and twice she turned just before reaching it, retracing her steps to the street. Every uniformed employee outside the black marble-and-chrome entrance watched her peregrinations with suspicious amusement. The bored chauffeurs attending several Rolls-Royces parked in the alley also watched, eyeing her in the discreetly aloof manner peculiar to male servants of the rich. She knew exactly what they were thinking, smug, tight-lipped lechers that they were, and she hated herself for being so indecisive as to give them reason for indulging in such thoughts, yet for the life of her Rena could not make up her mind.

Her initial impulse this morning had been to take Hodge Mc-Neill at his word, to act as though she innocently believed he was interested simply in hiring her as his secretary, and to work for him only so long as he scrupulously played the role of proper employer. She certainly wanted a more exciting job, and Hodge seemed as interesting a man to work for as any. Yet she understood his motives as clearly as she read the facial expressions of these lackeys, whose eyes followed her every footstep for the past fifteen minutes. In twenty-odd years of life she had learned more about the motives of men than most women learned after three score and ten. For some reason which she could neither understand nor control, and which she had never labored to cultivate, men found her irresistibly attractive. She often wished it were otherwise. Orphaned at six, she had been adopted by her father's best friend, a wealthy and respected businessman of Tel Aviv, whose wife loved her as a true mother, and who himself spared no expense on her upbringing, lavishing more gifts and affection on her than he spent on all three of his own children. She was barely fourteen when he fell to his knees in front of her, embracing her legs, pathetically crying out, "Rena, you are all I have or want in this miserable world! Do you understand what I am telling you, Rena?" She understood too well. That day she packed her valise, and never returned home.

Walking toward Trafalgar Square, Rena noticed the eyes of many respectable-looking gentlemen in pin-stripe suits and bowler hats roll magnetically in her direction, fixing with sheepish longing on her face, waiting for the slightest sign of encouragement. Sometimes she wished she were born Christian so that she could have retreated to a nunnery. No, she loved the world too much for that. If men would only leave her alone! No, that is not entirely right either, she thought. She had been in love once, and anyway she really liked male companionship. All her best friends were men, and those her own age, who were wise or docile enough to accept the fact that she did not care for them sexually, were in many other ways precious to her. Yoram, and Ephraim, for instance — what would life have been like without those two? They were as brothers to her, or children, both at once in fact. More like pets sometimes, or slaves. What would they not do if she but asked it within earshot of them? Did she feel like seeing a play, or listening to a concert? She had to mention just one word, and Yoram had his car running: "So hurry up, Rena, or we'll be late!" Did her back ache slightly? Were her feet sore from walking? Ephraim would sit gently rubbing the muscles that needed massaging. Now she missed them. Not as she missed David, of course, yet she had no choice other than to leave David, to create a new life for herself, starting all over perhaps. What else could she have done? Anyway it was too late now, and here she was with the pigeons wandering aimlessly around the base of Nelson's column.

Two teen-agers wearing skin-tight trousers and black leather jackets whistled long and low as she passed them, and on the other side of the column's base, two monks wearing broad-brimmed black hats and tasseled cords around their robes smiled sweetly and bowed. Dear God, she thought, what should I do? The hands of Big Ben pointed to ten-thirty. If he really wanted a secretary, Hodge wouldn't wait forever. Oh, he doesn't need a secretary and you know it, and he knows you know, she reminded herself; which was why she had turned back from the entrance both times. Had she been willing to settle for what he did want, there were certainly better opportunities waiting at her beck and call anywhere in Soho! She had now quit three successive jobs in London. It was a fine pot of soup she had jumped into!

"Bang! You're dead!" a small boy shouted, standing a few paces in front of her, smiling the most endearing smile she had seen since leaving Israel.

"Hi," she said, stooping to touch his bright cheek tenderly. "What's your name?"

"Ethan," he said, "and I'm seven."

"Are you really? My goodness, what a big boy!"

"I was just fooling," he said. "I'm four: but I'll be five in two months."

"Why that's even more remarkable, Ethan. I never would have guessed you're only four." His hair was the color of David's, bright as a field of wheat in the morning sun. She held out her hand to him, and he laughed, extending his own to touch her wriggling fingers.

"Ethan, come back over here!" a voice summoned from behind her.

"Aw, why can't I stay?"

"I must leave just now anyway," she said. "Nice to meet you, Ethan."

"Did you hear me, Ethan?" His mother again, no doubt. What would she tell him when he went back? Never talk to strangers, Ethan, specially not women who look like that one?

"Bye, Ethan," she called, but he was crying too bitterly as his mother scolded him, to notice her go. What an awful responsibility it must be, she thought: motherhood. Sometimes she suspected her fear of becoming a mother was really what had made her leave David. Am I irresponsible? she wondered. Her stepsister had another word for it: spoiled. *Everything's always come too easy to you, Rena. That's the trouble with you, you're spoiled!* Hateful word. It made her think of rotting vegetables.

I might as well hear what he has to say, she decided. If he tries to touch me, I'll leave. Rena started her third pass at the hotel entrance and, without so much as a glance at any of the lackeys, walked into the lobby. The boy operating the lift stared with such obvious pleasure at her dress that Rena wondered if she had been too bold in wearing her new Paris chiffon for so early a business appointment. She loved pretty clothes and gay colors. The fabric was somewhat transparent, but the neckline wasn't really too low, and the hem was no higher than most new dresses. She would hide her legs when she was old and ugly! She walked along the hushed hallway, wondering why she felt so nervous as she tapped lightly on his door.

"Come in. It's open!"

The room was crowded with boxes, and seeing several strange men, Rena thought she had come to the wrong number. Whispering "Excuse me," she was about to leave, when Hodge appeared, and snapped, "Oh, it's you. You're late."

"Sorry," she muttered. "The traffic."

"Never mind. Close the door. Have you eaten?"

"What? Oh, no. I mean, yes. That is I . . ." She noticed the table covered with elegant silver dishes and tea service. There were scrambled eggs and bacon, and muffins and jellies of several varieties, at two places. Hodge went back to his chair, gesturing for her to sit opposite him.

"Might as well eat," he said. "I ordered it for you."

"That's very kind of you," she began, but he was not listening to her, focusing his full attention on the two men whom he had not bothered to introduce. She decided to take a hot muffin and some jelly, sit silently and listen.

"How strong is it?" Hodge asked the men. They were holding some sort of meshed cloth between them.

"Ah, *veddy* strong, sir. Quite remarkable in fact; our *newest* discovery. May we demonstrate it for you, sir?"

"Of course."

"Ah, thank you, sir!" He was a tall muscular man, meticulous in a double-breasted dark suit, blue-striped shirt with a detachable white collar, and yellow gloves. His cohort was slightly shorter, but other than that his mirror image. Their bowler hats and tight black umbrellas were resting on one of the beds. Bracing his knee against one side of the bed, the taller man gripped the mesh with gloved hands, while the other man did the same from the opposite side of the frame. "Set, James?"

"Set!"

Then they started to tug, leaning back as far as they could, tautly stretching the mesh, till both their faces were bright red. They were so well matched in strength that neither could budge the other. Rena felt like cautioning them not to overstrain but feared that Hodge wouldn't approve of such advice. He was watching the tug-of-war very seriously, though he paused to sip his coffee. She was too nervous to eat. She wondered if Hodge was in the net business?

"Now *sir*," called the tall man, his voice echoing the strain of physical exertion, "would you be so kind as to try cutting through the center with a knife?"

Hodge took a serrated bread knife from the tray, and actually started sawing at the mesh where the threads seemed most thin.

"Careful!" Rena shouted, expecting both men to fly backwards and crack their skulls against the walls or floor, but the knife could not sever a single thread. "Oh, that's amazing," she said, wondering if he was a magician or something like that.

"That's fine," Hodge told the men, still ignoring her.

"Thank you, sir. It's our veddy best synthetic, you know. We've had orders for it from your space agency people in America. Its molecular structure is impervious to temperature."

"Six," Hodge ordered. "Now let's see the guns."

The short man noted the order on a long list he was keeping, while the tall one extracted a stubby rifle from one of his boxes.

Rena gasped, but quickly stuffed a muffin into her mouth. The two men looked at her and smiled reassuringly. Hodge appeared to have forgotten she was in the room.

"Let's feel it," he said, taking the gun.

"Notice how light it is, sir? Our newest aluminium alloy."

"Did you bring a target?"

"Of course, sir." He set up a cork-centered steel plate at the far end of the bed. "Shall I demonstrate, sir?"

"I'll do it," Hodge insisted, inserting what looked like a hypodermic syringe into the barrel, cocking the bolt, and firing almost before he peered at the sights.

"Oo, you made a bull's eye!" she shouted, applauding impulsively.

"Did you notice how silent the discharge was, sir?"

"I'll want five of those, and fifty darts."

"Quite, sir."

She wasn't very flattered to note that he treated the men as brusquely as he did her. He seemed to have no human feelings, yet last night she'd been certain . . . What a strange man he is, she thought.

"I'll notify you of the boot sizes tomorrow. You won't forget the tents and collapsible ladders?"

"We'll have the lot for you, sir. You can rely on Benson & Moore, I assure you . . ."

"I'll need everything by Monday."

"*Monday,* sir? But today is Thursday!"

"Correct, and tomorrow's Friday. We fly to Delhi Monday, and I'm taking all these provisions with me. I don't care about the cost. I expect you'll have to work on this order during the weekend, but I'm prepared to pay a hundred pound bonus for guaranteed delivery to the airport Monday morning. My secretary here . . ." she almost spilled her coffee, as he turned to point, nod, and smile directly at her. ". . . Miss Gold, will be waiting at the freight receipt gate with your bonus at nine. I'll be there by ten myself if your truck is delayed. But we fly at noon. Understood?"

"I *dare* say! Jolly good, sir! By jove, you Americans *are* enterprising people . . ."

Hodge shook hands with the tall man, easing him toward the door. He helped carry the boxes into the hall, and then the two men were gone.

"You haven't eaten a thing," he said, returning to sit opposite her.

"I've hardly caught my breath," she whispered. "Do you do everything like this?"

"Everything's a big word."

She blushed, looking down at her trembling fingers. "I mean your business."

"I have no business."

"But then how can I be your secretary?"

He laughed, and leaned back to look at her, almost the way he had the night before, lighting a cigarette. "First tell me what sort of accent you have."

"Why? Do you think I sound funny?"

"No, I like the way you sound, Rena."

"It's Israeli."

"It's beautiful!"

"Hodge, is this the only reason why you asked me to come here?" She started to push away from the table.

"Hold on, baby! Now who's rushing things? Just making polite conversation till you finished breakfast. My offer of last night stands. I want to hire you as my private secretary; which means you do things like meet Benson & Moore at the airport on Monday."

"B-but I don't understand. What sort of work do *you* do? What were those guns and nets for? I don't understand anything! How can I be your secretary?"

"Fair enough. At the moment my work is organizing and leading an expedition to Nepal to hunt for the Yeti."

"The *what?*"

"You may know him by his other name, the Abominable Snowman."

"Oh, I see," she said, nodding vaguely.

"So you've *never* heard of him? Oh, well," he glanced at his wristwatch, sounding again as coldly impersonal as he had with the salesmen. "He's probably the missing link: half-man, half-ape. His major habitat is Nepal, the great Himalayas. People who live in that area, mostly Sherpas — you've heard of Tenzing . . ."

"Yes, yes," she said, wishing she hadn't sounded so ignorant before.

"Well, they've believed in him for many years. The rest of us have been skeptics, with a few exceptions, till now, mostly because Nepal was sealed off from Europeans till after World War Two. In the past ten years several expeditions have been launched, all unsuccessful . . ."

The phone was ringing. Hodge went to answer it.

"Yes, Tony? Yes, she's here now. No, I'll just be a few more minutes. Okay!"

"Look, Rena, I don't have time now to explain so listen: Your job will be bookkeeping, errands, phone calls, general man-Friday work. You'll remain in New Delhi as our liaison with T.J. when we go to Nepal . . ."

"What?"

"We fly to India on Monday. T.J.'s the man I just spoke to, Tony Judson, our private moneybags; all heart, solid gold. You get the picture. What's funny?"

"Nothing, everything. You don't know a thing about me, yet you talk as if . . . as if you have known me all my life."

"Our trip shouldn't keep you away from London more than two months, at most three. All expenses paid, and pocket money — say a hundred dollars a month. Okay?"

"It sounds wonderful, but . . ."

"What's troubling you?"

"Don't you want to ask me questions? How do you know you should trust me?"

"Tell me one good reason why I shouldn't?"

"There is none," she said irately.

"I didn't think there was."

His smile was so ingenuous, she could not help thinking, I could almost fall in love with him.

"You will take the job, won't you, Rena?"

"Yes," she replied.

"Good. Now you'll need a visa. Take a taxi to the Indian High Commissioner's office. Ask for Vice-Consul Das. Here, let me write that for you. Better call first to be sure he's free. Introduce yourself as my new secretary. Tell him I sent you for a three month visa. Ask him to cable Delhi for approval immediately. Check?"

"Check," she whispered, falling into step with the frenetic pattern of his speech. It made everything he said sound exciting.

"Next — shots. You'll need typhoid and cholera."

"I've had them," she reported proudly.

"Better double-check with the Center for Tropical and African Diseases anyway. Buy yourself lunch, and take taxis! Time's what we're trying to save, not money. This should hold you." He dropped two five-pound notes onto the table.

"But I won't need so much . . ."

"You'll need more tomorrow. Keep a record of expenses, and don't cheat yourself. Understand?"

"Understand."

"Good girl. I've got to run. Use the phone here for Das. Be back by four. The rest of the team should be here then, and you'll get the lowdown on our plans. All set?"

"All set. Are you leaving now, Hodge?"

"Of course. Good luck, baby!" And he was gone.

He left without saying one word about her dress.

CHAPTER 8

THE more Seth pondered it, the more firmly convinced he became that the only answer he could possibly give Hodge today was no. It was his immediate reaction last night when Hodge told him by phone what the expedition was after. It was his considered conclusion now that he'd slept on the proposal, despite all of Stella's interest in the idea, and his own curiosity. Hunting Yeti in Nepal was not the way to begin his year's research in Orissa. He was an anthropological scholar, not a zoological adventurer. The only reason he was entering the Savoy now was to have a drink with his old buddy. He would explain that to Hodge at once, and leave as quickly as possible.

Relieved at having made up his mind, Seth crossed the lobby at a more rapid gait. He hadn't realized how slowly he'd been moving, till he noted the clock over the desk registered four-twenty. Hodge's room was on the third floor, he remembered, searching his pockets in the lift for the book requisition slip on which he'd noted the precise number. He had so many crumpled slips of paper.

"You wouldn't know Mr. McNeill's number by any chance, would you?" he asked the lift operator.

"No, sir, I have just come on duty."

"That's all right. I think I remember it." Three-seven-one came to mind. He would probably hear their voices anyway. He found all sorts of notes to himself about articles he had been meaning to check, important references. One of these days he would have to go through all his pockets and carefully collate these slips. He would have to try to be more systematic. He was always making notes of things, and losing them. Especially department and committee meetings.

Seth stopped in front of the room numbered 371, but heard no voices. He tapped lightly at the door, still fumbling through his pockets.

"Hello," Rena said. "Are you Seth?"

Looking up to confront that face he could not answer. The eyes were innocently wide as a fawn's, fawn-colored. The smile was as shyly tentative as the first glow of dawn. It was a face as intimately familiar to him, as unconsciously part of himself, as his own heartbeat. He could feel a pulsating rhythm hammer through his body as he stared unspeaking, virtually in shock, at this reincarnation of the first woman he had ever loved, Anita. Had he been less abashed he would have uttered her name, so certain did he feel that this was the girl he had last seen fifteen years ago.

"I'm Rena," she said, breaking the spell, sounding somewhat flustered as she avoided his stare. "Hodge asked me to wait here for you. They've decided to meet in T.J.'s room. Do you know where that is?"

"No." His voice was barely audible. His mouth had gone dry.

"Come. I'll show you. It's just down the corridor. They are all there, drinking. Hodge promised not to start talking without you. He says you're the most important one on the team." She spoke compulsively as they walked, as though she sensed he was unable to speak, and did not want to embarrass him by her own silence. "Hodge says you are his best friend in the world. Is it how you feel about him?"

"What?"

"I mean — well, sometimes — this has happened to me anyway — somebody feels very close to me. You know, a friend. And I don't feel to him, how do you say it, the word for 'so-close'?"

"Intimate."

"That's right. I see it must be true; you are a professor?"

"Yes."

"I would think you are too young to be a professor. In Israel our professors are mostly very old."

"I usually feel very old."

Even her laugh was like Anita's, softly modulated, warm as deep wool. Her walk also, her slight yet voluptuous figure; they could have been twins. Instead of Seth's shock wearing off, it became deeper. He felt as though the door she had opened miraculously transported him back across fifteen years of his life.

"Here it is," she said.

"Here's the man!" shouted Hodge as he opened the door, gripping Seth's hand, keeping a firm hold on his upper arm, leading him into the sitting room that overlooked the Thames. "Seth, you're a sight for sore eyes! You haven't aged an hour, man! Come. Meet the rest of the crew."

"This is Niels Larsen, our great Dane. Best damn photographer, hunter, and climber in three continents; I'm sure you've heard of Niels. Just don't try drinking him under the table. I made that mistake a year ago in Copenhagen! Niels, Seth Goodman."

"Pleased to meet you," the tall man said, his grip as hard as the deep lines of his face, which looked painfully worn and pallid, unsmiling despite Hodge's effusive flattery.

"And here's Bruno Jaeger, the only one of us who's seen our prey in the flesh. Tell Seth how close you actually got to him, Bruno."

"So. From where I stand now to that wall. This is how close we have been."

"In daylight?" Seth asked.

"No, no. Yeti never moves till night. This also happens to be a very dark night, low clouds, like so." He held his arm slightly above his head. "Also the wind is very strong, and it blows to me, yah? So he cannot smell me. He hears no noise till I am nearly on top of him. But then I must take out my rifle. This makes him look. Ach! Such a face like this you have never seen!"

Watching the contortions of Bruno's scar tissue as he grimaced to imitate that face, Seth felt much the same way.

62

"Could you photograph the footprints?" Niels asked.

"Just that night I carry no camera. Always before, and you can be sure, ever since, I have a camera glued to my pack! But just this night I leave it behind!"

"What brought you out that night?" asked Seth.

"This too is strange. I think it must be his call that wakes me. Only a few days before we have lost a man, and I think maybe this is a human cry. So I don't wait to wake anyone else. This was, of course, very foolish."

"You're not the first man who didn't think of everything at eighteen thousand feet," Hodge remarked. "But we'll all benefit from your experience, I can see that. Damn glad you could join us! Bruno, this is Seth Goodman."

"My pleasure," Bruno said, shaking his hand vigorously, bowing slightly, and actually clicking his heels. "Goodman is a German name?"

"Jewish," Seth replied. He saw how warmly Rena smiled as he said it.

"Yah? But you look — what I mean to say is, you don't look —" Bruno stopped suddenly, licking his lips, smiling uneasily as he realized the room had become tensely silent.

"Actually, Seth's a full-blooded Hindu," Hodge injected, tapping Seth's muscle-tightened shoulder convivially. "Aren't you, buddy? That's why we need you so desperately, man. You're the only Indian on our team!"

"Now hold on a second, you blackguard; what about me, eh?" His face a warm wreath of welcome, Peter rushed over, extending a hamlike hand.

"This is Peter Partridge, Seth. As unbowed an international scoundrel as I've ever encountered! No brains, of course, but good-natured. He's done so much tramping around Scotland I suspect he's the Loch Ness monster. We're going to use him as a sex lure for the Yeti."

"Good God, I think he means every word of it!" Peter roared, grinning infectiously as he pumped Seth's hand. "The bloody Irishman knows me too well!"

"Hodge knows everyone but himself," Seth said, wondering what made him say it. It was as though the heady atmosphere of this room had stripped him of social inhibition. Or was it directed at Rena; an open warning to her about Hodge?

"That's what I need you for, buddy. You're my I.D. card," Hodge responded, and though it was said flippantly, Seth believed he meant it. "Last but most important, Seth, meet Tony Judson; the man whose generosity is making it all possible; only man I know who's made a fortune without losing his youthful spirit of adventure and pioneering."

"Hell boy, never had none! Maybe that's why I'm on this hunt," Tony roared, shaking Seth's hand with Rotarian vigor. "Welcome aboard, boy. Have a drink!"

"Thanks very much, but I'm afraid I've sailed in under false colors . . ."

"Hold it, man. Make no decisions in life without at least two glasses of champagne under your belt! There's an efficient secretary for you." Rena had filled a glass for Seth. "You've met my secretary, Rena Gold, haven't you?"

"Yes. Thank you."

"Seth and I are old friends," Rena said, handing him the drink.

"Oh? How's that?" Hodge asked, the faintest edge sharpening his tone.

"We walked here together from your room," she replied, laughing.

Hodge looked relieved. Then he spoke a bit louder, and his voice acquired that tone of command so familiar to Seth from their hours in the briefing room. "Gentlemen, now that we've all got our drinks, why don't we make ourselves comfortable, and get on to business."

A round table, with seven chairs spaced about it, was set near the windows. There was a scratch pad and ash tray before each seat. Seth resolved to make his exit at the first opportune moment. He scribbled "No" on the blank paper in front of him, then raised his eyes to see Rena staring at his face.

"In simplest terms, here's the picture," Hodge began, leaning forward, tautly extended fingertips together. "The Nepalese government has sold us the exclusive right to hunt the Yeti during this fall season; from now till December. We have to start our hunt on

Nepalese soil no later than October first, two weeks from yesterday, otherwise our option lapses and anyone with five thousand rupees can pick it up."

"Good God, is anyone else after it?"

"At least one other team, I've been told. But don't ask me who. The Ministry won't say a word beyond that. Now I've booked us on Air India for this Monday. Sorry, T.J., I mean you've booked us!"

"No offense, boy. You're the captain of this team. I'm just goin' 'long for the ride."

"Okay, we're booked at any rate. Our provisions are ordered, and I've asked the Indian Vice-Consul here to join us for dinner tonight so that we can be certain all of you have Indian visas by Monday morning."

"I don't understand how you can do that," Seth said, incredulously.

"Das and I are friends. I've done a few things for him," Hodge explained, winking. How many women, Seth wondered, were embraced in that particular wink? He remembered some of Hodge's extracurricular services to visiting Pentagon brass in India during the war.

My answer is still No, he thought, underlining the word he had written on his pad.

"We haven't had confirmation on the flight from Delhi to Kathmandu yet," Hodge continued, "but that's only a few hours, and we'll have some stores to collect in Delhi anyway. I'm sure we'll be able to lift off to Nepal by the end of next week. Which gives us two months of clear weather before the heavy snow sets in. That's all the hunting time we should need."

"Yah, but it takes us more than two weeks to walk from Kathmandu to Khumbu," injected Bruno.

"Right. Which gives us six weeks in Sherpaland."

"But I must ask one question, Roger."

"Fire away, Bruno. That's what we're here for."

"I do not ask it to argue for delay — but would not possibly spring be a better time?"

"Could be, weatherwise. I know you had a bad fall with the Swiss five years ago, but we'll have to risk that. Spring is optioned

65

by another team — again, I don't even know which country. For us it's now or never."

"Then I agree we go now."

"Check. Niels, how do you feel about this schedule?"

"I am ready. I do not return now to Copenhagen. I have here a friend who supplies film to British studios. I call him tomorrow morning. My cameras are with me."

"Excellent. Peter?"

"Good God, I've been ready for years. The only person outside this room who even knows I'm in London at this moment is a crazy American female I met yesterday." He shook the forelock out of his eyes and wearily muttered, "God, what a woman!"

Seth joined the general laughter that shook the table at this sudden revelation of Peter's plight. Whatever else it might become, he thought, this hunt wouldn't be dull!

"How about it, Seth? Are you with us, buddy?"

"Hell, I'd like to be," he was startled to hear himself reply. It happened sometimes when he was lecturing. He would think a subject through quite carefully before the hour began, outlining it on his note cards, even starting at times by reading from them. Then the topic itself took hold of him, and his thoughts flew off at an unanticipated tangent. "But I can't," he added quickly.

"Why not?" Hodge asked.

"Well, for one thing, as I told you yesterday," he began staring into his drink, because he knew they were all watching him intently, especially her, "I still haven't got my damn visa."

"You'll have it by Monday."

Seth rubbed the bristles under his chin with the back of one hand as he stared narrowly at his handsome friend across the table, wondering if Hodge could possibly be in the employ of India's Ministry of Foreign Affairs, or the U.S. State Department. Now that he thought about it, Hodge's life made more sense as a spy than anything else.

"If I had my damn visa I'd be in India right now."

"Great! Then you're ready to go?"

"My bags have been packed for three weeks, Hodge, but I'm going to Orissa, not Nepal."

"What the hell's in Orissa?"

"Santals. I'm doing an ethnography of the Chota Nagpur tribes, and the impact of mining on tribal mores." He left it at that, noticing their blank looks.

"Surely that can wait, buddy."

"It has. For me." From the way Hodge spoke and the rest of them looked, Seth suspected they considered his hunt as crazy as he considered theirs. It is with our manias as with our watches, he thought, none runs exactly the same, yet each believes his own!

"Look, Seth, you're the anthropological expert," Hodge began, and Seth knew that having opened with praise the sentence would probably end in insult, "but you wouldn't exactly call your new study the most urgently important thing in the world, would you?"

"I wouldn't call anything that," he said, his eyes wandering to Rena's lips. They were distended slightly, like fingers reaching out to him.

"Finding the Yeti is," Hodge insisted.

"Why?"

"Because I'm convinced he's the missing link. We're going to make scientific history, Seth; not just zoological, but anthropological as well. Ours will be the most important discovery about man's development since Darwin."

"*If* he exists."

"He exists. Ask any Sherpa. They'll tell you. Ask Bruno! No one believed America existed before Columbus, or that the moon could be reached before Sputnik! Or that Everest could be climbed! You name the invention or discovery that's helped bring all of us from caves to modern London, buddy, and I'll find you the names of a thousand jerks who said, That can't be done! It doesn't exist! It's impossible! That's no argument, and you know it. You're the scholar on this team, not me!"

"Maybe that's why I'm more skeptical," Seth retorted lamely, feeling the force of Hodge's assurance pummeling against him. "But even if he does exist I can't just drop everything I'm committed to now, Hodge. I've got a foundation grant for my study, and a year's leave. I've got an obligation to my university. I can't run off to Kathmandu."

"What happens if your visa doesn't come through by normal channels for another month? Suppose it doesn't come through at all. Suppose some grade-C clerk in Delhi's lost the form. What do you do then?"

Seth gnawed off a strip of his nail, wishing Hodge would leave him alone, instead of pursuing him now like the infighter he was; the short, swift jabs landing with deadly precision. They had sparred many times, and though Seth had the height and weight, Hodge had the speed, and a kind of mad daring, a wild sort of determination that left him impervious to pain, unconscious of punishment, refusing to admit he was outmatched. It was a quality of spirit more than physical toughness, which Seth had always admired.

"Do you give up your sabbatical? Do you go back home to teach? What do you do then?"

"I suppose I'd have to work on something else, some other project. I don't know."

"Sure you know! It's exactly what you'd do. You're a free agent, man!"

"Within limits," he said, meeting Rena's eyes again.

"Come off it, Seth! I know you as well as you know me. You don't think I'd have wasted a week tracking you to that two-bit dive in Bloomsbury if I thought you were such a slave to schedule that you wouldn't change course in midflight, do you? Man, you were my navigator when we both damn near got busted out of the service for tearing up orders and knocking out that Jap position near Imphal. Or have you forgotten that?"

Seth grinned. "I never liked orders."

"And what about that book you wrote last year?" Hodge paused to drain his champagne glass.

"I didn't know you read boring monographs."

"I don't, and yours isn't. Save the false modesty for your co-eds. I wish to Christ I could have written a book half as good! But do you know *why* you wrote it?"

The bastard's got *chutzpah,* Seth thought, smiling in spite of himself.

"You wrote it because you wanted to preserve some record of a tribe that was dying out. You wanted to catch their way of life before it disappeared. Maybe because you believe it's more sensible than our way, maybe just out of scientific curiosity, just because they happen to exist, people like us, only different. Is that right, or isn't it?"

Seth nodded, wishing half of his graduate students could have stated his thesis as accurately in twice that many words. He sensed now that he knew what Hodge was getting at, and it frightened him. It was what he had dimly been thinking ever since speaking to Hodge last night, though he had kept it securely hidden till now. He was certain, for at least a hundred sensible reasons, that his only possible answer to Hodge was *No*. Since seeing Rena, for a hundred and one reasons!

"The Yeti's a damn sight rarer than any tribe, man. If we find him, if we capture just *one* — there may not be a helluva lot more left — but if we get hold of just one *alive,* we can learn more about human evolution, and primitive man's motivation and behavior than every anthropologist has doped out from studying tribal cultures over the last half century!"

Seth felt like a butterfly being impaled to the board, like a microbe brought into focus under a high-powered lens.

"How exciting you make it sound," Rena whispered, her eyes and voice quite naked with admiration as she turned to Hodge. "You want to catch him alive?"

"Yes. Alive and speaking! Seth, we'll never have this chance again. Next year someone else may catch him; in a few years they might all die off, and with them the secret of primitive survival. Isn't that worth six weeks of your precious sabbatical?"

"It would be, if . . ."

"What?"

"If it wasn't so damn *crazy,* that's what!" He jerked back from the table, compelled to stand, to move like a caged beast toward the picture windows facing the Thames embankment. A tourist boat from Westminster was passing under Waterloo bridge, its bow already swallowed by the arch of concrete, rising like the open mouth of a whale from the ruffled surface of the murky water.

"Hodge, it's madness! You don't know that country up there as I do! You'll never find that son-of-a-bitch in six weeks, even if there are a thousand of them. It's like looking for five-leaf clovers. No, it's worse than that!" He remembered finding a five-leaf clover once at his uncle's place. "Oh, Christ, I don't know what it's like!

Mac, so help me God, it's the craziest, God-damned foolish idea you've ever had, and man, you have had some wild ones!"

"What do you say, buddy?" Hodge had come to stand at his side, resting a hand on his shoulder. "Are you with us?"

"I'm with you," he said.

CHAPTER 9

JANE wriggled into the blue Mandarin sheath she'd bought in Beaulieu, but never quite had the courage to wear till now. The silk hugged the soft curve of her small stomach and smooth thighs without a wrinkle, as though its lustrous substance had been poured onto her body. The dragon design curved up her pelvis and slender waist, its open mouth surrounding her left breast. She'd put her hair up, with a diamond diadem over the forehead fringe, and secured her pendulous sapphire-and-diamond earrings snug to her earlobes. The jewels were part of the treasure she'd inherited on her twenty-first birthday. In the nine years since then she had worn them only twice. In a family famed for its Puritanical restraint, Jane Tylor was nicknamed Sister Saint Jane. Until John's death, she had never missed Sunday Mass. The Archbishop himself had agreed to sanctify their wedding at the cathedral in San Francisco, and John was driving back to Santa Barbara after conferring with him, when his front tire blew on the coast road, and his car skidded over the palisade. The wedding became a funeral. Two weeks later Jane left for Europe, and in the past four months had not set foot inside a church.

What's keeping him? she wondered, spraying more perfume around her ears and neck, then ringing the desk clerk to check her watch. Peter had promised to call for her at five. It was now twelve minutes past. He would have found her in the diaphanous negligee had he come on time! The tingling increased near the tips of her small breasts, and a glow of vibrant warmth flowed through her body with the rekindled memory of last night. She had only read of it before, never experiencing so complete a sensation of simultaneous release and attachment as she'd felt in Peter's arms.

She lifted the phone again to call his room, but decided to wait. Undoubtedly the conference with Hodge was taking longer than he anticipated. Peter Partridge. Jane and Peter Partridge, she thought.

She sat facing the long mirror. When she crossed her legs the side slits of her dress revealed her thighs to the dark silk of the stocking tops. She felt her breath come faster, and a strange film of abstraction clouded her eyes. She jumped to her feet, paced across the room to the marble sink and drank some cold water.

Oh, why was he taking so long? It was five-thirty! "Mr. Partridge's room, please," she told the operator. The buzzing brought no response. He must be on his way, she thought, slamming down the phone, and rushing to touch the powder puff to her nose, and spray perfume along her naked arms. I love your limbs, Jane, he had said, kissing every inch of her. She thought she heard a tap on her door, and almost caught her spikes on the scatter rug dashing to open it.

No one was there. Glancing down the corridor, she saw a maid, her key swinging like a crucifix from her belt, absent-mindedly tapping the wall as she ambled along. Closing her door quietly, Jane leaned full against it, and biting her lower lip, wondered if she might have misunderstood him this morning in the rush at Nice airport. Perhaps what he had said was "Meet you in the lobby at five" not, "in your room." Of course! He was surely waiting there this very moment, pacing like a lost soul, but too polite to ring her room and prod her to hurry! Poor darling, she thought, draping her chinchilla stole over one arm, rushing out.

For the past month she had dreaded the prospect of returning to London, the first stop in her decompression journey back to Santa Barbara. London for a week with Mother. Then Washington with Daddy and her brothers. Then, home, alone. Happily Mother had left for a long weekend in Surrey with her stuffiest friends, and though word had been waiting for her to join them at once, Jane was able to beg off by phone, pleading exhaustion. Now everything looked beautifully bright. She'd never felt less exhausted. She wondered how Daddy would react to the news of her going to India?

She knew what the rest of them would say, especially Mother, particularly when she learned about Peter! It no longer troubled her. They'd been thinking it for years without the slightest justification, ever since she went off to paint in Santa Barbara, a "mere child" of twenty-five living alone! No Tylor girl had ever done that before. What would the Smiths think? How would the Longs react? High time she gave them something real to gossip about! Daddy was the only one who'd ever truly cared about her. He would understand. She would write him tomorrow. Daddy would love Peter.

The lobby teemed with officers in uniform, ladies in evening gowns, gentlemen dressed as Londoners alone bothered to dress, every evening a special occasion. She loved ritual, and festive formality. She hoped Peter had dressed really smart this evening. But where was he? She imagined she caught a glimpse of him disappearing behind one of the massive black pillars of the lobby, and felt girlish enough to want to cover his eyes with her hands and whisper "Guess who?" The man who turned to confront her was a total stranger, his hussar mustache far larger than Peter's, his eyes grotesquely bulging. "Oh, I beg your pardon," she said. He looked mildly amused. She felt confused, foolishly wandering from pillar to potted plant, staring at men's faces. He wasn't there.

Then a bellhop passed her paging someone else, and she stopped him to ask if he would call for Peter as well. Surely he hadn't forgotten their date? He couldn't possibly. What if he'd been in an accident? A shudder of terror swept through her. *Mary, Mother of God,* she thought, instinctively crossing herself, forgetting for the moment how useless prayer had proved. She had prayed half the night while they searched the highways and scoured the ravines. If anything happened to Peter, if *he* were to die —

"Jane, old girl, do forgive me."

"Peter! Darling, are you all right?"

"Yes! Do I look wrong?"

"You look wonderful! But where in heaven's name have you been?" She clutched his arm firmly, wishing he would take her back to the room at once, without wasting another instant.

"We've been having a drink in the bar with some Indian friend of Hodge's, and good God I had no idea how late it was. I do like that dress, you know."

"Oh, it's just something I haven't worn for a while."

"Smashing," he said, with a wink that warmed her blood. "Come along, I want you to meet Hodge. He's American, but quite civilized actually."

They were in one of the large horseshoe booths near the entrance of the bar, three men with a girl seated between them, a girl who looked much too young and attractive, Jane thought.

"This is my friend, Miss Jane Tylor," Peter announced. She smiled demurely as he introduced her to Mr. Judson, Miss Gold, Hodge, and Mr. Das. Judson and Das were gentlemen enough to make the effort of pushing themselves to their feet. Hodge remained seated. She hated him instinctively, sensing he felt the same spontaneous dislike for her.

"That there's a real becomin' dress, Miss Tylor," T.J. said, taking her hand and patting it paternally. "Say, you wouldn't by any chance be related to Frank Tylor of Washington, would you?"

"He's my father," she said.

"He *is?* Well, now how 'bout that? Hodge, this here's Frank Tylor's girl! Gosh A'mighty it's a small world!"

"Ambassador Tylor?" Hodge asked, sounding respectful.

"Daddy used to be an ambassador," she said coldly.

"He is a senator now, isn't it?" asked Mr. Das, speaking English with an Oxford-Indian accent.

"Everyone seems to know more about you than I do," Peter protested. "Why the devil didn't you tell me you were so famous?"

"I'm not," she laughed. "Daddy is." She squeezed his hand reassuringly before they were separated by the table. T.J. insisted she sit next to him.

"I hope you will do us the honor of coming to India with your friends," said Das, his thick lips puckered sensually at her.

"When are you leaving, Peter?"

"Our leader says Monday."

"So soon?" She felt a knot tighten in her stomach. "How nice for all of you. Are you a hunter, Miss Gold?"

"No," Rena replied, smiling.

"Rena's our secretary," Hodge explained.

Jane flashed her most ingenuous cocktail smile, wondering how long it would take to entice Peter away from these horrible people.

"Say, why don't you come on along with us, Miss — hell, you don't mind if I call you Jane, do you?" Tony asked. "Hodge, don't you think Jane should join us?"

"I'm sure Miss Tylor would be able to find room at Maharani's in Delhi, though I don't know if we dare impose any further on Das's good nature by asking him to expedite another visa."

"But that would be no imposition whatever for Senator Tylor's daughter," Das insisted.

Jane was waiting for Peter to speak. What if he doesn't want me? she thought, feeling that sinking left-out-of-it sensation which had ruined so many summers of her adolescence when her brothers planned glorious trips of adventure without her. That was when she started to paint, during one of those wretchedly endless summers. Peter, why don't *you* say something? she wondered, staring at him.

"Have you ever been to India, old girl?" Peter asked.

"Never."

"Bloody hot in October," he muttered, shaking his head low over his glass.

"I love heat," Rena said.

"I don't mind it," Jane added tentatively.

"Good God, I remember Calcutta once at a hundred and twenty, with at *least* ninety per cent humidity, you know, and there wasn't a blasted *thing* you could do but sit around pouring liquids into your insides, and, shall I tell you what happened to me once?"

"He's funny," Rena whispered to Hodge, laughing gayly, leaning both elbows impolitely on the table as she cradled her chin with her small fists and looked eagerly at Peter, who seemed to become more animated by this rapt attention.

"Well, my shirt got so bleeding wet, you see, that I took the blasted thing *off*. This was on the verandah of the Grand Hotel."

"The Grand?" asked Das. "Oh, I don't believe another word, old chap! You are putting us on, isn't it?"

"Wait! First let me tell you who I was drinking with. It was *before* independence, you see, and my mother happened to be related to the Viceroy's aide-de-camp, who was one of the Blimpiest colonels, so naturally no one dared say a word of rebuke as I wrang the bloody shirt out, filling an empty tumbler. Then — oh, I expect he must have been thoroughly potted by then, the Colonel drank it."

"Oh, *no!*" Das roared, his ample cheeks and chin rolls shaking gelatinously. "He drank it right down, you mean?"

"The *lot*," Peter insisted. "And what do you suppose he said, eh? As God is my witness! He looks at me like this!" Peter narrowed his eyes, and pushed forward his mustache. " 'Partridge,' he says, 'they serve undiluted *English* gin in this hotel, that's what I like best about it!' "

Das, Rena, and T.J. laughed along with Peter. Hodge smiled cynically, and Jane wondered if there wasn't perhaps more to him than she'd guessed. Peter had never seemed so hateful to her as he did at this moment. Her stomach was a rope of knots; her cheeks were blistering.

"Don't let him frighten you," Hodge said, addressing her almost warmly. "Delhi's not more than eighty now."

"Oh, Peter doesn't frighten me a bit," she said, feeling humiliated, betrayed, disgusted, but hardly frightened. *He's* the one who's frightened, she thought, noticing how sheepishly he grinned at her, how much like Peck's bad boy he looked with the hair falling over his eyes, as though he'd just been caught in the pantry with pie crust on his cheek. Oh, he was really too impossibly childish! *He's* frightened of *me,* she thought, and it eased the tension she felt so painfully, yet at the same time made her heart beat faster. Poor Peter, he's terrified of falling in love! That was why he was late this evening, and why he tried so desperately with his vulgar story to dissuade her from coming to Delhi. Oh, Peter, you *are* a child, she thought. You *do* need me!

"To be perfectly serious, Jane," Peter said. "I think you would find living in India more of a strain than you might imagine."

"I don't," she said lightly, putting her arm through T.J.'s. "It was really most considerate of you to suggest I might come along. I'd love to." Then she turned to Hodge. "Now you must tell me all about your expedition!"

CHAPTER 10

SETH refused to believe it till Saturday morning when the special messenger arrived from the High Commissioner's office with their visas. Then Stella started to pack.

"Do people speak English in Delhi, Dad?" Ethan asked, suddenly apprehensive.

"In one form or another. Don't worry."

It was a weekend of gathering together and packing up. For Hodge it was the fastest weekend of his life. No sooner did he slam down the telephone, than the door buzzer rang. He started making lists of his lists. At rare moments, when he paused to try to remember what he'd forgotten, he realized how fortunate it was that he'd hired Rena. She was fast, bright, and incurably good-natured.

"Rena, you should have been in the Air Force," he said.

"I was in the Army two years almost." Her calm smile was a stimulus he found invaluable to his morale.

When the expedition is over, he thought, I may marry this girl. For this weekend, however, she was far more important to him as a secretary. He was happy he'd hired her. She seemed happy, too.

"Excited, baby?"

"Oh yes, very. I love to travel. I think all Israelis do!" She laughed softly.

Tony spent most of the weekend on the telephone.

Peter and Jane spent most of the weekend in bed.

Bruno and Niels toured the pubs till Sunday forced them to abstemious rest through teatime, when back they went for more booze, and parting toasts. They staggered into the cab that took them to London airport.

"I tell you what I like about you, Niels," Bruno said.

"Go ahead — tell."

"You know how to drink."

"This is true." Niels squinted but could not erase the double image of the driver's head. He decided to close his eyes.

"Yah, but you would be surprised how rare . . . There are not so many men can drink like you, or me. I also know how to drink."

"When I started to drink I used to get sick," Niels said. "Now I get sick when I stop."

"This happens to me too, but try to tell Lotte! Women don't drink good, especially wives."

"My wife could drink."

"Yah? I did not know you are married, Niels."

"She killed herself last month."

"Ah, this is how they are — women," Bruno remarked. They spoke no more till they reached the airport.

The 707 taxied to the end of the runway, and stopped as the whining pitch of racing jets climbed higher. The plane trembled, its silver wings visibly vibrating. Then the jet speed tapered off. They started to roll.

"Lift off," Hodge said.

"Good luck to us, boy," T.J. shouted.

"Are we flying, Dad?"

"We're flying," Seth said. "Next stop New Delhi."

As soon as they reached cruising altitude, Tony left his seat beside Hodge, and walked ahead to the washroom. Stella unbuckled her belt and crossed the aisle, taking the seat T.J. had vacated.

"Excuse me, Hodge," she said, "but I've heard so much about you I almost feel as if I know you as well as Seth, yet we've hardly had time to say hello."

"Hello," he said.

"I can imagine how excited you must be, knowing how we feel."

"I feel a bit numb at the moment, Stella, sort of suspended."

She laughed appreciatively.

"What's Mom laughing about, Dad?"

"Maybe Hodge said something funny. Why don't you set up

your soldiers on this tray?" He released the back strap of the seat in front of Ethan, jolting it somewhat.

"Hi," Rena said, looking back at them over the top of the shaken seat.

"Oh, hi. Sorry I —"

"But I'm glad! Hi, Ethan."

"How does she know my name, Dad?"

"Ooo, so you do not remember me? Now I feel sad." She pouted.

"Should he?" Seth asked, again perplexed by this girl.

"Yes. We met the other day in Trafalgar Square, feeding pigeons."

"I do remember!" Ethan said, excitedly. "Hi."

"Can I come over and help set up your soldiers? I love to play soldiers. I used to be a soldier."

"Sure! You'll be the bad guys. Okay?"

"Okay," she responded, smiling, "if I must."

"That's usually my role," Seth explained, as she skipped around to join them. He wondered how long it would take Stella to rush back.

But Stella was too engrossed in her conversation with Hodge to notice that Rena had taken her seat. "Fascinating," she repeated. "But won't it be terribly dangerous?"

"No more than what you and I are doing right now."

She was too flustered to speak. Seth had told her many things about Hodge, but neglected to mention his charm.

"Few things are more dangerous than flying," he continued, apparently oblivious to her reaction to his earlier remark. "That's what I've always appreciated about the Air Force. It's made everything since seem simple."

"Yes, I can see what you mean, only . . . I don't think Seth has ever felt that way, do you?"

"Seth's a professor, he was born one. He's never happy unless he's worried about something, or someone."

"Oh, that's very good. I must remember to tell him that, if you don't mind, Hodge?"

"Christ no. He knows it better than we do."

"Yes, I suppose, in a way, he does. He has so strong a conscience about — everything, I guess — society, tribes, people, himself. I suppose that's why he works as hard as he does. He's never really taken a vacation. You're not like that, are you?"

"My whole life's a vacation."

"I think you really mean it."

"I really mean everything I say, Stella."

She blushed, nervously straightening her skirt, unfolding her legs. She was actually relieved to see T.J. approaching them.

"Oh, but I mustn't keep Mr. Judson's seat."

"Stay where ya are, young lady. Plentya room for me."

"No, please. Really. I was just going to wash my hands."

"Okay, girl, it's thataway! Hodge, what sorta magazine ya want?"

"None thanks, Tony. I'm going to try for some sleep. See you later, Stella."

"Yes, yes. See you later," she said, hurrying forward to the toilet.

"Now that you've destroyed all the bad guys, Ethan, why don't you change seats with me?" Seth asked. "You can look out the window for a while."

"Okay. Thanks, Dad."

"How about thanking Miss Gold for playing with you?"

"Thanks, Miss Gold."

They switched seats.

"He's a very handsome boy," she said.

"I'd always thought he looked like me."

"He does."

Seth put a cigarette to his lips, feeling that awkwardness again, as if their ages were reversed.

"How old are you, Rena?"

"Twenty. Why do you ask?"

"I'm thirty-seven."

"That's nice. How does it feel?"

Like twenty right now, he thought, looking at her nakedly beautiful smile, Anita's smile. He was too tongue-tied to speak when he sat this close to her.

"What do you think now?" she asked.

"How long have you known Hodge?" he lied.

"Is this what you were thinking?"

"No."

"Then why are you afraid to tell me what it was?"

"Because you wouldn't believe me."

"How do you know?"

"Because I was thinking I'm falling in love with you," he said.

She bit at her lower lip, but did not blink or shift her eyes from his gaze, at once pain-filled and adoring.

"Oh, I see everyone's changed seats," Stella said, stopping in front of them.

"Sorry," Rena muttered, jumping up lithely, rushing past Stella to the magazine rack.

"What a rude girl. She never even said hello to me."

"You didn't say hello to her."

"I was just going to . . . you certainly sound sensitive about her."

"Do I? Well, you know me, Stell — the sensitive type."

"Yes. Hodge and I were just discussing you."

"Exciting conversation?"

"It was, actually. I find him most charming, *and* handsome."

Rena glanced back at him, while flipping through the magazines. He wondered if she thought him a middle-aged fool?

"Well, if you're not interested — and I can see you aren't," Stella said, tilting her seat back, "I think I'll take a nap. Why don't you read something to Ethan for a while? Make believe you know how to be a good father, Seth."

Through lunch and dinner they flew. Toward early darkness, past zones of time. Across the Continent. Over the Alps. Into the night they rode above the clouds. Bruno and Niels slept, as did Hodge. Peter played blackjack with Jane. T.J. read the fashion magazines, studying advertisements as though they were stock reports. Ethan tired of games, of looking out the window, of reading. He yawned and rubbed his eyes. He became cranky and cried. He became nauseous and threw up his food. Stella tried rocking him to sleep in her arms. He dozed for an hour or so. Then woke and threw up again.

"He feels feverish," she told Seth.

"He's just warm from sleep. Let him stretch out across two seats. Here. I'll get some more pillows."

"Feel his forehead! He's burning up!"

She was right, of course.

"I'm thirsty, Dad."

"I'll get some milk," he said.

"Water," she insisted, taking a pill from her purse.

While the others slept they spelled each other at Ethan's side. He could not retain the aspirin any better than his food. They were afraid to take his temperature. He trembled uncontrollably.

"Seth, what will we do? Can't we ask them to put down the plane?"

"Don't panic, Stell. Try to get some sleep."

"He's my baby . . . What if . . . ?"

"Sh-h-h, he's sleeping. He'll be all right."

"Oh, my God," she whispered, shaking her head. "Dear God, if anything happens to him . . ."

"You won't be any good to him if you get yourself sick, Stell. I'll keep an eye on him. Take a nap now, I'll wake you if he stirs."

"Will you? Promise?"

"I promise."

She was asleep the moment she closed her eyes, exhausted by the strain of anxiety. He loosened his tie, and removed his shoes, prepared for the long vigil, five more hours to landing. He sat on the floor close to Ethan's head. The febrile breathing became deeper, thickly adenoidal, a heavy gargling sound that sent a shiver of panic through Seth's mind. He had listened one night to the death rattle of his father's breath, waiting in vain for the ambulance, which came too late.

God in heaven, he thought, staring at his son's fever-flushed face, if you're there, help us. He did not often pray anymore. His father had always prayed, every Sabbath; on all the High Holy Days, "Reb" Goodman donned his yarmulke and tallith, and sat faithfully davening in the basement of the Brooklyn synagogue. Their wealthier neighbors bought seats upstairs, in the spacious vault-ceilinged room, which he glimpsed at times when the door opened, hearing the angelic music of the sweet-voiced choir, the mellifluous resonance of the cantor. The folding chairs in the basement were jammed close together, the stagnant air foul with mouth odors and the acrid smell of snuff. No music was heard from those bargain stalls, just the busy babbling of shawl-shrouded men, croaking like frogs around a fetid pond, each competing for God's attention. *Adonoi Elihaynu,* they cried. Hear me, listen to me, God! He wondered how many such voices God could heed? Can He hear them all, Papa? *Don't be such a chuchum,* his father had said, inching the prayer book closer to his face, pointing his finger at each mysterious word, pronouncing them more distinctly so that Seth would follow the motion of his lips. He wanted to ask why God couldn't understand English? And why everyone had to repeat the same formulas in prayer? And all the names of the Hebrew patriarchs in precisely the same order? Often he argued with his father about religion. If God made the universe, Papa, who made God? And how could there be light on the first day, when in Genesis it said God made the sun and the moon and the stars on the fourth? Don't think you're so smart, the old man cautioned. Wait, you'll get older, you'll see there's nothing new under the sun. Everything's in the Bible, *boitchikla* — you'll see someday. Now stop giving me a headache with questions. Go play in the street! *And button up your neck!* But Seth only became more skeptical with age.

Still there were times when he prayed. Touching his lips to Ethan's scorching forehead, he wondered if this might not be God's way of punishing him for having said what he did to Rena. She was almost young enough to be his daughter. What madness had possessed him to flirt with such a girl? The sudden onset of Ethan's fever seemed incomprehensible now to Seth as anything short of divine warning. He vowed never again to indulge in such lustful treachery. He felt unworthy now of his father's memory; his father's sacrifice of comfort and happiness for them after their mother's death. He had never remarried, not wanting to inflict a stepmother upon them. Why do you think I work so hard? he asked Seth and his brother whenever they misbehaved. For you two boys, why else? You're all I have to live for, you two!

He dozed off, and woke fitfully, alternately chilled and sweating. The eerie light of the cabin, the unremitting drone of the engines added to the nightmarish quality of his dreams and waking he wished he would find Ethan better, hoping that the reality of this endless journey was itself a dream.

But then it did end. They started their descent as the first light of dawn filtered gray through the window shades, Ethan waking Stella with his plaintive cries. The stewardess brought him some juice, and he drank it eagerly, his lips parched from the fever. They tried another aspirin.

"If he can only hold that, it would break the fever," Stella said. "Oh, thank God, he seems a little better this morning. The sleep seems to have helped. But you look terrible, Seth. You haven't slept at all, have you?"

"I did—some. I better go and wash up."

Peering at his haggard visage in the washroom mirror, Seth realized more fully how insane he had been, speaking to Rena as he did. No matter how closely she resembled Anita, he was no more the young man Anita had loved than Stella was the child bride he had married. Age had scarred his face with dark shadows of wrinkles thick beneath his tired eyes. The day's growth of beard left his cheeks like fallow fields rank with the stubble of last year's harvest. He looked as old as he felt, as worn. He looked in fact so remarkably like what he was — a middle-aged professor, who had made a damned fool of himself — that he did not bother to comb his hair or straighten his tie, hastily leaving the washroom after splashing his face with cold water.

"Good morning," Rena said, smiling at him, as he approched her seat. "Is your son better?"

"I think so," he snapped, rushing past her line of vision. The trip had done nothing whatever to fade the luminous beauty of her eyes, the freshness of her glowing face.

"Please fasten your seat belts, ladies and gentlemen, for our landing at Delhi International Airport . . ."

They spiraled into the thunderhead of a late monsoon cloud bank. The plane jolted and vibrated, buffeted by pockets of angry turbulence that set Ethan vomiting again, pressing his ears and crying bitterly. There was nothing but dismal gray outside. The suburbs of New Delhi appeared as apparitions — dingy hovels, huddled buffalolike on the flat reddish-brown plain below. The air became moist and warm. The wheels touched, bounced off, and bumped over the none-too-smooth runway past old Dakotas, black pyramids of diesel drums, and tarpaulin-topped trucks. The engines roared, then wound themselves out.

No sooner did they stop moving, than the cabin door opened, and an Indian officer entered, armed with an aerosol bomb held upraised in one hand like a grenade.

"Please to remain seated," he announced, spraying the choking fog of disinfectant onto their heads as though he were dusting crops. The fumes made everyone gag. Ethan coughed and cried louder.

"Can't someone tell that stupid man to stop?" asked Stella.

The health inspector did a thorough job. When at last he had finished, he touched his fingers to the visor of his cap.

"Welcome to India," he said.

CHAPTER 11

LOTTE finished her fifth cup of coffee, or was it the sixth? She had lost count. Whichever it was, she was alone now in the cavernous dining room of Maharani's, except for the half-dozen turbaned waiters who hovered around her table, one of them returning to her elbow to refill the cup.

"No, that is quite enough, thank you." It was almost ten! She rose to leave. The waiters bowed. The assistant manager bowed. The manager himself escorted her from the air-conditioned room, gallantly bowing as he smiled and opened the door to the lobby, saying, "I hope you have enjoyed your breakfast, Frau Jaeger."

"Thank you, Herr Klug. There has been no sign of them as yet?"

"No word as yet, but the plane has arrived safely."

"Was this not four hours ago?"

"Of course, but you see there is customs clearance, and the drive from the airport may take more than one hour."

"So long as *this?*"

"Unfortunately, Frau Jaeger, we are now in India."

It was his one explanation, she noted, for all complaints or problems. Since her arrival last evening (she had come directly from Frankfurt after visiting her father) when her luggage was deposited in the wrong room, when the water for her bath was lukewarm, when she asked for more ice in her iced tea, he had remained polite, smiling, but his comment was invariably the same: "We are now in India."

She was beginning to understand better why Father had been so upset about her decision to accompany Bruno here. He had begged her to reconsider — to remain home until the baby was born. "It is no place to live, India!" he had shouted. Who would care for her when Bruno was in Nepal? Did she know any German doctors there? She had assured him confidently that there was no need to worry. But now, four hours after Bruno's plane had landed, with no sign of him, no word from him by phone or wire, Lotte felt less certain.

She paced from under the crystal chandelier hung like an inverted Christmas tree to the marble stairway carpeted in red velvet. In elegance of style and decor, the hotel had been a pleasant surprise, as was its Swiss manager. But Lotte could not rest easily without Bruno. Whenever he was away from her, the nightmares she'd had after receiving notification of his death during the war returned to haunt her.

She decided to leave the lobby, walking past the potted palms to the front entrance. A royal blue runner cascaded down the center of the semicircular marble steps outside. A scalloped canopy of blue stretched its umbrella across the entrance driveway, which circled an oval of rose bushes and carnations. The gravel path stretched like a sari fringed with palms to the main gate at the city road. Within the spacious gardens, eucalyptus trees and lush banyans blocked all view of the bustling world outside. To the right of the front stairs a line of taxis stood waiting, their dozing drivers at the wheels. Several sports cars and an old Bentley were left unattended at the other side. Not a leaf stirred. The air was pregnant with moisture, stiflingly close.

"Taxi, madam?" the doorman asked.

"No thank you."

She strolled aimlessly in the garden, and was about to return to the cool lobby when a cavalcade of four large taxis rolled through the gate and came to a gravel-scraping stop under the canopy's shade. Her heart beat faster as she started down the steps, but she recognized none of the occupants of the first cab: a man carrying a small boy in his arms, and a harried woman, who rushed out after them. Klug had just emerged from the lobby, and she heard the man tell him they needed a doctor at once.

Then the door of the second taxi opened and Niels stepped out to stare up at her, his face filling the immediate field of her vision. She had waited so expectantly for Bruno that now she thought she saw him, only as he was before the war ravaged his features. He seemed so miraculously restored to her, a Nordic god in human form, that Lotte all but flung her arms around his neck, crying out, "Bruno, you are well again!" She had dreamed of it often, hoping he would agree to undergo the plastic surgery he hated. Now she thought by some miracle it had been accomplished almost overnight in London. For an instant she was too paralyzed to speak. Then, like an actor emerging from behind his puppet mask, Bruno himself appeared at Niels's side.

"Ah, so here Lotte waits for us! Come, Lotte, meet Niels Larsen. We were just now talking of you, *Liebchen*."

"How do you do, Mr. Larsen. Bruno, what took you so long from the airport?"

"What do you think? — talk, talk, talk, jabber, jabber, jabber! This is what Indians love to do most. They are all born to be monkeys!"

"It was mostly my fault," Niels said. "I have brought many reels of film, and the customs officials wanted to confiscate it."

"Are you a photographer, Mr. Larsen?"

"Lotte, you have seen his pictures a thousand times! If you would not act so ignorant he might even photograph you."

"I'm sure Mr. Larsen is very particular about his subjects," she said, blushing.

"I am," he said, "and I would be flattered if you would allow me to photograph you soon."

He sounded so sadly earnest that she knew it was no flippant remark. She did not know what to say, feeling suddenly quite self-conscious, wondering if the heaviness she sensed inside her was as yet apparent.

"So! It is settled! You must pose for Niels, Lotte, before we leave, yah?"

86

"Bruno, don't be so demanding! Mr. Larsen hasn't had time to step inside the hotel yet!"

"This is when we must tie him down — before he becomes so busy he has no more time for us!"

Hodge, Rena, and Tony left the third cab, and went directly to the lobby.

"Rena, call Indian Airways. See how soon they can book us on a flight to Kathmandu, but not before Thursday, baby. We'll need a day or two of shopping here."

"I better phone the bank, boy," said T.J., "make sure my draft's come through."

The manager bowed before them.

"Ah, you are Mr. McNeill? My name is Klug."

Hodge asked how many vacant rooms he had and went to the desk to register.

Jane had stopped behind one of the potted palms just inside the entrance to whisper, "Peter, we *can't!* I won't do it!"

"Oh, good God, woman, don't be such a damned prude! They all *know!*"

"I just hate you when you talk like that, Peter Partridge! Have you been telling people —"

"God no, old girl! They have eyes! Don't be a bloody hypocrite."

"I solemnly warn you, Peter, one more word like that and I'll take one of those taxis to another hotel! I will not register in the same room as you. So if you want me to stay in *this* hotel —"

"Oh, all right, you win! What a fuss!"

"In case you think otherwise, Mr. Partridge, I have never in my life registered anywhere with any man. Oh!"

"Come on, Jane, no tears, eh? I apologize. It's just that I thought it would give us a bit more time —"

"And I suppose you don't think *I* care about that?"

"I didn't say that, did I?"

"But you meant it!"

"Well, if we were married —"

"What did you say, Peter?" she asked, brightening.

"I said *if*. Oh, good God!" You blackguard, he thought. Partridge, you'd better bloody well watch your step with this woman!

"All right, dry your sniffles," he said, handing her his handkerchief, looking around nervously. "Every ruddy Indian in this lobby is staring right at us! Come on, old girl — be British!"

Seth helped Stella remove Ethan's clothes. The interminable wait at customs had exhausted him, and he was sleeping again, seeming as feverish as the night before. The desk clerk had promised that a doctor would come within the half hour. They soaked towels and began swathing his limbs with them. He groaned and shuddered, but did not awaken.

"If anything happens to Ethan, Seth, I'll . . ."

"Nothing's going to happen. Ethan's a strong kid. Now soak this towel again, will you?"

From the crazed look of her eyes he didn't know which of them to worry about more. He wished he were back in the British Museum. He'd begun to curse the day that Hodge's telegram reached him. He'd sensed it meant nothing but trouble.

It was the longest twenty minutes of Seth's life before Dr. Vaidya arrived at their room. He was a quiet, efficient-seeming man, who assured them that the boy would be all right.

"The lungs are quite clear, you see," he said, folding his stethoscope and extracting a hypodermic needle from his case.

"What's that for?" Stella asked, nearly hysterical.

"Penicillin, madam. Is the boy allergic?"

"I don't think so."

"No," Seth said. "But will it bring down the fever?"

"Not before one day, I'm afraid. But we'll give him something else for that. Has he taken any water outside this hotel?"

"He was sick on the plane."

"I see. Then it's probably just a mild grippe. I'm sure he'll be fit in a day or two. Keep him in bed. Let me know if the fever doesn't subside by this afternoon. I'll look in again tomorrow morning."

"Where can we reach you?" Stella asked.

"Here is my card. Try to give him one of these tablets when he wakes up; it should help settle his stomach. Be sure to press fluids, but no milk for the time being. Is it quite clear?"

"Thank you," Seth said.

"Not at all. Is it your first visit to India?"

"Not mine, theirs."

"We have a saying that an unfortunate start brings a happy ending, isn't it?"

"Let's hope so," Seth said, showing him out of the room.

"Oh God, I hate this country," Stella muttered after the door closed. "I wish we'd never come!"

CHAPTER 12

IT was almost noon when Rena tapped at Hodge's door to report her failure.

"They have two seats to Kathmandu next Friday," she said, "and one on a plane the Tuesday after, but no room for five for a month."

"Impossible."

"That is what I said."

"And —?"

"I spoke to four people at Indian Airways — including the flight director and the supervising manager —"

"Did you tell them it was urgent?"

"Of course."

"And?"

"They said they were sorry."

"Oh, for Christ's sake!" He tossed aside the provisions list he had been checking, and rubbed the back of his neck, pacing angrily across the room, returning to take a cigarette. "Get that manager for me now, will you!"

"You want me to call them again, Hodge?"

"Isn't that what I said?"

His voice was like sandpaper. She had never seen him so angry. His eyes made her recoil in fear. She lifted the phone and asked the operator for the Indian Airways. "No, I — I don't know the number," she said into the phone.

"I thought you just phoned them," he snapped.

"I did! I have been on the phone with them since I stepped into the lobby! Where do you think I have been — in the pool?" She was trembling with rage, mostly because she felt so stupid. He talked to her as though she were his servant — not that she would ever speak to a servant so rudely! She had not even been to her own room as yet. The grounds were so beautiful outside, but she did not even go for a stroll in the garden! And no one had offered her so much as a cup of coffee! She was tired and hungry — why? Simply because she worked so hard to please him, to do his hateful chores — and this was the thanks she got! "Yes — yes, I am still waiting!" she told the operator. It was all she had seen of India so far — its telephones.

"What the hell's taking so long?"

"Ask the operator!" She was on the verge of tears.

"Okay, I will. Let me have that damn thing." He almost wrenched the phone from her hand. "Hello!" he shouted.

She hated him then more than anyone she had ever known. If she weren't so terrified of him, she would have struck at his smug, self-satisfied face. Most of all she hated him for making her feel so hopelessly inept. She hurried to the door before she would say something ugly and horrible to him.

"Where are you going?"

"To my room," she whispered, without stopping, or looking back. She slammed his door as hard as she could.

"Hello? Yes — I want your supervising manager . . . Mr. Mc-Neill. And please hurry — this is urgent!" He wondered what was bugging Rena? She'd run out of the room as though some demon was after her. "Hello — yes. Yes, I'm holding." It surely couldn't have been anything he'd said? He hardly had time to say a word to her. Women were peculiar creatures. The static reaching his ear through the phone sounded like a burning bomb fuse. He kept finding his line tuned into strange conversations — suddenly the low buzz of the dial tone returned. He tapped furiously at the phone. "Operator, I've been disconnected! . . . Indian Airways, dammit! . . . No, I don't know the number — you just had them on the line for me ten seconds ago!" He glared impatiently at his wristwatch.

It took forty minutes for Hodge to learn precisely what Rena had told him. Incredibly enough, I.A. refused to add an additional flight to Kathmandu, despite his offer to pay for every seat. The manager claimed that it was not a matter of money, but of insufficient aircraft. No other line made the internal runs. Yes, they were nationalized, he'd been told. No, there was little hope for any cancellations, since the waiting lists were already much longer than usual. That's socialism, he thought, slamming down the phone, shaking his head, and deciding to go see what was wrong with Rena. He would have to get her to call his friend at the Home Ministry, and make an appointment for him this afternoon. Nothing was impossible in India, he knew, if you reached the right people. Her room was next door.

"Who is it?"

"Hodge. Open up, will you."

"I'm still unpacking," she replied. The door remained closed.

"I have to tell you something."

"What?"

"Look — I can't stand out here shouting at this door! If you're naked, throw on a robe —"

"I'm not naked."

She opened the door, and was, much to his surprise, still dressed exactly as she had been in his room.

"Well, what the hell was that all about?"

"What do you have to tell me that is so urgent?"

Her voice sounded strained, her eyes looked inflamed.

"Hey, you haven't been crying, have you, baby?"

"Is this what you came to tell me?"

"Of course not." She was trembling, visibly. She looked pathetically frail, slight, like a child alone in a high wind.

"Well? What is it, Mr. McNeill? I'm waiting to hear?"

"What the hell's this 'Mr. McNeill' bit?"

"It's your name, not? And I work for you — so-o-o, this is how I call you."

"Rena, that's no way to talk to me, and you know very well —"

"No? But to yell at me the way you have done before, for, for nothing — this is all right?"

So that was it! He could not help but laugh, he felt so relieved.

"And you think this is funny? Or is it my accent makes you laugh — how bad I speak English?" She wanted to throw something hard at him.

"I love your accent, Rena —"

"Don't lie to me."

"I love everything about you, you wild woman. Don't you know that?" He gripped both her arms, drawing her body close to his. "Rena." He kissed her startled lips.

"Hodge, don't . . ."

"Be quiet. We've both talked too much." Her body was softly pliant to the pressure of his fingers.

"Please," she whispered, turning her face aside, pushing futilely against his arms.

"Crazy girl. I wasn't yelling at you, but at Indian Airways."

"No, but you thought I was stupid, and — Hodge, please. I can't breathe."

"Then don't." He covered her lips again with his own, losing his balance in a kiss so soft and deeply penetrating that they started to fall. He tightened his grip, moving her back toward the bed, toppling onto it, holding her.

"Hodge, no — not like this —"

"What's wrong with this, baby?" Her legs were like silken magnets under his.

"Please, let me get up, Hodge —"

"You're the most beautiful girl I ever met —"

"No, *please!* Be serious."

"I am, baby."

"Don't make me fight with you. You are too strong — I can't . . ."

"I love you, Rena. Kiss me."

"No . . ." He pressed his lips greedily over her mouth, bruising his tongue against the sharp edge of her teeth, feeling her pelvis tremble under the firm pressure of his body, pinning her legs to the bed. His blood hammered against his temples as she writhed beneath him, clawing at his muscles, trying to push him away, biting as a tigress. No woman since Margie had ever aroused him so swiftly, so completely. Through all the layers of their restraining clothes, he could feel her womanhood. The burning passion welled up in him, churned madly inside his loins, until that moment when it cracked with explosive fury — the flood waters rushed free with sudden, inundating power, racing warm and turbulent, white with foam . . .

"Baby, I love you," he whispered, releasing his grip, moving away from her prostrate form, feeling the moisture, the perspiration ooze from every pore of his body.

"Is this what that is called?" She barely whispered it, staring wide-eyed at the overhead fan, moving slowly, like a giant spider upon the ceiling.

"What?"

"Love?" she asked, her lips strangely contorted.

"I don't read you, baby." He sat up, and brushed his clothes straight, lighting a cigarette, offering it to her. She waved it aside. He took a long drag and puffed the smoke in her direction.

"Never mind," she said, getting up, going to the other side of the room, where she withdrew into the depths of a soft armchair, staring at him, spent and calm now, the burned-out volcano. She felt cheated, like merchandise used and discarded. More than that, she hated him now, for in spite of herself he had stirred her, aroused her warmth, her passionate longing, her most fervent desire, yet before experiencing the fulfilment she had resisted but wanted, needed, he had broken away from her. Watching him now she felt coldly contemptuous.

"What are you thinking about, Rena? You look very mysterious."

"Do I?"

"Yes. Mysterious and beautiful. You're a beautiful girl."

"Thank you."

"You're not angry anymore, are you?"

"Should I be?"

"Of course not." He came to her, sitting on the arm of her chair, stroking her hair, as though she were a pet cat.

"Good. Then I'm not."

"But why do you sound that way?"

She shrugged. "It must be my accent."

"No — but I know what it is."

"You do?" She turned her face to him to see if it was true. He was very handsome, and strong. She liked the way he looked. If only he could be less greedy, less selfish, she might almost —

"I know what you want, baby."

Do you, Hodge? She stared at his eyes with slightly parted lips. He has narrowly calculating eyes, she thought, as though he is always estimating how much the things he sees are worth in dollars.

"You want me to marry you, Rena, and I will — after the expedition's over, and we've succeeded —"

She would have laughed very loud, but knew that was too cruel — even for him. "And if you don't succeed?"

"We will succeed — and I'll marry you."

It wasn't "We'll get married," or "I'll ask you to marry me," but *I'll marry you*. She did not refrain from smiling.

"I'm not ready for marriage, Hodge."

"You will be — in a few months, baby."

"No, I don't think so." He looked momentarily hurt. That is something, she thought, if I can hurt him.

"We won't argue about it now, baby. There's a helluva lot of work we've got to do first. I couldn't budge those sons-of-bitches at Indian Airways —"

"Oh? I see." He looked and sounded more like the Hodge she'd remembered that first morning at the Savoy — almost the same. But not quite.

"To hell with them, baby. No point wasting another minute arguing with those jerks. We'll go over their heads, to the Home Ministry. Now get this — I want you to call the Ministry, and ask for Bose — N. K. Bose — that's B-o-s-e — he's a deputy-something — under secretary, I guess. Tell him I'm here, and want to see him today — any time, at his convenience. You can set up the appointment at the Ministry, if he likes — or if he can't make it this afternoon, invite him here for dinner. Okay?"

"Okay."

"Now powder your nose, baby, and we'll get some lunch. You must be starving."

She had never felt less hungry.

"Look — I'm going to change my — I'll get into a fresh suit, and be back in a few minutes, okay?"

"Okay."

"Hey, come on — cheer up, baby! Where's that bright smile?" She smiled.

"That's more like it!" He planted a mild kiss on her lips — a burned-out volcano kiss. "See you in ten minutes, baby!"

He closed the door behind him, softly as a lamb.

Men, she thought — they're all crazy.

CHAPTER 13

THEY were having lunch in the grand ballroom.

"So — when do we leave for Kathmandu, Roger?" Bruno asked.

"Not sure yet, Bruno. There's a slight problem."

"What's 'at, boy?"

"No planes."

"Yah? But how is it? I spoke just now to Klug, and he tells me they go twice every week direct from here."

"I should have said no seats — they're booked solid for a month."

"Good God, no!"

"How nice," Jane said.

"I think we'll be able to work it out," Hodge said, "to Miss Tylor's disappointment. I'm going to see a friend at the Home Ministry this afternoon."

"Who's your contact, boy?"

"N. K. Bose. Do you know anyone there, Tony?"

"No — not really. Is he big enough to swing it, ya think?"

"I hope so," Hodge said, adding to himself, because if he's not, we're in trouble.

"Yah, this is India. To buy a postage stamp you must know someone, or have a friend who is the friend of another friend!"

"Blackguards! Hodge, are you sure there's no plane?"

"I'm afraid so, Pete. Rena and I have both been through Indian Airways' chain-of-command with all the dynamite we have."

"When do you see the minister, boy?"

"Unfortunately he's not the minister, Tony. I see him at three."

"Then you should be back here by five?"

"I hope so."

"I'll be waiting for you in my room."

"Right, Tony. I'll let you know first thing."

"You girls ready to order?" T.J. asked, smiling at Jane and Rena, who flanked him, and signaling the waiter, in cutaway, who rushed to their side.

"But tell me, Roger, what is the plan if you do not get the plane from your friend?"

"Yes, we'll have to think about that."

"Does it mean we might have to go back?" Niels asked, apprehensively.

"Blast no! We can always drive a lorry up if we bloody well have to, can't we, Hodge?"

"Let's hope we don't have to —"

"Amen! But I mean we bloody well *could!* Couldn't we?"

"Seth? You know the terrain better than I do — what do you think?"

"There's a road," Seth said, "but I'm not sure how bad the rains have been this past week or two. When the monsoon's heavy some of those culverts are impassable."

"For how long?"

"Hard to say — a day, a week."

"Yah, this is true, and even when the road is clear this trip takes us one week at least."

"Which means extra provisions," Hodge said. "We'd probably need two trucks."

"Boys, let's not start countin' our twisters till they come. Have yourselves some good grub now. Trouble al'ays looks brighter on a full stomach — that's my motto."

"Agreed," said Hodge, ordering.

"How is Ethan feeling?" Rena asked Seth.

"The fever's down a bit, I think. Stella's with him. I promised to relieve her as soon as I finish —"

"Could I help?" she asked.

"No thanks." He did not look at her as he spoke.

"Yah, I notice you carry him in this morning," Lotte said. "He is a fine-looking boy. You have had the doctor?"

"Yes."

"Good. I speak later to your wife."

"Roger, when you go today to see your friend, let me do something else, yah? I could order provisions we need here," Bruno suggested.

"Right. I was going to ask you and Peter, in fact, if you would do that. I've drawn up a list of things — there's an excellent man in Connaught Circle — Misra."

"Yah, I know Misra —"

"Wonderful. Rena can give you the list after lunch. Pete, is that okay for you?"

"Mmm — fact is, you know, I had rather promised to show Jane a bit of old Delhi today," he began, coughing nervously into his fist and glancing somewhat sheepishly at Hodge. "The Red Fort and all, you know?" His cheeks became red as he said it.

"Oh, I see," Hodge said, nodding knowingly. "Well, I suppose Bruno can manage alone."

"Hey, boy, I wouldn't mind seein' a few sights myself," T.J. said, turning to Peter. "Why don't the three of us go together?"

"Uh — yes," Peter said, his cheeks growing scarlet. "That *would* be just lovely, of course, but you see I *do* have to phone a chap or two first now, and — well, it's just *possible,* you know, their being such old friends and all, that I *won't* actually be able to get free today —"

"I think Peter's plans haven't quite jelled yet, Tony," Hodge said, winking.

"Oh! Hell, don't worry 'bout me, boy, I'll find my way around!"

"So, this is settled," Bruno said. "Niels, you must take your pictures of Lotte today, yah? Then we see how they look before we leave."

"Ach, Bruno!"

"But he has agreed, *Liebchen.*"

"Yes, whenever you wish," Niels told her.

"But my hair —"

"Never mind, never mind your hair! It looks today more beautiful than when you spend so much money to have it set!"

"I must say it couldn't look better," Peter affirmed, twitching his eyebrows. Jane kicked his shin under the table. "Ow!"

"An' how 'bout the looksa this here food?" Tony said, digging into his shrimp cocktail. "Why, you know, t'hear folks back home talk about India's food shortages, you'd think a man'd damn near starve comin' here, but that there menu's good as any I've seen in London or New York!"

"Yah, only nothing to drink!"

"Hell, we kin get plentya that in our rooms, boy."

The others were still eating when Seth excused himself, wishing Hodge good luck.

"I'll need it, buddy." He left for the Ministry at two. Bruno decided to accompany him as far as the Circle.

"Do you like me to bring my camera to your room now, Lotte?" Niels asked as they started across the lobby together.

"No, but why should you bother? I could come to your room — or — ach, but it is foolish to trouble you so."

Her reticence, and more than that, the subdued quality of her smile, the aristocratic mold of her face, her manner, at once modest yet touched with hauteur, suddenly appealed to him. Till this moment he too had thought Bruno's request opportunistic, almost crude in its attempt to exploit his talent after so brief a friendship. He was, of course, accustomed to such requests from friends, still he resented them as impositions — though he knew they were meant as flattery. Looking more closely at her face now, however, he wanted to photograph her. It was not merely a pretty face. There was much strength in its features. Sadness too. And pain.

"It will not take long," he said. "I would enjoy doing it, Lotte — if you don't mind?"

"You are most kind, Niels."

"No. I have never been kind."

"Why do you think so?"

"Oh — I don't know. It is an impresssion I have of myself, and what others who have known me best confirm." They walked slowly along the veranda facing the rear garden that led to the pool. The sun had burned off the morning haze, blazing naked onto the lush foliage of tropical vegetation. The plantain trees and brilliant gol mohurs in bloom, the passionflowers with their moisture-bloated stems and blossoms of crimson, orange, and purple languidly exuded an atmosphere of sensuality and warmth that touched an all-but-forgotten chord in his spirit, and stirred Niels, awakening him to a sudden, intense awareness of this exotic world around him.

"How beautiful it looks — in the sunlight," she said, as though intuiting his thoughts.

"Almost too beautiful."

"But why? Can anything be too beautiful?"

"I think so. Yes."

"How?"

"Like too much brilliance," he said. "It will destroy any picture you try to take, and too much beauty — sometimes that is equally destructive."

"I see."

"This is my room. Please come in. I will just set up the tripod. The camera is loaded."

"What made you choose photography, Niels?"

"I wanted to paint — when I was a boy — at sea, but — I was not good. The camera is much easier."

"No art is easy," she said.

"Have you ever —?"

"Ach, I have no talent. I play piano, of course —"

"I love to listen to piano music. Can you play Scarlatti?"

"Yah, of course. But here I have no music, and I have not played for some time — at home Bruno does not want me to play —"

"Does he?"

"Yah, and he composes. He did not mention it to you?"

"No."

"No, because it depresses him now. He has finished nothing in so many years — since the war. Before then he was a prodigy. He won a scholarship to study in Vienna. Everyone thought he will be — another Mozart, a Beethoven, perhaps. Ach, such talent he has — remarkable genius! Then comes the war. Did you fight in the war?"

"I was your prisoner," he said, peering at her through the camera.

"Madness — this is the only word for such things. It is all our fault, I know — such meaningless waste, such destruction — for what? At least if we were any wiser now, yah?"

Her smile was plaintively ironic. He shot, and swiftly advanced the roll.

"Did you take my picture?"

"Yes. I will take many — as we talk, if you don't mind? Be yourself, Lotte. Do not try to pose. I move the camera around you this way —"

"But don't you need a light meter? Can you take the picture so fast?"

"The meter is built into this camera. Speed and aperture adjustments are automatic. You see, it does everything for me — I am practically unnecessary."

"No, I sense you are a true artist, Niels. But how ingenious this small machine has become — it is no larger than my own camera."

"It is German," he said.

"So at least we have done one thing good for you. I am glad."

Her smile was joyous, radiant. He snapped again. That was a good one — Beatrice illuminating Paradise. He felt exhilarated. He was not even thirsty now. He went to the window and changed the angle of the blind, subduing the light slightly. He studied the contours of her face, the play of light on her cheeks and neck, the noble sweep of her brow. She could have been Helen of Troy, he thought.

"Does my hair look terrible, Niels?"

"Beautiful."

"You should not flatter me so. I might think you mean it."

"I do," he said, clicking another shot. "You are the most photogenic model I have had since —"

"Since?"

He left the camera, and turned away from her, standing without moving, seeing nothing.

"Niels, is something wrong? Did I say something to upset you?"

"No. Forgive me, Lotte. I — sometimes I feel slightly dizzy."

"But then you must lie down," she insisted, going to him, touching his arm gently. "Can I get you something? I have pills in my room for headaches."

"No, it is all right. I — perhaps I will take just a light drink. Will you join me?"

"Of course, but for me *very* light, yah?"

His hand trembled as he poured the whiskey, spilling some of it onto his dresser.

"I take plain water with mine," he said, "but if you wish soda, I will call . . ."

"Plain water is fine for me, too."

"Skoal," he said, handing her the glass.

"To your artistry, Niels. It is a rare gift — art."

He smiled, somewhat cynically, she thought, and finished his drink in one gulp. Then he refilled his glass.

"I drink too much," he said.

"We all have reasons for what we do. Tell me, Niels, what were your reasons for joining this expedition?"

"I had to leave Copenhagen."

"I see." But she said it with a questioning tone.

"This was the first opportunity," he continued, shrugging. "It seemed as good as any other."

"And the Yeti? Do you believe in his existence?"

"Who knows? There are many mysteries."

"Yah, this is what I often think. Birth and death — God." She looked at him bemusedly. "Love."

She waited patiently for him to speak.

"I was going to say, since Ulla — my wife. She is dead now. She killed herself."

Her expression became so ethereal, so maternally affectionate, suffused with such understanding love and tenderness, that he wished then he could have taken her picture, sensing that whatever other shots he made of her, none would be so richly revealing of this woman's soul, none as true. She faced him unmoving for an instant, then went to him, kissed his lips, softly, tenderly — withdrawing almost as soon as they touched.

"Thank you, Niels," she said.

"For what, Lotte?"

"For trusting me enough to tell me."

"No, it is I who am grateful to you — and Bruno. I have not been able to talk this past month to friends I have known all my life, the way I can talk to you both."

"Yah, this is how we feel to you, Niels! It is what Bruno said to me just before lunch — how one reason he is so happy he has joined this expedition is that he feels so close already to you. This *Gemütlichkeit — die Geselligkeit,* what we call — it is much too rare in life."

"Stay just so, Lotte," he said, going quickly to the camera, taking another picture. "Yes, that is lovely! I would like someday to photograph you in my studio — with floodlights."

"I love to visit Copenhagen, Niels — and you must come to us in Frankfurt, yah? We must remain now always friends! Do you promise?"

"I promise," he said, smiling. How unfamiliar it felt to him, that smile. How good it felt.

CHAPTER **14**

"YES, do come in, Hodge," Bose sighed, opening the door to his file-crammed office, extending a limp hand to his guest. There were ribbon-wrapped manila folders piled onto every flat surface in the small room, including the floor. Bose quickly removed a stack of files from the chair beside his desk, offering Hodge a seat. He looked much older than Hodge had remembered him three years ago. His hair had thinned, and turned gray. His face was careworn. "Well now — what brings you to India this time?"

"I'm actually on my way to Nepal, N.K."

"Another hunt, is it?" Bose had been District Officer in the region of Hodge's last tiger shoot, and their maharajah host had invited him along for the sport. He was quite lively then, animated, and cheerful. He'd just received word of his promotion to the Ministry in Delhi, and told Hodge to be sure to call him as soon as he returned to India — so that they could arrange some more sport! "You know, I haven't had a real holiday since that weekend we spent in Himachal! The pressure here at the Ministry, Hodge, is unbelievable! I have not had a minute yet today for my lunch, but let me order some tea for us."

"Don't bother —"

"No, I insist! It's the very least hospitality I can offer." He tapped nervously at the bell on the edge of his cluttered desk. A barefoot servant appeared at the door, touching his hand to his turban. Bose ordered some tea and sweets.

"Naturally, I would ask you to have dinner at my home tonight, Hodge, but the Minister has entrusted me with the responsibility of preparing his answers for tomorrow's question period in Lok Sabha, and I've hardly finished, you see. These files —"

"I'm glad you're doing so well, N.K. That's quite a responsibility."

"Yes, yes, but the work is unbelievable! I tell you frankly, on days like this I feel as if the entire weight of our government sits on my shoulders alone! The pressure is fantastic! Sometimes I don't see my family for days. My wife's mother has come to stay with us now. I have barely spoken two words to her! This is how we work today in India! Of course, ours is the largest Ministry, no doubt, and the most important, you see, so that is where the pressure comes in. The P.M. is always consulting with my Minister — every day. You must have read how close they are. Like you and I, isn't it? There is nothing the P.M. doesn't consult with him about, and quite frankly, Hodge — but this is strictly confidential — just between us — when the P.M. retires I think my Minister will succeed him!"

Hodge acted suitably impressed at this revelation, wishing N.K. would stop talking long enough to let him state his business.

"But I don't say that to make my own small job sound more important, you realize," he continued compulsively. "After all, I'm still just the D.U.S., isn't it? So, what does it mean, you will ask, in terms of numbers remote from the Minister? Well, you see, my immediate superior is the U.S. for P.A. Parliamentary Affairs. I see you were puzzled by that. We are used to all these abbreviations, of course, and I always tell my assistants — especially our new probationers — 'Learn to abbreviate! That will save time when you talk! Otherwise you cannot get your day's quota of work accomplished!' Where was I? — Oh yes, then there's the P.U.S., and the J.S. —"

"Very interesting, N.K.," Hodge interrupted, "but seeing how busy you are, I don't want to take more of your time than —"

"No, don't go yet. We'll have our tea first —"

"Actually, there is something I wanted to ask of you, N.K."

"Is it? Of course — ask anything you like. If I can possibly be of any service to you, Hodge, it will be my greatest pleasure. Ah, here is our refreshment now, you see!"

"I flew in this morning, N.K., and I've been told by Indian Airways that there are no vacancies to Kathmandu for the next month —"

"What? That's preposterous! When do you wish to go? I'll see to it personally that you have a seat! I am entitled to fly wherever I must, and if necessary I will get you a seat in my own name!"

"Thank you very much, N.K. I'm most grateful to you for that —"

"No, it's nothing at all! What is a friend for, if not help when you need it? I only wish I had time to take you out for a shoot this weekend, but with Lok Sabha in session, you see —"

"Naturally. The thing is, N.K., I need five seats, and —"

"Five? My goodness, have you brought your whole family? But I thought you weren't married, Hodge?"

"No, I'm not. These are my friends —"

"Ah! You're beginning to sound more like an Indian every second — oh, excuse me!" The phone was ringing. "Bose here! . . . Yes, sir! . . . Yes, yes, of course, sir . . . Yes, I am working it up right now, sir . . . Sir, it will be ready today! Of course . . . When? At four, sir? . . . I see . . . Yes, certainly! . . . Positively. I will bring it to you personally within the hour! . . . Yes, sir. Thank you, sir." He hung up. "That was the Minister! He needs one of the answers by four. He's going to the P.M. and must show it to him today. It's a very delicate issue —" He had started moving files from one side of his desk to the other, opening various colored ribbons, and glancing nervously at the precious papers inside the manila folders. "Now where did I put that? Oh yes, here it is — oh, my — it's not finished!"

Hodge set his tea down, and stood, bending over the desk.

"N.K., I know you're very busy, but it's rather urgent that I get to Nepal this week —"

"Yes, yes, I see. If you were going alone —"

"My friends must accompany me, and there's quite a load of provisions — over a ton —"

"My goodness — a ton, is it? What are you going to do? Build a hotel there?"

"We're going after the Yeti."

"Oh! Well now — let me think a moment. That's a big operation. The J.S. would have to arrange that, you see. He has direct control over all internal airways, and you'll need half a plane — yes, yes, you must see the J.S. I couldn't touch that — no. The J.S. is there, you see, and he's very particular about the things he takes direct charge of —"

"What does J.S. mean?"

"Joint Secretary! I'll call him right now. If he has a minute, you can speak to him today —"

"Thanks, N.K." It was, Hodge suspected, the most he could have hoped for from Bose, as he watched his harried friend, the D.U.S., tap nervously on the crowded desk top, waiting for the J.S. to answer. There's no bureaucracy like an Indian bureaucracy, he thought.

"Excellent . . . Thank you very much, sir. . . . Yes, yes, he will be right there this minute!" He hung up with a triumphant smile, and slammed his palm against the button top of his bell. The servant opened the door. "Take Sahib to the J.S.," he ordered.

"You're a friend indeed, N.K.," Hodge said, clasping his hands together in the namaskara salutation. "When you come to America, if you ever need a plane ride, I'll be your personal pilot."

"Good! I may accompany the Minister on his next trip abroad, isn't it? Well — good luck, Hodge. Let me know what the J.S. says. I'm sure he will help you, if he can."

"But you say he's in charge of the airways. There's no one he has to send me to, is there?"

"No, no, no — he is directly second to the Minister himself, you see. He will take care of everything himself. No doubt of it!"

Hodge followed the bare heels of the elderly servant along the austere corridor of the Ministry, past open-doored rooms crowded with clerks hammering away at old typewriters, surrounded by ancient filing cabinets on top of which were stacked enormous volumes bound in peeling brown leather. The air was heavy with the dust of papers, yellow-edged and crumbling, permits and licenses, records and receipts, despatches and documents of state, memos and tabular lists. It was a beehive bursting with papers, a labyrinth of cubicles through which the files that ordered society moved in mysterious paths from desk to desk, somehow acquiring by the devious dervish dance of their motion the power to perpetuate the ritual of government. He had worked in such an office once in Washington — for six months during the war. Any field of combat was preferable, even the China-Burma-India zone. He'd vowed never again to become the human conveyor belt in a paper factory!

The servant opened the door to the spacious, unlit, almost empty room — and for a moment Hodge thought it was a deserted waiting room outside the office of the J.S., but then he saw the slight figure seated behind the large clear desk.

"Mr. McNeill?"

"Yes, sir. It's very kind of you to see me on such short notice —"

"Please be seated. Now, what can I do for you?" He was skeletal thin, so remarkably frail a figure that he appeared almost to be a child at his father's desk — but for a fringe of white hair around the sides and back of his head, just over his ears.

"I'm going to Nepal —" Hodge began, explaining as quickly and succinctly as possible about the expedition, and his urgent transport requirements. He paused every few sentences as he spoke, politely waiting to see if the J.S. had any questions or comments, conditioned by N.K.'s loquacity to expect at least one or two irrelevant monologues. But the slight skeletal head merely rested upon one arm propped onto the desk top, the eyes widely alert and never wavering from Hodge's face, the mouth firmly closed. He remained in fact so extraordinarily silent, that Hodge began to wonder if he were listening, till he found himself suddenly at the end of his statement.

"Is that all, Mr. McNeill?"

"Yes — essentially."

"I see." He removed his chin from his palm, and smiled wanly.

"If you will please put what you have told me in writing, and send it to my Secretary, I will look into this matter."

"But I've just told you — I've tried to explain how urgent —"

"Yes, yes, I have heard you, sir. But you see, there is nothing I can do until your request has been submitted formally —"

"Can't you consider my statement just now —"

"Forgive me for interrupting you," he added, firmly. "I had not finished what I was going to say. Your request — or complaint, if you prefer, must be submitted to this office formally in writing. Since you are somewhat in a hurry, I would suggest that to expedite this matter you send us your letter in triplicate."

"And how long will it take you to act —?" Hodge felt the blood rising through his collar, but carefully refrained from raising his voice. He knew enough about India's bureaucracy to appreciate how sensitive official mentality could be.

"That will depend upon the complexity of the investigation, Mr. McNeill. It could take one week, or one month. I have no way of knowing —"

"But even one week could ruin us! If we don't reach Kathmandu by October our option to Khumbu lapses, and then anyone else —"

"My hearing is quite excellent, Mr. McNeill. I must ask you not to shout please."

"Sorry," Hodge whispered, feeling the perspiration racing down his back, covering his forehead and palms. He wiped his face and hands with his handkerchief, cautioning himself to calm down, reminding himself that he was not addressing an idiot junior clerk, but the man who was second-in-command of this Ministry, the man empowered to make the final decision in cases of this sort — since the Minister surely had no time for such trivial problems! Whatever you do, don't antagonize him, Mack, he thought.

"Forgive me, sir," Hodge said softly. "I'm afraid I haven't made clear to you how important it is for my team and myself to reach Kathmandu this week." He had to inhale deeply, as though he'd been climbing at rarefied altitudes.

"Perhaps not, but you may put anything you wish in writing —"

"There is no time! This is Tuesday afternoon, sir. I want to be in Kathmandu by Friday — I'm prepared to pay whatever —"

The J.S. rose to his feet. He was not much taller standing.

"I cannot initiate investigation without a written statement," he said. "This is a matter of procedure. I'm sure you will appreciate that we have rules of procedure in this department, Mr. McNeill."

"There are exceptions to every rule! This isn't my first trip to India! N.K. knows me very well — he'll vouch for my credentials! I have my permit here from the government of Nepal — it cost me five thousand rupees to get this thing. I've worked four years putting this expedition together."

"I understand all that."

"Then why can't you simply pick up that phone and call Indian Airways? Tell them to put another plane on their flight to Kathmandu this Friday. That's all I ask of you! It would take half the time we've spent arguing . . ."

"In my country, Mr. McNeill, we have very little of aircraft. Our technological resources are much limited. Indian Airways doubtless could utilize three times the number of flights presently available. If I were to grant your request in the manner you suggest, sir, I would have to do the same for every other visitor or Indian businessman who urgently desires to travel —"

"But how many others have asked you for this today?"

"No, that is beside the point, sir. The others do not ask it, because they understand our rules. I do not make the rules of our government, you see. I am merely a civil servant." He sounded like a textbook in elementary civics, like a student reciting answers he'd memorized for the civil-service examination. His voice was a worn record, his face a mask.

Hodge refused to believe it. He could not accept this absurd formula, this rote rejection, this unthinking impersonal response that threatened in the most bland and banal of language to halt his expedition's progress now that he had come within a few hours' flying time of its actual launching.

"Please," Hodge said, leaning forward on the barren edge of the desk that separated him from the one man who could do so much to facilitate or frustrate his ambitions "Help me, sir. It's a small matter, an insignificant request perhaps to you, but this is all I've worked at now for years. I've staked my entire future on this expedition, and my supporter, Mr. Judson, has risked a small fortune.

We've brought ten people here today and over a ton of provisions —"

"I am sorry, Mr. McNeill," the little man replied, and for the first time he sounded human.

"Sir," Hodge continued, suddenly wishing he had taken the time to learn this man's name, so that he could address him more intimately than by title, "there surely must be something you've wanted in life, some luxury perhaps for yourself or your family —?"

"Oh, yes, so many things! We are a poor country, you see, and none of us in the service receive very high salaries —"

"Of course," Hodge said, nodding, feeling the accelerated throb of hope in his chest. Behind every human façade, however formidable it might seem, lurked the man himself, the creature of passions and foibles, of desires and natural weaknesses! Knowing it was, he had learned, the master key to human relations, the lubricant of all social intercourse, the passport to success. "With the cost of living constantly rising, I can well imagine that there must be many things you and your wife would like to have, but possibly cannot afford —"

"Indeed yes, Mr. McNeill. I have never possessed an auto, you see, and I have never given my wife a gas-burning stove, though she would find it easier than her charcoal oven now that we are older — and — yes, there are so many of things! My sons have never owned a bicycle — because we are a poor people, you see. Though my personal salary has increased many times over since I have been in the service, still we deny ourselves all luxuries to give what we can to the peasants around us, who would actually starve otherwise."

"Then if you will allow me," Hodge said, extracting his large breast wallet, "I would like to give you —"

"Wait, Mr. McNeill! I have not yet finished!" His fingers trembled visibly as he raised one hand, and his voice was strained as he continued, speaking louder. "But there is one thing, sir, in which I am not half so poor as the richest man on this earth! And shall I tell you in what that is? That thing is honor, sir. Honor!" he repeated.

Hodge felt his cheeks flaming. He had to lower his eyes, unable now to meet those tired, yet somehow shining beacons illuminating this small man's dark face. He replaced his wallet without opening it.

"Perhaps you do not understand that word, is it, Mr. McNeill?"

Mutely Hodge shook his head. A whole damn world full of corrupt officials, he thought, and I had to pick an honest one!

"Now leave this office, sir, before I must say something to dishonor us both," ordered the Joint Secretary.

CHAPTER 15

"THAT'S a shame," Tony said, as Hodge finished recounting his interview with the J.S.

"It's murder! You don't realize who that son-of-a-bitch is, Tony! The only one left is the fuckin' Minister, and right now he's with the P.M. I don't even know if I can reach him tomorrow! Christ, I coulduv killed that little —"

"Easy does it, boy. Have another drink, Hodge. No point workin' yourself into an ulcer, y'know."

T.J. refilled his glass, and Hodge was amazed at how calmly he seemed to be taking this news of their setback. Monetarily, Tony had as much to gain from the success of their joint enterprise as he did, and far more to lose. The most remarkable difference between multimillionaires and all other people, Hodge decided, watching how T.J. smiled as he handed him the fresh drink, was their ability to remain unruffled at the prospect of losing a potential fortune. He had never respected Tony more than he did at this moment, but it hardly diminished his own disappointment, frustration, and fury. It merely made him more acutely conscious of how vulnerable he still was to the behavior of others, to setbacks inflicted by decisions beyond his control.

"No point'n gettin' ourselves all in a lather over the problem, boy. Let's try'n address ourselves to its solution."

"Agreed. But where the hell do we go from here?"

"Well — that's the question all right. Now if Indian Airways won't take you boys, I suppose we could always try hirin' a private plane?"

"Maybe," Hodge said, "but this isn't America. I don't even know a maharajah who owns his own airplane."

"Mmm — what else is there? Of course, there's the Indian Air Force —"

"Sure. Do you know the size of that, Tony? We left them fifty Dakotas after the war."

"Hell, boy, we'd only need one!"

"Great — and how do we get it?"

"Seems t'me I met an Air Force Indian at one of our Rotary International sessions back a few months ago. What in hell was his name anyway?" T.J. scratched at an armpit, screwing up his face in thought. "Guess it was Sinha — somethin' like that. Maybe I could give him a call tomorrow?"

"At this point we'll have to try everything," Hodge said, feeling none too sanguine about Tony's memory or the strength of his contact, even if Sinha was its name.

The phone rang.

"Hello," Tony said. "Hi, boy. Come on up. Me and Hodge are havin' a drink — bring the gang . . . Sure. We might as well gas up before dinner!" Then he called room service for more glasses and ice. "That was Bruno — just got back. Cheer up, Hodge — we only live once!"

"That's what I'm afraid of."

Within a few minutes Bruno arrived, followed by Seth, Niels, and Rena. No one had seen either Peter or Jane since lunch. They were all anxious to hear Hodge's report, but became as morose as he was when they did.

"Yah, this is Indian bureaucracy, Roger. Hopeless! It is a waste of time to try more with any of them. If you like my opinion, I suggest now we take the train to Patna, and there we try to hire a truck or two to Kathmandu."

"Not a bad idea — we could be in Patna tomorrow night . . . What did Misra say? Can he deliver the goods tomorrow?"

"Yah, he is ready even to give us everything today."

"What about a private plane?" asked Seth.

"That's what Tony suggested — I suppose we should try it. We can always jump on the train tomorrow night if nothing turns up —"

"Can we be sure there are trucks to hire in Patna?" Niels asked.

"Of course not," Hodge admitted, "and if our present streak of luck holds, I expect we won't find any land transport in all of Bihar ready to take us to Nepal!"

"We should be able to find something," Seth said, anxious now that Ethan's fever had fallen somewhat to get on with the hunt so that he could have more time for Orissa once it was over. He was also anxious to get away from Stella for a while. They had just had another argument.

"I agree we must take a chance," Niels said. "At least we will be moving in the right direction."

"Okay. We'll give ourselves tomorrow then to find a plane ride," Hodge decided. "If we still have nothing twenty-four hours from now — we go by rail to Patna, and after that we'll play it by ear — agreed?"

"Sounds sensible t'me, boy — let's drink on it!"

They had lifted their glasses, when someone knocked at the door.

Hodge found two Indians standing outside, one short and gray, with a head almost the size of his torso, wearing a double-breasted Western-style suit and a garish thick-knotted tie, the other a lanky young man in open-collared Nehru shirt and slacks.

"Mr. McNeill, please," said the large-headed man, officiously.

"I'm McNeill. What can I do for you?"

"Ah, good afternoon, sir!" he bellowed, sounding like a man at least twice his size, sweeping grandly into the room as though everyone were assembled there simply to await his arrival. "And a very good afternoon to all in this distinguished gathering! I am Mukherji. Subash K. Mukherji, of course, and this hapless soul, whose lugubrious spirit haunts my footsteps," he announced, swinging one dwarflike arm in the general direction of the young man who followed him like a self-effacing shadow, "is Krishna, my disciple in the dubious art of journalism. My card, sir!"

Hodge took the card, on which was printed the name of its

bearer, designed in a large font as ornately archaic as his dress and manner.

"Thank you," Hodge said, "but what was it you wanted —?"

"Philosophically, sir, my wants are the universal desiderata of all great religions — peace, love, and salvation. But alas, how rare is the realization of such simple goals, is it not? This wretched worm, for example," he declaimed, motioning again toward Krishna, but never deigning to look at him directly as he rolled on in tones as smoothly flowing as the sacred Ganges, "how many eons of tortured damnation will *he* be obliged to suffer before so much as glimpsing the empyrean plains of paradise? Behold the helot, my friends, and mourn for him as I, Mukherji, have mourned! To all outward appearances sane of mind and body, yet beneath that façade, the festering cesspool of young India's tortured soul. He's useless! I've told him so a thousand times, poor idiot, still he worships me, and who knows? Perhaps such bhakti will liberate him a thousand lives hence!"

He paused and seeing an empty chair made himself comfortable. "But I sense, sir, that your question is of more practical purport, relating rather to my immediate wants, not my cosmic desires, so permit me to explain my mission. I am, as some of you may know from my published corpus, a philosopher-poet by birth, forced through the wretched exigencies of circumstance to earn my livelihood in journalism, and I have come — nay, I have been commissioned by the Barons temporal of our fourth estate to commune with your spirits, my friends, to interrogate your souls, to elucidate the obscure and obfuscate the obvious, or — in the pressroom vernacular of your own country, sir — to do a story on you! Now tell me, Mr. McNeill, what mission has lured you to India?"

Halfway through his long-winded speech, Hodge was tempted to lift this impertinent dwarf with one hand, and put him out. He'd seen all he wanted today of Indians! But on reflection it occurred to him that Mukherji might be helpful, for he remembered seeing that name now on many widely read columns. At this point, publicity might be of some value to them.

"We're trying to reach Nepal, Mr. Mukherji, to hunt for the Yeti."

"So I have been informed, sir. A laudable ambition, no doubt, but do you honestly anticipate success?"

"If we can get on a plane to Kathmandu — of course we do. Our only obstacle at the moment is Indian Airways —"

"Ah — so they've banned you, have they? Most intriguing! Did they state any reasons?"

"They haven't *banned* us. They just don't have any seats!"

"Oh." Mukherji seemed disappointed. After a moment's reflection, however, his face brightened. "Ah, but that is the excuse they have given you, the *official* explanation, the formally declared *causus belli,* is it not? Yes, yes, of course! Prevarication, Mendacity," he declaimed, raising one finger aloft, "thy name is India!"

"Dammit, boy, you need a drink," Tony suggested.

"No, thank you, I dare not consume alcoholic beverages! There is little enough blood in this meager body of mine to support the unique brain to which it has been appendaged! The curse of infant marriage, sir! We all suffer from the same congenital afflictions in this morbid country. Even I, Mukherji, and that one, of course —" He wagged a finger in the direction of Krishna, who had squatted in the lotus position next to his chair. "I have labored to liberate him from the tentacles of this national morass by intellectual shock treatment — without the slightest success as yet! You can see for yourselves — he not only considers himself inferior, he *is inferior!* Racial self-attrition, that is our problem par excellence. It may take us five thousand years, my friends, to reach your physical stature alone! As for brains — one Mukherji in a hundred million, sir, has managed to advance himself to my level — but contemplate the psychic price! Mill could read Latin at four, and I, Marx, Mill, and Spencer, yet think of it, my friends, an infant possessed of all the fruits of universal knowledge with barely the motor mechanism for walking! But we seem to have digressed. Krishna, where was I?"

"Indian Airways," the young man whispered.

"Yes, yes — the political reasons for their refusal to give you passage — of course!"

"*Political* reasons?" Hodge shook his head abashed. He no longer knew whether to laugh or shout at this escapee from a circus side show.

"Indeed, sir. Ours is an age of politics, you must realize, and

whether consciously or not, we are all motivated accordingly —
myself included! I am what you might call a pastiche of Spencerian
Marxism, Neoplatonism, and Fabian Fascism. Even this languor-
ous illiterate, cringing like an ape behind me, even he has not been
untouched by the political fever, sir. Ask him his political faith! He
will not hesitate to inform you that he is a Congresswallah! Is it not
so, Krishna?"

"Yes, of course," the young man replied eagerly. "I realize naturally that our Congress Party is not perfect, but —"

"Spare us! Have the sense at least to conceal your darkness
under the bushel of silence, fool!" But then Mukherji turned expectantly to Hodge. "I suppose, of course, that you have been sent by
your government to investigate Communistic inroads into Nepal?"

"Where in hell did you ever get that idea —?" Hodge began.

"Never mind. I see you don't trust me sufficiently," Mukherji
injected with a shrug, looking morose. "Given my profession, of
course, why should you? Alas, I have yet to meet the C.I.A. agent
who was willing to admit his identity to me!"

T.J. roared. "Dammit, boy, you don't think we're *spies,* do you?"

"Mr. Mukherji, I'm sorry to have to disappoint you," Hodge
said, "but I'm afraid this interview —"

"No, no, please do not take offense, my friends! I will print none
of it, not a word of truth ever passes my pen undeleted by the
shrunken-skulled gentlemen who edit my columns. I have long
since made my peace with our lord god Dissimulation. I will write
of your adventurous enthusiasm, your earnestly disinterested ambition to advance scientific learning, your penchant for exploration,
your fascination with the unknown, and by tomorrow evening millions throughout India will sip their tea sitting on their dung piles,
wishing you all well and dreaming of hunting for Yetis! Have no
fears, my friend, Mukherji is well trained in every aspect of the
craft of literary lying. I asked only out of personal curiosity. To be
perfectly frank, you see, I myself have thought of venturing into
Himalayan heights to explore the front lines of Chinese treachery.
Why shouldn't they absorb Nepal, after all, and India as well, for
that matter — we're all too effeminate, too lazy, too climatically
enervated to stop them."

"That sounds like Communist propaganda t'me, boy," said Tony.

"Bravo, sir! Spoken as a true American! My Communist enemies would be infinitely flattered to learn that I, Mukherji, have become allied to their floundering cause!"

"Well now — if you really believe all that hogwash about India's bein' so damn weak, boy, why in hell don't you do somethin' about it?"

"Ah, there is a question for *you*, Krishna! Permit me, sir, to divert your query to my disciple, for he is more representatively Indian than I, you see! Tell our American friend, Krishna, why you don't do something?"

"What *can* I do? I am willing to work but no one offers me a job, and as to fighting — I have not much of strength or inclination to such things."

"Your oracle has spoken, sir! He is nineteen, but his bones have no sap in them! His spirit is devoid of strength! He is India incarnate! Alas, there is little hope for us, since the British have gone. We are racially inferior, I tell you. Visit Calcutta's railway station — talk to the refugees who were born there, reared on the urine-covered platforms. Go to our half million villages, sir — interview the Untouchables who wait all day for a kind Brahman to draw some water from the well for them! Ask them why they don't do something! Any other species on earth would have chosen death long ago — and actually, it's the only solution. We can't feed all the people we have anyway. Mass sterilization is the only possible answer."

"Yah, this is what we tried in Germany," Bruno said, nodding. "This experiment —"

"You mean murder," Rena shouted, rising. Her voice broke. She was livid, trembling.

"No, I did not mean — Of course, none of us knew —"

"I don't believe you," she whispered, rushing to the door.

Hodge called to her, but she dashed from the room without turning.

"I'll speak to her," Seth said, putting down his drink, excusing himself, though not to Bruno.

"Did anything *I* say offend the young lady, Mr. McNeill?" Mukherji asked.

"It's getting late," Hodge replied. "I think we're all a bit tired —"

"Naturally, sir, I understand. No more digressions, I assure you! But I shall require a few facts for my column tomorrow. Firstly, the names of your teammates . . . ?"

Hodge answered him briskly, determined to end this interview as expeditiously as possible.

CHAPTER **16**

SETH caught up to her just as she opened the door of her room.

"Rena! May I talk with you?"

"What? Oh — if you like." She shrugged. "Come in."

"I know how you feel about what Bruno said, Rena, but —"

"Then why but?" Her lips were tautly distended, accusing fingers of anger. Her eyes blazed. "And if you know so well, why did you not tell him something? That Nazi! If I am a man I would do him more than shout!"

"The war's over, Rena."

"Oh-h-h-ch! This is what you come here to tell me?" She rolled her eyes skyward, and shook with barely controllable rage.

"Will you stop acting so self-righteous?"

"*I* should stop! How pious you are! So full of charity, and — and forgiveness for murderers! Next you will say to me — turn the other cheek, not? Love your enemy? Why do you waste your sermon on me, Professor? I am not Christian!"

"I'm not either, damn you!" He gripped her shoulders, wanting to shake some sense into her, the way he shook Ethan at times when he lost control of his own temper — but she appeared so startled, so shocked at this sudden display of passion, that instantly he let go, whispering, "I'm sorry."

She looked amused, biting at the nail of one finger as she eyed him, inclining her head slightly.

"See," she taunted. "You act like a Christian. How quick you apologize — How noble you are."

"I only wanted to help. I thought you might —"

"How generous."

"Stop it," he said softly.

"What?" Her voice now was as tender as it had been harsh a moment ago. There were beads of fine moisture on her upper lip, clinging like dew to the soft fringe of down that covered her face. Her eyelids were almost closed, her mouth partly open.

"Rena," he whispered, touching her shoulders very tenderly this time, bending to kiss her lips. "Rena," he repeated, kissing her cheek, her eyelid, her neck, her ear, whispering her name again and again as he did so.

Her eyes probed his face with a look at once blissful and terrified.

"Seth?"

"Yes, Rena?"

"That's all — I just wanted to hear how it sounds — your name."

"You make it sound — special."

"It is. Seth. I love it."

"And I love Rena."

"The name?"

"And the girl."

She lowered her face, pressing her chin almost to her neck, not looking up at him when she spoke. "In Israel this is not a word we use — just-so."

"I am not using it just-so, Rena." He touched her chin with his fingers, lifting her face slightly, cupping it in his hand, like a lotus held by a worshipper before the altar of God. She was really more beautiful than Anita, though the resemblance was remarkable. "I will always love you," he said.

"How can you know that?"

"I know it."

"Why do you look so sad now, Seth?"

"It's my disposition."

"That's not right."

"You say it as if you know me better than I know myself."

"I only know what I feel — what I sense about you."

"Which is —?"

"Strong passion," she said, "and life, much life. I do not know so good how to say it in English. See, now you are laughing at me."

"Wrong. I'm just happy — that's why I smiled."

"Then I was right, not?"

"Perhaps. Now tell me about you. How many men have loved you, Rena?"

"Should I be modest in answering that — or truthful?"

"Truth alone conquers," he said. "The motto of India." He lit a cigarette, and looked away from her.

"Now you are angry with me, Seth."

"No."

"Why did you not ask how many men I have loved? That is a much simpler question."

"Is it?"

"Yes."

"All right — how many men have you loved?"

"Only one. May I have a cigarette, too?"

"Of course — I'm sorry." She looked older, sadder. "Do you still love him, Rena?"

"Maybe — I don't know. It does not matter now."

"What happened?"

"Ohhhch!" She smoked like a fish, gulping and exhaling in swift short puffs, tapping nervously at the edge of her ashtray before there was ash enough to discard. "He was engaged to my friend when we fall in love, and — she swears to me she will kill herself unless — what? Unless I stop to see him. And — so I am stupid enough to feel sorry — so I say to him I do not love him, and — so now I am here."

"Did they marry?"

"Yes."

He went closer to her, taking her small hand in his, lifting it to his lips, kissing the soft pad of her palm.

"And you, Seth?"

"I've been married ten years, and have a son."

"Are you in love with her?"

"Stella's a very good wife, and mother —"

"But do you love her?"

He released her hand and stared dumbly at the dresser top lined with its strange assortment of cosmetics, perfume bottles and atomizers, nail polish and lipstick, eye pencils and hair brushes. In their room, Stella had put Ethan's toys on the dresser. Her makeup kit consisted of little more than a comb. Oh God, what the hell am I doing here? he thought, turning away.

"Seth, do you love her?"

"Yes."

"Then you must be very happy with her?"

"That's right."

"Why do you lie to me so?"

"Rena, I just wanted — I better go back and see how Ethan's doing."

"You wanted what?" She stood before him, searching his face with eyes unashamed to stare nakedly, unafraid.

"About Bruno — I didn't want you to — to be upset —"

"So you came to comfort me?" Her voice was incredulous as her smile. She moved her fingers lightly along her hips with feline coquettishness, swaying ever so slightly closer to him as she did so. Her eyes were sensuously sleepy. He felt the force of his blood tingling as it raced through his body.

"I better go," he whispered, his voice guttural.

"Then go!" Her expression hardened.

"Rena —" He wanted to rush to her, to hold her firmly again in his arms, to break all the bonds that restrained him, the invisible chains of obligation, the wet straitjacket of circumstance that chilled his every impulse and locked his passions like the arms of a madman tied helpless to his body. He wanted to tell her then of Anita, and of how she restored him to the beauty of seventeen, when flames of promise boiled his blood, and everything was Tomorrow rather than Yesterday —

There was a knock at her door.

"Yes? Who is it?" she snapped.

"Hi," Hodge said, entering the room. "Everything under control, baby?"

"Yes, of course. The Professor has given me a lecture on good manners!"

"That's my buddy, Seth." Hodge playfully punched at his arm. "I always said you'd make a great rabbi, man — didn't I?"

"Did you? Not?" She laughed, wrinkling her nose coquettishly at Hodge, who smiled warmly in reply to her overture.

"I was just leaving," Seth said. They did not attempt to detain him.

He shut the door firmly, and walking away from it outside felt coldly alone as he heard the warm music of their youthful, exhilarated laughter.

CHAPTER 17

"HE just fell asleep," Stella whispered as Seth entered the room. Then appraising him suspiciously she asked, "Where have you been?"

"With the gang," he replied. "Some crackpot named Mukherji came to interview us. It's only five-thirty, Stell. Why don't you go for a walk until dinner?"

"I will — if you don't mind."

She left without coming close to him. Not even a hand-blown kiss, or a wave good-bye. The formal changing of the guard by strangers on sick watch.

Stella walked up the garden path. Near the pool she heard familiar voices — Bruno, Lotte, T.J. — raucous banter, hollow giggling. She hurried away from them as fast as her feet could carry her. Not that any of them would have noticed had she gone to join them. They cared only about themselves! Even Hodge, whom she'd thought so nice, hadn't so much as asked about Ethan, when she appeared at the table for lunch. None of them wanted to be bothered by anything unpleasant! Hodge had flirted so overtly with that little tramp Rena, that Stella saw he was really a shallow person. Lotte was the only one who seemed half sensitive, but she rushed away with Niels, almost as fast as Peter did with Jane. They left her alone, in fact, to finish her lunch at the big, empty table — rude, selfish people.

Stella walked glumly through the ornate lobby of Maharani's, repelled by its overstuffed furniture, bizarre onyx pillars, and up-side-down wedding cake of a chandelier. Ostentatious and hateful, she thought, passing the manager, whose oily grin and pompous bow were as artificially cool as the air in his precious dining room. She decided to go for a walk outside the hotel grounds, wishing now that she hadn't encouraged Seth to waste a precious day of his sabbatical on this preposterous hunt for a nonexistent creature. By the time she reached the street beyond the front gate, Stella felt tears streaming down her face. She stopped to dry her eyes.

It happened often to Stella — finding herself alone in a room full of noisy, laughing people, alone in some abandoned corner at a faculty party, even at times in her own home, when they invited their "best friends" to dinner. Eventually, she crept away some-where remote from the sound of their artificial gaiety, to cry it out — alone. Yet for years she had dreamed of this trip to India, of seeing wonderful new things, meeting exciting, stimulating people, helping Seth with his field research — how could the same sort of depression be recurring here? Why did she feel so old, so alone? I wish I was dead, she thought.

Then she remembered Ethan — not Seth. For years it had been Seth, his need of her, which proved to be Stella's saving grace. Now she knew him better. He needed no one — except for an occasional tribe of savages, or some illiterate villagers somewhere. Ethan still depended on her though, and so long as he did — while he was still a child — Stella would manage to stay alive. After that, she thought, after that — we'll see.

A precariously wobbling trolley rattled by, crowded with bare-foot passengers standing on running boards, clutching at wooden poles. Poor souls. Most of them looked as though they would be blown away, yet they hung on as if God knew what reward awaited them at the end of that wretched ride. Stella turned downhill at the corner, walking past the pool from the street outside the wall, its happy sounds muted by distance. She remembered the summer she spent at camp, when she was fourteen, her first real summer away from home. Everything about the natural setting was so beautiful, so lush and green and full of magic wonder that for more than a week she could not believe her good fortune. Nothing so beautiful had ever happened to her before. She made a friend in her own cottage, a lovely, sensitive girl named Esther, who enjoyed all the things she did — Sinatra, and *The Brothers Karamazov,* and *Lost Horizon,* and the Museum of Modern Art, and chow mein — they swore eternal friendship, and promised to tell each other everything, just everything that really moved them deeply, to share all the excitement of that glorious summer. She could hardly wait to tell Essie of her attraction for a junior counselor, whose table was next to theirs in the dining room. Essie listened as sympathetically as ever, but then just shrugged and said, "He's cute, only not my type." Next day on the way to the lake she heard rustling noises in the pine grove, and though it wasn't the sort of thing she ordinarily would do, something made her stop, and creep silently closer till she was hidden by a tree. She waited, crouched there like a culprit, hoping her heartbeat wasn't audible to anyone else as the rustling sounds faded. Then she heard Essie's soft laugh, and muted question, "Who do you like better, me or Stella?" Though she couldn't see him, she did recognize his voice answering, "Geez, what do you take me for, a creep? I wouldn't touch old piano legs with a ten-foot pole, Essie! She gives me the jeepers!" Esther's laughter was more than she could assimilate in silence. Stella ran from that grove too quickly to care about the noise she made. She ran to her cottage, packed everything she owned, and waited with her luggage all that afternoon and on into the evening, not moving, not eating, speaking no word to anyone, till her father finally drove up to take her home.

The echoes from Maharani's were lost now, as Stella walked toward a totally different world. Unpainted shacks of peeling stucco, whose broken-hinged shutters hung like pirate patches over blind eyes, tumbled against one another to the river's muddy arm, which gleamed like a sequined chola band in the sunlight at the bottom of the steep grade. Squat, shadow-dimmed doorways gaped their toothless mouths at the dust-laden heat haze along streets that changed from concrete to cobble, from cobble to pounded earth. A frail wisp of a woman, her sari drawn Madonna-like around her face, labored slowly up the hill, bearing three glistening water jugs of salmon-colored clay, stacked steeple high on her head. Stella stepped aside to let her pass with ample room, for the feat of balance seemed as impossible as the strain of that arduous ascent. Yet the woman walked on, apparently oblivious to the burden she bore with all the deft grace of a model trained to cross a room with a book on her head. Down the middle of the dirt road a coolie strained backwards to keep from being crushed under his cart of timber beams, to which he had harnessed himself like a dray horse, his torso polished mirrorlike with the sweat that clothed his otherwise naked body.

By the time she reached the river Stella felt less sorry for herself. Though she often considered her life a total failure and her days an intolerable succession of miserable waste, she had read and seen enough to know that relatively speaking she was well off, in many ways fortunate. She had never gone hungry, nor suffered physical deprivation of any kind really. She had a brilliant husband, a healthy son, a perfectly decent little home, her own washing machine, and a new refrigerator. She owned more dresses than she ever wore. Now she had even gone abroad, not just to Europe, to Asia as well! She had no possible right to pity her plight — none whatever! Now everywhere she looked she could see people crushed low by burdens of poverty, immobilized by illness, paralyzed by utter despair, or driven to frenetic motion by desperate need. Why, compared to any one of those women bent double by the water's edge, pounding their wash over rocks, she lived the life of a queen!

Yet walking onto the rock-strewn fringe of soiled sand, she could not quite convince herself it seemed, for inexplicably once again her eyes began to water. What right did she have to cry? None at all perhaps! But she could not help herself. She could not control her tears. She had expected so much of life once. She had hoped for so much, dreamed of so much. Not materially. Her mother had all the material luxuries any woman could ever want, but she never envied her mother. During adolescence Stella hated her, but later understood that her mother wasn't the vicious, cruel, resentful woman she'd once thought, merely a selfishly indifferent person, as incapable of loving her own daughter as she was of loving her husband. After that Stella pitied her for what must have been the awful emptiness of a life devoid of true love. She had always pitied her father, in a different way, for his weakness mostly, for having wasted his life in adoring a woman who lacked the simple capacity, not to speak of desire, to respond to his love. Whatever success he'd attained in his business was never appreciated by the woman for whom he had worked countless hours for more than forty years. The home in Manhattan he furnished so extravagantly for her, the trips to Miami Beach and the Catskills with which he indulged her desperate boredom so lavishly, the furs and jewels with which he adorned her evoked little more than grander demands, and greater expectations.

For years Stella had dreamed of a career in music. When her savings permitted, she went to Carnegie Hall every time there was a piano recital. She begged her mother for lessons, but she pretended not to hear, and her father would do nothing against his wife's wishes. She overheard them arguing about it, her mother as usual winning the argument. "Are you kidding, Max? Please, don't make me laugh. You know Stella and her dreams of glory! Why throw out good money on piano lessons for that one — she's tone-deaf. She can't carry a tune! I'm the one should have had piano lessons — forty years ago! Anyway, if you're so flush, why don't we go up to Grossinger's for the weekend? Bertha says they have a terrific new show —" She imagined her mother was right about her voice. She never sang in the house after that. She stopped thinking of music, and decided instead on a career in pure science. She read about Marie Curie, and wanted to model her life after hers. She started doing experiments at home, but ruined the new rug, and almost set fire to her room. Then she did so poorly on the high school Regents exam in physics that she knew it was hopeless. Her ambitions turned to drama. She had an excellent memory, and every time her parents were off on a trip she would declaim for hours from *Romeo and Juliet,* or *A Doll's House,* or *Major Barbara.* The latter made her think seriously of the Salvation Army, and she would visit the Bowery waiting for the Call to enlist. Till one day she ate something down there that gave her ptomaine poisoning, and they had to pump out her stomach at Bellevue, and after that her father made her promise to stay away from "Bums and Flop Houses!" Anyway she wasn't pretty enough to act. She had known it secretly even before she was turned down by an amateur theater group in the Village. She tried writing a play, but threw it into the incinerator, before finishing the second act. She failed at everything she really wanted.

Monsoon-swelled and muddy, the turbulent Yamuna rolled by before her eyes, sacred consort of Mother Ganga, with whose waters it would merge at Allahabad. She watched the boatmen guide their drum-loaded flat craft with long bamboo poles, deftly dipped into the river like straws, extracted dripping mud, only to be immersed again with the rhythmic motion of a ballet, done to the chant of half-mesmerized workers, who were born to their lot in life and accepted it with the same fatalism as the bullocks and buffalo sipping in contentment at the edge of the sand. What arrogance made her think she was justified in expecting any more of existence? What sinful pride was it that so feverishly inflated her ego to aspire beyond the mediocre limitations of self, dreaming of the joys of romantic fulfillment — of perfect and reciprocal love? Yet for many years with Seth, she believed that had come within reach. She believed it with all the naïveté, the fervor, the glorious self-deception of eighteen. Loving him as she did, she could not believe he would love her less completely, less honestly. To Stella it seemed then that all her previous failures in searching for a career were more than compensated for by her good fortune in finding a husband, someone to whom she could selflessly devote her life as wife, lover, and friend. She wanted only to make him happy . . .

Stella closed her fist over the sand, and watched as it seeped with insidious stealth through her fingers. The harder she pressed her hand shut, the more quickly it disappeared. Hastily she brushed her palm clean, and rose to walk away. Several children of the washerwomen working at the water's edge stared furtively at her, their cherubic faces and enormous eyes focused like sunflowers in Stella's direction. She smiled and waved at them. Giggling they rushed behind a large stone and peered out the way Ethan would when they played hide-and-seek. She extended her arms and called to them, but none were brave enough to come. She'd never really thought about having children till she fell in love with Seth. Then she wanted a large family, all sizes and shapes of him running and tumbling about her house, rolling around her like teddy bears and baby pandas, singing the songs she taught them, laughing at the stories she read, needing her love. No, they were too timid to come. She felt hollow as she turned back to the road along the river.

"Excuse me, memsahib," a man whispered, startling her to a halt. A slight, timid figure, he stood just a pace behind her, nervously clutching his worn Panama hat in bony hands, his fine-featured face sadly smiling. "Please excuse me?"

"Yes, what is it?"

"I am Anglo-Christian," he muttered, as though it were the most important information he could possibly convey about himself. "My father, you understand, was English, and I was baptized —" Except for his dress, a shabby white suit of Western cut, a badly soiled tie, and the sweat-stained straw hat turned haltingly between his hands, he looked fully Indian. "I worked fifteen years for English ladies — as chauffeur, butler, cook. I have references." He extracted several yellowing papers from his breast pocket. They had turned almost black at the folds, where they started cracking as he opened them.

"I'm sorry," she said, "but I don't need help —"

"But if you will just take one moment to see. I have always been honest, sober, very efficient —"

She glanced at the first letter he held out for her perusal, noticing those very words, which he'd memorized. She noticed the date as well — 1947, the dawn of Indian freedom.

"I can see these are very impressive references," she said.

"Thank you, thank you very much, memsahib. I would not expect salary — only board for myself and the family — we have four children, and there has been no work for me now that so many English memsahibs have departed —"

"But couldn't you find some Indian family — ?"

"You see, I am Anglo-Christian. Indians do not hire us. They consider us as foreigners, and yet —" he smiled at the obvious irony of his doubly displaced position.

"I am truly sorry," she said, "but we'll only be staying in Delhi a short time, and at Maharani's I really have no need of servants."

"Perhaps if you hear of some friends who are looking for some-one — allow me to present you my card please?"

"Of course. I'll do whatever I can," she said, knowing how meaningless a promise that was to such a man, yet it seemed to cheer him.

"Thank you, memsahib. Thank you, and God bless you."

She felt at once elated and depressed as she hurried away, clutching that card, which he'd entrusted to her care so eagerly, with such desperate faith, as though she were able to do anything to help someone, as if she were a person of means, or power — some-one like T.J., rich enough to do so much good in this miserable country. Why did people like that always choose to waste their money on useless ventures like hunting for Yetis? Stella wondered. How many Indian families could live for a year on the money the Judson Foundation allocated just for this expedition? The mere thought of it staggered her imagination. Suddenly she wondered if it might not be possible to convince Seth or Hodge, or T.J. himself, of the greater value of using those resources for something hu-mane? She was so close to them after all. There would be no prob-lem in presenting the idea. Perhaps it was simply that such a thought never occurred to them.

The first thing, of course, was to decide where to start. The ideal way to help men like the Anglo-Christian she had just met would be to bring wealthy Americans or Europeans to India so that they could live in large houses and hire many servants. Yet why would such people move here? And after they left, then what? No, per-haps creating more jobs of a different sort was a better answer. But what other work could people who served the rich all their lives do? Special schools would have to be established, technical schools where useful skills could be acquired. But that would mean finding able teachers, and choosing property on which a suitable school could be built. Then to employ such skills, industries or businesses would have to be developed, and a market established to absorb the things produced. What things? And who could afford to buy them if most people were starving or unemployed to start with? It began to seem like a vicious circle to Stella. The more she pondered details the more confused and discouraged she got. Why was every-thing so complex? Even something as simple as trying to find a way to help people, when so many people needed help? She would have to talk to Seth about it. Why didn't they talk about such things anymore? Things not immediately concerned with themselves, or Ethan? Maybe that's our trouble, she thought.

It came like a revelation. It made her stop walking. Perhaps that was why they'd been drifting apart these past years. They no longer discussed important things! Startlingly, she felt more truly awake now than she had in months, and looking around, she noticed that she'd stopped in front of an open gate leading into a spacious courtyard. She heard the soft chant of children's voices musically reciting something, and realized that the rectangular two-storied building surrounding the courtyard was a school. Hesitantly, she stepped inside the gate. The court was pounded earth, empty but for a simple birdbath of white stone erected in its center. The building was made of old timber, gray like the driftwood washed onto a sand beach, encrusted with salt over time, pock-marked and cracked by nature's erosion, elegant in its unvarnished simplicity. No speck of litter marred the symmetry of this site. An atmosphere of peaceful tranquillity pervaded this court, far different from the ostentatious peace of Maharani's, somehow integrally emerging from its surrounding environment, a purer part of the natural landscape of India, rather than a segment of Europe artificially transposed to a totally foreign scene. Instantly she felt at home here. A soothing calm suffused her spirit, as she walked quietly toward the chant of children reciting the English alphabet.

There were about thirty of them, all smaller than Ethan, seated on long low benches behind unpainted tables in an otherwise bare, unlighted room. The girls with their black braids and starched white cotton dresses sat on one side of the room, the boys in white shirts and blue shorts on the other. She had never seen so well behaved and attentive a class. The teacher was a thin, young Indian man, who led the chant, and was so absorbed in watching his pupils, that he did not immediately notice her standing silent in the dim doorway. For a moment she wondered why the children were allowed to study in so dark a room. Then she saw that they all had cardboard pages set before them, their small fingers moving slowly over braille letters as they recited.

Oh, my God, she thought, they're blind! With a shudder the awful realization swept over her, and Stella had to press her hands to her mouth to keep from crying it out. Hot stinging moisture filled her eyes.

"Ah, we have a visitor," announced the young teacher. "Please come in, madam. You are welcome here." The small heads turned in the direction of the door, and many of them stared at her blankly with beautifully open eyes.

"Say, good afternoon," the teacher told them.

"Good afternoon," came the timid chorus in reply.

Stella could barely control herself sufficiently to respond in kind. Her throat was choked with emotion. Her heart fluttered fiercely.

A soft bell sounded suddenly, and the teacher announced, "That will be all for today, children. Now join hands please and rise."

Carefully they stood up, holding each other's hands, waiting in patience at their benches until the teacher led them out, line by line, into the courtyard, where a young woman appeared and, taking the hand of the first child, led the class off to another side of the building.

"You have not been here before, madam?" He was a gentle-voiced young man, who, but for his thin mustache, looked barely more than a teen-aged boy.

Mutely she shook her head, watching the long line of children slowly snake into the doorway at the other side of the yard.

"You wish to look around the school, perhaps?"

"Yes, if it isn't too much trouble."

"Not a bit. If you will come with me, I will introduce you to Dr. Pearson. Dr. Pearson is our director, and can tell you more about the school than I. This is only my first year. My name is Iyyer."

"Thank you, Dr. Iyyer."

"Oh, I am not a doctor," he said, leading her to the outside stairway up to the second-floor veranda. "No, I have just finished my A.B. degree at Madras, but one of my professors, Father Lucas, was good enough to recommend me for this position, and Dr. Pearson has given me a trial appointment. Had you heard about our school before you came?"

"No. I was just walking by."

"Yes, that has happened here before. It is a very peaceful spot, don't you think? There, you can see the river."

"How lovely," she said, "but none of those children can —"

"No. Unfortunately not. All students here are totally blind. This is Dr. Pearson's office." He knocked gently.

"Come in!" It was a strong masculine voice, but behind a rolltop desk filled with books and papers sat a gray-haired little woman, wearing steel-rimmed glasses and a loose-fitting gray suit. "Oh, hello. Whom have we here, Iyyer?"

"Ah, forgive me. I did not ask your name, madam."

"Stella Goodman," she said, crossing to take the outstretched hand of the old lady, who had jumped vigorously to her feet and greeted her with a warm, heavily wrinkled smile.

"Edwina Pearson. How do you do. Sit down, please. Iyyer, tell Rao to bring us tea, will you? He's forgotten me again today. I think his memory's going, poor fellow. Getting senile, I'm afraid. Rao's almost ninety, you see. Well!" She sat ramrod straight at her desk, and tugged her jacket down neatly, smiling tight-lipped at Stella as she appraised her with alert and penetrating eyes. She wore no makeup whatever, and her face was ashen gray, wearily wrinkled, yet through all the damage of time, Stella sensed that Edwina Pearson must have been a beautiful woman once. "Have you seen them?" she asked.

"The children?"

"The children."

"Yes," Stella whispered.

"Aren't they marvelous?"

"Yes," she agreed, though till now she'd only thought of how pitiful they were.

"You visited Iyyer's class, did you? The little ones?"

"Just for a few minutes."

"They're my favorites," Miss Pearson said. "But don't tell the others I said so!"

"I promise not to. How many others do you have?"

"Our total enrollment is seventy-four this term. But we only have room to put up fifty-five at the school."

"You mean they live here?"

"Of course. Most of them are orphans, you see. Where else would they live? Ah, here's our tea. Thank you, Rao. That will do nicely."

He muttered apologetically for being late and hobbled away bent almost double, his arthritic joints slow to uncoil.

"I hope you don't mind it strong," Miss Pearson said, pouring. "I loathe weak tea, but I'm afraid some of my visitors find this a bit much."

"It looks just right," Stella said. "Thanks." She sipped the burning, bitter brew, which tasted better somehow than anything she'd eaten at Maharani's. "Delicious!"

"Good. Ah, that *is* good! But you're the first American I've met who enjoys real tea. You are American?"

"Yes. We just arrived a few days ago. We've been staying at Maharani's —"

"Oh, *that* place!" She grimaced.

"I agree," Stella said smiling.

"The *we* is your family?"

"My husband and son, yes, and — well there are some others."

"How old is your son?"

"Ethan's four."

"You must bring him to visit us."

"Thank you. I was going to ask if I might as soon as he's better. Oh, it's nothing serious — too much travel, I expect. He's almost back to normal now. How long has the school been here?"

"It was bought by our Mission before the war — or I should say, World War I, shouldn't I? We had twelve children when I came in 1930. I expect that's before you were born."

"And you've been here all these — ever since then?"

"Yes, it is many years! But do you know, remarkably enough, it hardly seems —" She removed her glasses and pinched the bridge of her nose, closing her eyes, more in reflection than from weariness, pertly opening them after a moment, and smiling as she re-tucked the steel frames behind her ears. "There's been so much to do! How the time has flown by!"

"How wonderful that must feel."

"Well, doesn't it for everyone? Oh, you're still too young, perhaps, but you'll see soon enough."

"I think it's less a matter of age than occupation," Stella said. "Ten years ago time seemed to go much faster for me than it does now. Dr. Pearson, I wonder — could you — would you possibly be able to use someone — I mean, do you think I might be of any help to — could I be of any service to your school?" She blushed, and suddenly felt, she suspected, much as the Anglo-Christian who'd approached her a few moments ago.

"Oh, we're always shorthanded here," Miss Pearson replied. "But have you ever worked with blind children before?"

"No," Stella whispered, her heart sinking after its momentary rise.

"Well, neither had I, of course."

"You mean — ?"

"We couldn't afford to pay you anything, you realize."

"Oh, *I'd* be happy to pay," Stella replied, hardly able to believe her good fortune, holding her breath as she stared again into the warm, kindly eyes.

"But you'd be welcome to bring Ethan along if you like, during play time. It just so happens that one of our play supervisors left us this week — to have her own baby — and, I must confess, I'd begun to wonder how we would ever manage. We desperately need another good pair of eyes at the moment. Would you really be able to spare an hour each morning and afternoon?"

Stella swallowed heavily and nodded her affirmation. For some ridiculous reason she could not bring herself to speak.

"Splendid! Well then," the old lady said, springing to her feet. "Let me show you around, Mrs. Goodman, and introduce you to some of the others."

"Oh, please call me Stella, Dr. Pearson."

"All right, Stella," she said, ushering her out, "but then you mustn't call me Doctor! Edwina's my name. Why not call me that?"

"Thank you — Edwina."

CHAPTER 18

"HAS anyone ever read your palm, Peter?" Jane asked, tucking the pillow under her breasts, peering intently at the open hand she kissed.

"Good God, no! You don't believe in that sort of nonsense, do you?"

"Oh, I don't know," she said, absentmindedly tracing one line of his hand with her fingertip. "It's interesting."

"What?"

"Your palm."

"Well, what the devil does it say, old girl?"

"Oh, lots of things."

"Speak up!"

"Why? You think it's nonsense."

"Never mind what *I* think. Let's hear what *you* think. Can you see any numbers?"

"Uh — uhh. But what an amazing lifeline — it just goes on forever. Look at the length of it, will you?"

"Which one?" He turned over so that his body half-covered hers, and stared at his palm with his cheek brushing her face.

"Peter — stop. I can't read if you distract me."

"Do I distract you, eh?" He whispered it with his lips against her ear.

"Oh Peter, you really are insatiable!"

"Is that so bad, eh?"

"Don't — that tickles! I thought you wanted me to read your palm?"

"Yes, I do — honestly!" He eased his body a few inches away from her. "I promise not to touch you again. Honor bright!"

"That's one promise you'd better not keep, you blackguard." She grinned and blew him a kiss with her puckered lips.

"No you don't, woman! I've got a will of pure iron, and I'm going to prove it to you now by not budging an inch till you've finished reading! Go ahead — let's hear the whole bloody story."

"Uhm — let me see — there's the lifeline. See how far it goes, and not even the slightest gap — oh, you'll live to be a hundred at least, Peter Partridge."

"I will, eh? That's good. What else?"

"Your career line is *very* confused," she said, peering closer.

"True enough, I suppose! Can you see anything like a dukedom in the future? You know, something with an assured stipend?"

"Certainly not! And I wish you'd stop acting as though that were the sort of thing you wanted out of life — as if you were money mad! Honestly, Peter, you know it's the sort of thing you could have had years ago if you really gave a tinker's damn about it."

"Good God, woman — how?"

"Oh, any number of ways! You know it! What about that Italian countess who proposed to you in Milan?"

"But she must have been eighty!"

"That proves it! If you really cared about money, her age would have made her all the more attractive to you, Peter Partridge! Now you hush, and let me finish reading —"

"What does it say there about our chances of getting a Yeti, eh?"

"There's no line for that," she replied, frowning, looking into his eyes suddenly instead of at his hand. "Peter, must you go on this hunt?"

"What do you mean?"

"Just that."

"Of course I must!"

"Why?"

Why? It was hardly the sort of question to ask a man with his clothes off. "Oh, you know —" he muttered.

"No, I don't!" She was doggedly persistent.

He tugged at the edge of his mustache, squinting narrowly as he spoke. "I suppose it's just the idea of stalking the blackguard — something no man's ever touched before — *no one!* Trapping the bugger, you know, and holding him!" He clenched his fists, grinning down at them, the knuckles bulging and white. "To do something like that — while the whole bloody world down below you there live out dull-as-dishwater lives, counting the blasted hours till the boring game's over, and puff — out goes the candle, eh? It's different! It's a challenge! I hate the thought of waiting round for the last puff — that's all most people really do, you know? Good God, I've begun to sound as maudlin as a bloody parson!"

"I don't think so," she said, looking almost terrified, her face suddenly lined with pain.

"Is anything wrong, Jane?"

"Not *wrong,* darling. It's — it's just that I've never been so happy in all my life, Peter, as I've been today! Could you possibly guess why?"

"No — and look here, I haven't shown you any of those sights I promised to take you to," he replied lightly. He'd suspected it might be dangerous keeping her in bed.

"What sights, Peter?" She ran her fingers along his thigh, probing provocatively at his groin.

"The Red Fort and Humayun's tomb — you know."

"Yes, we must see Humayun's tomb," she whispered, caressing him hungrily, baring her teeth as she laughed, the most lascivious laugh he'd ever heard.

She's a bloody phenomenon, he thought, feeling the moist pressure of her body full against him, amazed to find he could still be aroused by her passionate longing.

"Who was Humayun, Peter?"

"I don't know. Good God, he was buried — that's all I know."

"Bury me," she whispered.

The phone started ringing again. It had been ringing all day.

"We really should answer it," he suggested, halfheartedly.

"Bury and crush me," she said.

"You're a glutton for punishment, you know."

"Punish me, Peter!" She sank her teeth into the flesh of his upper arm, digging her nails deep into the muscle of his back. What a woman! he thought. Then he stopped thinking, and though the phone continued to ring, he stopped hearing it . . .

"Shall I tell you something funny, Peter?"

"Mmm — do." He closed his eyes, wishing she would let him sleep awhile. Walking across Nepal would seem restful after this!

"I always thought I was frigid, darling."

"Good God," he muttered.

"I did — truly."

Her laugh made him wince.

"Look here, old girl, why don't we try sleeping a bit before dinner, eh?"

"I couldn't *sleep!* Oh, Peter, I'm so happy! We're so right together, darling!" She clung fiercely to his neck, planting moist kisses on his face.

"You don't want me to be exhausted for my trip, do you?"

"Don't go, darling!"

"Now look here, Jane, I've bloody well taken Hodge's money for this trip, and room and board all week! You don't think I'd be blackguard enough to ditch the whole business now, do you?"

"I'll pay him every penny," she said. "I'll bail you out, darling! In fact, I'll even give him a handsome bonus — for bringing us to our honeymoon! Oh, Peter, don't you know what I'm trying to tell you, you impossible, wonderful fool?"

She sounded so earnest he had to sit up, tossing the forelock out of his eyes, trying with his most disarming smile to divert her from the single track of seriousness along which her mind had begun racing at such alarming speed.

"Be careful, woman! You know I have no scruples. If I let you buy me out of bondage to old Hodge, you may be stuck with me for the rest of my life!"

"You can't frighten me, Peter Partridge. I love you, don't you understand that? There — now I've said it! I've never felt so brazen in my life! I never thought it was possible for Jane Tylor to feel this way. I don't recognize myself, darling — did you know that? I'm not the Miss Tylor you met a hundred years ago, Peter. I just couldn't be! I don't know who I am, but I love being me! I love being me with you, Peter Partridge. I don't ever want to leave you — not for a day, not for an hour! Oh, Peter, we could live at my place in Santa

Barbara — there's a gorgeous view of the ocean, and an orange grove, and — we can be so divinely happy together, darling. We could fly away from here tomorrow if you'd feel awkward about Hodge —"

"It's not Hodge, Jane."

"Then what is it?"

"I am tempted, you know," he began, stroking the flaming red of her loose hanging hair. She was not a bad-looking wench at all. Like most women, she improved with love, blossomed. Almost beautiful, by God, he thought, appraising her closely.

"Only what?"

"Only me, I suppose. I don't know, old girl —"

"I hate when you call me that, Peter!"

"Sorry. But look here, Jane, it's not that I don't — that I don't feel as strongly about you, because the truth is I bloody well *do,* and you *know* it."

"I thought you did," she whispered, lowering her eyes, clicking her tongue loudly and picking a piece of lint from the sheet.

"Blast it, you *know* I do, Jane! I just can't chuck the expedition now that we're practically set to start."

She began to laugh so hysterically it frightened him more than her serious mood.

"Well, why the devil does that sound so funny, eh?"

"Because you really think you're interested in *money,* Peter Partridge — that's what I'm laughing about! I'm probably the richest woman who's ever proposed to you, and you've turned me down for an animal who probably doesn't exist! Now isn't that hysterically funny?"

"You've got a God-awful sense of humor, old — Jane."

"In America we say — if you don't laugh, you cry! I've always hated tears!"

"Now you don't sound a bloody bit like a woman."

"And now you're thinking in stereotypes again, Peter Partridge! Haven't I warned you never to do that with me?"

"Well, good God, you *are* a woman," he insisted.

"I just told you — I don't know who I am anymore — or what. I only know why, Peter! But I do know you, darling!"

"You've read my bloody palm, that's why!"

"No — it's not in your palm! It's in your voice — on your face. You're frightened to near death of me — oh, not *me* perhaps, but what you think I might do to you! You're terrified of marriage, aren't you? Of being tied down."

"Not really," he said, chagrined.

"Yes, you are! Come on, Peter, be honest, won't you?"

"Oh, blast — I suppose you're right. But look here, if you must know, Jane — I've got eight siblings who've all married and have broods of close to thirty among the lecherous lot of them! Honest to Christ! And not one of them halfway happy with his damned spouse, you know? As respectable a lot of miserable malcontents as you'll ever find anywhere — good God, what a wretched bore their lives are!"

"Shame on you, Peter! You told me at least three of your brothers were perfect fools who ruined themselves in the most romantic escapades!"

"Well, in my opinion, they did! But answer one simple question honestly, if *you* can? Have you ever known a couple that's been happily married over five years, eh? I mean *truly* happy!"

"I think so! Sure I have. Lots of Daddy's friends have always seemed happily married, though I'll grant you, you never know a marriage truly from outside —"

"Ah-h-h-h, now you've said it, Jane!"

"Stuff and nonsense! You sound like the most conventional male on earth, Peter Partridge, when you talk that way! It's horrid rubbish, and you know it!"

"Hold on, old girl. What the devil do you mean by conventional?"

"I mean precisely what I said. You remind me of the Princeton boys I used to date when I was seventeen. They sulked and pontificated all evening long about how wretchedly ordinary an institution marriage was, and how none of them would ever be trapped by any wily wench, just because she refused to go to bed with them — or, alternatively, because she happened to be a really good lay, who left them walking around the next day with burning balls. What nonsense!"

"Good God," Peter whispered, blushing. "Did I say that?"

"No, but you were thinking it!"

"Now, look here — I suppose you're a mind reader as well as a palm reader, eh?"

"Yes, and I ride on a broomstick! Oh — *pooh!*" She turned her face aside. He thought he heard her sniffle.

"Look here, Jane —"

"I don't think I feel like talking anymore now, Peter." Her voice was strained.

He felt more vulnerable at that moment than he had all day, not because he was sorry for her, for having hurt her — he'd never been moved by tears or a sense of guilt. It was the fear of losing her that shook his confidence now. He'd never really thought he wanted her enough to care about losing the bitch, yet as his arm stretched out to caress her naked back, he realized it was trembling.

"Oh, good God, Jane," he whispered, "you haven't finished reading my palm, you know."

"Yes, I have." She eased away from his hand, moving just beyond his reach.

The phone rang, and this time she answered it on the first ring.

"Hi, T.J."

He grimaced and put on his shorts, searched for a cigarette. He felt drained, his spirit as dry as his bones, as though all the marrow, all the life had been taken from him, the way he used to feel in Soho, walking down the long flights of stairs where the peeling paint of eggshell-colored walls was always plastered with flashy travel posters, and the working girls outside could tell from one look at him that he was good for nothing at all.

"No, I've been sight-seeing with Peter," she said. "Yes — oh — everything, but I'll tell you about it later. . . . When? . . . Oh, how nice . . . Yes, it sounds lovely, T.J. . . . Would you? . . . You're an angel. I'm just going into my bath. . . . In the lobby, yes! Lovely."

"What the devil does old money-belly want?"

"I think T.J.'s a dear man. Don't be so intolerant of wealth," she said, getting into her robe and walking briskly to the bathroom, as though she had just awakened from her beauty nap. "Better hurry and get dressed, Peter. He's taking us all out for dinner!"

"Oh, blast that blackguard and his togetherness! I'm going to sleep —"

140

"No, you're *not*, Peter Partridge! You're to go to your room now and get into your best suit of clothes and meet me in the lobby in fifteen minutes! I've just told Mr. Judson you and I went sight-seeing today, and *you're* going to tell everyone about all the lovely sights we saw — because *I* don't even know the names of them! And you're going to be charming, witty, and wise, and answer every question of fact that anyone asks of *me* tonight about sightful India, *before* I have time to open my mouth and put my foot into it! Now do you understand?" She sounded like a nanny scolding her charge for wetting his trousers.

Good God, old boy, he thought, sighing inwardly at how close a call his had just been, you're bloody well out of that one!

"Well, Peter — do you?"

"I'll see you in the lobby, old girl."

"In fifteen minutes?"

"Yes, ma'am," he replied.

CHAPTER **19**

"COME on, kids," bellowed Tony, "we're going to town tonight!" He had hired a chauffeured limousine, a long black bus of a car, spacious enough for all of them to crowd into. He, Bruno and Niels were dressed in tuxedoes, Lotte and Jane in evening gowns.

"Plentya room on my lap," T.J. told Jane.

"This is fun," she said, accepting with alacrity. "Shout if I get too heavy, T.J."

"You're light as a feather, honey," he said, paternally patting her shapely thigh.

Peter pretended to take no notice, announcing, "There's another lap right here — if any of you girls dare try it!" But Lotte was comfortably settled between Tony and Niels. Hodge held Rena on his lap on the other jump seat, and Bruno and Seth sat up front beside the driver.

"Where we headed, Tony?" asked Hodge.

"Some damn place called the Imperial, boy. I called that friend of mine — the Air Force guy I told you about — Sinha. And by golly he was still in his office — now how 'bout that for luck? He says we kin get all the liquor we want over at this here hotel of his, and there's good chow to boot — so, hell's bells, let's have a ball!"

"Great! Hey, that is luck, man! We can ask him about a plane then."

"Sure can. Hell, I forgot t'mention that t'him! We'll just wait till he's had a few under his belt, huh, boy?"

"Right," Hodge said, winking back at his patron. He could see that Tony wasn't nearly as stupid as he'd once thought.

"What is that enormous temple called?" asked Niels.

"Jane here'll tell us — she's been out sight-seeing all day. What's that thing called, honey?"

"Uh — that's the — uh, Jama Masjid," Peter explained grimacing as he strained his neck around to peer quickly at what Niels was pointing to. "Biggest — uh, Muslim mosque in Delhi, you know — lovely marblework inside, eh, old girl?"

"Yes, incredible really," Jane said.

"Did they show you the footprint?" Hodge asked her.

"The footprint?"

"Oh! Oh, yes, you mean the Prophet's impress on that old stone," Peter blurted out, tugging anxiously at his mustache.

"Hell, boy, let Jane tell us about it!"

"Why yes — it's very exciting," Jane said "A bit like Grauman's, of course, but most interesting really."

"And where else did you go?" asked Lotte.

"Well, to the Red Fort there — on the other side, you know —"

"And we went to Humayun's tomb," Jane said.

"Hey, you kids really got around, huh?"

"Good God, yes, we barely stopped moving!" He thought he could see her blush, right through all those layers of war paint. The damned bitch had put on a gown that practically left her bare-chested! She didn't look half bad, actually, even with Lotte and Rena so close by for comparison.

The drive through New Delhi, with its broad boulevards and parks, its monuments and Mughal-modern structures, amber-tinged with the violet of sunset, was sufficiently diverting to shift the focus of attention from Jane, who breathed a bit easier, but found at times that T.J.'s hand wandered annoyingly high along her upper leg. She was, in fact, beginning to regret her impulsiveness in choosing Tony's lap to make Peter jealous, wishing she could shift to more familiar and desirable territory, when they turned off Raj Path to the taxi-crowded driveway of the Imperial.

The hotel was much larger than Maharani's, its lush grounds even more beautifully adorned with flowerbeds, though being so close to the heart of the new city, it was less remote from the road, and obviously much more popular. The doorman, an enormous bearded Sikh, who looked at least like a general with all his sashes, medals and jeweled-and-feathered turban, bowed and helped the ladies out onto the scarlet carpet under a scarlet canopy.

"You wouldn't know where I could find Air Vice-Marshal Sinha, would you, boy?"

"Yes, sahib, he awaits you in the bottle room! If you will please to follow me?"

The room was an intimate bar, with less than a dozen tables, only a few of which were occupied. They were led to the largest booth, padded in panther skin, where a handsome heavy-set man in black tie, with a mustache even longer than Peter's, was waiting to receive them.

"Judson, old boy — so good to see you again!"

Tony introduced them to the Air Vice-Marshal, who kissed the ladies' hands, and sounded like a purebred Englishman. His complexion was so fair that in the dim lighting of the bar he looked no darker than Hodge. His large watery eyes and sensuously full lips alone betrayed his Indian origin.

"We'll have our champagne now," he told the servant, who brought their glasses and ice bucket.

"Hey, Sinha, this is all right," T.J. said. "Why in hell can't we get this sort of thing in our damn hotel?"

"Ah, yes, Maharani's did have a bottle room once, but I seem to recall that so few of the guests there had permits, they decided to close it for reasons of economy — some sort of foolishness like that, you know. This whole prohibition business *is* rather a bore, isn't it?"

"You must have a permit to drink here?" Bruno asked.

"I'm afraid so, Mr. Jaeger. Are you by any chance the Jaeger who was with the Swiss team several years ago?"

"Yah. So you see, Lotte, someone has heard of me!"

"Well, I daresay, most of you are rather well known in India. I've particularly enjoyed your snaps in the *National Geographic*, Mr. Larsen."

"That's very kind of you."

"And correct me if I'm wrong, but haven't you done a book on some of our tribals, Professor Goodman?"

"Yes, I have, but I never imagined it was the sort of thing that would appeal to the Air Marshal."

"Ah, but some of us — even in the military — *do* read, you know. It was rather a good show, actually, now that I think of it — though you were a bit *hard* on our bureaucrats, wouldn't you say?"

"No, sir, but I'm sure they would."

Sinha laughed appreciatively. "Quite so! Well, gentlemen — and lovely ladies — cheers!"

Hodge was so impressed at the breadth of Sinha's knowledge that he could not help wondering, as he lit the Marshal's cigarette for him, if he was Director of Air Intelligence.

"What sort of duties does the Air Vice-Marshal have, if I may ask?" he said.

"Ah, that's well put, Mr. McNeill," he replied, his laugh as smooth and unruffled as the velvet lapels on his dinner jacket. "Curiously enough, I must confess I don't rightly *know*. Of course, I've held the rank, you see, for less than a year, and I suspect we *will* have to work out something rather more *routine* for me. Every month or so the Old Boy mentions it, you know, but he hasn't had the time as yet to standardize our T.O. — we are rather a new arm in India, you see. I suppose that's how I find so much time to read."

"Sounds like good duty," Hodge said.

"Rather — yes. *I* like it, I must say. But tell me, what brings you charming people to India?"

"We're trying to get to Nepal," Hodge explained, "to search for the Yeti."

"Ah, so that's it, eh? splendid! Well, good luck to you!" He raised his glass in a toasting gesture. "That should be great fun! But won't it be a bit strenuous for *you,* Judson?"

"Hell, boy, it'd kill me! I'm stayin' right here till they come back. Just along for the ride — first damn vacation I've had in thirty years."

"Tony's foundation is sponsoring us," Hodge explained.

"Good show! I suspected you were an institution, Judson, but I never imagined you were a foundation! That rather puts you in a class with Ford and Rockefeller, eh?"

"Hell no, boy! Not by a damned long shot! Fact is there's more piddlin' foundations like mine in America nowadays than airplanes in India."

"Ah, but that's still rather a select group, you know!"

"So we've found out today," Hodge injected. "Incredibly enough we've been unable to book a flight to Kathmandu —"

"*Really?*" Sinha shook his head in disbelief, and Hodge decided to plunge with his ball through the gap in conversation, heading the way he used to as quarterback, knees up and elbows out, straight for the goal post.

"How discouraging for you chaps," Sinha said, as Hodge finished his story of Indian Airways and the Home Ministry, tactfully amending the latter, of course.

"It damn well won't help India's tourist trade none, if you keep runnin' air service this way, that's for sure," shouted Tony.

"No, I shouldn't think it would, old boy."

"Good God, there must be *one* bloody plane in this country that could be spared for two hours!"

"Yes, one should *think* so, wouldn't one," said Sinha, and Hodge half expected him to offer them Air Force transport, he seemed so sympathetic, but all he said was, "Shall we go to dinner now?"

The dining room was bright and gay, its décor of pink and gold an appropriate background for the elegant ladies in glittering saris, gold bangles and necklaces, who occupied most of the festive tables in this palatial room. A centerpiece of ice carved in the shape of a mermaid rose from the long table on which cold meats were enticingly displayed. A small orchestra played at one end of the seashell-shaped room and several couples were dancing. The maitre d' led Sinha to the one empty table ringing the dance floor, removing the "reserved" placard as they sat down.

"Sinha, this sure beats our joint by a damn sight!"

"Yes, Maharani's *is* a bit old-fashioned, I'm afraid."

"Hodge, we should'uv come here!"

But Hodge felt too depressed to answer. The festive atmosphere of the hotel served only to deepen his despondency. He should have waited, as Tony had suggested, to plead his case to Sinha much later in the evening. Now he had no appetite — for anything.

"You girls sit over here, where me and Sinha can keep you outta trouble," Tony ordered, putting Rena between them, Jane on his side, and Lotte next to Sinha. "The resta you sit wherever you like!"

"It's so exciting here," Rena exclaimed. "I love it when they play music during dinner!"

"Are you from Israel, Miss Gold?" Sinha asked.

"Yes. Did you recognize my accent?"

"Indeed. I've visited Jerusalem — most intriguing city."

"I love it! I was born there. I am what we call *sabra*. Do you know this word?"

"Ah, yes — lovely . . . Would you care to dance?"

"Thank you!"

Seth felt his stomach muscles tighten as he watched them walk onto the floor, hand in hand. He had not intended coming tonight, but within minutes of Stella's return from her walk they'd begun fighting again — over what? He couldn't even remember. A sour greeting was enough to set them off! Their argument woke Ethan, who began to cry, at which point she said, "Why don't you go out with your friends? You're not of much help to us here!" He needed no further prodding. Seeing Sinha hold her so close on the dance floor, he was tempted to jump up, to rush over to them, and tap the Air Marshal's shoulder — right there in public, in front of them all, he felt like announcing, "She's mine!"

"Come, Bruno, let us dance, yah?"

"Ach, I am no dancer."

"But you were the best —"

"Yah, what I *was!* Better to forget what I was, *Liebchen!* Niels knows better than I how to dance! Show her, Niels!"

"Bruno, stop," Lotte whispered, blushing.

"I am not very good at such things," Niels remarked, "but if you would like to dance, Lotte — ?"

"I love to dance, thank you." She was still blushing as he helped her out of her seat.

"Come on, Jane — how 'bout it, honey? Let's show these old sticks-in-the-mud a step or two!"

"Let's just do that, T.J."

"Attagirl! Say, honey, did I ever tellya the one about — ?"

"The old lecher," Peter muttered to Hodge. "I wouldn't trust that blackguard with my grandmother, you know!"

"She'd prob'ly be safer with him than Jane, Pete."

"That's what I bloody well like about you, McNeill, your Irish wit!"

"Yeah." Hodge rubbed his forehead with his palm, and sighed. "Hasn't helped me a helluva lot today though."

"Yah — now we must plan what we do," Bruno insisted, leaning forward with both arms solidly pressed against the table.

"I thought we agreed about that a few hours ago," Hodge replied, sensing that Bruno was becoming somewhat impatient with his leadership.

"No, no, Roger, I mean we must be sure and know *precisely* what we do — each of us, tomorrow, and — and then after we reach Kathmandu, what we are each responsible for, yah?"

Nothing like Teutonic precision, Hodge thought. "I'm sorry, Bruno, I don't read you!"

"Ach, this is because I do not make myself sufficiently clear, yah? Sometimes, I wish we could talk in German."

"I don't," Seth said.

"Roger, this is what I try to say," Bruno continued, ignoring Seth entirely. "On such trips it is good to have for each man something special he must take charge of. For example, I give you an analogy. You were in the *Luft* — in the Air Force during the war, yah? So, on a plane you have what? First comes the pilot, and the copilot — then what else? You have a navigator, yah. Gunners.

Someone to take care of the engines. Now — is it clear what I mean?"

"I see what you're driving at, Bruno, but on this sort of expedition I think we're better off leaving things pretty flexible — all of us more or less doing whatever comes to hand as the occasion arises."

"Hear, hear," Peter said, rapping his spoon upon the table. "Up the amateur — that's my philosophy."

"No, but this will waste precious time, Roger! And worse than that — it will destroy our effectiveness as a single unit, that can be *instantly* mobilized in emergency —"

"All right, all right . . . perhaps, but what we need first is to get Sinha to lend us a plane. Any ideas on how we can accomplish that?"

"He looks too rich to bribe," mused Peter, "but from the way he went for Rena I should think you might be able to offer him a little something he would like, old boy!"

"If that's supposed to be English wit — it's what I *don't* like about you!" Hodge snapped.

"Well, we're even now, you blackguard! But look here, McNeill, you sound rather serious about that girl! Like her, eh?"

"I'm going to marry her," Hodge replied.

Seth dropped the match he'd just struck to light his cigarette onto the tablecloth.

"Good God, watch out!" Peter snuffed the match with his thumb. "What's wrong, old chap?"

"N-nothing. I — it slipped." He tried to light another match, but could not get it to ignite after two strokes. His hands were trembling. Peter lit the cigarette for him.

"Everything under control, buddy?" Hodge asked.

"Sure."

"You look pale. You didn't get much sleep last night, did you? Maybe you'd better rack it in, Seth. We can't afford any delays over sickness —"

"No, I'm all right. I'm — fine."

"But what was that you just said, McNeill? Good God, are you serious?"

"Why shouldn't I be?"

"Now don't bloody well get offended again! I didn't mean anything invidious, old chap! It's great, you know! Congratulations!"

"Save that, will you," Hodge said. "And for Christ's sake, don't mention it in front of her. Nothing's set yet. In any event we won't marry till this trip's over."

"Ah, I am glad to hear that," said Bruno. "I was afraid you think maybe to take her with us to Nepal."

"Nope. Nothing like that — don't worry. The fact is, I don't even think she believes I mean it yet. I guess it's overwhelmed her a little. She doesn't know me too well —"

"Hodge, you *are* a blackguard, you know! She's a beautiful girl, all right!"

"Never mind, Partridge! That's why I've told you first! Don't try any trespassing!"

"Good God, old chap, I've got my hands full — you can bloody well believe that!"

Hodge roared, and slapped Peter convivially.

"Seth, buddy, you haven't said anything — what do you think?"

"About what?"

"My decision — do you think Rena'll make a good wife?"

"Yes, I do. She's a bright girl —"

"There's the old Professor for you! *Bright!* Well, that's an asset too, I guess."

"Has she agreed?" Seth asked.

"I told you — she was overwhelmed — but let's change the subject, men — they're coming back."

"Hey, that's not a bad little band," Tony shouted. "Jane, honey, you dance like a dream!"

"Just following your lead, T.J. That was fun!" She pecked at his cheek before they sat down.

"You dance beautifully, Miss Gold," said Sinha, holding out her chair.

"Thank you — but now I am too hungry! What is everyone going to eat? Hodge?"

She turned to him first, Seth noticed, as a good fiancée would. He bit through the tip of his cigarette, and quickly put it out before starting another fire.

Between courses they danced — Hodge with Rena, Peter with Jane, T.J. with Lotte — even Bruno finally consented to dance with his wife once, and Sinha tried all the women, though Rena was clearly his favorite. Seth alone remained seated, leaving the table only once — to retreat to the men's room, where he threw up everything he had eaten. He almost collapsed on the tile floor, but after several minutes regained his balance, and with ample cold water applied to his face, managed to return, looking little worse, he suspected, than he had since Hodge dropped his bomb. He felt more tired though — old, cold, numb-tired. No pain really, just a dull sort of fatigue.

"Do you feel all right, Seth?" Rena asked, as he returned to the table. "You look tired."

"No. I feel great."

"Hodge, doesn't he look tired?"

"That's what I told him hours ago, baby, but he's a big boy now," he replied, shrugging.

"But if you're not tired, then why do you not dance?" she asked.

"I never learned how," he said.

"Oh, buddy! Hey, that's a good one, men! You should'uv seen this professor here during the war," Hodge informed them. "Christ, he was really something — Hey, man, remember that night in Calcutta, when those babes offered to — ?"

"No. I don't remember that, Hodge."

"Okay, okay! He's *modest*," Hodge said, covering his mouth with the side of an open hand facing Seth's direction, winking at Tony and Rena.

"What brought you chaps here during the war?" asked Sinha.

"Air Force," Hodge replied, telling him where they were stationed.

"Not *really?*"

"Of course," Hodge said.

"But, by Jove — then you must have been at Imphal in '45!"

"Damn right we were."

"But I was there too, you know! Adjutant to the C.O."

"Jesus Christ, was that *you?*" Hodge said, slapping his forehead. *"Sinha* — of course! Well, I'll be damned! Man, that's a mental block if I ever had one! You were the son — the one who almost had us busted out for taking that plane off course! Seth, he's *that* Sinha!"

"Ah, yes — were you those two Americans who caused all the stir — ? We never did meet actually, did we?"

"Hell no! We avoided you like the plague, but C.O. told us you'd written him about our little jaunt! God damn, it *is* a small world!"

"By Jove, it is at that," Sinha said, extending his hand to Hodge with the warmest smile he'd flashed all evening. "McNeill. Yes, I do remember that name! I knew it sounded rather familiar!"

"Well, I guess you had as much reason to block us out as we did you, Marshal."

"Let's forget rank, old boy, shall we? I must say, I rather admired your courage in taking things into your own hands the way you did!"

"It was really more his fault than mine," Hodge explained, pointing to Seth.

"Both of you, then," Sinha continued. "You know, McNeill, I'd rather like to be of some assistance to you — if I may? We don't have awfully many planes, you know, that we could really spare for your sort of venture," he paused, "but I shouldn't be at all surprised if we can't find one Dakota to lift you chaps into Kathmandu. When were you planning to leave, eh?"

"Tomorrow," Hodge whispered, his hopes suddenly so high, he hardly dared to speak.

"Well — that is a bit close, you know. Would the day after do?"

"Just fine," Hodge said, almost shouting.

"Splendid! Shall we shake on it, McNeill?"

"Marshal, you're a godsend!" Hodge stood up to go over and shake his hand.

"Three cheers for the Marshal," Peter said, raising his water glass. They all joined in, and the other guests in the dining room turned to look as though they were mad, or the happiest people in New Delhi tonight — or more probably, both. And before they had finished with the second cheer — the entire crowd chimed in. Then the band struck up a rousing marching tune, and everybody began to applaud. It was undoubtedly one of the most joyous scenes anyone had ever witnessed at the Imperial.

It's a goddamn touchdown, Hodge thought, and much to his own amazement, there were tears in his eyes.

After dinner, Sinha insisted that they return to the bottle bar with him to toast the success of their expedition. He broke out the Scotch, and they all had whiskey and soda.

"Dammit," said T.J., "the only thing I'm missin' now's a good cigar! I brought me a few boxes from London, but damned if I took enough provisions for tonight!" He searched the pockets of his tuxedo. "It's this stupid monkey suit I changed into!"

"If that's all you want, Judson," Sinha said, "do come up to my room for a moment, old boy. I have all sorts of Havanas in my closet — you can take your pick of the lot, eh?"

"Hey, boy, you mean that? Kin you spare a few?"

"God, yes — come along! I insist! You'll excuse us a moment, won't you?"

"Good God, we're set as long as this liquor lasts," shouted Peter.

"Yah, if it is all right that we stay without you?"

"Never fear, chaps," said Sinha, extracting his membership permit and leaving it on the table. "Order anything you like with that!"

"Hey, that's better'n a Diners Club card," shouted Tony, taking hold of Sinha's arm as they walked none too steadily out of the bar. His voice sobered once they were headed across the lobby toward the elevators. "Thanks, Marshal — we appreciate your cooperation," he said.

"My pleasure, T.J. I didn't want to commit myself to tomorrow, you know, to avoid any possibility of alerting them. I think it went off quite well, wouldn't you say?"

"If I were a Hollywood talent scout, Marshal, you'd be under contract right now! It was a neat show."

"Good." They reached the elevators. "I suppose we'd best go up, hadn't we? Hmm." He twisted the pointed tip of his mustache, frowning meditatively.

"Damn right, we've gotta get those cigars," Tony said. "What's troubling you?"

"Nothing. I was just trying to remember if I had any *imported* cigars left in my room?"

Tony roared with laughter as the elevator took them to the top floor. "Hell, any old cigar'll do, Marshal. I could manage to smoke one pure dung Indian home-product, if that's all you've got!"

"Goodness, no, we have much better weeds than that —— the best you can buy in this hotel, at least, but the Havanas have been rather in short stock — well, here we are, let's see what we can find, eh?" He opened the door, and busied himself at once in rummaging about on his dresser, searching the drawers, and muttering to himself as he found several empty Corona boxes, which he tossed into the wastepaper basket.

Tony went to the window, staring out at the crowds strolling peacefully along Raj Path, beyond the stately royal palms that lined the front walk like a giant guard of honor. The city seemed placid enough, the sky clear of all turbulence.

"How's it going up there, Marshal? Any word yet?"

"No, not a thing! We've tried everything we've got, T.J., but they're on to us, I am afraid —"

"The Nepalese?"

"Yes — it's that damned Mandeva! He's become quite a nuisance, actually."

"Can't you get rid of him?"

"I wish you'd tell us how — if you have any bright ideas, the Old Man would certainly appreciate hearing from you."

"No — other than this expedition, Marshal, I'm afraid we've drawn a blank. You'll have to handle the General your own way. We can't risk any more of those operations right now. They get too damn much publicity."

"Rather! Of course, that's *our* difficulty as well, you know. This *is* annoying," he muttered, slamming the last of his drawers shut. "Not a decent cigar in the room!"

"Don't worry — as long as you have something — ?"

"Yes, I've a whole box full of these things — not bad, actually, once you develop the habit."

"I won't smoke enough of them for that, thank God. I'll send you a box of my Havanas tomorrow."

"Would you, T.J.? That's awfully good of you, you know!"

"Hell, it's no *airplane!* Come on, we better get back before they start worrying." He took a fist full of Sinha's cigars and put them in his inner pocket.

"I must say, I'm rather keen to see if they'll find anything," Sinha said, as they stepped out of his room.

"Hell, if it's where we think it is, Marshal, they damn well should, shouldn't they?"

"Yes," Sinha replied, though he sounded less emphatic now than he had last month when Tony spoke to him from Washington.

"No use worrying it, Marshal. Best to let them have a look-see, and keep our fingers crossed."

"Oh, I agree to that, T.J. We've got to get someone up there, and the sooner the better, you know!"

"Right."

Neither of them spoke in the elevator going down. The lobby was almost empty, however, as they started to cross it toward the bottle room, and without turning to look at Tony, barely moving his lips, Sinha asked,

"You're quite sure none of them suspects anything, are you?"

"Positive," Tony replied.

CHAPTER **20**

THE drive back to Maharani's was a wild and noisy one. Fortunately the car was heavy, the roads empty. They reached Maharani's in record time, just before midnight.

The fragrance of perfumed air welcomed them as they stepped none too steadily from the car. The stars shimmered like jewels on a sky of soft velvet. But for the crickets' song, the night was silent.

"Let's go for a swim," Hodge said. It was his night — he didn't want it to end.

"What a lovely idea!" applauded Rena. Tony offered to bring his liquor to the pool. Lotte alone excused herself, explaining she felt tired.

"Yah, the little mother needs rest," explained Bruno, not without acerbity. He escorted her back to their room, but promised to meet them all at the pool.

"Maybe I'd better rack it in also," Seth said.

"Aw, come on, buddy — we've gotta celebrate tonight! A good swim'll pick you up, man! You have to show us that double-somersault jackknife of yours!"

"Can you do such fancy dives, Seth?" asked Rena, her face glowing.

"I doubt it," Seth said, "anymore." He felt like asking her then if it were true — what Hodge had told them. He knew he could have no rest until he asked her, no matter how tired he was. But he would have to wait till they were alone.

"Come on, buddy, don't go soft on us! Hell man, I've been waiting almost twenty years to win back that bottle of Haig & Haig you took me for at the Grand!" The old competitive gleam brightened Hodge's eyes as he jabbed playfully at Seth's stomach, catching the muscles relaxed. "You're getting out of shape, Professor."

Perhaps he could find a moment to ask her at the pool, he thought. "Okay, I guess I could use a swim at that."

"What fun," Jane shouted. "I haven't been midnight swimming in months! We should all go in our nature suits!"

"Hey, that's for me, girl! By gosh, let's go, honey!" Tony grabbed her hand and started up the steps.

"Wait, T.J., I was only joking!"

They all laughed, and went inside to change.

A greenish glow, surrealistically eerie, almost as disturbing as the Northern Lights, hung over the pool, from which wisps of steam rose hairlike to merge with the darkness above. The white concrete deck was deserted, except for air mats and sun chairs of aluminum with brightly colored backs of plastic. The bar was set with ice and glasses by the time they arrived, bearing their own bottles. The men came first, Hodge and Bruno diving right in; Seth, Niels, and Tony pausing for a drink before braving the water. Peter raced up to the high board the moment he appeared, shouting in simulated horror as he looked down, "Good God, *help!*" Holding his nostrils, he jumped feet first, kicking his legs like a circus clown, making an enormous splash, which reached the bar.

"Do it again, boy," Tony shouted as Peter's head surfaced, "one more jump like that an' I'll have just enough water for this damn drink!"

"Whose dive did I miss?" asked Jane, emerging from the foliage in a single-piece lemon-colored suit.

"Pete here just fell in, honey! Show 'im how t'dive!"

"I can try," Jane said, climbing the ladder nimbly, pausing to tug her suit down at her buttocks before running the length of the board to jump off in a swan dive.

"Say that's not bad, woman," Peter remarked.

"The water's delicious," she said, climbing out and removing her cap, shaking her luxuriantly long hair loose, and going over to take the drink Tony had mixed for her.

"Honey, you're my dream come t'life," Tony said, putting his arm around her dripping waist.

"To dreamers everywhere," Jane said, clicking her glass against his.

"Hear, hear," shouted Peter, running over to join them.

"Come on, Seth," Hodge called, climbing the ladder to the fifteen foot board. "I'm still after that bottle, man!" He ran forward and did a neat body spin ending in a clean dive.

"Yah, that is good, Roger," shouted Bruno. "Now I must try it." There were pink potholes of wrinkled skin splashed like moon craters across the otherwise smooth surface of his stomach and back. He stood like a trapeze artist warming up at the top of the ladder, first rubbing his hands dry, then leaning back at arm's length, springing forward with muscular speed to jump off and execute a double spin, cutting without a splash into the green water.

"Bravo," Niels shouted.

"Hey, he's good," said Hodge, turning to Seth. "How about it, buddy, let's make this a three-way contest — okay?"

"I'm out of shape, Mac," he answered.

"Good God, but *she*'s not," whispered Peter, his eyes widening as Rena stepped onto the lighted platform surrounding the pool wearing a bright pink bikini and golden pumps, whose spikes sent faintly visible vibrations up through her almost naked body at each measured step.

"Hey, baby," Hodge called, "that's quite a suit!"

Every eye was upon her as she walked around the edge of the oval-shaped pool, like the beauty queen coming to receive her

156

crown. Smiling coquettishly as she approached them, Rena asked, "Is it all right? I bought it in Paris."

"Honey, it looks good 'nough t'eat!"

Peter emitted a long low whistle.

"I like to have my camera now," said Niels.

"Do you think it is pretty, Seth?" she asked in a whisper.

He was not sure now whether he loved or hated her. Perhaps, after all, he thought, she is nothing but a juvenile tease. She seemed to enjoy her singularly provocative powers. He could not speak to her. He turned to refill his glass.

"Good God, woman," said Peter, coming over to place one finger upon her bare midriff, "is that *really* you, or my intoxicated imagination?"

"Ooo, that tickles," she laughed, backing away.

"By God, it's *real!*" he shouted, grinning warmly.

"Thanks for the drink, T.J.," said Jane, setting her glass down so hard upon the bar that it sounded like the report of a muffled rifle. "If you'll excuse me — I'm turning in!" She grabbed her towel and wrapping it tightly around her shoulders, ran back toward the hotel.

"Jane!" Peter shouted. She did not stop or turn. "What the devil —? Why do you suppose —?" He looked around at their bemused faces, appearing to be the only one there who did not understand what had happened to Miss Tylor! Then he shrugged, as though he could not have cared less. "Women artists, you know," he muttered, joining Seth at the bar.

"She acts as though she's in love, Pete."

"Oh, good God, aren't they always? Show me a woman, old chap, and I'll show you a born trapper! Cheers!" For all the bluff of his words, he sounded morose.

"Ever been married, Pete?"

"God, no! I may be a bloody fool, but I'm not senile!"

"Hey, come on, men!" Hodge shouted, clapping his hands for attention. "We're having a diving contest — me, Bruno, and Seth! Who else wants to compete?"

"I love a competition," said Rena, rushing over to take a poolside beach chair facing the board.

"Go ahead, boys, me an' Rena'll be judges!" Tony caved into the chair next to her, his stomach protruding like an inflated inner tube through his unbuttoned sport shirt.

"Me too," shouted Peter, pulling up the air mattress at her other side, and squatting on it cross-legged.

"Okay — the best fancy dive out of three tries wins," Hodge announced. "Does that sound fair to you, Bruno?"

"Yah, this is fine."

"Seth?"

"I haven't been on the high board for a while, Hodge — I'll watch." He sat beside Peter.

"Come on, buddy, none of us have been practicing for this meet! You can't chicken-out on me!"

"Dammit, boy, don't be a spoilsport! If I was your age, I'd be up there myself!"

"Tony, you sound younger in spirit than he," Rena said softly, though not so soft that he did not hear her.

"Never mind, Roger, if he is afraid, we try anyhow, yah?"

"Okay," Hodge said, "what'll we dive for?"

"Might as well make it a bottle of Haig & Haig, Mac." He set down his glass and stood up.

"Hey, buddy!" Hodge rubbed his hands together, smiling. "That's the old spirit, Seth!"

Old is right, he thought, feeling none of the tension, none of the excitement he once had felt before any contest, the spirit of competition that still flowed, he saw, like the rapids beyond Niagara through Hodge's veins. Seth had known it once himself, and every examination, every sport, every casual game or serious venture he embarked upon became a battle for Victory. When did it die in me? he wondered.

"Want to go first, buddy?"

"No, you guys kick off," he said, feeling stiff in every joint.

"Bruno, why don't you start? I'll follow you, and Seth'll come after me. How's that?"

Bruno raced nimbly up the ladder. From the top he called down, "Any special dive, Roger?"

"The best you've got, Bruno. Better try a triple-somersault jackknife though, if you want to beat buddy Goodman here — he's got the double down pat!"

Bruno grimaced, braced back, and ran forward, jumping high. His muscular coordination was excellent. He beautifully executed a single-somersault jackknife, which everyone but Rena applauded. Nazi or not, Seth thought, the bastard's a good diver.

"Ach — too low," Bruno commented, climbing out.

"Well, here goes nothing, kids," said Hodge, who had eagerly raced to the top board before Bruno surfaced. He balanced himself on tiptoes at the back end of the board, spreading his arms like an eagle poised for flight. Then running the plank, he sprang off, rolled his body into a ball, turning full circle twice before he pulled out stiff as an arrow to slice through the water without a splash.

"Beautiful!" Rena gasped.

"Terrific! Bravo! Great dive," they all chorused.

"Nice going, Mac," said Seth, offering Hodge his hand as he climbed out of the pool.

"Not fast enough for the jackknife though," he replied, shaking his head. "Didn't have enough spring off that damn board!"

Climbing the ladder, Seth thought it was simply that he'd matured, Hodge hadn't. His values, his perspective had changed. He no longer felt obliged to prove himself this way, nor in any other way, for that matter. Even in teaching, and scholarly research, he'd stopped striving to become the most inspiring classroom instructor, the greatest authority, the foremost expert in his field. At thirty he had dreamed like that. Nearer to forty now, he knew better. There were colleagues in his own department, ten years his junior, who had published two books, others who were far more popular with students.

He gripped the curved aluminum bars at the top of the white concrete pillar and stared along the matted canvas-covered board to the emptiness beyond. There was a time when he'd felt more at home up here than he did on the sundeck. He'd won more points at the Calcutta meet than any member of the Base team — five more than Hodge. The coach had talked about Olympic possibilities after the war! He'd even written about that to Anita, as if she'd be impressed by anything as stupid as a high-diving champion! He returned home to find her married to her intern — "He's just the most brilliant man I ever met, Seth. He's going to specialize in brain surgery! I know you'll just adore each other! I've told him so much about you, Seth. I do *so* want all three of us to be *friends* —"

He took two long strides and a jump, hugged his knees to his chest and spun round once, twice, then splashed like a dud bomb into the water before pulling out. Bubbling down through the warm liquid he retained his fetal position, and wished he could simply remain at the womblike bottom of the pool till everyone had gone to bed. Then he kicked up and reached hungrily for the surface. There were no shouts of approval as he emerged.

"Neat somersault, buddy," said Hodge, not quite able to keep the edge of satisfaction out of his voice.

Seth stared numbly at the indifferent tower, whose mocking high board looked like a huge tongue stuck out in laughter at his poor performance. He couldn't face any of his judges. The passion for victory might have died in him, but the shame of defeat was still distressingly strong. He brushed the hair off his brow and watched Bruno do a perfect double-somersault dive, which he scored even higher than Hodge's first dive. The Nazi'll beat us both, he thought.

Then Hodge started his pre-dive show again, posing like a ballet dancer, beginning his run but stopping a scant few inches from the precarious end of the board to walk back calmly and take a second warm-up. Rena gasped. Tony whispered, "That boy's got somethin'." Hodge bent over, touching his fingertips to his toes, straightening, inhaling, running, and springing off with such force that he flew almost five feet above the board. It was a spectacular jump, but the sheer force of it seemed to upset his equilibrium, and instead of recoiling Hodge twisted half around, coming down in a half-twist swan dive, which was beautiful, but not quite what he'd intended.

Still and all the judges applauded, and Rena yelled "Whoopee!" They were not the most discerning audience. Hodge wasn't nearly as pleased with himself this time. Coming up at Seth's side he shook his head, muttering, "I flubbed it."

"You looked good though."

Get it over with, Seth told himself, walking around the pool to the knurled rungs of the tall ladder. What earthly difference did it make, after all, whether or not he proved to three men he hardly knew and a half-naked girl he wished he'd never met that he could dive better than Hodge McNeill and Bruno Jaeger? It's unimportant, he thought, trivial, childish, and in the long run — unimportant! His position at the university was secure for life. His modest contribution to scholarship would endure beyond his remaining years. What the hell more did he want or need? Twenty years ago the high board was the closest thing within reach to be conquered, the double-somersault jackknife dive and Anita — those were his great ambitions. Now neither of them mattered. What does matter? he wondered, and he felt cold. It's this damn expedition, he thought. I should never have joined it! He began to feel as though he were tricked into a trap, lured back in time, forced to relive a past which he'd blissfully forgotten. As if all the locked doors of decisions irrevocably made were suddenly flung open, and he stood once more facing thresholds he'd long since abandoned all hope or intention of crossing.

He could see the Big Dipper and the North star. He'd once learned every constellation in the sky. Show Seth Goodman three stars anywhere and he'll bring the damn plane home without maps or a radio, Hodge used to exaggerate after a specially nasty flight. God, the things they'd planned doing — after the war! He filled his lungs, locked his jaw and ran forward. A dive is no better than your spring, the coach always reminded him. Try and break the damn board, kid! Hit it with all you've got! Make it crack! He went high enough this time to pull out after the second roll, but there was no room for the jackknife finish. He could barely straighten before the water lapped over his arms, and he felt his knees buckle, his lower legs smacking the surface with a splash that ruined his chance of even matching Hodge's first dive. Yet he wasn't smarting with shame as he came up for air, greeted by shouts of approval from all, except Hodge, who looked and sounded earnestly professional as he said, "Not bad, buddy, but you bent your knees."

"I know, Mac." He was amused at how apprehensive Hodge suddenly appeared.

Bruno looked grimly determined as he paused before his final jump. His face reflected all the proud anger, the fierce determination, the dogged arrogance, of the former S.S. man he was. Then he raced forward and jumped, but it looked as though he simply tried too hard, as if he were hoping by this individual feat of valor, by beating these two Americans, to recoup some of the loss his nation had suffered in the war. He could not quite match his own brilliant last performance, redoing the double-somersault straight dive, somewhat less neatly.

"Nice try. Bruno," shouted Hodge. "You're one helluva diver, man!"

"Ach —" It was all he could say, coming up and shaking his head in disgust at his failure.

None of them uttered a sound as Hodge stood for what must have been more than a minute, fists locked over the rising curved rails of the ladder top, leaning back at arm's length, like a tautly drawn slingshot, gulping air as though he were pumping himself up, then catapulting off at alarming speed, hitting the outward tip of the board with a resounding thump, catching it flatfooted instead of by his toes, and springing so slightly that he knew there would not be time enough for the double roll, so he decided instead to jack-knife after a single, which he executed beautifully, as he had before. They all cheered. Tony shook his hand heartily, patting his wet back. Seth joined the chorus, but read the look of growing apprehension in Hodge's eyes, and felt like telling him, "Don't worry, skipper, you win! I'm not even going to try to beat that — it doesn't mean a damn to me."

He almost said it, in fact, was ready to waive his last try, to plead fatigue, but then it caught hold of him, the sudden febrile desperate desire to win — it seized him like a trap of the meanest ambition all but hidden from his own consciousness by carefully disguised camouflage of self-effacement, virtuous conduct, modesty, and shyness, cutting like a surgeon's scalpel to lay bare the raw bone of what he truly wanted, as savagely primitive as any child's serious play, as the mortal struggle motivating tribal braves for the Princess, whose body was the reward vouchsafed to physical prowess alone. Climbing the ladder for the third time Seth thought of nothing but the acrobatic feat he would have to perform to push himself just a bit higher than the ordinary spring of this board should lift him, for the single jump he'd last attempted was as forceful as any his weight could command, yet it hadn't carried him quite high enough. He would have to spring twice, gaining enough momentum from the first bounce to land with greater impact on the tip, for his blast-off. The risk, of course, was overshooting the end if his first jump was too hard, which was, he suspected, why neither Hodge nor Bruno had tried it.

He estimated the spot for his first jump carefully, ran forward and landed with both feet flat upon target, rising high enough to come down with the added impact he needed to fly birdlike off the tip, reaching for the Dipper with outstretched arms before curling into himself, rolling full around twice, snapping out and touching his toes with his fingertips, legs and arms as rigid as knife blades, then straightening to slip without a splatter into the pool.

His heart was pounding wildly as he came up, gasping for air, his ears plugged with water, mercifully spared the shouts of his drunken witnesses, stomping and clapping like warriors now that the battle was over. Rena bent above his head as he started to emerge from the pool, her bosom all but touching his upturned face, her eyes wide with adulation.

"It was beautiful, Seth! The most beautiful dive I ever saw!"

"I've gotta hand it to you, buddy," Hodge said.

Then he felt sick. Not from the strain or tension so much as from his own awareness of why he had done it, from the sickening consciousness of what he had seen and learned of himself, of the debased and predatory creature lurking in the darkest recesses of his spirit. Each shake of his hand, each tap on his back only added to the miserable feeling of treacherous self-betrayal, of supine insecurity and weakness that had driven him so desperately to prove his virility and power. His ears rang with shame, and he felt a sudden upwelling of bile, a wave of nausea.

"I'm sorry," he whispered. "I — I don't feel too well — I better get to sleep."

"*Layla tov,* Seth," she called out, running after him, catching up to him on the garden path, just beyond the lighted area, out of earshot of the others. She was panting from the run, almost as hard as he was. "It means 'Good night' — in Hebrew." She smiled innocently.

"Is it true, Rena? Are you going to marry Hodge?"

"*What?* Are you mad? Who — ? Did he — is this what *he* told you?"

He nodded mutely, unable to speak — this time for the joy that welled up inside him.

"I don't love *him*," she said, softly. "I don't love any of *them*, Seth! Do you not understand this?"

Then he understood, and extended his hand to her. They walked back to the hotel together.

CHAPTER 21

"You are wonderful, darling," she whispered, peering down at him in the softness of her room's darkness, her voice like velvet. He could see her face, smiling blissfully, the naked radiance of love's completion brightening her eyes, like diamonds glowing with some inner light. He felt the softness of her hair upon his bare body.

"I love you, Rena."

"And I," she whispered mellifluously, *"Anee ohevet otkha."*

"I love to hear you speak Hebrew."

"Do you know Hebrew?"

"Shalom," he said, virtually exhausting his vocabulary. How eager his father had been to pay whatever it would cost to be sure that his sons had a Hebrew education! *My sons, the Yeshiva-buchers!* When he was four Seth "read" his brother's lesson books for guests in their living room. He had learned the books by heart from hearing his brother recite them. His father hoped he would become a rabbi someday — "What *my* father wanted for me, *boit-chikla,* only I never had your brains! For you it will be easy — you take to it! This is a marvelous thing to be — a rabbi!" The Depression, and his mother's firmness in insisting that her boys receive free public school education by the time he was ready for second grade, saved Seth from that strange fate. He'd often blessed her for

it. Now the only Hebrew words he remembered were those for peace, and peculiarly enough — boy and girl. "I also know *yeled* and *yalda*," he told Rena. "What I was — and you are."

"Bah! It makes me angry when you talk so! You are the youngest man on earth!" She kissed his lips.

"Only with you, Rena."

"Good! For other women you *should* behave old!" She laughed joyfully. "Seth! *Anee ohevet otkha!*"

"What does it mean?"

"I love you. It is something I have not said a long time."

"Tell me again," he asked, "so I may say it to you — in Hebrew."

"Ah, but for you it is *anee ohev otakh!* You see, in Hebrew it is not the same for a man and woman — I mean, the words are not the same."

"The rest is," he whispered, feeling the pressure of her body, responding in kind.

"Yes." Her lips moved closer, till they locked against his mouth. Their eyes closed as one. Their bodies moved as one. He felt as much a part of her being as she was of his. Clinging together, the fluids and flesh of their bodies merging, they filled the vacuum of a universe, which seemed no longer existent beyond the limits of their limbs. They loved — was it for an instant or all eternity?

"Oh, Seth."

"Rena."

"You make me so happy, Seth."

"*Anee —*" he began, "*ohev —*"

"That's right!" She smiled, nodding, prompting him, as he hesitated, with "*otakh*. It is a very strong word, *otakh* — not?"

"Yes, very strong." Then he said it all together, slowly at first. He repeated it faster. Her face became even more rapturous with delight.

"Oh, my darling Seth! I wanted you to take me in your arms when I first met you in Hodge's room . . . Did you know it? I almost trembled, thinking it is what you would do! I was nearly terrified of you, yet I felt — I felt immediately so close to you! And then how you answered Bruno, when he asks if you are German —

do you remember? I wanted to kiss you then. Before today I have kissed you many times, my darling — did you know?"

"Not as often as I've kissed you —"

"Yes?" Then they kissed again, and did not talk for a long time.

"I have never thought I could love anyone so," she whispered. "There is no end of passion within me — for you, Seth. It is like — like waves on the ocean, each one coming higher, stronger —"

"Like the mountains," he told her. "In Nepal, you can see them so — range beyond range, each dwarfing the one before, till no sky is left, only a mountain wall that covers the universe and stops the sun in orbit — it keeps rising, growing — I thought I was so exhausted, Rena, hours ago, I thought I would have no strength to hold you in my arms, yet now I feel more alive, more awake, more in love with you —"

"I think it must be — we are the happiest people on earth tonight, Seth."

"Yes — and the luckiest."

"Because we are the most in love. But now you must try to sleep, darling." She cradled his head against her full bosom. "Sleep in me, Seth."

Even with Anita, at the peak of their romance, he had never found such completion, such perfect harmony of passion in love. He was too young then to respond to her ardor as he could now, for with youth's impulsiveness he would often leave her when she wanted him most strongly. Age tempered his fire, experience taught him control, and holding the lithe body in his warm embrace, he felt he could live inside her forever.

"I could sleep in you, Rena — and wake in you."

"Yes," she whispered, running her fingers along his face, feeling the outline of his lips like a blind person reading by touch alone. "All night, and all day, darling — and every night, every day."

So they slept, and woke, and slept again, locked in love. Their wakeful moments were like dreams, and dreaming they woke to find each other, to kiss, to touch, to dream some more. . . . Till the first faint glow, the cold gray clammy fingers of dawn stealthily came to her room, rudely arousing him.

"Oh, God," he said, sitting up, rubbing his knuckles against his eyes, "what time is it?" She was fast asleep, her head half buried by her pillow. He left the bed, and went to wash his face. The water felt like needles against his smarting eyes. He could barely see his visage.

He did not have the heart to wake her. He kissed her naked arm gently, and stepped out on the porch, feeling like a thief as he glanced in both directions. But no one was in sight. Nor was it any wonder. The sky was but faintly gray. He walked quickly to the lobby. A single servant stood vacuuming the rug. Even the desk was as yet unattended. The clock over the entrance registered half-past five. . . .

Perhaps she's sleeping, he thought, carefully opening the door of their room, relieved to find it quite dark inside. He could hear Ethan's adenoidal breathing. Stella lay on the bed, her back turned to him. She seemed fast asleep too. He tried easing into the bed without shaking it.

"Well," she said, turning to confront him, her eyes wide, her voice very much awake, "I thought you were dead by now!"

He said nothing. He stared at the unmoving fan blades overhead, wondering if they were sharp enough to cut off a man's head.

"Well? I'm waiting," she said.

"For what?" The excuse, of course. The story. The lie! Yes, it would really be kinder to lie — but he was not good at that. He would have liked to think it was professional ethics — his scholarly code of honor — that kept him from lying now. What was it he always told his students? *Ultimately, a scholar has one master, and only one — truth!* No, it was just that he wasn't very good at fabrication — he could never make it sound really convincing — the way Hodge might have! Relax, baby, I was just out with the boys for a few drinks!

"What do you mean *for what?* You come in here at midnight, and tell me you're going for a 'quick-swim,' and five hours later you creep back into this room like a filthy robber —"

"I didn't want to wake you!"

"Oh, thank you very much! How wonderfully considerate! You just leave me here to cry my stupid eyes out all night long, wondering if — if you're dead — or — or God knows what else by now!

167

And then you have the gall — the filthy rotten *gall* to tell me you *didn't want to wake me?*" The volume of her voice had risen steadily, ending in so loud a shout that Ethan woke, crying.

He closed his eyes, covering them with his hand, rubbing at his brow. His head began to throb. He went toward Ethan's bed, but was arrested by Stella's warning —

"Don't you touch that child, you monster!"

He went to the medicine chest then, and took some aspirin, while she comforted Ethan, who asked, "Is Dad a monster, Mom?"

"Hush, darling," she said. "Never mind — don't cry. Momma's here to protect you — hush now." Her tremulous words of reassurance served only to make Ethan cry harder.

It seemed only an appropriate way to Seth for so beautiful a night to end.

CHAPTER **22**

HODGE was following Air Vice-Marshal Sinha down the long musty corridor. Yellow-edged papers were stacked shoulder high at either side of them, and they moved so quickly that pages kept fluttering off the stacks in their wake. Hodge paused to pick up the documents, but each time he did so Sinha moved farther away from him, and Hodge had to run to catch up. "Just a formality," Sinha was saying, "won't take a minute." The rattle of old typewriter keys grew louder as they passed down the hall. Half a stack of flimsy papers swayed and scattered across the floor. Bending to pick them up, Hodge dropped his wallet, and his personal papers scattered amidst the debris. He gathered them together as rapidly as he could, but in his haste found he had taken some official documents as well. "Hurry," called Sinha, "this won't take a minute." Nervously, he replaced the Ministry's documents on different stacks, and stuffed his own back into his wallet. Then he was standing in front of a bare desk behind which the Air Marshal himself sat, his visored cap thick with silver wings scrambled together. "Here's your flight pass, McNeill," the Marshal said, holding out what looked like a plane ticket. "May I see your birth certificate, please?" He emptied his wallet onto the desk, and pushed over his passport. "Your birth certificate," the Marshal repeated. He fumbled through the other papers, finding his driver's license, which he offered in evidence. "Sorry — we need your birth certificate!" He opened the officially sealed permit from the government of Nepal, but the Marshal's eyes wouldn't so much as bother to focus upon it. Desperately he picked up each of the other papers, credit cards, receipts, bills, notes, pictures — where was his birth certificate? "I must have dropped it in the hall," he explained, starting to sweat now for neither of them said a word, just staring in disbelief at his confusion. "Back there — with all those other papers," he said, turning and running back to look for it. But the corridor was empty. The stacks had been carried off. There wasn't a scrap of paper anywhere, only yellow specks of paper dust. He ran, half stumbling, the full length of the dim hallway, dashing back again when he reached the outside door. Panting for breath he turned to open the nearest door of the many cubicles from which the typing noises echoed, the muffled hammering of keys and dim ringing of carriage bells. He pushed the door open wide, and found Seth and Rena lying there, naked on the bare floor, in the otherwise empty room. She looked up at him and laughed, the metallic laughter of hammering keys. Then Seth started to laugh. The hammering became louder . . .

Hodge woke to find himself covered with sweat, sunlight flooding through his windows. The phone was ringing.

"Hello — oh, yes, Tony." He blinked at his wristwatch. It was half-past nine. He must have fallen asleep just after dawn. Most of the night he had lain awake, listening to the sound of their voices, the sound of her mattress, through the wall of his room. "He what? — Oh, good. That's fine — What? — Oh, no, I'm okay. Just a little tired. — What? — Oh, yes, yes, it's great news! Sure is, man. Thanks a lot. I'll see you in the dining room — Okay."

He hung up, and lit a cigarette. Sinha had just called Tony to tell him they had the plane. Everything was set for departure to Kathmandu tomorrow at ten! Everything's Roger — all the way, he thought. Everything's A-okay!

He felt no elation. No excitement. No joy. It would be different, he knew, once he had the Yeti — that would be the Big One, the Fix that was waiting up there in Nepal with Hodge McNeill's name on it — waiting to dispel all the aches and pains, all the frustrations and failures. Once he got that juice in his arm, once that was in his blood — man, she could lay the whole Indian Army, and it wouldn't spoil his day for a second!

He dragged the smoke into his lungs, leaving it there to sit in his gut, to burn through his insides, for all he cared. Till he could hold it no longer, and almost coughed up his balls, choking, gagging, clutching at his throat as he ran to the sink, and stood doubled over it, till the blood was in his eyes, and the whole basin looked red.

He turned the cold water on, filled the sink, then immersed his head. He did that three times, before drying off. He dressed quickly, and went to her door. He tapped very hard.

He waited. Then he tapped again, harder, feeling the door against his knuckles — wishing it were her head.

He was about to kick it open, when her voice, sounding sleepy said, "One moment — who is it, please?"

"McNeill!"

"Oh — Hodge, it's you! I thought it is — some madman. I — " She touched her disheveled hair self-consciously, hastily drawing her robe a bit tighter to hide her neck. "I — I must have overslept. When is it, Hodge? I'm sorry —"

"It's nine-thirty. We're leaving tomorrow morning at ten. There's a lot to be done yet. We've got to get cracking!"

"I see — so the plane is set? Yes? Of course — I will just get —" Hastily, she started gathering her clothes up, her pants and bra, her garter belt and skirt. The robe kept coming loose each time she bent, and she dropped things as she paused to draw it together, but one button was missing below the cord, and though she pulled it tighter, her legs kept emerging, naked almost to her pelvic bone.

The bed looked like a battlefield, sheets and pillows crushed beyond repair. He could see strands of hair on the rumpled sheets — pubic hair.

"Enjoy yourself last night, baby?"

"What?" She looked as though she didn't know, had no clue as to what he was talking about! "I will take just one moment, Hodge, to dress — if you will please excuse me — ?"

"Go right ahead — don't mind me." He sat in her easy chair, amused at how troubled her face became, how frightened she suddenly seemed of him.

"Hodge, please wait outside."

"Nah, don't let me bother you, baby! Go ahead — you can do anything you want within sight — or sound of old Mac — you know that, kid!"

"I don't understand how you talk now," she said nervously, clutching her clothes as though they were weapons in her small fists, keeping her robe very safely shut as she stepped away from him. "Please wait outside, or — or in the lobby?"

She was moving cautiously toward the bathroom, he saw, going back slowly so as not to alert him, not to indicate how terrified she'd become. But he sensed her every thought, with the innate sixth sense of a hunter anticipating the moves of his prey, he knew she was trying to get close enough to the bathroom door so that in one stride she would be ready to barricade herself, lock herself safely out of his reach. She had all the instincts, all the passions of a dumb animal.

Only he was too fast for her. As he jumped up, she screamed, almost paralyzed with fear while she tried to race back — to the bathroom door he reached two steps ahead of her. He slammed it shut, and saw the terror widen her eyes as she moved now in another direction, toward a cul-de-sac between the clothes closet and her bed. He laughed heartily at how easy it was to trap her, and at the stupid expression of panic distorting her face.

"What's the matter, baby? Why so worried? Guilty conscience?"

"Not at all," she whispered. "For what?"

"Suppose you tell me, huh?" Her lips looked so grotesquely twisted and ugly as she gnawed at them, he could not help wondering why he even gave her the satisfaction of showing that he actually cared enough to feel jealous. Jealous of what? he thought. A cheap slut! A bitch of a Jewess. He was tempted to fire her, then and there — send her back waiting on tables in Soho! This was the thanks he got! Goddamn whore!

"What happened to you last night, baby? You ran off so fast, no one had a chance to say good night to you. Poor Tony was asking me if you were angry — or what? He didn't even know if you enjoyed the party? Said you didn't even thank him — or anything."

"I'll thank him today," she whispered. Her back was pressed against the wall now.

"Where'd you go, baby?"

"To sleep. Please let me pass, Hodge — I must dress now."

"To sleep — with who?"

His heart was hammering in his neck, his chest, hammering against his eyeballs.

"It's none of your business!"

He felt the spittle of her answer dampen his cheek — aimed like bullets against his ego. He was tempted then to kill her, to lock his hands around her slender neck, emerging like a cobra's body from the collar of her robe, to choke and wring that neck till the poison-bloated head above it rolled dismembered onto the floor. He'd rarely felt so strong a temptation — not since the afternoon he caught Margie in bed with the kid from the apartment below. It would, after all, be a service to mankind, to rid the earth of a slut like her!

"Everything about you's my business."

"What does it mean?"

"It means, that's the kind of ball game I play, kid. Strictly Big League. I'm a pro, baby. I don't dig the Minors!"

"You're mad."

"Damn right I am, kid — at you!"

"Please stop it, Hodge — you — you're frightening me."

"What's he got, Rena, that I haven't got?"

"Who? I don't understand anything you are talking —"

"Seth!"

Her face whitened, her lips were livid. "Leave me alone — now. *Now,* I say, or I scream."

"I can give you more than he ever will!" His head was throbbing, his body burning with passionate longing for her. His skin felt like flame. "When this expedition's over, we can go around the world, baby — just you and me! The slick magazines alone have promised me a small fortune, don't you understand? I'll be able to take you anywhere — buy you anything, everything you want! What the hell can Seth offer you?"

"Please! Go from here!"

172

"Has he asked you to marry him?" Her momentary silence was all the answer he needed. "He never will! Believe me, baby, I know that jerk — you don't! He's small potatoes, kid! He's not in our class, Rena! He's a sweet-natured slob! A good guy, sure — but they always end last!"

"Not in diving," she said, her smirk sending needles of pain through his groin.

"I won't give you another chance, Rena. You don't deserve this one —"

"I don't want it."

She said it so smugly, so complacently, so self-satisfiedly, with such sickening confidence — it made him shudder, tremble with rage and hatred for all she was, all she stood for in the whole lousy world, a world of whores and bastards, of pimps and prostitutes. What a smug little cunt she is, he thought, and more as a reflex than from premeditation his arm stiffened and jerked out at her, the rigid back of his hand catching her cheek, not really very hard — hardly more than a touch. But she made it seem worse than it was, wrenching her head around, pressing the other cheek flat against the wall, squeezing two drops of moisture out between her tightly shut wrinkled eyelids. Only she did not utter a sound, not a cry. He watched the cheek facing him blaze to crimson. How beautiful it looked. He felt like kissing it then. But he wouldn't give her the satisfaction! She's not worth it, he thought. She's not even worth the wages I pay her!

"How strong you are," she whispered, opening her eyes, glaring at him. "Now what do you do? Choke me? Punch me? Rape me? What next do you do to me — to make me *love* you?"

"I didn't mean to do that." His hand was tingling as though it had been burned, as if he had held it directly over a fire.

"O-o-och! Does it make you less a coward? Because you didn't mean? *Get out of my room!*"

"What has he got, Rena?" He felt light-headed, as though he would not be able to stand much longer. He was perspiring profusely. His shirt clung to his torso, dark stains of sweat spreading like rifle targets from his armpits, the cloth hugging his spine, like the rubber of his diving suit. He went down after octopus and shark, covered in that black rubber suit, with the harpoon gun in

173

his hands, the tanks strapped to his chest. He had caught a shark once. It almost cost him an arm. The razor-sharp fin cut through his muscle to the bone. He still felt the rheumatoid pain in his left arm — when the weather was very raw. He felt a twinge of it now, like an itch that could not be reached, no matter how hard he scratched — always just beyond reach.

"You wouldn't understand," she said, sounding very strong, as if she was not in the least bit afraid of him. As if — had he felt like doing it really — he could not have killed her with one blow, one stiff-handed slash at her neck, one bare-knuckled punch of his fist between her eyes, or into the butterlike warmth of her womanhood!

"Goddamn you," he said, every inch of his flesh trembling from the agony of control he exerted to keep himself from lashing out at her smug-smiling face — clenching only her wrist with one hand, twisting her arm — just the slightest twist, almost gently. "I asked you what he's got, Rena — that I haven't?"

"Ow-w-w!" It was the groan of a sick dumb animal. But then baring her teeth at him, she spit full in his face. "I love him," she shouted, "and you I *hate!*"

He released her arm. He stared unblinking at her, silently, for a moment. He did not wipe one drop of her saliva from his face — it was still warm from her mouth, the closest she's come to kissing me, he thought. He could not stop laughing then, that seemed so funny. He almost split his gut with laughter, stumbling toward her door.

CHAPTER 23

As far as Hodge was concerned, once he'd slammed that door on her, Rena was no better than Margie, no more worth worrying about. It was time to get cracking!

He called Bruno and told him to notify Misra to pack up the provisions, asking him to get over there as early as he could to be sure they weren't cheated.

"You've gotta watch these Indians, Bruno — they're no more

trustworthy than Jews!" Bruno understood, assuring Hodge he would be at Connaught Circle in half an hour to keep a bull's-eye focused on Misra's scales.

Niels was ready. He'd tested his equipment, he explained, had taken some shots that he wanted to develop today — just to see if the film was all right. Did Hodge know of any place that could print pictures fast here?

"Try Klug, the Manager — he knows everything about Delhi."

"Ah — that's a good idea. Thanks," Niels said.

"I hope Lotte likes them," he added, just in case Niels thought he wasn't on to him. Danes could be pretty sneaky too!

"Uh — yes, yes I hope so."

"See you later, buddy."

Peter's voice sounded so low, Hodge suspected he woke him.

"Grab your socks, and let go of your cock, Partridge — we're leaving tomorrow — Sinha's come through."

"Good God — I'd better pack."

"Right. And get some rest today, man. From the sound of your voice I'd say you could use a few hours outta sack!"

"You blackguard! I wish it were bloody well true! Oh, Christ, what a night."

He sounded so blue, Hodge couldn't resist the pleasure of asking what had gone wrong?

"Blast women, old chap! We can't take them or leave them and remain sane, you know!"

"I know."

"Damned American bitch — I bloody well know what *she's* after!"

"You."

"How right you are Mac! It's that obvious, eh? And here it's taken me half the bleeding night without sleep to work out! Good God! Can you imagine anything more calculating than that woman, more bloody well invidious?"

"Yes, I can. But forget about her, friend. It's time to get cracking!"

"Roger."

Hodge kept his hand on the hung phone for fully a minute after that. He was calm now. Perfectly calm. He had complete command over his emotions. The reins he let slip half an hour ago were firm in his fist again. No throbbing. No sweat.

Still he couldn't quite bring himself to speak to Seth — not yet. He lifted the phone, and asked for the desk. He told the clerk to have a message delivered to Professor Goodman's room from him.

"Get packed and ready," he dictated. "We check out tomorrow at eight. Departure from Palam at ten."

"What signature, sir?"

"My initials will do — H.M."

What else? he wondered, slamming the phone down harder than he'd meant to. He could use some breakfast — Tony would still be waiting for him. They had a few money matters to straighten out. He would get his secretary to cable the Royal for a few rooms in Kathmandu — it was easier thinking of her as his secretary. A month from now that bitch'll be begging to kiss my ass, he thought. Well he would just let her beg, till she was blue in the face!

Peter saw her leaving the dining room as he reached the top of the marble stairway leading to the lobby. She was, of course, accompanied by Judson, who kept a fat hand around her waist, and responded to her chatter as though she were the wittiest woman on God's bloody earth.

"Go on ahead, honey! I'm waitin' for Hodge. We'll see you at the pool later!"

She muttered something else that sent him into flab-vibrating stitches. The old lecher even blew a kiss at her! What a balloon, Peter thought, safely ensconced behind a pillar on the balcony, from which he could watch them both without being seen. Judson went to the desk to pick up some newspapers, and Jane was starting up the stairway now, holding herself like royalty as she climbed! It was the true test of a woman's rearing, he knew, how she looked walking upstairs, when she didn't know she was being watched. She had poise — he had to grant her that. From the look of her posture, he would have thought she'd been born an English Lady.

"What the devil kept you so bloody preoccupied last night, that you couldn't answer your phone?" he asked, accosting her as she reached the balcony and started toward her room.

"I beg your pardon?" She glanced at him as though he weren't there.

"Come off it, old girl," he snapped, adding "will you?" to take the edge from his tone. He even twitched his eyebrows to mollify her.

"Off *what?*" She looked positively lovely when she got that spark of anger in her eye — incredibly attractive, he thought. If he weren't so burned at having phoned her room half a dozen times last night, calling her practically every half hour, till he could no longer bring himself to face the damn operator's snickering, even from the remoteness of telephonic contact, he would have complimented her on her appearance this morning!

"Oh, now look here, Jane! —"

"Don't you dare raise your voice to me," she whispered, so devastatingly swift and soft it cut him dead in midthought. "You'd best learn some manners before speaking to me again, Mr. Partridge! I'm in no mood for your rudeness now, nor for your petulance!"

"*I'd* best learn manners, eh? Who in God's name bloody well turned on her heel last night, leaving me without so much as — ?"

"Oh-h-h-h-no-you-don't. You know very well what precipitated *that*, Mr. Partridge! Don't you play little boy Innocent with me, Peter!"

"Oh, good God! So I bloody well whistled at the girl! So what? If I'd been half as stuffy about you and old money-belly down there — pawing at you all bloody evening —"

"You have a filthy mouth, Peter Partridge! It should be washed out with soap for that! T.J.'s older than my father, and if you could even so much as *think* —"

"Well, it's what *he's* bloody well thinking right now, that blackguard! I saw the lecherous look in his eye when he just blew that kiss to you! I'd bloody well like to blow that balloon to Agra — with my fist!"

"Oh? So now you've begun *spying* on me, have you?"

"Good God! I just happened to be *standing* here! I haven't had any breakfast yet! I — I was going down to the dining room when I saw you come out, and thought I'd just as soon wait to say good morning to you up here where — where we could be alone!" He felt his cheeks glowing as he stammered through that apologetic explanation, knowing full well that he'd peered at her window many times last night — after each of his phone calls remained unanswered in fact — to see if she was still sitting up in bed with her reading lamp on! He had even knocked at her door once, around three A.M., but she ignored his voice as persistently as she did his ring.

"I have nothing to say to you, Mr. Partridge, that can't be said in public — in front of T.J., or anyone else!" She said it as haughtily as though she were addressing a butler, who'd forgotten his place.

"Blast it all, woman —"

She walked on toward her room, as if he no longer existed, as gracefully proud as the Queen of England herself.

"In God's name, Jane," he called, catching up to her before she could put her latchkey into the door, "will you marry me?"

"What?" She sounded faint.

"Will you have me for your husband, woman?"

"Would — would you — would you repeat that — *slowly?* I — I'm not sure I heard you."

"I love you, Jane. I want to marry you — if you'll have me."

"*If?*" Then her eyes flooded, her lips trembled, her voice broke. "Did you say *if?* Oh, you crazy, wonderful man! You incurable blackguard, you! Oh, Peter Partridge, my darling, of course, I'll marry you! I've loved you ever since you lost your last chip, you fool! I've loved you every second since then!"

She flung her arms around his neck right there in the corridor, kissing him full on his mustached lip — clinging so tightly to his neck, he thought it would break — till they both heard a serving cart full of breakfast dishes rattling toward them. Quickly she opened her door, but before entering the room she looked into his eyes. Then he lifted her in his arms, and carried her over the threshold . . .

Klug himself, Niels learned, was an amateur photographer. He kept his own fully equipped darkroom at Maharani's, and was more than delighted to offer Niels the run of it.

"Do whatever you like here, Mr. Larsen," he said, graciously.

"Someday, perhaps — if it is not too much to ask — you will allow me to exhibit one of your photographs in my lobby?"

"I will be flattered," Niels replied.

"No, no, it is *I* who will be flattered!"

Fortunately the assistant manager came to call him away soon after that — to arbitrate some crisis in the kitchen. Niels developed his prints, and returned to his room with the five best shots of her well before noon.

They were still moist as he spread them carefully on the glass top of his desk. He arranged them symmetrically, then studied them with a critically approving eye. Yes, they were good. No, they are better than good, he thought. They are excellent!

That disturbed him somewhat, that impulsive outburst of pride, so he turned away from the pictures. He paced across his room. He lit a cigarette, and pretended now to be strolling quite casually toward the window of a studio — not his own studio. He was a stranger here, going for a walk, and he would naturally wish to look at any pictures he might find on display — the work of photographers unknown to him! He would try to judge them in that sort of mood — from that distance of dispassion. Slowly he returned to the desk, looking straight ahead of him till he was right in front of it. Now he looked down.

No, they were more than excellent! They were brilliant, he thought, and it excited him as nothing else ever did — or could. He stared at them the way a miser stared at his hoard, like a lover, staring mutely at his object of adoration. He appreciated every aspect, every quality, of their artistry — the sharpness of focus, the texture of light, the subtle nuances of expression, the brightness and shadow of them. He concentrated upon one picture at a time, studying first the individual characteristics that made it a work of art, and finally absorbing it as a complete, a totally satisfying aesthetic experience. He was, in fact, so deeply preoccupied with this most pleasurable concentration that he took no immediate notice of the faint knock he heard at his door. He assumed it was the dhobi, perhaps, or a maid, who would leave quietly if he simply ignored that intrusive sound.

But the knock persisted. He opened the door resentfully — only to find Lotte standing there before him.

"Ah, forgive me for not answering at once! Do come in — yes, please do! Ah, what a delightful coincidence! I have just finished printing them — come! Look! But be careful — they are still wet!"

"Yah, let me see! I won't touch them," she promised, going over and bending closer to study them — saying no word as she looked quite carefully at each picture of herself.

He felt as tensely apprehensive as he had the first time Ulla came to his studio to see her proofs. For all his professional experience, Niels had never outgrown that sense of lurking insecurity, of almost physical terror, which gripped him the moment a discerning subject stood silently contemplating the fruit of his labor. He felt as though his entire life was distilled onto those fragments of photosensitized paper, as if all he was or was not, the total value or worthlessness of himself as a person, was being weighed, measured, appraised, determined by this judgment. Nor did his fame, past achievement, or reputation, serve to mitigate the tension he experienced anew after each sitting. Once he had thought it was immaturity, but by now he realized that nothing would liberate him from the ordeal of this particular trauma. He was, after all, fully confident of his craftsmanship by now. His fame was established. He was independently wealthy. But all of that was unimportant to Niels. His one ambition, his one desire in life, was to create art. To achieve with camera and light the plastic reality of sculpture. To capture the dynamism of life's frenzied motion at any instant of time, and preserve it for eternity, frozen like a body kept under ice. What was more beautiful, more elusive, more evanescent than a woman's smile? He had filled many albums with the faces of smiling women — each smile uniquely revealing some facet of its subject's soul. Yet for Niels the acid test of his success or failure, the judgment that mattered most, remained that which was passed by his last subject herself.

"Oh, but I did not dream —" she said, looking up at him in awe. "— I never imagined — they would be so — so alive — so wonderful! I feel when I look at them, Niels, as if — as though you have seen me —"

Color flooded her glowing face as she reached up to caress his cheek, pressing her lips, like satin cushions, to his mouth. Never had he felt so soft a kiss, so submissive a quality of pure femininity, like the breast of a mother offered to the suckling child, given as naturally, with the same nourishing instinct of selfless love. As a child he accepted it, hungrily but without lust, her tribute to his talent rather than an appeal to his manhood. It vindicated him, comforted him, restored his faith in life's value and meaning. For he was eager now to take more pictures of her, and to discuss those he had taken, to speak of the nuances of light, the miracle of human laughter, to reveal to her his innermost ambitions, his dream of artistic achievement.

Perhaps, after all, Niels thought, it was not too late to start again. In Bruno he had found a friend. In Lotte there was more than friendship, for her beauty inspired him to work. And in their love for one another he seemed to discern a symbol of universal hope, the healing powers of beauty in life. He would photograph Bruno as well one day, and the two of them together, and later, when the child was born, the trinity — his mind's eye formulated the scene and he could almost place his floodlights properly, so vivid did it become for him, with Bruno's face shrouded in darkness, just one glimmer of light to bring out the force of his eyes, Lotte glowing, motherhood incarnate, the purity of her soul shining sunlike from her full visage, radiating life's warmth to her baby. Each month he would add other scenes, fresh images from the life cycle, doing with his camera what Vigeland had done in bronze, and someday perhaps a permanent exhibit hall could be built for his work, light-filled yet laced with shifting shadows, like the Tivoli, his own Frogner Park!

"Do you really think they are good, Lotte?"

"Beautiful," she said. "Do you know what I feel, Niels? I feel you have seen me naked." She toyed distractedly with one button of his shirt as she spoke, twisting it first this way, then the other, accidentally, it seemed, extricating it from the loop.

"Ah, you mean the naked soul. Yes, I have tried —"

"I mean the body as well." As if impelled by a will of its own, her hand inched through the opening in his shirt, her fingers probing the muscles of his chest. "Your body is so smooth, Niels, so firm. Were you surprised that I came now to see you? I had to say good-bye alone to you, Niels. There is so much I must explain to you about myself — about Bruno —"

"No, but I was just going to call you. I too have many things I want to speak with you about, Lotte — plans, and —" Her fingers made him nervous, confused by the urgency, the passion, of their mute statement. He felt almost infantile, the way he used to when his mother insisted on soaping his body in the bath, though he was big enough to soap himself.

"Yesterday, when I kissed you, Niels, what did you think of me? Do you think me an unfaithful wife?"

"No. No, but I understood perfectly, you did not mean —"

"How can I explain this to you?" she continued, not seeming to take any interest in his willingness, his eagerness to absolve her completely of any suspicion of adulterous guilt. "For thirteen years I am married, yet never once before —"

"Please do not torture yourself, Lotte! I understand it meant nothing."

"Nothing?" She looked more perplexed than she sounded. Her lower lip and chin trembled so, that for a moment she could say no more. "Oh, but this is not what I meant, Niels. No, I see why you say that — to protect me from myself, and, and for Bruno — yah, for him, but — look at me, darling. I know now that you have seen me as no man but Bruno has ever penetrated. I can keep no secret thought from you, Niels. I can hide nothing from you any longer. Tomorrow morning you will leave, and —"

"Lotte, sit down please. You are so pale. Why do you tremble this way? Should I get — ?"

"No, no, I just — I feel so hot —" She sounded faint, and with the same unconscious gesture, she'd used in loosening his shirt, now opened the buttons of her silk blouse, tugging it free of her skirt while she did so, then lying down across his still unmade bed. Her brassiere was of white satin in its lower half, but composed of lace above the nipples, which showed brightly through the threads, like tongue tips pressed against wire mesh. She seemed unaware of the fact that her blouse had fallen open, shaking her head as she stared at the ceiling.

"I — I will turn on the fan," he said, hurrying to the wall switch. "Lotte, is there something I can get — water?"

"I will look so different when you return," she said, talking as though to herself, as if he were not even in the room. "I will be so ugly — bloated, and —"

"But you must not think that way, Lotte. To be pregnant is part of the nature cycle, and, and for some women it is the most beautiful time. I have taken pictures of pregnant ladies in Copenhagen, and I am anxious to take you —"

"What do you say? I cannot hear you with the fan — Niels, come sit by me — give me your hand. Let me see your face when you talk. I love how your lips move. Before he — before — Bruno's lips were just so — Is it a crime to love more than one person, Niels? Say truthfully what you think?"

"A crime, to love?" He went warily to the bed, sitting where she could see him, yet not too close, staring at the rumpled sheet under her back, its asymmetry somehow repulsive to his sense of aesthetic balance. Whenever Ulla left the bed unmade he would quickly straighten the covers himself, as though to hide the scene of their — he looked quickly away, saying, "No, I think it is a worse crime not to love."

"You do, darling?"

"Yes. I mean — we can love many people — in different ways —"

"Yah, it is so." She brought his hand gently to her lips, kissing his fingers with maternal tenderness. "You have such long fingers, Niels, such beautiful, sensitive fingers. Did you ever play piano?"

"I took lessons for two years, long ago, but I was never gifted —"

"I must feel your fingers on my heart," she said, placing his hand full upon her breast, while staring at him with so plaintive a smile of devotion that he could not draw himself away. Still he felt no surge of passion or desire for her, only an artist's appreciation of her beauty, and the kinship of attachment wrought by mutual loneliness, the bond of spirit, what he believed to be more truly the definition of love than any crass craving for the conquest of flesh.

"Do you feel how fast it is beating, Niels? I am so frightened —"

"But why?"

"I don't know, which only makes it worse. I feel as confused as I am afraid — for you, darling, for Bruno, for myself, and the baby — the baby, yah! Only two months ago I thought it would make us so happy, fulfilled, hopeful. Now I only wish —"

"Lotte, you must not —"

"I have to say it to someone, don't you see? I cannot speak any more to Bruno. He thinks I have tricked him, betrayed him —"

"No, but I am sure you only imagine —"

"Ach, I know it is true! I know what he thinks even before he will admit to himself. I know his every mood, his spirit is like that of a wounded tiger, and at any moment he may turn to devour, to destroy — anything, everything around him. You must be careful in Nepal with him, Niels —"

"But I like Bruno, and he likes me!"

"Yah, of course. And I love him, but that is only what makes him more dangerous, because he has come to think that those who are closest to him only feel sorry for him, and this is the last thing on earth he wants — this pity, from anyone. He refuses to believe it is possible to love someone whose flesh has been torn —" She sat up and leaned closer to him. "Let me touch your body, Niels. Just let me rest my cheek against your smooth skin — just for two moments, darling?"

She asked it so innocently, so pathetically, he could not reject her. His fingers were stiff as he tried to open his shirt. She had to help him, like a mother undressing her child, and when his torso was stripped naked he felt more infantile than before. He felt no emotion, no passion, not even fear, only the longing for escape from such exposure.

She pressed her cheek to his chest, sighing as though released from incarceration, her fingers moving hungrily over his back, down his spine, her lips caressing his chest, her teeth biting into the nipple of his breast.

"Lotte —" He tried to ease away from her.

"No, don't move! Please — let me. Lie back, darling. Please."

The words sounded to him like grunts. She was spreading saliva on his skin, groping with frenetic fingers at his belt, clawing his body. He had to close his eyes, grit his teeth, trying to control his revulsion. Why did it have to degenerate into this? Why was the purest, most beautiful friendship with the loveliest of women somehow doomed to this transmutation into sexual ugliness? His dreams of art associated with Lotte, Bruno and their child vanished, were mutilated, defaced, destroyed by this noxious, vulgar lust.

184

"Will you stop it!" he shouted.

She pretended not to hear, and he had no recourse but to grab hold of her hair with his fist, the hair silken and thick as Ulla's had been, like his mother's hair. He remembered how his mother sat combing out her hair each evening, preparing to set up the golden braids before dinner. He would come to her dressing table to watch, counting with her to one hundred on each side, then he was permitted to help fashion the braids, while they shared secrets, and he would sit on her lap as she told him a tale from Hans Christian Andersen, and sang a lullaby.

He tugged harder till Lotte's head jerked back convulsively, and her eyes filled with lust's film of moisture stared in wonderment at him, her sensuously parted lips glistening.

"Niels, I love you," she gasped.

He let go of her hair, but other than that could not move or speak. Inside he had turned to ice. All he could contemplate now was death, the only escape from this bondage to passion, which changed the most beautiful of God's creations into twisted, writhing creatures, shameless as dogs in heat.

"Darling, what is it? What is wrong with me?"

It was the question Ulla always asked, and it softened him, for he feared now that unless he responded, unless in some way he tried to convince Lotte that it was not her fault alone, he might be guilty once again.

"No, but — it has nothing to do with *you*," he insisted, reaching out to comfort her, to stroke her arm softly. "You must not think you are to blame, because I — I cannot —"

Finally, she appeared to understand. She broke away from him, whispering, "Oh, my God — what have I done?" hastily buttoning her blouse, running out of the room as though driven by a flailing whip.

She had not even waited for her pictures. He returned to his desk to stare at those angelic smiles, those spiritually beautiful faces which bore so slight a resemblance now to the woman, whose claws had left their searing imprint on his flesh.

One by one he turned the pictures over — till all of them were hidden from his sight. My last exhibit, he thought.

Niels removed the top from a half-empty bottle of whiskey on his dresser, and putting the glass neck to his parched lips, he drained the golden hot liquid into his mouth, swallowing it greedily, the way an infant drinks his milk.

CHAPTER 24

SETH was alone with Ethan when the message from Hodge arrived. The risk of leaving the "monster" with her son had not deterred Stella from going out to her new job shortly after he'd come back. Nor had he tried to detain her. They had spoken not a word more, in fact, other than her bland statement that he could baby-sit, and she would be back before dinner. She had questioned him no further. He had volunteered no more information. The confrontation he had dreaded for the years of their marriage, the prospect of which alone at times had veered him from a course that seemed headed toward a catastrophic realization, was that simple, that almost ludicrously mild.

Almost, he thought, knowing that there would be a delayed reaction, that their showdown had been deferred, rather than averted. Stella would take her own sweet time, before letting go at him with both barrels. She would store it up. She would let all the bitterness, all the vituperation ferment inside her heart, till it was boiling hot, dripping with acid — then she would pour it out, right on top of his head. He was hardly deceived into any false sense of serenity about prospects for the future by the calm that pervaded before the storm. He had married a woman of many virtues, but charity was not strongest among them.

Nor did he want charity, knowing he deserved none. He was old enough to know that. He was conscience-laden enough to understand fully what he had done. It was not without an all but paralyzing sense of guilt that he accompanied Rena to her room, but in spite of it. He made no attempt to delude himself by blaming his behavior either on intoxication or the exhilaration of winning the diving meet. He had gone with her for reasons irrational perhaps, but hardly evanescent. He had taken her the way he took air into his lungs, the way he craved food for his body — as naturally, as indispensably as any nourishment which ever helped sustain his life. Nor did he regret one moment of it. Stella had good reason to resent his action — better than even she supposed. He'd never loved any woman as he did Rena — not Stella, not even Anita.

But how can I tell her that? he wondered, and he was still pondering the imponderable when the message from Hodge arrived.

"What does it say, Dad?" Ethan was sitting on his bed, arranging his soldiers in battle formation around the mountainous bulge he'd made with his sheet.

"I'm leaving tomorrow, son. We've got a plane ride to Nepal."

"Where's Nepal?"

"It's a small country — just north of here."

"Can Mom and me go?"

"No. I'm afraid not, Ethan. You'll have to wait here with your mother till I get back."

"Aw! Gosh, that's not fair, Dad!"

The fever had thinned him, and now that it was gone, Ethan was pale and subdued. That, and the sadness of his expression now, made him look so much older that Seth had a premonitory vision of his son as a young man. It was as if the veil of time had accidentally been lifted, revealing Ethan to his eyes as an adolescent, or as though, looking back past the incremental transitions wrought by ten thousand days he saw himself again, staring out at life's mysterious prospects with all the wonderment and perplexity of maturing youth, all the innocent expectations and doubts of untested potential. It was a singularly ambivalent vision, a revelation at once of the continuity and transience of life. He saw himself reborn, and dying. He wished then that he could explain to his son — everything he knew, all he had slowly, painfully, at times tortuously learned about life, about — everything.

"Not fair," the boy repeated.

"Not everything is in life, son."

"Why not, Dad?"

"I'm not sure I know the answer to that one, Ethan."

"But you know everything!"

"No, I don't." He was tempted to say, I don't know anything, but too much truth he knew, like too little knowledge, could be dangerous.

"Mom says you do," the boy insisted. "She told me — She says you're the smartest man in the world! Mom wouldn't lie to me, would she?"

He had to swallow very hard before answering. "No, Ethan, your mother would never lie to you, but at times she does tend to exaggerate —"

"What's that, Dad?"

"Well, it's like — like when she told you that about me."

"And when she called you a monster?"

"Yes — that too."

"Why did she, Dad?"

It was time to change the subject!

"How's that battle going, son?"

"Fine. But why *did* she, Dad?"

"Which are the bad guys, son?"

"Why don't you tell me, huh?"

He could be quite persistent for a four-year-old. Probably because he was four! Sitting opposite him on the bed, Seth looked at Ethan quietly, wondering how his life would be in thirty years. As different, no doubt, as his life was from his own father's.

"Huh, Dad? Why?"

"Because — I just don't know," he lied. He'd never consciously lied to his son before, but there seemed no less painful way of silencing him now. Ethan sensed it was a lie. Four-year-olds were like tribals, like villagers — they didn't understand lots of fancy things, but they knew when you were telling the truth — at least when you were sincere about what you told them. They always smelled a lie, they had olfactory bulbs for it, like a bloodhound's.

"Come on — I'll be the bad guys."

"I don't feel like playing anymore." He grimaced at the soldiers and knocked them down, sending several flying off the bed.

"Want me to read you a story?"

"Nope."

He'd never refused that offer before either! It's a day full of firsts for all of us, Seth thought. Ethan no longer looked at him, but sat with his eyes lowered, picking at a loose thread on his pajama pants. Seth groped for something to say, some magical formula, by which he could close the gulf that he'd opened between them — the gulf that would only grow wider from this day onward. Was there no way of closing it, or preventing it from starting? He was tempted then to tell everything, just as it happened — about Anita, and how much he'd loved her once. About the bitterness of his disappointment when he realized she hadn't loved him enough to wait. At twenty he thought she would wait forever. About the chord of memory and longing struck by Rena. About the ineffable beauty of their love. . . .

"How do you feel today, son?"

"Fine. Kin I go outside now?"

"Maybe tomorrow —"

"Aw, gee! I wish I was home. I don't like it here."

"You will — once you're all better, and your mother can take you out for trips. There are all sorts of wonderful things for boys to see in India. Elephant rides, and monkeys —"

"Why can't you take me, Dad?"

"Because — I told you, son, I'll be leaving tomorrow — for a while —"

"How long?"

"I don't know exactly. A month perhaps."

"Gosh — that's awful long! A whole month? Why can't you stay here with us, Dad? *Why?*"

"Well — when you get to be grown-up, Ethan — when you're a man, there are many things you have to do. Like work, and —"

"Are you going to work, Dad?"

"No, not exactly."

"Then you kin take me! Okay? *Please!*"

"I wish I could, Ethan."

"Pretty please?"

Seth rose and straightened out the sheets. He fluffed the pillow.

"Better lie down for a while now, Ethan. It's time for your medicine."

"Aw — I hate that medicine, Dad."

"I know, but it's good for you. You wouldn't want to be sick again, would you?"

"I don't care."

"Remember what happened to Pierre when he said that?"

"A lion ate him up." He said it almost longingly, as though any fate would be preferable to his present plight.

"Hey, come on, son — it can't be all that bad!"

Can it? he wondered, pouring out the milky fluid on a spoon, wishing there were as simple a remedy for himself.

Stella returned at four. Ethan had fallen asleep. Seth watched the door open, waiting for her to speak. She merely looked at him, contemptuously, he thought, saying nothing. She went over to peer down at Ethan, touching his brow.

"How long has he been sleeping?"

"About half an hour."

"Did he seem all right?"

"Fine."

"Did you give him the penicillin?"

"Yes."

She had nothing more to ask of him.

"We're leaving tomorrow, Stell. Hodge sent me this note."

She took the note, read it, and tossed it aside.

"Why didn't he call you, or come over to tell you himself?"

"I don't know — I guess he's been busy."

"It sounds as though he's angry at you —"

"Does it?" He hadn't really thought of that, but picking up the note again he saw she was right. "Probably just busy —"

"Who were you with last night?" She asked it in the faintest of whispers. It echoed like the clap of thunder in his ears.

"Stell —"

"No, that's the one person in this hotel I'm sure you weren't with!"

"Look —"

"I'm listening now. I'm waiting, Seth."

She's always been good at waiting, he thought, staring at the firmness of her mouth. The years before they married, at college together, after Anita made a confirmed bachelor of him, she waited undemandingly, with remarkable patience. *There's no future for us Stell,* he warned, but her answer was clear-eyed and calm. *The present's enough for me, Seth.* She agreed with all his philosophiz-

190

ing about the evils of marriage and family, about the ills of society. She was as free thinking, as iconoclastic, as unfettered by conventions as himself. At least she seemed to be. He could talk to her about anything — from his radical ideas of politics and society to his libertine views of sexual relations. He explained, among other things, that he never expected to earn money enough to support a wife. She understood. She waited. He took pre-med courses one semester, but quickly lost interest in science, suspecting it was only the urge to show Anita that he too could become a doctor, which had started him in that direction to begin with. He shifted to humanities, drifting, drinking, writing poetry, growing a beard. He even played the guitar for a while. Stella wore jeans and kept her hair in a ponytail locked with rubber bands. They talked and sang half the night, made love for much the rest of it. She kept waiting. Then he read Franz Boas and Kroeber, and was converted to anthropology. Stella converted with him, only by his senior year she was still a sophomore. When he won the fellowship for Chicago, they celebrated on pizza pie and beer. But later that night she cried. *Because you'll go away, Seth, and I'll never see you again!* He told her to come along — Chicago had a good anthro department. She only wished she could, but her parents would never allow it. They called her a tramp even now — just seeing him this way, while living at home. She cried so bitterly that he suggested — in as offhanded a way as he'd said, "Let's have pizza tonight" — "We can get married, if that's all that's worrying you."

"I'm still waiting, Seth!"

"I'll be gone now for a while, Stell. It'll give us both some time to — think things through, and — after I'm back we can talk about — the future," he said. It jarred him, saying that. It used to be one of her favorite phrases during their first years of marriage. *Seth, darling, let's talk about the future now! Let's make some plans for the future!*

"It's that little tramp — that Miss Gold! She's the one, isn't she?"

He could say nothing at all. So much welled up in him then, so many thoughts, so many words, clamored in tangled confusion at the back of his brain, that like too large a crowd jamming, rushing, pushing toward one narrow exit, no word passed through the open portal of his mouth. Dimly he wondered if she would remember how many people had called her a tramp once? He had to stand up, to walk. He felt himself choking, as though he were still deep underwater after that first futile dive. He kept sinking deeper, and all the air was out of his lungs. He fell lower and lower into a bottomless tank. As though he were stone dead. Only he remained conscious of life all around him. Perhaps that's how it is, he thought, to be dead.

"Well, if you won't admit it, the least you can do is *deny* it!" she shouted, tears rolling in bitter confusion down her cheeks, her voice so plaintive it sounded as if she were begging him to lie to her, pleading with him to have the decency to give her some pretext for hope, to fabricate any excuse, however flimsy, however nebulous, a straw of faith to hang onto — for she too appeared to be drowning. "God in heaven, Seth — what's happened to us? Why can't you talk to me? Why won't you look at me?"

He bit so deeply into the soft inner flesh of his cheeks that he tasted the hot flow of his own blood. The physical pain of it came as something of a relief to him. Mutely, he shook his head, and walked out.

Rena's door was partially opened. He heard her voice, saw her sitting on the bed, speaking into the telephone. She looked up and covered the mouthpiece.

"Come in, darling," she whispered. "Close the door." Then she spoke back into the phone. "Yes — yes, two rooms will be fine. Yes, for tomorrow and the day after — Yes, Mr. McNeill —" She spelled Hodge's name, and sighing heavily, hung up.

"O-o-och! What a day!" She rushed to him, embracing his neck with her arms, kissing him passionately, ardently. Then she jerked her head back and looked at him with bewilderment in her eyes. "What is it, my darling?"

"Nothing." He kissed her more warmly now — hungrily.

"Oh, Seth — Seth! What will I do when you're gone?"

"I love you, Rena."

"I love you." She stared into his eyes as though trying to memorize every line, every mark, every feature of his face.

"Where have you been so long? I have been waiting here all day for you to come — it's been such an awful day!"

"I know. I couldn't come before now — I've been with Ethan."

"Is he all right?"

"Yes."

She jumped away from him, rushing to peer through the drawn blinds of her window.

"What is it?"

"No-n-nothing. I thought I heard footsteps —"

"I heard them, too. Are you expecting someone?"

"No. Of course not!" She ran back and kissed him more fervently. But he sensed the tension, the anxiety of her mood, the partial distraction even in her kiss.

"What's happened, Rena? Have you seen — anyone?" He could not mention Hodge's name.

"He came here — this morning." She gnawed nervously at her lip, lowering her eyes.

"Hodge?"

She pressed her head, like an animal seeking shelter in its cave, against his chest, nodding in the affirmative.

"And? — What did he say, Rena? Did he — do anything to you? Look at me, darling. Tell me what happened?" He felt himself grow rigid, like a steel ramrod, every muscle in his body had locked taut.

"No — it's all right, Seth. He didn't — he didn't touch me."

His heart had stopped beating for a moment. Now he relaxed. He had not expected Hodge to be exactly pleased with their joint departure from the pool last night. But anxiety, like all things, was relative. He had hardly bothered to consider Hodge's reaction till now. Yet he knew Mac could be acerbic, trenchant, foul-mouthed. He saw from Rena's pained expression and manner, sensed from her reluctance to speak of it, that Hodge had administered one of his notorious tongue-lashings to his secretary. Sticks and stones can break my bones — it was a comforting ditty.

"Pay no attention to what he says, Rena. He can sound pretty mean, I know, but his bark's worse than his bite."

"Hold me tighter, Seth. Hold me tight as you can, darling."

She was trembling.

"Rena, what is it? What did he say to you?"

"Not-nothing — no, a lot of things, but — never mind now! As long as you are holding me, darling, it does not matter. Nothing else matters in this world to me, Seth, when I am in your arms! Did you know it?"

"I know." It's just the rest of the time, he thought, wishing that instead of his going alone to Nepal, the two of them could fly off to Israel tomorrow!

"Seth?"

"Yes, Rena."

"Seth, you must promise me to watch him — to take very good care of yourself there."

He could not help smiling at her exaggerated apprehension. It was the least of his worries.

"Don't be afraid, darling. I've known Hodge a long time, and I think I can take pretty good care of myself by now." He almost reminded her that he had lived among headhunters for two years.

"No, but he is — *mad*. I think he is quite mad, darling!"

"Aren't we all?" It made her smile, just a glimmer of laughter brightening her eyes.

"Ah, but this is in a different way, not?"

"Yes — in a beautiful way."

"Oh, Seth, I wish — I wish you would not leave me now — ever."

"Amen," he whispered, knowing he would have to go from this room very soon, that he could not risk spending another night with her, or there would be no predicting what Stella might do — to herself, to Ethan —

"But I'll come back to you, Rena, — soon." God willing, he thought.

"I will wait only for that moment, my love. My Seth."

Then they kissed, and spoke no more.

CHAPTER **25**

SINHA sent an Air Force bus for them at seven on Thursday morning. The bearers started loading the provisions, sealed by customs for transshipment through India, into its gaping hull a few minutes after the bus arrived at Maharani's. By the time breakfast was over, the loading was done. The team's personal baggage was stowed on the rear seats of the bus. It was all handled with military precision. At eight-thirty, with dew still shimmering on the foliage of the flower beds, they said their farewells, and were ready for the drive to Palam.

"All aboard, boy?" Tony asked Hodge.

"All except Peter! Where the hell did he disappear to?"

"Christ, he was just here, wasn't he?" Tony and Hodge started looking around in every direction, shouting his name.

"I think they're ready, old — Jane," he said, chucking her lightly under the fallen chin, noticing the hubbub he'd caused through the glass panels of the revolving front door. She'd insisted on walking back inside, refusing to say good-bye to him out there — in public. "Come now, you've got to be British from now on, you know!"

"This is for you to wear, Peter Partridge — for good luck!" she pressed the golden crucifix necklace into his startled hand.

"Good God —"

"It was grandmother's," Jane said. "You will wear it — up there, won't you, darling? It's very old, and specially lucky."

"Yes, of course, I'll wear it," he promised, staring at the bright pendant with heathenlike wonder. "It's — lovely, you know, but look here, I don't have —" A bloody thing to give you, he thought.

How stupidly inconsiderate of him, not to have brought her so much as a token gift to consecrate their engagement! There really had been no time — no time away from her side, since he'd proposed. And his first law of travel was to carry nothing inessential in his suitcase. As he swiftly took mental inventory of his possessions, Peter realized that he had nothing less functional in his baggage than a turtleneck sweater or toothbrush! He felt barren as a beggar, shamefacedly putting her lavish gift into his pocket. But before removing his hand, he felt the polished surface of the ten franc chip, which had started him on a lucky streak at Monte Carlo many years ago. It had remained in his pocket since as a sort of amulet of good fortune.

His fingers fondled the plastic chip as worshipfully as a monk feeling his rosary. He should have kept two of those blasted tokens! Then he touched the crucifix again, and felt a bloody miser.

"Here, Jane, take this. It's not worth much, but it's brought me luck —"

"What in the world? A roulette chip? Oh, Peter — I adore it!" She kissed him impulsively, and he felt the moisture of her cheek.

"Don't you lose it, woman. I'm going to reclaim that chip for a diamond ring when I get home, you hear?"

"I won't lose it, darling. I love you, Peter Partridge!"

"Dammit, Pete, let's get cracking!" Hodge had finally found them, breaking it up in the midst of a warm embrace, all but lifting Peter onto the bus by the scruff of his neck.

"God bless you, darling," Jane called.

The pneumatic door hissed itself shut. The gears gnashed their teeth, and ground into position. The bus shuddered, and a cloud of exhaust rose from its rear to blend with the low-lying mist of morning. They rolled away.

Seth raised a tentative hand to his locked window, moving his fingers slightly in the direction of Ethan and Stella, of Rena as well. He had entered the bus without speaking to either woman, only the mute look of pain — a different sort of pain from and for each — serving as their parting salutations. He'd held Ethan in his arms till the last moment, trying to get him to stop crying, till Stella finally wrenched the boy away from him, firmly holding his hand. But now Ethan broke free of Stella's grip. He started racing after the bus, heading, Seth thought, straight for the rear wheels! He felt his heart pound, flutter, and stop. Stella caught him none too soon, and lifting him off the gravel path, slapped a stiff hand against his bottom. Then Seth could see no more. The bus swung around the semicircular drive, and gunned up the palm-lined path to the road outside.

Past the fortresses and tombs of Mughal glory they rolled. Past Ashoka's pillar of limestone with its edict enjoining Peace and Universal Brotherhood in cryptic letters over two thousand years old. Past the ruins of Indraprastha, first capital of ancient India, where the Brothers Pandava reigned by divine law, destined to bring eternal happiness and justice to mankind — four thousand years ago. Only the stones endured. History spread its pages of rubble on both sides of their bus. Over newly paved roads they raced, past marble statues to British power, and fields once vibrant under the tread of Scots Guards and Coldstreams, parade grounds that heard Kitchener's cries of command, hosted the Durbar of Curzon, and greeted George V. Through the city conquered by Babur the Tiger, sacked by Timur the Lame, plundered by Ghaznavids and Ghors they rolled. The parakeets and monkeys, cyclists, and purdah ladies in motor scooters, dhoti-clad Congress-capped men in taxis survived — unknown, unsung legatees to all the centuries of conquest and conflict, all the dreams of imperial glory. The fog lifted. The sun burned bright, desert orange, minaret high, as they reached the airport.

Sinha was waiting to clear them. He looked taller in his uniform. His stride was longer, and walking beside him Hodge felt himself almost running to keep up. Everywhere soldiers with bayoneted rifles snapped to smart attention as they passed, the Marshal responding with a wave of his ivory baton. There were no delays, no difficulties, no problems of clearance here. The provisions were loaded in record time. The Dakota was waiting on the open field. Sinha escorted them to the gangway. He shook their hands, one by one, as they climbed the boarding ladder, Hodge last.

"Well, good luck again, old boy!"

"Thank you, sir. I don't know how to properly express my thanks for all this —"

"Nonsense, McNeill! It's nothing at all! Have a good flight, and good hunting!"

Had he paused to think about it, of course, Hodge would have realized that all went so smoothly, so efficiently, so incredibly well, something had to be wrong! But there was no time for him to pause. He entered the old pack camel of the sky, and almost before he was seated and strapped in, the engines began to rev, the blocks were pulled clear of their wheels, they taxied to the runway, and took off.

"Good God," Peter shouted, "next stop Kathmandu, chaps!"

My God, Hodge thought — so it is! The salmon stone and orange soil of Delhi tilted below, streaked with the mercurial glint of sacred rivers touched by sun. They circled slowly, heading east.

"Roger, how fast we go?"

"These birds can do one-eighty."

"Yah? So the distance is, what — four hundred miles?"

"Just about. Kathmandu for lunch!"

Checkered squares of green, paddy ripe for harvest, rippled below, the geometry of cultivated soil disturbed only by an occasional cluster of mud and wattle, marking a village. The paddy chessboard was threaded with rivulets of irrigation canals, and from their low altitude they could see bullock carts and the shadow dots of people along the roads. Soon they veered slightly northward and the green changed to dappled fields, the splayed skin of a giant leopard. The cities were far between, but when they appeared there were budlike domes beside smoke-belching blades of modern factories, and rail yards where boxcars of freight sat like toy blocks, while ribbons of smoke trickled from archaic engines that seemed to be standing still. A cloud bank veiled the Himalayan terrai, hiding Nepal from their view.

The sun glittered through the churning blades of the prop engines, whose drone filled the hollow of the drab olive cabin. Each turn of the props vibrated through the old fuselage, and the smell of burned oil seeped into the low-pressured atmosphere they inhaled. In an age of jets, the Dakota felt more like a vehicle of land rather than air transport, yet slow as it was, imperceptible as their progress toward the clouds seemed at times, the minutes became an hour, and as the second hour dragged toward its halfway point streamers of cloud reached their wingtips. Then the cotton wool closed in on both sides. They entered a thunderhead, whose turbaned top rose several thousand feet above their cruising altitude. Turbulent pockets of air caught them on a roller-coaster ride designed to test the toughest of stomachs. They gripped the vibrating arms of their seats, kept all belts securely fastened. The engines hummed and moaned, alternately racing and standing still it seemed. The plane was buffeted from above and below, rolling from side to side like a cork loose upon high seas. For twenty minutes they saw no ray of sunlight.

Then, unanticipated as its advent, the storm was behind them. They emerged from darkness through a mist of crystalline light, a garland of rainbows. They flew north over green-garbed foothills and jungle valleys as lovely from this distance as they were treacherously ugly below, insect-infested swamps, the domain of tiger, virtually unmarked by human habitation. At the horizon, shrouded with veils of purplish haze, loomed the Himalayas, jutting like a global spine over the earth stretched prone.

At twelve-thirty they started their descent toward Gaucher. The valley of Kathmandu shone like a tourmaline under the ostrich-plume fringe of cloud that hid the most spectacular peaks from their view. The terraced sides of the vale's bowl rippled like folds on a walrus neck. It was an amphitheater of the gods, whose eyes peered up at them from each side of the question mark painted onto the tower of Svayambunat's stupa, as they circled low.

The Bagmati snaked its silvery sinew of life through village clusters of Newari huts, hovering yaklike on the plains skirting the capital city of this hermit kingdom, an incongruous congeries of Rana palaces in Italian Renaissance style, Hindu Shaivite temples, Tibetan pagodas, and rows of hovels in ocher-clad stone. The temple-decked city glowed like a birthday cake, reflecting the sun from a hundred tarnished towers of brass and gold, like candles lit for divine festivity. Circling to the tarmac they winged past Pashupati's stately compound of shikara-topped shrines to Shiva as Lord of Beasts, set in the shade of giant eucalyptus and sacred pipal trees, its burning ghats on the river bank facing the lingam-covered hill beyond. There was an unreal lucidity, a quality of timelessness about this remote and rarefied atmosphere with its ancient symbols of eternity racing past the wing of the Dakota.

They touched down, vibrated, swerved, and raced to a bumpy

halt at the end of the all but deserted airfield. A single jeep and a crew of barefoot porters bearing a ladder started toward them.

"It is Kathmandu, gentlemen," their pilot said, opening the door, and saluting them as they stepped out of the plane.

The jeep drove them to the customs shed, a tent, which looked as though it had just been pitched in anticipation of their arrival. Rifle-bearing Gurkhas flanked the flap, through which they were obliged to stoop in order to enter the large tent.

A young officer, whose smooth olive face and slight stature made him appear almost juvenile, certainly inconsequential, greeted them, smiling, and bowed politely.

"May I have your passports, gentlemen?"

They gave him the passports, and Hodge showed him their permit from the Nepalese government as well.

"Ah, yes, thank you so much," he said, smiling sweetly again. "If you will excuse me one second, please?"

The provisions began to arrive inside the tent from a different flap. They were piled carefully onto a plank table set on top of wooden horses, which also seemed to have been rapidly improvised for them. The crates and cartons, sealed with steel bands by Indian customs came off much more slowly than they had been loaded at Palam. Hodge estimated, in fact, that somewhat less than half of them appeared inside the tent, when the young official returned, followed by a more portly and elderly man.

"You will please come this way," said the elder.

He led them across the tent, toward the flap on the far side. Two jeeps were waiting just outside.

"Good God, you mean we're through already? I say, that was bloody well fast!"

"Hold it," said Hodge, "what about our provisions?"

"Everything will be quite safe here," the official assured them politely.

"What do you mean safe? We need that gear —"

"First you must come."

"Come *where?*"

But then he noticed the two Gurkhas with pistols pointed at them, standing on the rear bumpers of each jeep, and his mouth remained dumbly open. Christ, Mac, I knew it was too good to be true! he thought.

"Good God, chaps," whispered Peter, aghast, "I think we're under arrest!" He was right.

CHAPTER **26**

IN a matter of minutes their bumpy ride over monsoon-rutted roads from the airport had ended at a low compound, which was clearly police headquarters. The officials, who accompanied them in the jeeps, answered none of the questions Hodge and the others kept asking, other than by cryptic smiles and polite nods. They were herded into a brick-walled room, which was too large for a cell, appearing rather to be an office from its furnishings, an old desk and chair, a telephone, and a small cabinet. There they were left alone.

"Can they just arrest us this way?" asked Niels.

"Bloody uncivilized blackguards," muttered Peter.

"Yah, what is the law here?" said Bruno.

"They have something called preventive detention," Seth remarked, "which waives habeas corpus, but why use it on us? Mac, have you any idea what's going on?"

"Shit no. But if someone doesn't come to explain it to us in five minutes, I'm walking out of here!"

"You won't walk far, old chap. Those Gurkhas know how to use their firearms."

Just then the side door opened, and a thin young man, who looked no more impressive than the first customs official they'd encountered, entered the room, surveyed them all silently, and sat calmly behind his desk. He wore an open-collared short-sleeved shirt, whose only insignia was a silver medallion on each of his cloth epaulets.

"Excuse this inconvenience, gentlemen. You will have to be detained until we have time to clarify several of questions."

"What questions?" Hodge snapped. "This is one hell of a reception to Nepal! I pay your government five thousand rupees for a permit, and no sooner do we get here than the permit's taken from me and we're all hustled off to jail! You're the one who better start clarifying! Are you responsible for this piracy? What's your name? Who are you? Why were we arrested and brought here?"

"Ah, then you are Mr. McNeill, is it?" He seemed singularly unfased by Hodge's tone of indignation. He had removed a sheet of paper from his desk drawer, unclipping the ball-point pen from his shirt pocket, and starting to take notes.

"Damn right, I'm McNeill! Who are you?"

"I am Deputy Inspector of Criminal Investigation, sir. My name is Ran."

"Good God, we're no bloody criminals! I want to see the British Consul!"

"Ah — and you are Mr. Partridge?"

"Bloody right! Of Partridge Green, and I'd better be sprung from the lockup right now, Mr. Deputy Ran, or you'll bloody well hear about it from your commissioner in the morning!"

"And your name, sir?" he asked, turning to Bruno. His lashless eyes and beardless face seemed no more perturbed by Peter's righteous wrath than they were by Hodge's. Quietly, methodically, he ascertained each of their names, answering none of their questions as he did so.

Hodge felt his temper rising to its limit of endurance as he glared at this half-baked provincial backwater cop, but knew that without their passports and permit they were all helpless as manacled maniacs. He'd never been more acutely conscious of the value of personal freedom. He suspected, of course, that it was all simply one of those ridiculous bureaucratic mistakes, that their identities had been confused perhaps with those of a gang of international gold smugglers, that in a few hours, or a few days, everything would be straightened out, apologies would be proferred profusely, and there would be no need for America, Great Britain, Denmark, and West Germany to declare war upon Nepal in order to liberate the five of them! Yet a few days were precious to them now, and he found even a few minutes of such utter helpless humiliation galling. But he swallowed his bile, and kept a close rein on his fury.

"Mr. Ran," he said, "what possible reason can you have for detaining us this way?"

"Yes. Perhaps you can help me answer that question best, Mr. McNeill, by telling me what you have come here to do?"

"The answer's on that permit! We're here to hunt for Yeti! What the hell do you think we've come for?"

"Do you always travel by Indian Air Force planes?"

"What?" So that was it — the damn plane! But why, he wondered, should the Nepalese resent their arrival by official Indian auspices? Nepal had always been India's vassal state. Their relations were more than friendly — they were mutually dependent in a thousand ways — what the hell was he talking about? Whatever it was, Hodge knew it couldn't possibly affect them. He decided to play it straight. "No, of course not. It just so happens that we couldn't book passage on Indian Airways —" He explained the whole story, right down to the coincidence of Sinha's having remembered him from Imphal.

"And do you expect me to believe that?" Ran asked.

"Damn right I do! It's the truth!"

"Oh, good God, what the devil are you driving at with your blasted innuendo, old chap? Mac's bloody well told you precisely what happened, and you sit there without blinking a blasted eyelid accusing us all of being liars, or lunatics! I've taken all of this bloody nonsense that I intend to tolerate, and unless you damned well —"

"Easy does it, Pete," Hodge said, sensing that Ran was not quite as impervious to insult as Partridge appeared to think, anxious to resolve this mess without further complications, such as charges of assault and battery! "If you don't believe *me,* sir, perhaps you'd be good enough to tell us why *you* think we've come to Kathmandu?"

That seemed to puzzle him, to shake his confidence somewhat, Hodge sensed, as his eyes shifted swiftly from one of the faces to another. He appeared to be trying to work out some plausible justification for his arbitrary arrest. Hodge suspected now that this young officer had acted on impulse, overextending his actual authority, eager no doubt to try something spectacular in order to win commendation or rapid promotion. From the troubled look on his face at this point, and his reluctance to state any charge, that seemed the most logical explanation. Well, you're going to pay for it, buddy, he vowed.

"I'm sorry, I cannot — I am not empowered to answer that question, Mr. McNeill —"

"Well, I insist on speaking to someone who is, dammit! This little game of yours has gone far enough, mister! I want to be taken to General Mandeva — immediately!"

That did it. He was so taken aback, so clearly shaken at the mere mention of the General's name that Hodge felt like laughing at his captor's obvious bewilderment. The letter from Sir Charles, which fortunately was still in his breast pocket, did more to bolster Hodge's self-confidence right now than the entire Strategic Air Command.

"*You* wish to see the General?"

"That's what I said!"

"B-but —"

"No buts, please! Better get me over to him quick, friend, or you'll find yourself unemployed this time tomorrow! The General happens to be a personal friend of mine." There was no harm, he decided, in so slight an anticipation of the truth. When Mandeva read Sir Charles's letter, after all, they would be friends.

"I see," said Ran, sounding more in control of himself, looking almost amused, as he lifted his telephone. Hodge felt the sudden impulse to amend his statement about their friendship then, for he was afraid that it might ruin everything if Mandeva insisted he had never heard of anyone named McNeill! He was about to retract it, actually, to explain that they had a mutual friend in Sir Charles Baker, but Ran was already speaking into the phone in Nepalese, and he knew how suspicious he would sound admitting he had lied — so he locked his jaw and hoped for the best. Men like Mandeva, he suspected, met so many visitors from abroad that they could never keep track of everyone. Nor was it usual for anyone, especially a foreigner under arrest, to lie to the police! He would simply assume, Hodge hoped, that he'd forgotten McNeill's name, but would be curious about seeing the face.

Hodge thought it all through with the adrenaline-charged alacrity of a climber dangling from the end of his rope. His mind raced at split-second speed, and though he felt the sour acid flowing equally fast into his empty gut as he watched Ran's bland face and incomprehensible lips, he kept his own face a mask of perfect composure and confidence. He was fighting against time. He was determined to win their release as quickly as possible. He would rot in hell for lying before risking another day's delay, before allowing this punk to stand between him and Yeti-land! Still he held his breath, awaiting the verdict, as Ran slammed down the phone and looked up at him.

"The General awaits us. Come with me, Mr. McNeill."

"Give 'im hell, Mac," shouted Peter, clasping his hands triumphantly over his head, grinning with adulation.

Hodge smiled, but refused to tempt the gods with a word of hubris. He said nothing more to Ran either as they drove to the palace, fixing his gaze on the mountains, cloud-decked and purplish white, towering in awesome serenity above the valley. All he had dreamed of for four years was about to come true. It was there, within sight of his eyes at last! No man would stop him now — nor any woman. The beast he had come to track was waiting in his lair, innocently sleeping! Sleep on, you bastard — sleep while you can! He hadn't been inside a church since his confirmation, but Hodge suspected he knew how God felt — knew better than anyone on earth that sublime and utter loneliness, that omniscient feeling of power.

The palace, built in imitation of Buckingham, intruded to block his view of the mountains, as the jeep swung through the gates and across the spacious courtyard. Hodge turned his full attention to the immediate challenge of conquering Mandeva. He anticipated no difficulty, however, for he was certain Sir Charles recommended him highly, and felt that the General's willingness to see him alone was a death blow to Ran's impetuous arrest. He almost felt sorry for the young man, who looked so glum, seated at his side. The damn fool would probably be demoted now.

They left the jeep beside the sentry box at the inner gate, advancing on foot through the stone archway to the open court, at the far end of which a palace guard was waiting to escort them through corridors furnished in faded Louis Quatorze and Georgian décor, past a gallery of royal portraits, the Gurkha Rajahs of Nepal, who traced their origins to the solar deity Vishnu. Mandeva's office was a high-ceilinged ornate room off the gallery corridor with a wall of French windows overlooking a formal garden, whose walks were guarded by Grecian statues mounted on marble pedestals. The General's back was to them as they entered. He seemed absorbed by the play of green parakeets on the rim of a stone birdbath just beyond the windows. His hair was white, his neck like aged leather, tarnished and with folds too deep to be erased. He wore a red velvet smoking jacket and yellow silk scarf. His facial expression looked black, however, martially menacing, as he turned, ordering, "Seat him here!" He pointed to the one chair in the room, which had no upholstering on it, a roughhewn chair of teak. Iron chains were secured to the flat-topped arms.

Hodge grimaced, turning to confront Ran, who held a pistol pointed at his back. There were other guards as well in this room he noticed. All of them had drawn beads on his body. He was too stunned to speak, too shocked to do anything but sit where he was told, feeling the chains dig into his wrists as the irons were fastened securely.

"Wait a minute, I have —" He had not even been able to remove the letter from his jacket pocket, but suspected from the look on Ran's face as well as Mandeva's that it was best he hadn't reached for anything in this company. They looked at him as though he were a traitor, or potential assassin. He could not quite bring himself to laugh now, or shout indignantly, for that matter. He merely watched Mandeva's eyes closely, and asked,

"Why? What have I done, General?"

"Why did you ask to see me?" Mandeva stepped closer, and Hodge marveled at how much taller he was than the others. He was the tallest Nepalese Hodge had ever seen.

He was tempted to ask the General if he received all guests so hospitably, but rejected flippancy as the lesser part of valor, given his condition.

"Why did you tell this man you're my friend? I've never seen you before!"

"I'm sorry, General," Hodge began, wondering what sort of

punishment he might have received had he identified himself as Mandeva's enemy. "But I do have a letter of introduction to you from Sir Charles Baker, and since I'd been arrested without cause or provocation —"

"How do you know Baker?"

"I've known him four years." He was about to explain that Sir Charles had aroused his initial interest in the Yeti, but Mandeva cut him short.

"Who sent you here?"

"No one, sir. I've been granted permission — at least I've assumed till today that I *was* granted permission by your government, General, to search for Yeti in Solo Khumbu —"

"But I was told you arrived at Gaucher in an Indian Air Force plane?"

"We did, sir, but as I explained at some length to Mr. Ran —" Since he was not interrupted this time, he went through all that once again, feeling the sweat trickle down his brow, along his eye, as he spoke.

"Your stories become less and less plausible each time, Mr. McNeill," the General snapped. "When will you people stop it? I should have thought I've made it clear enough by now to any and all of you that Nepal is no longer your pawn! We are an independent nation-state, and we will retain our independence, our integrity, and that means our resolute determination to deal by ourselves with all of our neighbors — *including* China! We no longer want your 'protection,' sir, not yours, not India's, not Britain's! We know full well where that would lead us! We will not become another Korea, another Vietnam, simply to gratify your wishes, to placate your anxieties, McNeill! Now I have stood as much of this as I am willing to tolerate, sir! And you may tell your masters in Washington, in Delhi, whichever agency you serve, you may tell them this is what Mandeva swears to them — I send you and your cohorts back with your lives *this time,* but this is the last time! The next batch of spies I capture will be executed!"

Halfway through his speech, Hodge had thought Mandeva was crazy, but by the end of it he doubted his own sanity, his hearing ability, his comprehension of English! Though Mandeva's elocution was clear enough, Hodge hardly understood one word he said. His head kept spinning as he tried to fit the sentences into some order of sane logic. For the life of him, he could not.

"Whatever it is you're talking about, General, it — it's simply not true," he gasped.

"I know, it's never true! None of you admit anything!" The tall man sighed and tapped his hands, one inside the other, behind his back. "Even the ones we caught last month with their code books and film — you remember those, don't you, Ran?"

"Yes, General — the Indians —"

"That's right, all of them Indians that time! Did any one of them confess? Not one! Scoundrels! I should have hanged the lot!"

"General Mandeva," Hodge called, fearing that if he allowed them to continue much longer in that vein, the General would become too distraught to reach. "Please, sir, if you would just read the letter in my breast pocket, from Sir Charles —?"

"What letter? Oh, yes, you said — See if he has any letter, Ran."

Hodge no longer felt the least shred of pity for the young officer, whose hand probed his inner pocket. He felt like biting off that skinny arm. His wrist bones ached as he strained to free himself.

"Here is an envelope, General."

"Oh?" He seemed surprised to notice that it was sealed, addressed by a familiar hand. He opened it quickly, and the harshness of his expression softened as he read. He took a long time reading that letter, much, much longer, Hodge thought, than it had taken Sir Charles to write it.

"Baker seems to know you quite well," he said, almost sweetly.

"Yes, General, he's known me four years, sir. It's really thanks to him that I'm here, actually. He was the one who roused my interest in the Yeti when he read a paper —" Hodge told the General every detail of every conversation he could remember having with Sir Charles Baker. He spoke literally with all the conviction, all the urgency, all the desperation, of a man pleading for his life.

"And you saw him last — when?"

"Last week, General — didn't he date the letter?"

"Yes, he did. I was wondering if you happened to remember it?"

Oh, my God, Hodge thought, licking at the sweat that rolled like water down his lip, sensing that Mandeva's decision about him, about whether or not to believe him, whether to release him, to allow him to go on with the hunt, or pack him off to Delhi on the next possible plane, might very well depend on his answer to this simple, childishly ridiculous question — the *date!* When was it they'd met at the Club? Fifty years ago? No, that was just how long it felt! Oh, God,—faster, Mac! Don't take all day on this one! He closed his eyes tight. For a moment he could not remember today's date! He wanted to scratch his nose — the tip of his nose itched so badly he thought he would break his arm trying to raise his fingers close enough— He felt himself losing all control—the whole shooting match, every ball game he'd ever played, every aquatic meet — everything he'd worked for, wanted, dreamed about — it was all blowing sky high because his brain refused to function in the simplest of possible ways! *What the hell was that date?* He felt as though he were ready to cry.

"Don't you remember it?" Mandeva asked again, sounding surprised.

"Of course I do, General. It was — Wednesday, sir, the seventeenth!" He said it without reckoning, without consciously thinking, drawing upon some deeper process, some primitive survival instinct for that memory.

"So it was—indeed," whispered Mandeva, looking and sounding this time far more surprised, seeming like an entirely different man, in fact, to Hodge. "Ran, release him, would you?"

"You say — release him, General?"

"Yes, yes, hurry."

Rubbing his wrists, he did not know whether to laugh or cry, but did something of both, as he rose, shaking his head, scratching with delicious delight at the tip of his nose, mopping the sweat from his face with two handkerchiefs.

"You say Baker stimulated your interest in our Snowman, McNeill?"

"Yes, sir," he responded, surprised to realize that though he was unleashed, Mandeva still seemed to be undecided about him.

"Curious," mused the General, tapping the page of Sir Charles's letter against his wrinkled palm. "But why *you,* McNeill? Why are you going after him?"

The eyes of the tall man were hooded, lashed, unlike the eyes of the others in this room — Caucasian rather than Mongoloid. They held Hodge's eyes in as shrewdly probing a stare as he'd ever remembered seeing. Then Hodge knew that Baker's letter vouchsafed his freedom, but that Mandeva himself would decide as to whether or not he could continue his expedition. He appraised the General as the sort of man who passed final judgment on all things himself. It's now or never, he thought, and his mouth went dry as he reviewed before his mind's eye all the standard, pat, often-expressed reasons he'd given to so many other men for his launching of this expedition.

"I'm not sure I know, sir."

"Yet you've gone to considerable trouble and expense in arranging this trip, haven't you?"

"More than I've ever expended on any project in my life."

"But you're not sure of why?"

"No, sir."

Mandeva lowered his eyes for a moment, standing and turning that over silently, like a detective sifting evidence. Hodge suddenly feared that his complete honesty was his ruination, that it made him sound more suspicious, perhaps, more like an agent or spy! He wished now that he could retract his answers.

"I see you're a mystic, McNeill," the General said, smiling.

"Perhaps, sir."

"Or a fool."

"Yes, sir, more probably that."

Mandeva laughed. "How old are you, young man?"

"Forty-five."

"Well, I hope you live to be forty-six!" Then he extended his strong hand. "Forgive me for mistrusting you, McNeill. We have had some unfortunate intrusions of late, but I see you are not one of them. You are welcome in our country! Accept my apologies for this rude treatment, and extend them to your companions as well! Ran, release his men, and see to it that they receive whatever assistance they will require before leaving for Khumbu."

"Whatever you say, Excellency." He bowed very low, as though ashamed now of showing his face to General Mandeva.

"Thank you, General. I don't know how to —"

"That is unnecessary. A month from now you may wish you were in jail. Then you may be tempted to curse me. I prefer to accept neither your praise nor blame. We Hindus believe, you see, that each of us by his own actions decides his destiny. Your karma is to search for the Snowman. I will not stand in its way, McNeill — but tread warily. The gods are jealous of those who presume too much."

"I will remember that," he promised. He wanted to say more, but Mandeva's back was turned to him now, the General's renewed preoccupation with his parakeets seeming to indicate that their audience was at an end.

Hodge left the palace with a guard of honor. He had never felt quite so good before. But driving back to release the others, he could not help wondering if he really knew why Sinha had given them that plane ride?

CHAPTER 27

SUN lit the golden finials on the tallest temples as they drove from the Royal that Saturday morning, headed east across Kathmandu. The air was cool as mountain water, its silence shattered only by the distant tingling of monastic bells, and a piercing bird cry, heralds of the dawn. They drove swiftly, crammed into an old opentop touring car, their rucksacks jutting like seracs from the rumble seat. Like demons of the dark they raced past grotesque icons of stone deities, as though seeking shelter before brightness came to destroy them.

"Let's hope Pasang and his boys don't leave Badgaon without us," said Peter, breaking the silence as they crossed the maidan and skirted the old bazaar of the sacred capital.

"Don't worry. He is much-much reliable," subaltern Yadev replied, mistaking Peter's banter for genuine concern. Yadev was an earnest, moon-faced young man, whom Mandeva had sent to them as official liaison for the expedition. It was Yadev who introduced Hodge to the Sherpa sirdar, Pasang Dorji, and Pasang who hired the forty-five coolies to carry their stores at least as far as Tyang-boche.

"They'll be there," Hodge said, slapping Peter's shoulder, gripping it so firmly that Partridge shouted. He felt so elated now that they were actually under way, so sure of his victory, he could have even slapped Seth in as good natured a way. The helter-skelter of hiring, distributing provisions to the coolies, and mapping their route had kept Hodge too busy yesterday and what remained of Thursday to relish the full joy of realizing that his hunt was about to start. He knew it now though. Every pore in his body tingled with delicious anticipation.

"Yah, and it looks we are in luck today with weather," said Bruno.

"Yes, yes, and October is much-much gooder month in Nepal," promised Yadev.

Crossing the stone bridge over the Bagmati they passed peasants from neighboring villages walking in with their buckets of buffalo milk slung from poles across their shoulders. The sun's rays reached the lower terraces of the valley. Patches of glistening rice paddy rose like velvet pillows among rows of earthen stadium seats, arranged it seemed for invisible giants to watch the daily spectacle of light reborn. The ever-changing play of light and shadows on the mountain walls seemed a pantomime of divine actors locked in mortal conflict. A banyan tree fluttered to life as a harvest of parakeets rose from its nest, like seeds blown from a dandelion.

Beyond Gaucher they rode, over the Manohara, flooded by monsoon rains, rushing froth-topped and singing down the plain, on to the village of Thimi, wakened to life, its solid two-story houses simmering smoke from tiled eaves, while Newari women with braids snaking their brows brought water from the bustling well. Peasants plodded to the fields, indifferent as nature itself. They took no note of the car's pretentious passing, inured to the ways of strangers lured to their land by some restless quest they neither understood nor envied. Only a small boy, driving an enormous buffalo with his stick, turned to smile and wave.

Seth returned the greeting. The boy looked Ethan's age. A sudden yearning to see his son again impelled Seth to turn, straining to watch the boy till a bend in the road made him disappear. He wished now that he had phoned Delhi from the Royal, just to hear Ethan's voice. The prospect of having to make small talk with Stella deterred him. Nor could he quite bring himself to call Rena. The sound of her voice alone, he feared, would have lured him back.

"There it is, you see — Badgaon," announced Yadev. "Does it not look the shape of a conch shell from here?"

None of them could see the resemblance, but Yadev insisted, faithful to the popular myth that this golden city of Nepal was laid out in the form of one of Vishnu's inconographic accouterments. Squatting Newari women threshed at meager mounds of rice, others patiently paced off the distance within the pole skeleton of a loom on which they drew their thread taut. They could hear the metallic ring of a smith's hammer. They stopped short to let several goats cross the road, and advanced again at the pace of a yak cart groaning along up ahead with its burden of bricks and straw.

"Give him the horn," ordered Hodge. "We can walk faster than this! Pull over, damn you!"

The driver swerved to within an inch of the carved doorway to a brass shop, whose terrified owner sat staring at their monstrous mud-covered vehicle as though it were the festival chariot of Kali herself, come to pulverize him under its bloodthirsty wheels. They gunned on past cross streets guarded by griffins, under elaborately carved eaves from which buxom caryatids were bracketed, poised as if ready to swoop down on their open car. The houses grew taller, more richly adorned with woodwork images of deities and demons, whose identity among Tantric cults often eliminated all distinction between the benevolent and malevolent forces of a supernatural world never further from the consciousness of Badgaon life than the nearest building's façade. They rolled from the narrow road into the temple-cluttered cacophony of the great Durbar Square.

"Good God," whispered Peter. "Look at it! I mean, will you just *look* at it!"

The gilded image of Bhupatindra Malla, greatest of the Newari Rajahs, glistened atop his pillar of polished stone, surrounded on all sides by pagoda temples, whose crimson-tiled roofs, hoary with age, sprouted whiskers of grass and green moss. A massive bronze bell hung suspended in deafening silence between pillars of granite. Fierce lions locked in stone guarded the gateways to temples, on whose plinths were spread bloated sacks of barley and rice, lentils and chilies, betel nut and paprika. Merchants in brocaded coats and fur-trimmed Newari caps hovered protectively close to their wares, warding off gaunt children and sacred cattle alike. The bronze doors of the palace entrance shimmered with golden flecks of light, and over the green copper roof winged lions pranced toward the sky, as golden lizards crept tenaciously over a dancing garland of gods and demoniacal goddesses.

There was no man-made center of artistic achievement to match this square in all of Nepal, yet Hodge was impatient to find his Sherpas and supplies, so they moved on, through another narrow canyon of tall houses to the larger public square east of the royal one, where the Bhairava pagodas stood.

"It is called by us Panchtala," Yadev explained, as all eyes fastened on the spindly pagoda rising so precariously above the five plinths of roughhewn stone. "It means five levels, you see, and was built by that same Malla Rajah who sits on the lotus-throne pillar we just now saw. This was to have been the temple of the Bhairab."

"Yah, but he was never put inside?" Bruno asked.

"Who is to say?" replied Yadev, shrugging nervously. "No one has been permitted to enter the temple for much-much time — maybe never. Some say yes, he is there, others no."

"Excuse me," said Niels, "who is this Bhairab?"

"No one knows," said Hodge.

"Oh sure, that is known," insisted Yadev. "He is the god, you see, who kills all demons."

"Then why lock him up?" asked Hodge sardonically.

"Why? Because — well, sometimes he gives trouble —"

"You mean because he may be the worst demon of all, don't you?"

"Yes, but — no," Yadev said, by now quite confused. "How is it you know so much about Bhairab, sir?"

"I don't know as much as I'd like to," said Hodge, leaving the car impulsively and starting toward the long stairway of stone, flanked on either side by giant stone statues, the mustached wrestlers of Malla at the bottom, each reputed to have had ten times the power of ordinary men, and above them the trident-painted elephants with ten times the wrestlers' strength, and at the next level Chou lions with the fierceness of ten elephants, and higher still griffins, each with the power of ten lions. Hodge touched one griffin's leg as he passed it, staring above at the many-armed figures of the Bhairavis Vyaghini and Singhini, whose fang-toothed grins and bulging eyes made them look more like animals than humans, though clearly their bodies were carved in human form. Credited with one hundred thousand times the power of man, each of them sat supreme at the top of the towering stairway, before the solid door locked for all time, sealing the chamber built for their consort, the male Bhairava. In vain Hodge tried to find some crack, a keyhole or fortuitous opening through which he might peer into the sealed sanctum.

"See anything?" Bruno asked. He had come up the stairs just behind Hodge.

"No luck."

"Maybe we should come back tonight and try to force open the door, yah?"

"Are you kidding? They'd cut us to pieces."

"But if *he* is in there?" Bruno spoke in a conspiratorial whisper. The others had left the car, Hodge noticed, but remained in the square, gathered around Yadev, who was pointing to the three-storied pagoda temple to Bhavani across the plaza. Only Bruno had intuited what Hodge did.

"Never mind, Bruno, there wouldn't be much left of him by now anyway."

"This is true, but — you think it is the Yeti, Roger?"

"What do you think?"

"Till now it did not occur to me, but — yah, it seems a good possibility. He is a very ancient god only of Nepal, and from what they say of him, and what I have read about human sacrifices to him — I think it possible."

"So do I."

215

"Maybe we could drill just a small hole in the door?"

"Too risky," Hodge replied. "Come on, Bruno, let's find ourselves a living one."

"I am ready, but if he is a Bhairava this may be a more dangerous hunt than we expect, yah?" He laughed heartily as they descended the stairs side by side.

"Only if we're demons," Hodge retorted, smiling.

At the eastern outskirt of Badgaon the road ended, and in the field beyond they found Pasang camped with his porters, ready and waiting. The motley crew of Sherpas and Sherpanis, Khambas, Gurungs, and Bhotias assembled from the bazaar at Kathmandu, had walked with their packs from the Royal arriving the day before, and after a good rest seemed in high spirits, eager as the team itself was to be on their way, headed toward their homes in Solo Khumbu. They put out their camp fires, and started gathering their utensils, hefting their loads, as the sahibs got out of the car and into the harness of their own rucksacks.

"Good walking day, sahib," Pasang said, grinning broadly as he came over to greet Hodge. "Not hot, not cold." His face was as cheerful and open as the country spread before them. Yadev had recommended him highly as an experienced sirdar, yet Hodge needed no references to see that Pasang Dorji was a man to be trusted with one's provisions, and if need be, one's life. He carried himself with the easy grace, the childlike manliness, of a person reared in mountain country, nurtured by danger and the precariousness of existence, together with the closest proximity to nature's beauty. A stranger to pride, jealousy, and fear of his fellowman, he was befriended by all.

"My things are in that bedroll, Dorji," Yadev said, making it clear from the start that as political liaison he would carry nothing but himself.

"I put with my pack," Pasang said, no trace of resentment in his voice as he lightly lifted the bulging roll with one hand.

"Why carry it yourself, sirdar?" protested Yadev.

"It be light."

So they started, Pasang up front and Hodge beside him. Bruno walked next to Niels in the second rank, then Peter and Seth. Yadev, as befitted his post, came between the team and the long line of porters. By way of conditioning exercise, Hodge insisted that each of them carry forty-pound packs from the first day. The Sherpas carried sixty-five pounds.

They walked east and slightly south, following the course of the Sun Kosi, whose waters sparkled with a golden light. Crossing terraced fields of lush farmland they soon came to the mountain of Manjushri, with a zigzag trail up its side broad enough for two-way foot traffic. There was a Buddhist chorten at the top, its saffron flag tattered slightly by the wind, which only wafted now in mild flurries of perfumed air. The far valley spread in fecund magnificence beneath them, in the distance verdant hills, and beyond those mountains of pine green. Farther still were walls of black rock and buttresses of snow, the Abode of the Gods, called Himalayas.

"Much world there," remarked Pasang as they paused to take in the view.

After only a few hours of walking it looked a long, long way that still stretched before them till they would come within range of their Snowman.

"Much world — never enough time," said Hodge. "Let's get cracking!"

So they continued to walk. And walk.

For seven days they walked through valleys of tropical growth, decked with primulas, golden and mauve, painted by wild rose, iris, and hibiscus, adorned with orchids the texture of silk. Prey to leeches, ubiquitous, insatiable, tenacious as tiny tigers, they trekked over mud trails, blended with their own blood. Across raging rivers they went on bridges woven of jungle vine, stone-hopping shallower streams and pausing to swim where the water was limpid, cool as the mountain fastnesses from which it sprang. Over hills sown in terraced barley and potato, past villages of bamboo huts plastered with red mud and roofed in thatch, serenaded by black and scarlet minivets, surrounded by butterflies bigger than bats, screeched at by monkeys, through forest of fern, moss, and fir they walked for one week.

Their feet and shoulders blistered, till calluses formed where the pressure of trail and pack dug into flesh that had softened from disuse. Their faces and arms were bronzed by the sun. Niels and Peter left their beards to grow. They all became leaner and tougher.

Hodge set a pace at which Pasang's porters balked at first, for they were men to whom the going was life's goal, who liked to stop every half mile or so, resting their loads on the pointed rod stools they carried, leaning back to enjoy the view while they broke for a smoke or a sip of chang, the rice brew that served in Nepal as beer. Ordinarily they averaged from one to two miles an hour, and walked no more than seven hours a day, stopping well before sunset at a village with ample camping ground nearby. But Hodge demanded an eight hour day, and insisted on covering an average of fifteen miles. To overcome porter resistance he promised each man a ten per cent bonus if they reached Tyangboche in two weeks. The trek became a test of stamina and something of a race.

On the morning of the eighth day they climbed to a pass over nine thousand feet, where gnarled rhododendron trees bloomed in flaming scarlet, and the view they confronted was different in kind from that to which their eyes had grown accustomed. The gorges were deeper, the mountain walls more precipitous, too steep for much terracing, sparsely spotted with isolated huts that clung like Alpine goats to rocky ridges. The snowcaps looked almost close enough to touch with outstretched arm, and cascades of silver water fell like dangling earrings of diamonds from dark lobes of shimmering stone.

"Solo Khumbu," said Pasang. "My country!" It was Sherpaland.

"How beautiful," Seth remarked.

"Terrifying," said Bruno, though that honest reaction appeared to embarrass him, so he quickly added, "but magnificent! Yah, magnificent!"

"How many miles to Tyangboche?" asked Hodge.

"Maybe one hundred," answered Pasang. "If bridges all be there."

"That doesn't give us time for sight-seeing! Let's go, men!"

Past Thoze and Dzunbesi they walked, over mountains covered with magnolia and rhododendron forests festively arrayed with floral splendor. Over rockhewn ledges with Mani walls of stone carved in Tibetan letters for the salvation of passersby. *Om Mani Padme Hum!* Oh, Thou Jewel in the Lotus, proclaimed the sacred stones, appealing to Amitabha Buddha for salvation in the blissful Western Paradise. No mountain pass was without its stupa of rocks, crowned by white ribbons of peace, as though proclaiming truce to all men below from the highest flagpoles on earth, the message left by humble wise men, crossing this most rugged yet peaceful patch of earth's tormented surface. They passed yellow-capped Lamas from Tibet, spinning their prayer wheels as they walked, and Sherpa yak-herders of Nepal garbed in Tibetan wool and fur. There were no national boundaries here, no border barricades, no customs officials, no visas, no passport watchers, no armies, or police, no bureaucrats, none of the artifice or tyranny of civilized society, none of the sophisticated complexity or barbarous chaos of urban industrial life, no murderous vehicles, no hotels.

They slept with the villagers, sharing the upstairs room of a Sherpa's home with his family, sharing his hearth, passing his bowl of chang from man to man as they sat on hide-covered floorboards and talked of the weather, of yaks, and of crops, and sometimes, if their host was not too frightened, of Yeti. None of the Sherpas they met doubted his existence, though none had actually seen him. One old man claimed his father had found a Yeti once, captured him with stout rope in his sleep, but that the Snowman woke before help could reach them, and that his uncle saw the Yeti stretch and break his bonds, lifting his captor overhead, dashing out his brains against a nearby rock. Soon after reporting what he had seen the uncle died as well.

"Of what?" Seth asked the old man in Nepali.

"Yeh-Teh," he replied, nodding. It was how they spoke of him here. The old man seemed surprised by the question, as though there could be no other reason for the death of anyone who saw a Yeh-Teh's face as clearly as his uncle had.

Of that too, all the Sherpas were in agreement. No curse was more mortal than that of the Yeh-Teh. They argued and disagreed only as to lesser details. Some said he walked upright, others claimed he was a quadruped. Most had seen his five-toed tracks, but many said the toes pointed backwards, some insisting they were directed ahead as he walked, just as human toes. Many found tufts of his hair left in rock crevices he had climbed, and though it was generally agreed that the hair was reddish in color, two of their informants argued persistently that it was very black.

They sat around the glowing embers of the hearth, smoke-charred fumes smarting their eyes, making them cough, in the chimneyless, all but unventilated dark rooms, and on some nights they talked till the fire went out, and the silent frost crept dagger-like into their bones. Once they thought they heard a voice other than the wind outside, a voice no one but Bruno recognized.

"Did you hear? Yah, I think it was him," Bruno shouted. They went out to look, but after finding no tracks anywhere in the vicinity of the house, Hodge insisted it would be foolish to start their search so soon.

"But if he is near, Roger, it would be madness to lose this opportunity —"

"I agree," Seth said, "and even if it wasn't a Yeti, this is as good a place as any to stop for a few days. The porters could certainly use a rest, and I know I could. You look pretty bushed yourself, Hodge — why push it?"

"We haven't come here to rest, Goodman," Hodge retorted. It was the first time he'd spoken directly to Seth since the march began. He felt himself tremble, and strenuously tried to moderate his tone, for he noticed the stunned looks on the faces of Peter and Bruno as well as Seth at the sudden violence of his outburst. "This isn't a picnic outing for boy scouts! We push on to Tyangboche — that's base camp! We're behind schedule now —"

"But good God," Peter injected, smiling, "it's our own bloody schedule, you know."

"It's my schedule," Hodge snapped. "I'm leading this expedition! If any of you think otherwise, better think again! Anyone too chicken-livered to take it better turn around and start back — the sooner the better as far as I'm concerned!"

"Yah, but of course you are the leader, Roger. I did not for one second mean to dispute —"

"Good God, old chap, relax, eh? We're not challenging you, you blackguard!"

"What about *you?*" Hodge asked, jutting his jaw in Seth's direction. "Turning back, *boy?*"

Seth grit his teeth. He felt his fingernails dig into the tough callus of his palms. No man had talked to him in that taunting tone of contempt since his cadet days of Air Force officer training. He'd taken it then for a year as a lower classman, the chicken shit and personal servitude, the sadism and tongue-lashings from upperclass-men. All just part of the system — the "character building" portion of their military education. He'd been too young at the time to know better, and the coveted wings seemed worth any personal sacrifice, any humiliation, any degree of degradation — for Air Force, God, and country! He remembered the motto that helped them all survive it then, that ordeal-by-shit — "If he's a prick kiss his ass, but if he's a good guy fuck him!" He suspected now, look-ing at the narrow glint of Hodge's eyes, that it was the motto his old buddy never stopped living by. He also sensed that Hodge was waiting for him to answer in the only way a man could answer that sort of verbal assault — with his fists. And it wasn't the challenge to his leadership that provoked Hodge. You're not that stupid, Mac, he thought. He wondered just exactly what it was Hodge had said to Rena. It was a question he would have to ask his old buddy — One of these days, Mac, I'll want you to tell me all about that conversation! It would have to wait though — till they were alone.

Seth buried his fists in his parka pockets. He said nothing to any of them, walking back into the Sherpa hut, getting into his sleeping sack. But he did not sleep that night. He lay unmoving, his eyes smarting, but open. He listened to the deep snores of those around him. He listened to the wind. He listened for Rena's voice, coming to him softly, like fire against his eardrums — *Sleep in me, darling.*

CHAPTER 28

OVER the roaring Dudh Kosi, bubbling milk white as molten metal below the treacherous bridge of wet logs on which they had to bal-ance themselves like high-wire acrobats with bamboo poles, they walked. Then at last they turned north to climb the buttress toward Namche and Tyangboche beyond it, toward the Imja Khola valley, toward Everest itself.

The mountainside village of Namche Bazar, Nepalese anchor point on the main Sherpa trade route to Tibet, loomed high above them late in the afternoon of the thirteenth day of their march.

They worked their way tortuously up the steep trail out of the gorge, hacking shrubs as they climbed, clutching at low-hanging branches for help, pushing their boots deep into humus and soft soil, panting, puffing, groaning under the weight of their packs, till they emerged onto a plateau at about ten thousand feet. From there the multi-leveled terrace of whitewashed buildings, looking down at them like rows of Mani stones from the rock face several thousand feet above, sprang with sudden clarity into view.

"Namche," pointed Yadev, squatting and out of breath.

"Not all that bloody big, eh? Good God, from the fuss those Everest chaps have made about it, I expected something of a metropolis, you know!" It looked more like a cluster of Midlands millhands' homes than a trade center.

"Which part is the bazaar?" asked Niels, focusing his camera on the undistinguished rows of virtually uniform houses.

"Not like that, you see," explained Yadev. "It is called Bazar because much-much caravans come to stop before they cross Nangpa La."

"To China," Hodge said, scratching at his neck.

"Tibet," Yadev corrected.

"Same thing," insisted Hodge. "They must get lots of Chinese traffic as well then."

"Yes, of course — mostly salt and furs, you see," but then his face seemed to darken, Hodge thought, and his voice went lower, sounding as though he knew something, as if he were about to tell something, which he did not want any of the Sherpas to hear. "Maybe they bring much-much other things too now."

"What sort of things?"

"Who can say as yet?" Yadev shrugged. "Maybe we learn much-much of that, isn't it?" He grinned sheepishly.

"What do you mean by that, Yadev?"

But before he could answer, Pasang rushed up to Hodge, interrupting them, reporting, "Sickness, sahib!"

Hodge followed the sirdar down trail to a tree against which one of the porters was propped, groaning, and visibly shaking.

"What's wrong with him?" Hodge asked, opening his pack and removing his first-aid kit.

"Fever," Pasang said.

Hodge touched the glistening brow of the sick man, and quickly withdrew his hand, as though it had been blistered by live coals.

The porters opened the circle they'd formed around their sick friend to admit the sahibs. Peter and Seth had followed Hodge down. The grim faces of the Sherpas, whose number continued to grow around that trouble spot, reflected the panic all of them felt now. Seth heard whispered comments in Nepalese about "Demon fever" and the "curse of Yeh-Teh."

Hodge removed his hypodermic, and prepared a nikethamide solution for injection.

"Better try aspirin first," Seth advised.

"I'll handle this," Hodge snapped, squinting at the clear fluid he drew into the tube.

The stimulant would get the man on his feet faster than anything else, Seth knew, but he feared that if it was a really potent bug the remedy would only overtax his body and might ultimately do more damage than good.

"Don't, Hodge. He may go into shock! We're close enough to Namche. Give him four aspirin and we can have him carried up there. It might cure itself in a day."

"Bullshit — this is mountain fever! He needs a dose, or he'll be dead in ten minutes! When I need your advice I'll ask for it! Pasang, roll up that sleeve! Clean his arm off with this!" He handed the moist cotton to his sirdar.

It was not unusual, Seth knew, for Sherpas, who were ordinarily impervious to illness of any sort, to die of fevers of undetermined origin in a matter of minutes. It happened, of course, only when they were driven too hard, when their remarkable resistance with its natural immunities broke down. The aspirin might prove useless then. He studied the sick man's face, wreathed in pain, the lips white with foam, the eyes half shut and glazed. He stopped arguing with Hodge, who deftly injected the needle, administered the stimulant, and remained crouched on one knee, testing his patient's pulse.

No one in that usually garrulous group of Sherpa onlookers whispered a word. They barely seemed to be breathing, all eyes focused on the bubbling foam of the sick man's mouth, all ears tuned to his faint groaning. Then miraculously enough, his groans

223

grew stronger, his lips parted, his face became moist with sweat. Soon the pain lines were replaced by a grin, and opening his eyes wide, he started to stand up. It seemed nothing less than a miracle, and Hodge was the doctor who'd performed it. Pasang pumped his hand with both of his own, Peter slapped his back warmly, everyone joined in the chorus of congratulations and thanks. The sick Sherpa bent over and kissed Hodge's hand.

"The hell with that," Hodge said, drawing his fingers away, and telling Pasang, "let him walk without any pack — split up his load! But let's get this crew moving, sirdar! We want to be in Namche before sundown!"

"Yes, sahib, yes!" Pasang clapped his hands and passed Hodge's orders down the line.

"Hodge, you can't make him *walk*," Seth said, coming within a step of his ear so that none of the others would be alarmed by his anxiety.

"For Christ's sake, Cassandra, I said he can climb without a pack, didn't I? What the hell more do you want? You expect me to carry him?"

He left Seth to formulate an answer to that by himself, hurrying back to the plateau. Peter followed Hodge, but turned after taking two strides, calling, "Come on, you blackguard — we're almost there, you know!"

Seth was tempted then to tell Pasang to rig a sling for the sick man, and leave his load with that of two other Sherpas on the trail, so that they could carry him the rest of the way. He would have done so, in fact, had he not known that for him to make such an order stick was probably possible now only over Hodge's dead body. Still he hesitated, but looking back at the cured Sherpa, saw him grinning and sharing a pipe with several of his brothers, and decided to mind his own business. Perhaps he was being unduly alarmed about the man at that.

They pushed on, up the trail that broadened and became much easier above the plateau. The soft earth was replaced by stone. The brush disappeared, and fir trees offered them shade from the sun, which had spent its fury for the day. Namche was almost at arm's reach when they heard the cry of terror behind them. They raced back, almost falling over one another, they moved so fast, but it was not fast enough. By the time they reached the sick Sherpa's side again, he was dead.

"Christ, Pasang, he mustuv been sick when we started," Hodge said.

The sirdar did not attempt to argue. He simply removed his pack, and bent to lift the body of the porter. He carried him alone all the rest of the way into Namche, walking now with his porters, keeping some distance from the team itself.

"Bloody bad luck that," Peter muttered. "They are a superstitious lot, you know — they'll blame it on the Yeti!"

"Yah, but this — it could happen to anyone, Roger! You should not let such a thing depress you now. See how well we have done, yah? So, now we are here — in Namche!"

"Right! Hell, I did the best I could for him!"

"Yah, this is what I say —"

They walked ahead, side by side, bolstering one another's conviction that whatever happened, it wasn't their fault.

"Poor man," Niels said, looking sadly at Seth. "I wonder did he have any family?"

"He did — all here — in Namche," Seth whispered. He had heard a few of the others speaking of the dead Sherpa's family here, of how eager he had been to see them again, after being away in Kathmandu for almost a year, saving up so that he could return home and marry off his daughter in proper style.

The village women and children had come down from Namche to welcome them, not the strangers, but their husbands, fathers and sons, the Sherpas, who like sailors in other lands were obliged so often, for such long periods of time, to leave families behind as they trekked off to carry the loads by which they earned their livelihood in this grudgingly inhospitable land that resisted cultivation. The children were all dressed in their finest clothes, and their hair was smoothed down flat and glossy with yak oil. Their round faces were very manly and earnest as they watched the long procession advance slowly up the road. The women were decked out in their brightest costumes as well, the jewelry they wore only on special festival days polished and shimmering in their hair, and on their arms over the richly colored smocks, at their necks and around their waists. They even had heavy silver ankle bangles and some of their bare toes bore rings with tiny bells on. It was a happy reception committee.

Till they saw Pasang's burden, and all of the joy was drained from their bright faces, all the laughter left their eyes, swiftly replaced now by tears. The lament of the mourners echoed across the high walls of the mighty mountains, and soon the lugubrious bells of the Lamas began tolling, as they came softly chanting their mantras for the dead from the Lotus of the Good Law.

What should have been a triumphant arrival turned into a funeral march.

CHAPTER 29

THEY were obliged to pitch tents outside Namche proper that night. None of the villagers opened their homes to the sahibs, who were treated as pariahs. More than half of their Sherpa porters left them as soon as they set down their loads, informing Pasang that they would go no farther on this expedition. It was cursed, they said — by the Yeh-Teh.

"But they've contracted for Tyangboche!" Hodge argued.

Pasang remained silent. He was clearly torn between loyalty to his promise, which as sirdar he would never break, and sympathy for his men, whose fears he seemed in good measure to share.

"They must know Sherpas die of mountain fever just lugging rhododendron branches," Hodge continued. "Didn't you tell them that, sirdar?"

"I do tell, sahib. They be afraid."

"Christ Almighty!" Hodge rubbed the back of his neck, staring anxiously at the mountain of stores piled in hasty disarray outside the two tents that had been pitched on a flat rock-strewn shelf just below the town. No twenty Sherpas on earth could lift that load to Tyangboche! "There'll be no bonus for deserters, sirdar! Did you tell them that?"

"They know, sahib. It not be money."

No, he knew it wasn't money they cared about! Damned

idiots! Illiterate fools! No wonder they all stayed so poor. They were hardly more than animals themselves. It was useless trying to appeal to them in civilized human terms! Nor would he give this one the satisfaction of seeing him break up over it! We'll just have to improvise, he decided. "You say there are twenty willing to work, sirdar?"

"Myself make twenty, sahib."

"Nineteen and you. Okay, Pasang — get dinner cracking. I'll pay off the others after we eat!"

"Yes, sahib."

Yadev had gone into Namche to dine with the Headman, and returned after dark to report that he learned a Yeti had been seen in the vicinity barely a week ago. Everyone was quite nervous at the time, he explained, and now with the Sherpa's death people were too frightened to speak much about it — even to him. The Headman refused absolutely to see Hodge.

"Yah, but you say only one week ago? Roger, this means he cannot be now too far!"

"Check. We'll have to change our plan of attack, men. We're splitting up. We won't be able to lift half our stuff to Tyangboche, and once we pay off up there I'll be lucky if Pasang can find a dozen Sherpas to work for us out of base camp." They had gathered around a kerosene lamp in the larger tent, and looking at the shadowy faces listening to him, Hodge noticed one was missing. "Where the hell's Goodman gone?"

"He said he was going up to pay his respects to the dead man's family," Peter reported, shrugging.

"Damn nut — they'll probably lynch him!" Hodge muttered. "We better keep an eye on him, Pete. I don't like the way he's been sulking. I've seen guys go off their rocker before, and if you ask me he's headed for some kind of a breakdown!"

"Yah, I have noticed this too, Roger."

"Okay, never mind the Professor now. We've got more important problems. As I was saying, we'll have to split up. Bruno, I'm putting you in charge of the team here —"

"Ah, this is very good of you, Roger!"

"Not a bit. You're the logical man for the job. You've got the experience —"

"Thank you, thank you, Roger."

"Niels, I want you to stay here with Bruno. You two have been climbing well together. I think you make the best team."

"This is an excellent choice, Roger! Niels, you and I, yah?"

"Of course. Whatever you think best," Niels replied, shaking Bruno's hand without any particular enthusiasm, but then, Hodge had noticed little enthusiasm or verve in anything Niels did since they'd left London. Scandinavians, he decided, were all icebergs.

"The rest of us will push on tomorrow. We'll camp at Tyangboche, Bruno, and if you sight him, or need us you can always send a messenger to reach us in a few hours. We'll do likewise. I'll keep you notified every week, at any rate, and if the hunting seems better up there, you might want to come up and leave a few Sherpas to guard the provisions you can't carry. Is that clear?"

"Absolutely," said Bruno. "And in the morning Neils and I make our first reconnaissance, yah?"

Their faces glowed with intensified excitement reflected by the flickering light of the lamp. The intimacy of the tent somehow added piquancy to their sense of mutual dependence and isolation from the rest of the world. It helped make more real for them their actual proximity to the goal of their voyage, which was now imminent as tomorrow.

"Good God, chaps, we've made it, you know?" Peter sounded as though he were trying to convince himself.

"Let's save that till we've got him, Pete. Bruno, remember to rely wherever possible on your natural cover. The bastard's eyes are a lot keener than ours. If he sees a tent or camp fire, he'll run like hell the other way."

"Yah, we be careful, Roger. We look for him at night mostly."

"You may be able to catch him sleeping by day though," Roger reminded him.

"Of course, yah! We look in daytime too!"

"Good God, when the hell do we sleep, eh?"

"You've been in sack most of your life, Partridge! A few weeks out of it won't hurt you!"

"That's a moot point, you know. The reverse could be argued —"

"What else?" Hodge said, ignoring and silencing him by the urgency and earnestness of his tone. He assumed the manner of a general briefing his staff on the eve of the big push. He snapped his fingers, bringing all eyes to attention. "Lures! Don't forget your lures, Bruno. We've got aluminum discs in the crate with the chain. They'll reflect the sun by day, but you might want to focus a flashlight on them at night. The odd shapes shining might just arouse his curiosity —"

"Which has killed many a cat, old chap!"

"Right, and may do in our Yeti as well. Oh, and while we're on that — try bait if you can. But you'll have to set traps for some rodents, field mice. He likes small animals, we know, disembowels them and leaves the entrails behind —"

"Yah, Yeti is the only animal to do this —"

"Yeti and man," Hodge corrected him. "I don't think he goes for yak, try everything — play it by ear. And Niels, don't forget your flashbulbs. A shot *of* him will almost be worth a shot *at* him!"

"This reminds me, Roger. If he attacks us — ?"

"Keep your nets handy. Toss at his head or arms!"

"Yah, but if we miss with nets?"

"Use your dart guns. The dose should keep him out for at least an hour or two. Chain him fast, and stake him secure. Don't try dragging him in alone. Send for us, and we'll all do that together, understand?"

Bruno kept nodding, his questions posed as swiftly as Hodge could answer them.

"But if the dart does not take at once, Roger? Do we run or kill?"

"I'd like him alive."

"Yah, of course, this is what we all want —"

"Run if you can. It may give you time to take a second shot with the dart gun —"

"But —"

"We all have our pistols," Roger said.

"Good! I just want to be sure it is agreed by you that if everything else fails —"

"Of course," Hodge said, wishing Bruno would have more tact

than to pursue this particular point with Yadev sitting among them. "Naturally, as Yadev here can tell you, killing a Yeti, even in self-defense wouldn't make us exactly popular heroes in Khumbu, would it, Yadev?"

"No, no, there is much-much concern here, you see, on that very point. As the Headman said to me only tonight, when he asks about your mission — 'I hope they do not intend to kill Yeh-Teh if they find him.' And I am very positive to him you will not kill — only try to capture —"

"Right! There's your answer, Bruno! Above all, men, remember we're scientists. This is a scientific hunt. We're not after game now." Though he said it with conviction, Hodge understood how Bruno felt, sensing the lust for blood in his voice, seeing its glimmer in his eyes. He too felt that same hunger. He rose, excused himself, and left the tent, going to the water jug Pasang had left outside the flap. He drank, and wiped his mouth with his sleeve, then stared for a silent moment at the awesome outline of mountain silhouettes, faintly gray and purple where the snow peaks were caught by the moon.

"I'm coming for you," he whispered, feeling the full flush of his power welling inside him. He was going to do something, perhaps tomorrow night — that no man living had ever done!

Then he heard the footsteps behind him, and startled he turned, drawing his pistol, aiming the gun at the tall shadowy figure, who stepped closer, seemingly unafraid.

"I have to talk with you, Hodge —"

"Don't ever sneak up on me that way, Professor!"

"I never sneak," Seth replied.

"No?" Hodge spit. He was tempted to use the pistol, but there was bigger game in this country. "Pete just told us you've been sneaking around the town — looking for trouble! From now on, buddy, you let *me* know before you go any place, understand? I'm responsible for this team, and I don't intend letting any one member of it put the rest of us into jeopardy, going off half-cocked! Now you don't even know what we've planned —"

"I promised that man's family we'll pay for his daughter's wedding, Hodge —"

"Are you crazy? What the hell did you have to do that for?"

"I didn't *have* to do it."

"They're getting his pay, dammit! Isn't that enough?"

"No," Seth whispered. "I promised them enough for a decent dowry, and the sort of wedding he would have wanted —"

"But couldn't afford!"

"That may be — yes."

"Oh, Christ! Thanks, buddy! Thanks a lot!"

"You keep the sarcasm, Hodge. Just give me the money. Five hundred silver rupees."

"*How* much? You're out of your simple mind to tell people like that — five *hundred?* Why that's almost all I'm paying every one of those filthy Sherpas!"

"The rest of them are alive, Mac. He's the one we killed. It's blood money. It doesn't pay for his life — but it's going to buy his daughter what he wanted her to have. Now will you go in there and bring it out to me, Mac, all of it — or do I have to take it myself? Because I promised to deliver it — tonight."

He said it very softly, slowly, deliberately, making it very clear as he spoke that he was not letting any of the others know he had taken this action upon his own authority, but making it equally clear by what he said that unless Hodge complied with his demands now he was ready to assert his independence of Hodge's leadership — openly. Hodge got the message all right.

"You're blackmailing me," Hodge whispered.

"Call it anything you like, Mac. Just get the money — now."

Hodge started to say something else then, but clamped his mouth shut, and returned to the tent.

"Big day tomorrow, men. Let's turn in," he told the others.

They all went outside the tent then to prepare themselves for the night. Hodge unlocked his strongbox. He kept the silver rupees in small bags of one hundred. He threw five bags into a larger one, re-locked the box, and came out. The bag was heavy enough to crush a man's skull — maybe even a Yeti's, he thought, hefting its not inconsequential weight. For the second time that night he was tempted, approaching Seth's back. The Professor was standing, hands buried in his pockets, gazing at the North star, which looked almost the size of a golf ball. You'll pay for them, buddy, he swore — every filthy one!

"Here are your shekels, Goodman," he said, tossing the bag at Seth's feet.

Seth stooped to pick them up, but he did not say thanks.

CHAPTER **30**

SNOW began falling at Namche as the expedition left for Tyangboche next morning, with Bruno and Niels heading off to the northwest on their first sortie. Flakes of dry snow fluttered softly like tinsel tossed to hail their procession, while the bells and gongs of a monastery rang out in dissonant carols.

"It is like a Christmas morning I remember when I was a boy," said Niels. "Snow makes everything more beautiful."

"Yah, but too much can be ugly. I hope soon it stops."

"I don't think it will last long."

But all that day it continued to snow as they climbed closer to the wall of Himalayan ice that marked Nepal's border, decorating pines and junipers, coating the grayish-black moraine of the lower mountains with a garb of white. After morning camp break, Bruno decided it would be best for himself and Niels to proceed with their bouldering, secured to one another by rope. The freshly covered rocks were slippery. They could not advance as far as they hoped before dusk began to close in. Their two Sherpas advised making camp on a barren ledge just above the tree line, where several overhanging boulders provided excellent wind shelter.

"It does not matter here," said Bruno, "if we put up a tent for tonight. Maybe tomorrow, if we have a clear day, we come close enough to Yeti to be more careful, yah?"

"Yes. I hope it is clear enough to take some shots tomorrow. We should have a good view," Niels remarked, staring at the impenetrable bank of gray clouds and bluish haze.

The Sherpas secured their tent and boiled tea, while Bruno and Niels chewed K-ration bars, squatting close to the fire. With dark-

232

ness, a freezing fog descended, and they were glad to have canvas under which to lie, easing into their sleeping bags shortly after the last cup of warm tea was finished.

For some moments neither of them spoke, but suddenly Bruno asked, "What did your wife look like?"

"Very beautiful."

"Nordic?"

"Yes."

"What was her name again?"

"Ulla."

"Yah — Ulla. She was quite young?"

"Twenty-two."

"Ah, so young as that? And already tired of life!"

Bruno heard only the heavy breathing of his companion. His eyes remained open, but he did not turn to look at Niels' face.

"So, you prefer not to talk about her?"

"No. I just — I am not sure I know why she has killed herself."

"Women are much simpler than men. For them it is always the same reason — love. This, of course, is more true if they are young and beautiful, yah? Lotte has tried to do the same. Does it surprise you?"

"Yes."

"Yah! Well, at the time I myself — oh, it happens not very long after we are married, you see. Of course, I should never agree to marry. I try to explain to her that we are not — how do you say? — suited to each other. Yah, I tell her this many times, but she thinks — as much as a woman *thinks!* They are more like the animal, yah? They feel. It is for them the blood pressure that runs the brain — so, but that is another matter. What did I begin to explain? Ah, of course! Each time I tell her we are not suited to marry, she thinks I tell this because of my face — the scars. She wants to prove to me I am not too ugly for her to love, to look at me every day. This is her personal sacrifice for the war, the Jews — whatever it is we Germans must crucify ourselves for — to Lotte all of this is connected with me, you see, because when she marries me then she purge herself of guilt —"

"No, but she loves you, Bruno."

"No, no, wait. You misunderstand what I say. About her love

you are right, of course." But here he paused to reflect, and continuing, his voice acquired a strangely acerbic tone. "Love! But never mind this word now, it has too many meanings to discuss. What I try to say is that Lotte *thinks* I do not want to marry her because *I* love and need *her*. This to her is dogma, you see! Ach, you do not doubt such belief. This is written on stone! *Verstehen Sie?*"

"I think so."

Bruno felt the fog, penetrating canvas, piercing the tight fabric of his bedroll, creeping insidiously, invisibly, through the heavy garments he wore, down to the scarred calcium of his bones, where it clung like dry ice pressed against warm flesh; he felt it and shuddered, gritting his teeth to keep from chattering before he could speak again.

"Yah, but just here, you see, at the crux of her life's religion, just at this crucial point of faith, she is wrong! Is this not the funny part, Niels? This is what is so ridiculous, yah? So — so comical!" He started to laugh, a staccato outburst like a volley fired from a machine gun.

Niels lay perfectly silent till the laughter had stopped, venturing then in a tone of disbelief to ask, "But then do you not love her?"

"Of course not. I have never loved her. This is what makes her attempt suicide, the night after I admit to her my true feeling — when is it? — oh, four-five month after we are married. She swallows a bottle full of my barbiturates, which I find empty less than an hour later when I need one for myself! She is unconscious, of course, but they are able to pump everything out — yah? Is it not very comical — life?"

"But — then why did you marry her, Bruno?"

"*Immer warum!*" he sighed.

"No, I can understand why," Niels injected. "In many ways she reminds me of Ulla — not just her looks. Ah, that too, but I mean her sensitivity to art, her tenderness —" He stopped speaking of Lotte as impulsively as he'd begun. As if sensing a trap, his teeth half buried in the alluring bait, he paused, saying nothing at all for fully a minute, breathing inaudibly through his nostrils. Then drawing back, veering cautiously to cover his tracks, he continued, "So far as anyone can see from superficial observation, I mean, that would be my impression of Lotte."

234

"Of course. This is naturally everyone's impression," Bruno replied lightly. "Ach, I do not say I am not also impressed by these things. *Ein schöner Rücken ist auch entzückend,* yah?" he recited, laughing again, somewhat more frenetically than before. "And Lotte looks also good from the front, this is true!"

"No, I am not talking of physical attraction."

"Then what is it you find in her so attractive, Niels?"

"I? But nothing. I personally do not find — feel, any — I was speaking only just now of you, her husband."

"Yah, this is true, I am her husband!" Suddenly whatever he said seemed comical to Bruno, for he continued to punctuate his words with volleys of nervous laughter. "But shall I admit to you something? Do you know why I marry her, Niels? You will never guess, so I tell you. After I am discharge from the hospital, I live in Berlin, I try to compose my symphony. Lotte comes to stay with me. This is to say, I stay with her, because it is her money that supports us — her father's money. Yah, whatever I need she buys it for me — piano, score sheets — everything for art! She pretends it is my music which makes her love me, but for Lotte there is nothing more important than sex. I say for Lotte. Who knows, maybe this is true for all women?" He paused, waiting for Niels to comment.

"But you were going to explain why you married her, Bruno?"

"This is the funny part — the grotesque comedy we call life — I have just now explained all!" His voice was barely audible above the howling gale, which had begun like the sibilant whisper of a Japanese chorus, and wailed on like the tormented cry of a demonic soul racing wildly through the mountain crags and ravines. "Comfort and inertia, Niels, these are the traps they use for us, yah?"

"No, but I have always been romantic," Niels insisted. "For me there is nothing more dangerous than beauty — in its purest state."

"This you find in music, not women!"

"Maybe that was why Ulla — but who is to say what makes another person lose hope and the courage to continue life?"

"Why do you speak so of suicide, Niels? This is the supreme act of strength, not weakness. For a man, at least — to take your own life, to overcome the inertia — what is more easy than to live, after all? Or more cowardly than natural death? We pride ourselves on our boldness in hunting, yah? And for good reason, you will say. I agree. This also takes strength, to face the tiger's leap, and trust your finger to pull a trigger, when every natural instinct tells to you, what? Drop the rifle — run! Or in war, to do this same thing when another man, also he carries a gun, jumps up in front of you — this is still harder, more of a challenge to nerve. But to kill yourself, who is alert always, ready to argue with you against it, yah? To make of your nerve steel and turn your body into the lethal weapon that defies your brain? Or still better to convert your own mind into your ally in his annihilation, *this* is the supreme test of strength. The Japanese are the only race who master this art, but it takes them centuries of breeding pure warriors, men who choose death, prefer it to dishonor — and this even is less than suicide in the highest sense, how Nietzsche has taught us — to die at the right time! No, this has nothing to do with cowardice, Niels — it requires the highest form of courage."

"I am not sure I can agree with you, Bruno. I have too often thought — many times in this last month — that the easiest solution to life is self-death."

"But still you live."

"That is true."

"So perhaps it is not quite this easy?"

"Perhaps not," he whispered.

Bruno did not pursue his point further that night, but lay silently absorbing the strange sound of the wind that roared down from the world's summit, wondering whether tomorrow or the day after that, or a week or a month later, these same winds, grown soft with the strain of their voyage, made heavy by the smells and sounds of cities they might cross, would reach Lotte's ears and lungs, bringing some echo of his voice to her consciousness. For he sensed now that courage had returned at last to his spirit, and if only he could muster enough of it he would never reach her again by more immediate means.

The faintest gray of dawn filtered through the flap of their tent, when a Sherpa's grinning face appeared, announcing, "Tea, sahibs."

The fog still lingered, but the snow had stopped. They advanced

236

cautiously along the ridge of moraine rock, and soon were obliged
to climb so precipitously that the increased altitude forced Niels to
stop less than two hours after they began. He dropped to his
haunches on the trail, and pressed both fists against his eyes. Bruno
felt the slack of his rope go taut, and turned to ask what was
wrong.

"My head is throbbing. I will be all right in another minute."

"Yah, I begin to feel the altitude myself. We have not yet acclimatized. We take some aspirin now and I tell the Sherpas to
make fire."

They paused for a leisurely breakfast, but when Niels tried to heft
his pack again he almost collapsed under its weight. His face was
pale, his hands trembled. His eyes seemed unable to focus properly. He appeared frightened, adolescently unsure of himself, like a
boy suddenly confronted with the reality of war, standing in silent
shock over the dead body of a nameless enemy, mutely staring at
the smoking rifle still clutched in his own hands. The similarity, the
vividness of that transmutation through memory, disturbed Bruno
so much that he was obliged to force himself to turn away from
Niels' face, jerking around abruptly to gaze up the mountainside.

"Wait here," Bruno snapped. "I go ahead a little while by myself."

"No, no, I will be able —"

"You will do as I say, you fool! Do you want to kill yourself?
You must rest!" He said it so passionately, so impulsively, that the
very harshness of his tone made it sound far more intimate, more
tender somehow, than anything he had ever uttered to Niels before,
even in their most convivial conversations. Both of them appeared
equally startled, almost physically jolted, by Bruno's explosive
emotionalism, and Niels made no attempt to answer, though his
eyes now focused unwaveringly on Bruno's tight-lipped face.

"I — I come back in a few hours," Bruno blurted, feeling himself blush, as he dug the spike of his ice axe into the hard ground
and trudged away quickly.

Though the Sherpas offered to accompany him, Bruno insisted
on going off alone. They were well within the Yeti's domain, and
the fewer the silhouettes the better chance there would be of approaching him, Bruno rationalized. But he did not expect to find a

Yeti so easily, and knew all too well why he chose to advance without witnesses. It was precisely the opportunity he had been waiting for, the ideal moment. All that remained now was to find the proper place. Unfortunately, they had stopped at the base of a fan-shaped glacial valley, and the fog had begun to lift, so that even after climbing more than an hour, he could still clearly see the campsite below, and knew that Niels traced his progress as easily. The mere thought of Niels served to accelerate Bruno's pace, till he found himself gasping for breath, and felt the blood surge with hammerlike intensity through his forehead. He stopped and swallowed several aspirin tablets, but one broke on the back of his tongue and the bitter taste made him gag, half choking. He clutched at his throat and his eyes began to smart. Then like a mirage, or a wavering image seen through undulating water, Niels' face appeared again, pale, timid, disturbingly beautiful in its helplessness, the lips sensuously moist and roseate. He saw Neils's body as well, not hidden under the shapeless parka he was wearing below, but hairless and smooth, softly muscular and pallid, the way he remembered seeing it at the pool after the celebration with Sinha. Only now it was stark naked.

Bruno felt his heart racing in his wrists. He heard the runaway pounding, like a piston engine that has lost its cushion of steam, beating against his ears. Each step he took seemed to add weight to his pack, and all that he knew about climbing and the dangers of overstrain at high altitudes told him to stop, to turn back, to give his body time to adjust to the more rarefied atmosphere. Yet he continued. This was, after all, the right time to die. He had made his decision below, in full command of his powers, totally rational, mustering his courage like a battalion of well-trained soldiers assembled on the parade ground for close-order drill.

A fluted buttress of ice loomed ahead, rising like a rocket on a moonscape, hardly a thousand feet distant, he thought, though after another hour of laborious slow motion it seemed no closer than that. The altitude could, of course, distort his perceptions, no less than it taxed his powers of perseverance, Bruno knew, for as he continued to walk toward it, the buttress of white seemed to move farther away. He could better gauge his advance by looking back at the diminishing specks of Niels and the Sherpas. Once he reached the buttress, he would be able to liberate himself entirely from their view, circling around its base until he was totally out of sight, cutting steps in the wall till he had reached a safe vantage point of height, then falling free. . . .

And what more suitable place to die than on this barren graveyard of granite and eternal ice, where life of any sort seemed an intrusion? He felt no fear. No remorse. No longing to continue the deception of existence. Yet he did not think of the path he pursued now as one of escape, but rather of total affirmation. Ever since he was twelve, when the director of his youth camp, after first seeking to tempt him with women, finally confessed his own love to Bruno, kissing him full on the lips, he had run in desperation from the truth then revealed to his consciousness. To musical composition as well as women he ran, embracing both with a frenzy fostered by fear. Then to the Army, for what clearer proof could he present to mankind of his masculinity! For years he succeeded so well as to all but convince himself, ordering boys he loved to advance against mortar shells that tore their beautiful bodies to shreds of raw flesh, leaving their entrails for maggots to feast upon . . . Bruno suddenly stopped moving. At first he thought it was another mirage: there on the gray boulder before him, bleached by the sun, gelatinously smooth and coiled like a group of sleeping worms, lay the entrails of some large rodent, possibly a mountain hare. He thought it was memory playing tricks again with his vision, till he touched the slimy substance, squeezing it hard between his fingers so that it oozed, and he knew it was real.

His heart continued pounding, but for a moment he dared not breathe, looking all around him with intensified awareness and suddenly awakened interest in the most minute detail of the terrain in his immediate ambience. The snow which had fallen yesterday remained as a layer of clear ice over most of the ground, though puffs of softer white filled rock crevices and some drifts of deeper snow ran plateaulike toward the buttress wall. There were several boulders hurled down from the mountain heights that loomed in neolithic isolation large enough to hide an elephant. The wind had practically died, and the silence was as solemnly portentous as that of an empty Gothic cathedral, whose organ pipes had ceased to vibrate, but seemed at any second about to burst forth with a shattering basso chord.

Tossing aside the entrails, Bruno scanned the ground for some sign of tracks. There were so many pebbles and small rocks nearby that it was difficult to discern any clear imprint, but he thought he could see the outline of a large foot barely a yard from the stone on which the entrails had been left. The ice at any rate had been broken in a suspiciously symmetrical manner, and just a few paces farther along toward the buttress he found what seemed like another footprint. Then beyond that, still another. He wasted no more time in removing his dart rifle, fastening it together, inserting a soporific cartridge, and placing a spare in his breast pocket. He checked his pistol as well, releasing the safety lock.

The sun emerged with blinding fury as the last veils of fog burned off, and he was obliged to use Polaroid goggles, advancing in the direction of the trail. Though he could not really find a sharp impression in soft snow, the track seemed undeniably that of a biped. He was tempted to call back or fire a flare to signal the Sherpas and Niels, but he feared that any sound at this time would surely alert his prey — whatever it was! The condition of the entrails made him feel certain that they had not been discarded long before he'd found them. He only wished now that he were better acclimatized, for he felt almost faint, light-headed. He paused to swallow more aspirin, and left a lump of sugar to dissolve on his tongue as he walked. But the strain of altitude and the sun's heat made him stop again after just a few paces. Then he decided to drop his pack. He took out the nylon net, his compass, flashlight, and a small packet of condensed food, leaving the rest of his gear on a prominent boulder, which he draped first with a red scarf.

Relieved of his burden, Bruno moved ahead with cautious alacrity, each of his senses keenly alert for any unusual sight, sound, or smell. Near the foot of the massive buttress he came upon an imprint which made him gasp audibly as he bent low to examine it.

In overall length the impression was somewhat shorter than that left by his own boot, but it was broader, and sank almost twice as deep into the snowdrift, indicating that his game was far heavier and more powerful than a man, though probably no taller. There were clear marks as well, at least four, all about equal in size with somewhat greater spread between the second and third, rather than first and second toes. The heel was much narrower than the foot at its center, and quite nicely rounded. From all that Bruno remembered of the photographs he had seen published, and of similar tracks he followed five years ago, there was no doubt in his mind that the foot which left this mark belonged to a Yeti.

A sudden chill made him shudder. He felt his stomach contract, closing like an involuntary fist, and the hair at the nape of his neck seemed to bristle as he squinted ahead, sensing now that he was being watched, that his very thoughts were overheard by some being other than himself, though he could see nothing but ragged boulders, snow and ice, and the cobalt blue of sky in front of him. Terrified by a premonition of doom, he turned, jerking around so quickly that he lost his balance, falling back against the snow in which he half buried his rifle before he could brace himself. But there was nothing, no one, behind him. A cold film of moisture covered his torso. He sat without moving a moment, gasping for breath. Then he saw the bird, a bulky snow cock, impertinently peering at him from its hiding place at the base of a boulder, and he shook with silent laughter at his momentary terror, watching the awkward creature half fly, half run down the slope. Briskly, Bruno pulled himself erect, brushing the snow from his parka and trousers, tapping it off the stub nozzle of his gun. He turned again to reexamine his prey's footprint, but found that in falling back he had obliterated the mark. The first clear proof of the Yeti's reality, and he had destroyed it before they could so much as take a picture!

Infuriated at his bumbling stupidity, Bruno proceeded with his search more slowly and carefully. He was certain, of course, that having found so perfect a track, it would take but a few moments to locate more, many more. Peculiarly enough, however, though he scanned every inch of snow within a radius of ten yards of the imprint, he could not see another, barely discerning even as vague an outline as any of those he had earlier noted. But how was it possible? He kept returning time and again to the mess he had made by his fall, trying to figure out some way in which the Yeti might have retreated from that spot without leaving another clear print. Unless he had wings there seemed no solution — unless! It was just conceivable that he might have used a bridge of rocks, whose smooth tops were stripped of snow by the wind, to reach the buttress. Why he should take so tortuous a route was a question less easy to resolve, and seemed so improbable to Bruno that he refused at first to consider the prospect seriously, but realized then that the Yeti might have sighted him below, and shrewdly decided at that moment to elude him by leaving as broken a trail as he possibly could. It would certainly indicate remarkable intelligence, were that in fact what he did. Brain power, indeed, very close to that of man — but how else could he have escaped captivity so long?

Convinced now that the creature he followed was both conscious of his presence and much nearer to the level of his own intellect than he ever before suspected, Bruno worked his way to the buttress base by what seemed like the only probable bridge of stone that might have been used by an expert climber in crossing a riverbed, and then started carefully to examine the icy wall for any signs of finger or toe marks. The sun, which now played on the wall like a blowtorch, made his job all but impossible since its glare was so great, and its heat melted the topmost layer of crisp snow, causing it to run like warm icing down a cake's sides, erasing telltale indentations with each passing moment. Still and all, Bruno thought he could see several marks which might have been made by tightly curled toes gripping the ice. More important, however, in making him decide to climb toward the left instead of the right was what he judged the inherent logic of choosing such a route for ascent, rather than the inconclusive nature of the evidence he found. Born climber that he was, the Yeti could safely be credited by instinct with taking the best path up any mountain wall! Bruno now followed that path as well.

He was able to work his way up a very narrow shoulder for several hundred yards without using his axe, kicking toeholds only at a few precarious points, finding ample projections of stone for his hand grips. He had slung the rifle over his neck, and tucked the axe through the loop of his waistline rope, advancing very cautiously so that at every hold he felt sufficiently balanced to be able to take his weight entirely on his legs, freeing his arms for the gun, if that were necessary. But then the shoulder was cut off by a slightly broader protrusion of ice, which ran almost vertically to the top of the buttress, it seemed, and obstructed his vision of anything on the other side. In his haste to pursue his prey, Bruno had not taken the elementary precaution of reconnoitering far enough around the base of the mountain, or he would soon have found this formidable projection, and might well have decided to climb in the opposite direction! At least he would have known how thick the projection was which now stood before his face, a huge white barrier to any further normal progress. He tested the ice with his axe. It sounded solid enough for cutting steps, but he knew how risky that could be alone under ordinary circumstances. Hunting the Yeti it would have been sheer madness, since his hands would not be free to use the rifle.

Bruno glanced down. His elevation above the valley was probably somewhat less than one hundred feet. He turned his head the other way, and realized that in coming up on this side he had worked himself out of Niels's range of vision. Then he remembered, with startling clarity, what the tension of the hunt had temporarily obliterated from his mind. He remembered why he had come this way alone. His mouth went dry. His knees fluttered. He forced himself to look down again. The boulders below all appeared surprisingly pointed! They had seemed quite round from the valley floor. Now they were more like bayonets, he thought, or Samurai swords, hilts buried in snow-crusted soil. The wind had started again. Its icy sting flung fine needles against his face. The sun became weaker as clouds moved their ghostly shadows over its face, and suddenly the world below was dark, bluish-purple through the tinted lenses he wore. His blood seemed to stop flowing. His limbs were numb, his fingers stiff as the ice they gripped through the fleece-lined leather gloves he wore.

"Yah, now, Bruno," he said aloud. "You do it *now!*"

Then, as though in answer to his voice, he heard the cry — a piercing, strangely plaintive call, unlike any sound he had ever heard before. Lonelier than the wail of a wolf, wandering desolate above the timberline. Almost a man's voice, it seemed, resonant and rich of tone, like the single high note of a clarinet heralding a symphony, wordless and undefined it came to his ears — like the tortured first effort of humankind to articulate the inchoate, the unknown, the incomprehensible, the very birth cry of language.

It lasted just a few seconds, but that was long enough to jolt Bruno from his resolve to jump, if only because it aroused his curiosity again and providentially awakened in him once more the instinct of the hunter. He could, after all, choose any time to die!

Retracing his steps carefully down the buttress shoulder, Bruno decided to return to the campsite to lead back the others, rather than going farther now himself. He suspected his Snowman friend would not run too far while he was gone. There was somehow a quality to that cry which made him feel that the Yeti might also be looking for something — someone perhaps.

CHAPTER **31**

HODGE cursed the snow throughout the march to Tyangboche. He had driven them all as he did to get here before such weather would inhibit their progress. It was, Yadev insisted, much-much unusual for this time of year! Pasang agreed. October should be a clear month in Khumbu! Wind should not be blowing from the north as yet! But it did. And after they reached the lamasery town, perched like an eagle's haunt on a plateau facing the Imja Khola, the wind grew fiercer, the snow continued to fall — without letup.

All that day it fell. And the next. It fell so thick, they were confined to camp, to the tents they pitched outside the sacred grounds, where they huddled like yaks, waiting for the storm to lift. Seth pitched a tent of his own. Peter stayed with Hodge in the large tent. He played solitaire, while Hodge worked on some calculations, using his strongbox for a desk, seated cross-legged in front of it.

"I wish to God that bloody wind would stop! It's driving me buggers!"

"We averaged 15.8 miles a day from Kathmandu. Wonder if that's any record?"

"For all the bloody good it's done us now that we're here, we might as well have enjoyed the walk a bit more!"

"You sound tired, Partridge. Take a nap. This is your chance to catch up on that sleep you were so worried about."

"Right now, I'm tired of sitting on my ass. Come on, old chap, let's cut for high card, eh?"

"I don't play cards. It bores me."

"Good God, I should think you'd be sick of those stupid figures by now."

"The whole world is going to want to read about these figures, Partridge. Someone has to keep our record."

"Well, if we stay here much longer, you know, I shouldn't think anyone would give a farthing for them." He was doing his best to lighten Hodge's mood, but instead of laughing, Hodge turned at him angrily, and snapped,

"If that's all you have to say, Partridge, say it to yourself!"

"Ease up, old boy! You're getting a bit snappy, you know? Maybe you're the one who needs a nap, eh?"

"Go to hell!" The two-day growth of beard, his unkempt hair, and the redness of his eyeballs gave Hodge's face the wild look of soil gone to weed. He wore several layers of different colored sweaters, whose cuffs and necklines emerged in motley confusion. He looked, as he sounded, Peter thought — quite mad.

"I bloody well thought I was there," he replied.

"Where?"

"Hell, you know." He grinned, but Hodge didn't think that funny either.

"Shut up, will you! I'm trying to write —"

Peter frowned, shuffling his cards together. He'd always liked McNeill, but there were limits, even to the easygoing dimensions of a Partridge's temperament! He sighed and pushed himself to his feet, stuffing the deck into his pocket, putting on his windbreaker.

"Where the hell are you going?"

"Oh, I don't know — out."

"Don't get lost, dammit!"

"I'll manage, old chap, to find my way —" Then he hesitated. He was going to add, *will you?* But McNeill was writing his diary again, and Peter mutely shrugged, leaving him as he wanted to be — alone.

Exactly why God had sent this snowfall to hinder me, I could not quite fathom as yet, Hodge wrote, pausing to gnaw at the eraser of his pencil, narrowing his eyes as he stared at the wavering wall of his tent. He wanted to be as perfectly honest in recording his memoirs of this trip as was humanly possible, for he sensed that this document would soon be read by millions and millions of people, but more important than that — it would be handed down for posterity, and reread by each new generation. *Perhaps He was testing my stamina? Perhaps He was trying to see if Hodge McNeill was the sort of man to lose heart easily, to turn back at the first flecks of flak . . .* He liked that. It was well put. He had a real flair for words. Maybe, when this expedition was over, he would try his hand at a book or two. Something inspirational — about himself. Why not, after all? He wrote better than most of the books he ever read. He could do anything better than practically anyone! Just a few minutes with his diary had lifted his spirits immensely. He decided to write on . . . *to lose hope as other men would, even as other members of this very team were doing now, to turn tail and run for home? Was that His purpose? Well, if it was, He had judged the mettle of His Man wrong!*

Hodge read the whole passage, over, nodding and smiling as he did so, but he wondered if it might seem presumptuous of him to capitalize "Man"? Some people might resent that — petty people. Though actually it looked better to him this way — His and Man both capitalized. He decided to leave it alone. He wanted the diary to be as pure and direct a statement of how he felt as possible. . . .

"Mind if I join you, eh?" Peter asked, peering into Seth's tent.

"Oh, hi, Pete. Come on in — my pleasure. I was just brushing up my Nepali," he said, closing the well-worn little dictionary and setting it aside. "How goes it, friend?"

"Grim — I must say!" Peter shook the snow off himself like a huge bear emerging from his bath, opened his jacket, and sat facing Seth. "I think this snow's got us all half buggers. Mac's in a bloody rage!"

"Oh? What now?"

"Christ if I know! Ask him, if you dare! I've tried, and the blackguard damned near chewed my head off! Just this bloody weather, I suppose."

"It should clear soon."

"God, I hope so. Care to cut for high card, old chap?" Peter pulled out his deck.

"Sure. I don't have much money, I'm afraid —"

"That's all right. We'll just make it a rupee a cut, eh?"

Seth went to find his change. He had about twenty silver rupees to his name. He stacked a small pile of them on the canvas between their knees.

"Shall I cut — or would you prefer to?"

"Doesn't matter. You might as well. You've got the cards."

"I see you're no gambler, old boy!" Peter rubbed his palms together, and eagerly shuffled the deck, cutting for himself.

"Ah, the red queen! Good God, what an opener!" He spread the cards and held them out for Seth.

"King."

"*No!* Bloody beginner's luck! Double or nothing, eh?"

"Why not?"

Peter drew a seven, Seth a ten. They doubled the stakes again, and this time Peter drew four, Seth a jack.

"Blast! I don't believe it! How much am I into you now, eh?"

"Uh — seven rupees, I guess."

"Double again!"

"Maybe we should make five the limit on one cut, Pete —"

"Don't Jew me down!" He said it without reflection, one of the hundred clichés he'd learned since childhood, but then he noticed the swift reaction of Seth's face. "Oh, good God, I am sorry, old chap — I wasn't thinking —"

"Never mind," Seth said. "Let's not play for money, Pete. It's more fun when we make it a matter of skill, pure and simple. Give me the cards, and I'll teach you a game my old man taught me when I was a kid — it's called Pisha-Paysha."

"You're a bloody blackguard, you know?" Peter replied, laughing boisterously, handing over his deck, paying careful attention to Seth's instructions. . . .

They were still playing, and laughing, when Pasang looked into the tent and announced that the blizzard was stopping, and Hodge was ready to go. They bundled up and went outside. The last of the snow clouds blew over the plateau, like a flag waved to signal the start of an auto race.

The lamasery, rising multitiered and finial-crowned with the cluster of monks' homes nestled against its saffron walls, glistened with snow like a bright-cheeked shepherd surrounded by his fleece-clad flock. The chant of sutras rang through the crystalline air. Kwangde's massif, profligate in the power of its peaks, hovered in sparkling inviolability above this enchanted paradise of scenic beauty. Chomolungma, Mother Goddess of the earth, flung her snow plume eastward, like a tempting nautch dancer hurling aside her veil for monarchs privileged to see her naked face. Ama Dablam, still virginal despite all the suitors who had fought to conquer her perilous profile, speared the sky with a haughty finger of emerald ice. Kangetega towered its pearly gateway to heaven itself, all but obliterating the blue, which peered so timidly over its fluted spikes.

"Good God, it was still worth it, you know — if for nothing more than this bloody view!"

Seth agreed. He had never seen so unspoiled, so primitively perfect a portion of natural splendor anywhere on earth. The Alps seemed almost insignificant, bustling with civilization, by contrast.

"I'm taking Pasang and Yadev with me up to Pangboche," Hodge announced. "I want to see the scalp they've got there. Partridge, you and Goodman reconnoiter this area for the next few days. Try the vicinity of Ama Dablam — Yetis have been reported around there. See if you can pick up a trail. But be back here in four days if you find nothing by then — understand?"

They nodded. The Sherpas had finished loading up.

"You'll have two porters — it's all we can spare. I'll be at the Pangboche monastery if you need me. Got it?"

They had it.

"Okay, let's not burn any more daylight standing still! Good hunting," Hodge shouted, waving to them, as he started off in the fresh ankle-deep snow, followed by his entourage.

"Good God, Seth, I must say I am glad it's just the two of us, you know? I don't bloody well like the way that blackguard keeps barking orders of late!"

"Same here, Pete. God, it feels good to be out of that tent! Great day for a walk really."

"And smell that beautiful air, will you!"

They started toward the Imja valley, side by side, setting a hearty pace.

"Look at this country! It's all ours, you know, far as the bloody eye can see! By God, we are lucky beggars! When I think of people who slave all their blasted lives for a quarter of an acre to call their own —"

"Theirs and the bank they've mortgaged it to."

"Hear, hear! Blast all the bloodsucking banks! What was it Robbie Burns wrote, old boy? 'A fig for those by Law protected' —"

" 'Liberty's a glorious feast!' " Seth chanted.

"That's it, lad! 'Courts for cowards were erected —' "

" 'Churches built to please the priest!' "

"Hurray! Down with the bloody churches to boot! The whole damned Establishment's a fraud for fools to hide under, if you want Partridge's considered opinion! Piss on the prelates of Parliament, old boy — that's what I say — and I hope they bloody well quote me in *The Times!* Up the Outdoors! By God, I feel lucky today. I feel it clear to the marrow of my bones! We're going to find ourselves a Snowman tonight, Seth! Let's track the blackguard down in the dark, eh?"

The Sherpas had begun to look somewhat alarmed by the inordinate shouting of their sahibs, Seth noticed, glancing behind him, smiling with a reassuring wink, which must have only added to the anxiety of those who followed after.

All that day, and most of the night, the next day as well, they climbed, watched and waited like truants on an outing in the backwoods. Nothing it seemed would ever dampen their spirits again, and like bears just emerged from hibernation, like birds newly returned to their natural haunts at the first sign of spring, they raced and flitted about, following every track in the snow, snooping into every crevice in the rocks, examining every sign of Himalayan life, from the lowliest lichen and pelletlike droppings of a mouse hare to the soaring circles of an eagle's flight. They sighted musk deer and a snow leopard, butterflies painted bronze, and a silver fox, which led them a merry chase for several hours. But no Yeti.

"Let's lay out lures for the beast, and wait for him to come to us, old boy."

"If we can catch a few mouse hare, we might give him some bait to boot," Seth suggested. They set several traps near rocks where the pellet droppings were profuse, and caught one rodent to lay near a juniper bush, which they draped with shimmering lures. Then they dug a pit in the snow and loose rock above the lures and covered the opening with a taut nylon net, over which they sprinkled a layer of loose snow. Retreating several hundred yards to a boulder that offered sufficient shelter for both of them, they spread their bedrolls for the nocturnal vigil. They left the Sherpas to camp out of sight, and agreed to spell each other on night watch.

With night the fog rolled in, thick and cold, its blinding billows of moisture closing like steam curtains around them, almost tangible enough to clutch, lung choking, like sand shoveled into an open grave. Nor could they hear any sounds, other than the intermittent and distant rumbling of avalanching ice and stone from the precarious slopes far above. With each major fall the ground trembled, a shuddering reminder of the shifting and tenuous nature of the very landscape itself here at the top of earth's still buckling surface.

"You awake, old boy?" Peter whispered, while one of the more protracted slides continued to make itself felt.

"Yeah, I feel it."

"Good God, do you think we better move?"

"It should stop."

"Sounds as though half of Everest is falling."

"Mountains are a natural amplifying chamber."

"That's a bloody consolation! I wish to Christ we could see what was happening, you know."

"What time is it?"

"Four-forty. Should be light soon, Pete."

"Not soon enough for me, I can tell you! Ah, thank God that one's over!"

"Sh-h-h-h. Did you hear anything?"

"It's my heart, old chap."

"No — *listen.*"

The avalanche had stopped entirely, but they were both wide awake, and strained to detect another sound, a whispering swish, like something dragging its feet through the snow. Seth sat up, silently emerging from his bedroll. Peter was already out of his, on duty. They took flashlights and rifles, and started slowly toward the trap. The fog was so thick that the light beams barely penetrated two steps ahead of their boots. The swishing sound was louder now. It seemed to be coming from the direction of the trap.

Neither of them spoke, but each step they took crunched audibly into the icy crust over the otherwise soft snow. After every few steps they stopped to listen. The sound was still there! But it grew no louder. Seth wondered if they were going in the right direction. He checked his compass, then cupped his hand to his mouth and spoke directly into Peter's ear.

"We better make a dash for it. The trap should be straight ahead. I'm afraid he'll hear us anyway if we keep moving slow —"

Peter nodded. Then bracing themselves, they ran up fast as they could, rifles cocked and held snug under their armpits. The light beams played on the lures dangling mobilelike from the shrub branches. They were panting hard as they searched for the bait.

"It's gone," Peter gasped.

"And there's the culprit's tracks," said Seth, bending close to the beam he held just above the snow. "Wolf."

"Bloody sneak thief!"

"This isn't going to be as easy as we hoped, Pete."

"I'd like to get a blast at his scrawny hide," Peter shouted, shaking his fist at the darkness in the direction of the retreating trail.

"Come on. Let's get some rest. The Sherpas'll be up soon."

"I hate that damned wolf, you know it?"

Seth laughed, a laugh of frustration, not exuberance. Like Peter he felt a sense of futile rage, which began now insidiously to displace the joyous feeling of liberation that only yesterday had animated them both.

Dawn did not dispel the fog. It lifted only slightly as day wore on and they advanced in the direction of Ama Dablam. They became less conscious with each passing hour of the remarkable variety of life surviving at this altitude (they were now above 18,000 feet), and more acutely aware of the overwhelming barrenness of the terrain they traversed. There seemed no limit to the dimensions of emptiness stretching around them. No sooner did they climb to the top of one ridge of rock and snow than there beyond it was another desert expanse revealing more, infinitely more, of the same. The cold, fog-filtered light faded from the sky, and they seemed only to have come to the bleakly inhospitable spot they had left many foot-wearying hours before. It was different, they knew, geographically, but in no other way.

"Good God, old boy, I'm beginning to think we could spend the next twenty years combing this blasted country, and never make more than a bloody dent in its side."

"It gets easier to understand why no one's caught a Yeti, doesn't it?" Seth unbuckled his pack and stretched out on the ground, staring up at the low-hanging mist. "If he exists, I mean."

"Well, he *must* exist — mustn't he? All these damned Sherpas wouldn't just invent him to — just to trick us! And what about the Englishmen who've seen him? *They* wouldn't lie, surely? . . . Good God, he's bound to be around here — somewhere."

"I suppose so."

"Come on, don't say it that way, old boy. It depresses me."

"We make camp here, sahib?" a Sherpa asked.

"Might as well," Peter said. "I've got to get these damned boots off before my toes freeze." He started unlacing his boots, but before the Sherpa could leave to prepare dinner, called out, "Look here, old boy, you believe in this blackguard, don't you?"

"Sahib?"

"The Yeti — the bloody Snowman — whatever the hell you call him —"

"Yeh-Teh," Seth said.

"That's it — the Yeh-Teh!"

"Where, sahib?" The Sherpa looked terrified.

"No, I haven't seen one! Oh, never mind! There's proof enough for you, isn't it, Seth? Just mention the blackguard's name, and it sets their teeth chattering. He *must* exist."

"Why?"

"I just told you why! Oh, what a relief — these blasted toes haven't moved in four hours. Ah-h — that's it, lads, wriggle!"

"No, I mean why do *you* care so much, Pete? Granting for the moment he exists — I expect he does myself — but why is it so important to *you*?"

"What the hell are you talking about now? I wouldn't be walking my bloody toes blue if I believed he *didn't,* would I?"

"I suppose not. Maybe I'm just asking myself."

"Well, I wish to God you'd answer yourself then, and stop getting me all mixed up."

"I wish I could. Six months ago if anyone told me I'd be surveying the Khumbu glacier zone searching for Yetis I'd have said he was crazy. Now I'm beginning to think I must be crazy."

"Look here, old boy, I wish you wouldn't say things like that!"

"Sorry. I guess I'm overtired. Must be this altitude. I don't think I'm really acclimatized."

"No, it's not the blasted altitude." Peter picked up a stone and tossed it angrily downhill. "I know what you mean, old chap! I feel exactly the same way, if that's any help."

"Misery loves company," Seth said, sitting up and staring closely at Pete's apprehensive face. "What made you do it, Pete? Did you really expect we'd find him?"

"God, no. I don't believe I thought very much about that part of it, actually. Just in an offhand way, I suppose, in London. And three years ago perhaps, when Hodge and I first discussed it — this seemed as good a way of getting back to India as any! I had a girl here — Maya — oh, blast her! Of course I thought we'd find him! I still do! Good God, I don't even know what I'm saying anymore! What the devil's got into me? Look here, I thought you were going to answer your own bloody questions. What about you, Seth? You're the professor."

"That's right, Pete. That's why I ask other people questions. It's been a long time since I've had to do any answering myself. It's our method, man — the guild secret." He shook his head, laughing bitterly. "Those who can't answer questions, ask them. And those who can't ask, become administrators!"

"What the hell is that supposed to mean?"

"It's a parody on Bernard Shaw's parody on pedagogy."

"I wish to Christ you'd use a few simpler words."

"That's another guild secret. It's called how to lie with vocabulary. In some things it's too hard to be simple. I guess I've just been running away."

"What from?"

"Me, I suppose. That's the joker. This time I've run so far there's no one left but myself — and you, pal. See what you let yourself in for? Wouldn't you rather have me ask the questions again?"

"No you don't, you blackguard. I don't let my fish off the hook that easily. What the devil are *you* running from? I should have thought you had everything you wanted out of life? Well, it's true, you know. I'm the one they've always accused of running — from work, marriage, family responsibility. Good God, you name it, and Partridge has run from it! Ask any one —" he glanced about as though looking for corroboration "— back there, I mean. Someone who can speak our bloody language. Christ, what a morbid spot we've found ourselves for a picnic! Just like the fields of Sussex, eh? You know what I'd like for dinner now, old chap?"

"A pint of Guinness?"

"Yes, that too. But first I'd like a prime rib of Scotch beef — about so thick, eh?" He gauged his finger spread to a gap of several inches. "Blood dripping from the center, the fat singed brown at the edges — the lovely sort of morsel that makes your mouth juices flow just to see it on the bloody platter, you know? And Yorkshire pudding steaming from the oven, golden crisp at the top but butter soft beneath, moist as a woman, only sweeter — oh, Christ, I am going buggers!" He gnawed at his knuckle and fell silent.

"What did you want to be when you grew up, Pete?"

"Jack Turner — he used to groom the horses up at old Hornsby's place on the knoll. Later, of course, I wanted to be the Duke of Norfolk. And you?"

"A fireman — mostly the one on top of the hook and ladder, the one who does the steering in the back."

"Chang, sahib!" The Sherpa brought them each a bowl of greenish fluid."

"Thanks a lot, old chap! And don't cut my roast beef too thin tonight, eh?"

"Sure, sahib," he responded politely, grinning.

"Well — cheers!"

"Lachaim."

"I keep forgetting you're Jewish, you know."

"Everyone does. It's my hair color. I'm a throwback to some Prussian baron who took his *droit du seigneur* seriously."

"No, I think it's just that the Jews I knew were all scrawny money-grubbers — you know what I mean, don't you?"

"Too well, I'm afraid. Pete, you're an anti-Semite. I've been meaning to tell it to you now for a long time."

"Oh, Christ!"

"He was Jewish."

"What? Good God, I suppose He was at that, eh? But look here, I've never been a bloody bigot, you know. I've slept with women of every color, race, and religion —"

He said it so earnestly, Seth couldn't keep from smiling.

"Forget it, Pete, some of my best friends are anti-Semites." The subject seemed somehow ludicrous, and purely academic, here in the barren heart of Yeti-land. Seth wondered if animals ever practiced discrimination. "Hey, I just thought of something, Pete. Maybe the Yeti's Jewish! He's a wanderer, after all, keeps to himself — as a matter of fact, even the name Yeti sounds a bit Jewish, doesn't it? I had an aunt named Yetta."

Peter laughed so hard that he spilled half his chang, and Seth soon joined him, till they were both rubbing tears of mirth from their eyes.

"Listen, you blackguard, when Jane and I get married, I want you to be my best man — now what do you say to that?"

"It may ruin your chances of a happy marriage."

"Blast you — I'm serious!"

"In that case, I accept — with pleasure."

"*Sahib, sahib!*"

Both Sherpas came racing toward them, shouting at the top of their ample lung power, pointing frantically up valley in the direction of Ama Dablam.

"What the devil —?" Peter was on his feet, scanning the rocks before the Sherpas reached their side. Seth wrestled with the buckle of his pack, trying to remove his field glasses, for though he strained to see what the Sherpas were pointing at, he could distinguish nothing moving among the boulders above.

"There, there," they kept shouting. "See? *There!*"

"*What?* Dammit, you blackguards, what in hell's name do you see?"

"Yeh-Teh!"

"Where?" Peter started to run up the slope, but stopped after taking several long strides, realizing that he was still in his stocking feet. "Oh, God — blast this snow! Where the hell are my boots?" He returned hastily, brushing the snow off his feet as best he could, rushing to get the boots back on. "Can you see him, old boy?"

Seth had the binoculars to his eyes, but was still trying to focus them properly. The lenses were dusty. He had to pause a moment to wipe them.

"Which way?" he asked the Sherpas. "Where is he now? Point."

But the Sherpas only shrugged, staring mutely in the direction they had earlier been pointing to.

"Have you lost sight of him?" Seth asked, slowly sweeping the area through his lenses.

"They bloody well scared him off with that stupid shouting! Any sign of him, Seth?" Peter tied his laces as quickly as his gloved fingers permitted, then jumped up again, saying, "Let me have a look, eh?"

"Here," Seth said, handing him the binoculars. The light had been fading so fast during the last few minutes that he could hardly make out the contour of the boulders, and saw nothing at all of a creature moving among them.

"Oh, blast, it's too damn dark to see anything through these! Come on, let's get after him. Pack up, men," he told the Sherpas. "We'll eat later."

But neither of them moved.

"Are you blackguards deaf?"

"They won't come, Pete. We'll have to go it alone. Let's not waste time arguing." But while securing his own pack, Seth did address the sullenly silent Sherpas, asking them in their own language if they were certain that what they had seen was a Yeti. They nodded their affirmation, insisting they had seen a large, dark creature, moving on two legs among the rocks. It was a "Yeh-Teh." Seth ordered one of the Sherpas to leave for Pangboche immediately, to walk all night at as brisk a pace as possible, to inform

Hodge and Pasang of what he had seen, and lead them back to this spot with fresh supplies. He told the other man to remain here, adding, "If we're not back tomorrow, you come after us — understand?" He nodded, but appeared none too happy about the latter prospect.

"Okay, Pete, let's not waste any more time! Have you got enough stores to hold out for a day up there?"

"I better have, you bloody Semite! Here we go, lad!"

"Here we go," Seth repeated.

Off they went.

CHAPTER 32

"I do not know when it comes to us," Father Nyima said, fingering his beads as he spoke. He sat cross-legged on the luxurious folds of the thick skin which draped the Abbot's throne. His finely lined yellowish face was luminous, the texture of clarified butter. The wisps of his Mandarin goatee, like the penciled strokes of his mustache, were white. No trace of hair emerged beneath the curved line of his scarlet cap, the high-peaked lama headdress, whose long narrow earflaps lay folded back across his shoulders, revealing their golden silk lining. His gaze, fixed upon Hodge, was unwavering, infinitely calm, gentle. "It was here when I was called to Pangboche many years ago."

"I see," Hodge said, focusing again upon the scalp that had been brought to them on a faded pillow and set upon the ornately carved table before the Abbot's throne. Hodge had been obliged to wait less than two hours for this showing. Father Nyima had not forgotten Sir Charles Baker!

"May I examine the scalp more closely, Father?"

"Please do."

It was sparsely covered with short reddish bristles, conically shaped, nearly coming to a point at the top. The skin was parchment dry, shrunk by time, yet the scalp was still large enough to be worn by a man.

"I've never seen anything quite like it," Hodge said.

"There is said to be another at Khumjung lamasery, but I have not looked at that. I do not leave Pangboche." The Abbot must have been at least eighty, though when he smiled he seemed remarkably young. As a reincarnation of the Buddha, his temporal age was considered irrelevant.

"It is kind of you to let me see this scalp, Father Nyima."

"But Dawa Sahib has sent you, my son. He is our greatest benefactor. This building has been repaired many times with the funds he provides. Only convey to him my blessings when you return home."

"Thank you, Father. I will do that, of course. I know he will be most grateful, but I too would like to contribute something to the support of these houses of worship, if you will permit me?"

"Of course — you may buy a butter lamp before you leave."

"I would like to do more, Father. I have one hundred silver rupees here —" Hodge said, removing the string bag from his rucksack, placing it on the table beside the scalp's pillow. He carefully replaced the scalp as well, bowing in namaskara salutation after doing so. He too sat cross-legged, on the woolen mat spread before the upraised throne.

"You are most generous."

"It is only a token."

"We are erecting a new chorten. Your gift will help finish it."

"I am honored, Father."

The Abbot smiled serenely, lifting a small pellet from the ritualistic silver dish at his side, and extending it toward Hodge between his waxlike thumb and forefinger. "Take this, my son. Swallow it."

Without hesitation or question, Hodge consumed the pill as ordered.

"Chitta Adhishtana Abhishinyacha Om," intoned the Lama, beginning the blessing in Sanskrit, but continuing in English. "May life's indestructible essence penetrate your heart! May your perishable body be covered with armor of the seven pure doctrines! May you attain release from the pain of birth and death and rebirth!"

Hodge remained with his head lowered in silence. The mesmeric drone of the Abbot's chant echoed softly in his ears. He inhaled the fragrant incense of sandalwood, and felt strangely tranquil, an almost palpable diffusion of calm spreading with soothing suddenness through his body, as if induced by the dissolution of the sacred pill in his stomach. It happened so swiftly, in fact, transforming his spirit so inexplicably from turbulence to quiescence, that he suspected the pellet he'd taken was a peculiarly potent tranquilizer drug. Surely, he thought, it is some narcotic root or herb. Unless this was a mystic experience, such as those he had known in childhood, mostly in dreams, when he felt himself dissolving, transmuted from form into essence, and waking sensed he was no longer a person with mind, body, and name, but part of the room he slept in, the soil over which it was built. He felt that way at times flying solo. Hodge looked again into the Abbot's eyes.

"Why is it you hunt for the Yeh-Teh, my son?"

"I am not certain yet, Father."

"If you would find yourself you will have no need to seek another."

"Do you know who I am?" Hodge asked impulsively.

"I know what you are."

"But not who?"

"There is no difference."

"Father Nyima, do you believe the Yeh-Teh exists?"

"Only as you and I do."

"Which is?"

"Illusion."

"I see." Hodge became uneasy, impatient, suddenly restless, as though the potion had worn off, and reality flooded back to this ornate, dim room, where he was wasting precious time conversing with an old fool dressed like a circus clown, wrinkled as a monkey. He had seen what he came to see, and was anxious now to be on his way again, but his business was not quite concluded.

"What is it you wish to ask me?" Nyima said, sensing Hodge's hesitation.

"I would like to take this scalp back with me, Father — only for a few months — till it can be analyzed scientifically. No harm will come to it, I assure you. I am prepared to pay the monastery whatever you wish — within reason, of course — for its rental."

"But the scalp is one of our most sacred possessions —"

"I realize that, and I know it is worn once a year at your festival, in April, I believe?"

"That is correct."

"I promise to return it here before then."

"The scalp has never left this village, my son."

"But if we do not find a Yeti, this would be our only concrete evidence —"

The Abbot closed his eyes, raising one hand slowly so that the open palm faced Hodge, like a traffic policeman's signal to stop.

"Forgive me, my son, but it is impossible for me to grant your request."

This time Hodge smiled, cynically, and asked, "Why?"

"Our villagers believe the scalp has magic powers to ward off evil forces. If it left, they would live in constant fear of destruction."

"Do you believe in its powers, Father Nyima?"

"I believe in Buddha-ness."

"But you haven't answered my question."

The old man lifted a small silver bell from the folds of his robe, and tinkled it softly. The monk, who had brought the scalp, entered the sanctuary, head bowed. Nyima asked him to return the relic to its vault.

"I must go now to prayers," he told Hodge.

"If *we're* just illusions, aren't the evil forces that too?" Hodge blurted out, feeling as he always did after finding himself seduced, however temporarily, by institutionalized religious rigmarole, that it was only a hoax designed to trap the gullible. "Well, aren't they?"

"We will speak of it later — if you return, my son."

"I'm leaving today. I have no time to come back for another chat!"

"*Om,*" the Abbot whispered, and rising effortlessly, he stepped from his throne and walked away so quickly that Hodge remained seated on the floor all alone. But a moment later a monk appeared to escort him out of the monastery.

Hodge was burning as he left. He felt as though he'd been lured into an opium den, and rolled, hustled by a Nepalese version of

Fu Manchu! He was no more certain about the scalp's authenticity than he'd been a short while ago about his own identity. The entire sortie here, two days on the trail, two hours more waiting for this interview, seemed a preposterous waste of invaluable time, the stupidest possible diversion! Outside the thick wooden door, squatting in the open air compound, he found Pasang, talking with a Sherpa, who gestured in exaggerated animation as he spoke in strained expletives.

"Sahib, they have seen Yeh-Teh," Pasang reported.

"Who? Where?"

"Near Ama Dablam — he take us."

"Now you're talking, sirdar! Let's get cracking!"

"Yes, sahib — did Father show you scalp?"

"Fuck the scalp. I want the son-of-a-bitch that goes under it!"

CHAPTER **33**

NIELS stared spellbound as the gray leg emerged from a narrow fissure in the snow-covered rock. Quickly it was followed by another leg, and still another. Then the oval-shaped body of the spider itself appeared, hairy as a tarantula. It crept slowly toward him, and whether from the shock of finding anything so small alive at an altitude of twenty-one thousand feet, or because of the lethargy induced by the rarefied atmosphere, Niels did not move away, nor make any preparations to destroy him. He simply stared at the spider, dimly wondering if it might not be poisonous. Just beyond arm's length, it stopped, and Niels thought he could see the beady eye blink, as though it were appraising him.

Suddenly, from the same dark crevice another spider appeared, and the first seemed to back around in order to confront it. Then they moved toward each other, like wrestlers circling for position from which to tackle, and as Niels watched wide-eyed, they meshed legs and bodies in a silent, deadly embrace. Till one collapsed in a gray ball, legs curled inward. The victor paused for a moment over his adversary's corpse, then proceeded to consume the dead spider, till every morsel disappeared. Slowly, like a man made sluggish by a lavish feast, the predatory spider returned to his rock home. Wedging his bloated body through the crack from which it had emerged, he was gone.

"Ach, no trace of him," Bruno sighed, returning from the corniced ridge to their camping shelf on the icy slope. He packed away his binoculars, and removed his gloves, blowing on his fingers as he briskly rubbed his hands together.

"I have just watched something very strange," Niels said, recounting what he saw.

"Yah, this I have heard. Amazing how hardy are these spiders — they live above any other creatures. So! I am sorry I did not see this."

"It was terrible."

"But why? This is how they survive — like cannibals, yah? It is nature's way."

"No, it did not seem natural."

"But if it is the only nourishment they can find — why not?"

"I know. I just did not like it." Niels shuddered, slapping his sides with his arms to help restore circulation. He felt as if he would never be warm again. The sun's slanting rays were like spears of silver, shafts of light without heat. "Bruno, let us go back to camp on the moraine tonight."

"He cannot be far from here," Bruno whispered. "I am positive. You will see —"

"Ah, but this will be our third night in the open, and last night too you were positive —"

"You heard him yourself last night."

"I said I thought I heard him. There was so much wind —"

"No, no, it was him! I hear him clearly — very close."

"Then why have we seen no tracks?"

"He is so shrewd — like a fox! He knows which way we come after him, and each time he goes in a different direction —"

"I am not so sure. Bruno, it may be you imagined —"

"*Nichts!* I swear to you, Niels, the track I saw was so clear as my hand, and his cry which I hear — so sharp as your own voice speaking to me now! You have yourself seen the entrails —"

"Yes, but how do we know who left them? It could have been an eagle."

"Eagles do not leave such things behind. An eagle would carry the entire rodent to his nest. No, we must not give up! We are too close! Trust me — one more day, Niels! I promise to you if we do not find him by this time tomorrow, we turn back — yah?"

"Yes, I suppose one more day —"

"Good! But listen, we must rest now and hunt tonight. Now we are high enough, it will be clear, and the moon is more than half full — the snow remains light —"

"But the wind is much stronger at night —"

"We will go carefully, use rope. It is better than to lie here and freeze like last night."

"All right."

"Good! Good, so now we make a fire, yah, and eat something! You will see tonight, Niels — you will not be sorry," Bruno assured him, busying himself with lighting the small burner, setting the pressure cooker with its tea upon the faint bluish flame.

They huddled mothlike over the tongue of light, warming their fingertips on the aluminum vessel, which slowly absorbed some heat. It was a painfully slow process, even getting the liquid slightly warm under pressure. They sucked sugar cubes while they waited, as the sun slipped behind the sharp ridge and the frozen wind of dusk began to swirl flurries of snow overhead. A rug of dense cloud hid the valleys below them from sight, and as far as the eye could see there was no vegetation or sign of life. Only purplish peaks of fluted ice, windswept rock, and the cold clarity of sky. The tingling warmth of the pressure cooker made Niels tremble and feel colder than he had before. He drew his hands away from the flame and buried them in his fleece-lined mittens, but the fleece was tight and cold. His face felt numb. The wind burned against his eyeballs, and a dull, dizzy pressure lashed at his temples.

"Bruno, even if we found him — how could we get him down from here?"

"With rope."

Niels glanced at the icy slope descending to the clouds several thousand feet below. They had been forced to cut steps up the last thousand feet, and the idea of belaying a rope with so much dead weight dangling from it down that slope, without toppling after it themselves, seemed more than preposterous.

"I think it would be insane to try."

"Never mind — this is logistics. First let us find him —"

"But what is the use, if we trap him, and find ourselves trapped?"

"So Niels, you are afraid of death after all?"

Afraid of death? The question jolted him. Until now, he should have found it remarkably easy to answer with a loudly proclaimed "No!" He had always feared life, not death — the tests, and tortures, the trials, and frustrations of life. These frightened him. Not death surely!

"No, I do not think I am afraid to die."

"You are afraid even to admit it?" Bruno's smile was as tauntingly sarcastic as his rebuttal. "Yah, it is never easy, my dear Niels. Sometimes the more we want something the harder it becomes to admit —"

"Why are you so eager for me to kill myself?" His eyes narrowed as he watched Bruno, and instinctively he moved a bit closer to the rock wall.

"No, my dear, you misunderstand me. This is not at all my desire. I talk only of fear and courage in the abstract. This pistol, which I carry, for example —" He removed the automatic from his pocket, and held it lightly in his hand, the barrel aimed, quite by chance it seemed, at Niels. "Tell me, dear friend, which would you say takes more courage — to fire it, or to be fired upon?"

Niels stared at the black barrel's orifice, pointing directly now at his face, and his tongue was like stone in his mouth. He could utter no sound, feeling as he had when the spiders emerged, too fascinated, too terrified, to move a muscle or speak.

"But tell me, my dear, which do you guess? Why do you not speak, Niels? It is only a game, yah? To pull this trigger — who must be braver, you or I? Ach — you will not even guess?"

Bruno's laugh was that of a madman, and hearing it Niels felt certain it would, ironically enough, be the last sound but one he would ever hear on this earth. Yet even as he was thinking that, Bruno tossed the gun into his lap, and shouted, "So now, comrade, you point it at me, yah?"

264

He looked down at the gun, which had landed innocently on his lap, hardly able to believe it could suddenly seem so harmless. Shrugging, he set it aside, out of Bruno's reach.

"I do not like — such games," he muttered.

"I find them amusing."

"Yes, I see you do."

"You have sensitive lips, Niels."

"I beg your pardon?"

"Your mouth — the shape of your lips. I just remark how sensitive this is. Does it shock you, what I say?"

"No — uh — is the tea ready, do you think?"

"Yah, of course, the tea!"

Watching Bruno pour the tea in the fading light, Niels remembered the pockmarked German guard in their prison camp, who always said a few words to him when he came for his bowl of soup. He was a bull-necked, thick-featured man, with bushy black hair curling up over his neckline, the last sort of person Niels would have thought of as a homosexual. . . . And he remembered the first captain he had sailed with as cabin boy — "Never mind the polishing, boy. Come over here where I can get a good look at you! Ah, yes, I like the curve of those lips!"

"Why do you look so at me, Niels?"

"Oh, I did not mean to — I — thank you."

"Skoal!" Bruno clicked steaming cups, draining his own at one long gulp. "You are afraid of me?"

"No."

"Good. That is good! You have no reason to be!" He sat close to Niels, tapping his knee with a smile of reassuring camaraderie, but Niels shifted his position, moving his leg out of Bruno's reach. "We better try to get some sleep, yah? Another hour will be dark."

There was not much room on the ice shelf for their bedrolls. Bruno insisted they set them close together — to protect themselves best from the wind. Niels closed his eyes, but could not sleep.

"Ach, it is cold! Br-r-r, that wind — it cuts through me like a knife!"

Niels said nothing. He had placed his ice axe within easy reach of his hand.

"Niels, there is room for two of us inside one of these rolls, yah? I think unless we share body heat, we both freeze to death! Come, let us try."

"No, thank you."

"You are not cold?"

"I have been warmer, of course."

"So come, do not be a fool! I come into your roll, yah?"

"No, stay where you are."

"But why? This is how half the German army survived the Russian winter —"

"I am not in the German army."

"There is not so much difference between us, my dear Niels, as you pretend. I was myself born in Schleswig-Holstein — so I am at least half Dane, yah?"

Bruno laughed softly, then waited, but as Niels said nothing, he continued his monologue, "Why are we so afraid, all of us, to be what we are? From Hellenic times to our own, my dear, the greatest artists, the noblest geniuses, have all been men, lovers of beauty for its own sake, not slaves to some blind force of evolution, which dictates that passion and procreation are one and the same force of life! This is for the idiot herd, Niels, not for men like us. We see beauty everywhere, yah? In sound, in color, in a symphony, a pastoral scene — why not in a man's lips as well as a woman's breast? Do you listen to me, Niels?"

His fingers trembled as they touched Niels's forehead, running gently, swiftly, down his cheek, to caress the startled lips —

"I warn you, Bruno, leave me alone!"

"So there is much fire in you yet, my beauty!"

"And stop talking to me as if —"

"As if?"

"You know very well what I mean, Bruno!"

"You are the most beautiful man I have ever met, Niels — I love you. I —"

Niels gripped the smoothly oiled stem of his axe, deftly swinging it around so that its polished steel point was aimed directly at Bruno's chest. He held it poised like a spear in that position, and neither his arm nor his voice wavered as he warned, "If you try to touch me again, Bruno, I'll kill you."

266

Bruno laughed, less taunting than terrified it sounded, but his words, when at last they were spoken, were more trenchant than apprehensive. "So now you have the courage to kill, yah? You are not afraid now? Or is it fear which makes you so strong? Tell me, Niels, which will take more courage, for you to hurl the spear, or for me to absorb it? Who was the braver, the crucifier or Christ? When you have killed me, will you carry me down to place me on a cross, or do you leave me here for our friend to find and disembowel?"

"Why are you torturing me, for God's sake — what do you want?" He tossed the axe angrily out of reach, and crept from his bedroll, pacing the narrow shelf, slapping his back with his arms.

"All love is torture."

"You are insane! And stop using that word to me! I am not — what you think! You have guessed Ulla killed herself because I did not sleep with her — that is true! But it was not because — I have never had relations with any man either! Once in Africa I was sick. The fever has made me impotent, and ever since then I have lost all interest in —"

The wind kept howling as he spoke, but it was another sound entirely which interrupted his confession. The cry was unmistakably clear, and from its volume sounded almost as though it came from just over the corniced ridge above them.

Bruno was on his feet, strapping his pack secure even before the wailing ended. He lashed his crampons to his boots, and Niels hastily did the same. They fastened a nylon line to their waist ropes, draped the rifles around their necks, and taking their ice axes in one hand, flashlights in the other, started off, Bruno in the lead.

They clambered to the ridge without much strain, for the double line of steps Bruno had hacked out on his earlier reconnaissance was still perfectly firm. The corniced top was bluish gray in the light of the half moon, and curved off toward a col that led to a craggy peak several thousand feet above. The problem was trying to see below the shimmering edge of ice on which they stood, without moving so far out on the cornice as to risk a massive break that would hurl them into an abyss of darkness. From their present vantage point they had a clear view in every direction but that in which the sound seemed to have originated. Treading warily along the ridge, Bruno stopped to tap at the ice just beyond his weight, inching farther toward the ravine side.

Then they heard the cry again, and this time there seemed no doubt but that it came from just below them. There were really only two ways of getting a view of the underside of that cornice — or rather, in realistic climbing terms only one, namely to traverse the col and work their way along the inside slope of the higher peak by any of several precarious ridges, then to look back. The trouble, of course, was that the distance was too great for their flashlight beams to carry, and unless the moonlight was sufficiently clear under the cornice, they might see nothing but shadowy rock after going so far away. The other alternative was sheer madness, for it would involve crawling to the bitter edge of the windswept top in order to peer over. The risks involved in such a venture were so great that no mountaineer in his right mind would ever seriously consider attempting it. Yet Niels knew as he watched Bruno retracing his steps toward him, that he was going to suggest the impossible.

"I am sure he is down there," Bruno said, pointing with his axe directly below them.

"It may be."

"Yah, it is positive. So this is what must be done. We use two ropes, and both axes to belay me. Mine I bury so — here!" He raised the axe by its head, chest high at arm's length, thrusting it into the ice and snow like a pile driver, plunging his full weight behind it, sinking it almost to the very top of its shaft into the white ground. Though they were at least fifty feet from the edge, Niels half expected the cornice to collapse under the impact of that blow. "So!" Bruno grinned with satisfaction as he strained with all his weight upon the buried axe, which stood like a pole rooted in cement. "Good and solid, yah? Now the rope —" He deftly secured a spare line to the shaft, testing his knot this time by leaning back and tugging as hard as he could, the rope wrapped several times around his leather gloves. The other end of the line he fastened to his waist cord carabiner.

"Come Niels, now you belay from here," he said, pacing off five lengthy strides on a parallel line from the buried axe.

"You are not seriously thinking of crawling out there, Bruno."

"Of course, I am serious. There is no other way! Come — quickly — before he can escape!"

"It is insanity. The cornice will not hold your weight."

"It may," Bruno insisted. "Hurry — we have no choice!"

"We can go there — to the peak —"

"No, it is too far!"

"But what good will it do to see him, if you yourself are killed in the process?"

"Would this matter, Niels — to you?" He hesitated.

"It should matter more to you!"

"Yah, but it does not, you see," Bruno answered, grinning. "Once I believed we Germans are Supermen — that nothing on earth can resist our conquest. I try to immortalize this belief in music, yah? Then I find it is myth. We are beaten in battle, and for myself the music is dead. Still I think, perhaps anyway life is worth the effort — at any price, yah? I lie to myself, to Lotte, to the whole world — for what? To live. To exist. To survive! For what? This is not to me enough, my dear! I hide enough for one lifetime — so tonight I admit to you what I feel, what I want. In you there is all what I once was — perhaps together we could —"

"Bruno, it is not possible!"

"So!" He shrugged, and the grin disappeared from his face, the light of hope from his eyes. "Then let me at least try alone to capture what has never been caught, to prove —" He stared vacantly toward the edge that plummeted into nothingness.

"That you can kill yourself?"

"Perhaps, yah! Or — possibly that what no one believes can exist on this planet, does not only live, but is almost human, like I myself feel at times — a separate species — man that is not man alone — a new variety of sentient life. Possibly if I could conquer him, Niels — then I could find new reason for myself to continue, to try — I don't know what! But I cannot give up until I have done all what is possible to see —"

"And if there is nothing to see beyond that ledge?"

"You have heard him at least twice now yourself!"

"Unless it is the wind in some peculiar natural formation of the rock — passing through some resonating chamber — who knows what has made that sound?"

"You know as well as I do, my dear Niels. But you fear as much to find him as you do yourself."

"No, that is false!"

"Is it so? Then belay your axe, and let me try —"

"No. I would only be a party then to your death —"

"Ach! Then I go without your line! I use this rope alone, if it makes you feel less guilty!" He started toward the edge.

"Wait! I give up! But at least you must rig some Prusik slings first —"

"Yah, of course," Bruno agreed, smiling victoriously as he returned, looping the second rope around his thighs before playing it out to Niels's belayed axe. By the time he was finished he looked like a telephone repairman climbing to fit a new line atop a pole. They used a hundred-foot line for Niels's axe, rigging it double as a pulley, so that in fact there were three nylon ropes to hold Bruno's weight, and it was possible, even if the cornice collapsed under him, that he might be held firm, though Niels doubted if he would have sufficient strength at this altitude to drag Bruno back to the top.

He was not even certain, of course, that from the distance at which he remained, he himself was safe from going over, should a crack develop sufficiently far back. Cornices were notoriously deceptive, he knew, and many built up over time to a distance of twenty or thirty yards beyond the base of rock support. The snow and ice seemed solid enough right now, but as Bruno dropped to a prone position, and started crawling on his belly closer to the edge, Niels leaned back on his axe handle and mutely, barely consciously, began to pray.

He had not before realized, not fully at any rate, how much he still desired to live. So tenacious was the grip of life, that for all it had cheated him of joy, passion, desire, enough that was sweet remained to make him appeal devoutly, contritely, for a stay of execution now, a reprieve from the plunge to an icy grave. Just now, when death seemed closer, more probable, than ever before, the strangest sensations came to taunt him with tempting reminders of life — the taste of Tuborg, chilled and slightly acerbic, assailed his tongue, the sight of Tivoli through the trees on a clear night, the smell of the sea beyond landfall, where the air was washed clean of all impurities, the smiles and laughter of school girls running with their bags of books dangling from their shoulders and pigtails flying, the conversations with old Borg, the magic emergence of a photograph's dim outline from paper that a moment before had looked blank. If only there were some way of assuaging the guilt he felt about Ulla — life could become more than just bearable . . .

He kept the line taut as Bruno inched forward, feeling the strain of wind, whose velocity seemed to increase, perversely enough, lashing at Bruno's ballooned jacket and trousers, trying to hurl him off into space. But the cornice itself was holding! Bruno's arm reached out to the bitter knife edge of snow, and he actually peered over —

Then Niels heard the cry of the Yeti once more, louder than it had sounded before, more terrifying in its urgency and intimacy, like the greeting of recognition at the sight of a mate.

He shuddered, as the ground below him did. The crack was like a thunderclap reverberating from the mountain walls, echoing in the valleys below. He felt the world giving way, tilting off under his very toes. His arms strained helplessly at the axe that was toppling forward. He pulled desperately at the nylon rope, till his fingers felt as if they were coming off with his glove that jerked free. He saw Bruno's legs pointed skyward, and heard the shout that sounded like Bruno's voice, but was no more comprehensible to his ears than the call of the Yeti.

Niels lunged backwards, toppling, he thought, into the abyss, so swiftly did he fall, sliding back down the slope over ice on which he plummeted with toboggan speed, till he managed to kick in his crampon spikes, bringing himself at last to a back-burning halt. He was too dizzy to move, and felt for a while totally paralyzed, wondering vaguely if he had broken his spine, feeling a dull, numb pain at the base of his skull, where his head had banged hard against the slope. Still the cracked cornice echoed its thunderous fall, like a chorus of kettledrums hammered out by a pantheon of vindictive gods, heralding a Judgment Day already begun.

Now silence. More awesome than the noise had been. Awful in its fullness, its totality. This is how the grave must sound, he thought, from inside the coffin, to ears devoid of life. But his eye caught the brilliant glimmer of a star. Slowly, painfully, moving first one arm, then one leg, lifting his head a bit, then sitting up, Niels returned to life. His hand, which had lost its glove, was bleeding, and more than anything else the sight of that blood, pulsating weakly from his wrist, proved to him he was not dead. He squinted up the slope, blinking snow from his eyes, and though he had no axe anymore he knew that first of all he had to climb back to that ridge. It was the most painful climb he had ever assayed, and with each step he painted the mountain red, clutching at ice with bare fingers that felt nothing at all after a while. He panted smoke and lay practically flat upon the steep slope, pushing himself up by the claws of his crampons, wedging his knees into the tough brittle crust of bluish white.

The top was a gaping semicircle, a yawning mouth opened wide, where but a few moments before he and Bruno had stood so solidly secure. Both axes were gone. He crept to the very rim, for now it was strong enough, rising straight above the arête of solid stone, to hold an army of climbers. He peered down. The wall of white was like marble, freshly quarried, plunging for a hundred feet or so, and under that a grayish haze of flurrying snow.

And under that Bruno, he thought. Bruno, and his Yeti — if it was ever there. Then he quickly drew back, for vertigo had seized him, and he sensed that in another second he too would have plunged. He had to lie flat and perfectly still, eyes closed, till the nausea passed, and he could begin the long climb down. But not tonight, he decided, content merely to reach the ledge from which they had started barely an hour ago. He crawled into his sleeping roll, and pulled the hood closed over his head, trembling with cold, pressing his lame hand very tightly with his good one, trying at once to stop the bleeding and restore some warmth to the fingers that had lost all feeling.

He dreamed of the spider, who shared his ledge, crawling toward him — its face was Bruno's.

CHAPTER 34

SETH and Peter searched the icefall around the base of Ama Dablam's spire for tracks of the Yeti the Sherpas claimed to have seen from the moraine below. They searched in ever-widening rings for several hours, but to no avail. Nightfall made their task as haphazard and frustrating as the jumbled boulders of ice made it arduous.

"This is hopeless, Pete," Seth said, stopping and futilely shaking his head as his flashlight beam played on the tracks left by their own boots a few minutes before. "We're going in circles. I'm afraid he's lost us."

"If we could only get a whiff of the blackguard! He's supposed to stink to high heaven, isn't he?"

"So they say."

"Good God, it's like walking in a deep freeze up here! Look at the size of these bloody ice blocks, will you! Any one of them could preserve all the meat used in Partridge Green for a sweltering summer, you know? If we could only work out some way of transporting these lovelies, we'd both be rich as Rothschild, old boy! Or is that an anti-Semitic remark, too? Christ, you've got me afraid to open my blithering mouth anymore!"

"You sound inhibited."

"Actually, I expect I am, you know. What the devil is that, do you suppose?" Peter had been surveying their new locale with his flashlight, and held it steady on a triangular opening that seemed at first sight to be nothing more than a crack at the base between two leaning seracs. But as he walked closer to the aperture it looked more like the mouth of a cave.

"Hullo, anybody home?" he called, squatting to peer inside. "Good God, what a stench!" He backed off, pinching his nostrils, then turned, calling in excitement, "Say, old boy, look here!"

Seth was already carefully examining the ground in front of the low entrance to the lair, and in even more breathless a voice of discovery, exclaimed, "Pete, look at these tracks!"

There were several clear imprints, roughly the size of their boot-marks, but with what appeared to be toes in front — leading away from the cave entrance.

"Good God, they look human!"

"I think you've found his home, Partridge! You've sure as hell got a nose for hunting. Careful, he may be there!"

"That's right, by God, maybe you better take the lead! No, hold on! We'll flip for it — I have a two-headed chip here —" He reached instinctively into his pocket for the roulette chip, but found instead Jane's crucifix, and remembering their parting exchange of gifts, paused, looking disheartened.

"What's the matter, Pete?"

"Oh — nothing. Never mind. Come on, I'll go first."

He managed to squeeze through the entrance in a crouching position, and watching Peter do so, Seth reflected that had a man been in need of a cave around here, he could hardly have chosen a more appropriate one. Creeping into the ice tunnel himself, Seth was all but overwhelmed by the pungently powerful odor. Not even the sweat- and urine-soaked platforms of Calcutta's central station exuded such repulsive fumes, and meeting them here in a chamber composed of ice, Seth knew that its resident could not long have abandoned his cave. Though it was, they found, quite empty now, but for a scattering of juniper branches, strewn about at the far end of the oblong cavity.

"Good God, the blackguard brought up his own bed! Will you look at these, old boy — he must have dragged them a bloody mile!"

"It's not the softest mattress in the world, but better than sleeping on ice," Seth mused. "He's a clever devil all right. But let's not waste any more time in here, Pete. We should be able to follow those tracks. From the smell of this place he can't be too far."

274

"You sound less skeptical now, old boy!"

"Stop gloating, Pete. We haven't found him yet."

"Granted. But look here, you don't think this is the home of a mouse hare, do you?"

"No, but it could belong to a langur monkey, or a red bear."

"Blast your erudition, you blackguard!"

"I must admit though, I'm weakening!" Seth confessed. "Come on!"

Creeping out of the cave, Seth felt almost as if he were transported back through time to an age of glacial ice, an eon primitive and remote, when man had none of the tools, none of the techniques, that catapulted him from cave dwellings to the jet era of nuclear energy. He felt more intensely conscious of his weakness and isolation than he ever had, blinking out at the barren enormity of the cold landscape which enveloped him. Hunched over as he followed the trail, moving like an inchworm before the narrow beam of his light, he was acutely aware of extra demands now imposed upon his senses, grown dull by centuries of disuse, weakened by reliance upon all the crutches of civilized existence, overexposed and underdeveloped at the same time, his ears, and eyes, his olfactory buds, and tactile perceptors, so crucially needed now were, like his flat teeth, virtually deadened by disuse. His sole superiority over the creature he trailed came from what was really external to himself — his gun, his net, his ice axe, his flashlight, none of which he, Seth Goodman, had made! Without these, and the heavy boots he wore, the warm clothing that covered his naked skin, he would have been helpless as a monkey turned loose in a modern factory. So with his empathy for the Snowman came a heightened sense of difference, a sobering awareness of the powers and plight of this creature — whoever he was — who slept in an icebox on juniper branches, and wandered barefoot over terrain that would have torn through any modern man's soles.

How had it happened, Seth wondered, at the dawn of man's climb up the ladder of evolution that the Yeti's ancestors alone were trapped in this wilderness of snow, this frozen attic of earth's fecund mansion, destined to vegetate here for eternity, while his more salubriously located brothers shared the feast of nature's bounty, evolving to challenge the very solar system itself for command of the universe and all its planetary orbs? Why him, and not me? Was it by accident? Or design?

The cosmogonic questions which had haunted Seth as a child returned as he followed vague footprints in the snow, shaking his confidence in all the glib axioms he'd so long accepted as answers to the riddle of cause and creation. In the beginning — What? How? Why? Whence? Whither? For some years his answer had been an old man seated in the sky, white-bearded, wise-eyed, all-seeing, all-knowing, omnipotent as well. But why then had his mother been permitted to die? So the celestial throne became vacant, and the earthworm instead created life. But who put the Yeti here, and me there? And why must I track him now, in the night, half frozen, panting thin air, myself and Peter alone?

The trail led past blocks of solid ice bigger than the bus that had taken them from Maharani's, over crevasses too wide for them to jump across (though the Yeti did), that if not for their aluminum ladder would have halted their onward march. Up they labored toward the frozen fang of Ama Dablam, coldly imperious, indifferent, aloof, hanging over them it seemed in defiance of gravity. Or were the laws of lower places known up here? Seth felt as if he too were weightless, but barely able to move nonetheless, as if his body buoyed by reduced pressure above it lost its resistance to air, just when the air itself virtually ceased to energize his blood. He moved as though in a dream, effortlessly lifting his legs, yet apparently standing in the same spot. His head seemed to float, it felt so light. He was floating toward the beam of brightness shining clear upon the blue-gray ice. . . .

"All right, old boy?" Peter was grinning down at him, holding a crushed handkerchief close to his nostrils.

"What happened?"

"You passed out. It's the altitude. Take it slow, eh?"

"Oh. I'm fine — don't worry — no need to —" He tried to get back on his feet, but no sooner was he nearly vertical than his knees buckled again.

"Good God! No more heroics! Slow down, Seth. Let's just take a bit of a rest here, shall we? Lovely little cemetery this would make, wouldn't it?"

"Terrific. We oughta buy a few lots before the word gets around — Phew, did I really black out?"

"Like London in the Blitz!"

"How 'bout that? I felt great —"

"That's just what my friends on pot tell me, you know. I hope you start feeling miserable again soon!"

"It's coming back — never fear. Ouch, I think I hit my forehead. Any blood showing?"

"No," Peter said, examining his skull, "but there's a bloody big crack in the ice where you went down!"

"Yeah, my dean's always called me a hardhead. Hey, where in hell do you suppose he's taking us to, Pete?"

"The bloody top, I guess. Have a chocolate bar — Cadbury's best."

"You're a sport, Pete — and a patriot."

"Right, lad. Up the Queen, that's my motto!" He laughed and did a fast soft-shoe type of tap. *"Yeow!"* Grimacing with pain, he suddenly collapsed.

"What the devil's got you?"

"Don't know — my bloody foot — good God!" He gripped his left ankle with both hands, keeping his foot off the ice like a lame dog on the run. "I really didn't mean any disrespect to Her Majesty, God! I knew as soon as I said that — ow-w-w!"

"Better take off your boot, Pete."

"On this ice? You're buggers! I'd freeze my toes —"

"Just for a minute," Seth insisted, focusing his light on the snow-caked boot Peter kept so gingerly off the ground. "Let me help you —"

"Blast! I'm not that old, damn you! Ow!" He had set the boot down carefully, and began unlacing the leather thong. "I think I just strapped this blackguard too tight, you know! That feels better already."

"Take it all the way off, Pete."

"What in God's name for? There's nothing wrong with my toes!"

"I didn't say there was."

"But you were thinking it, damn you! Admit it!"

Seth could tell from Peter's tone of defensive hostility that the pain was far worse than Partridge was willing to admit, especially to himself. He moved closer with the light, but said nothing.

"All right — just because you're a bloody don, you think you can bully me, eh? Well, if it'll make you happy —" He removed the lace entirely and bent open the sides, but could not extricate his foot from the boot, though he tugged hard, with his jaw muscles pulsating through his cheeks, beads of cold sweat knurling his forehead.

"Let me help," Seth whispered, touching the heel gently.

"Say, old boy — take it easy, will you?"

"I'll try not to hurt you too much, Pete. Steady — there!"

It was worse than he'd feared. The bottom of Peter's sock had frozen solid against the inner sole of the boot, tearing itself away from the rest as the swollen foot came free. A layer of callused flesh remained inside the boot, exposing a ragged circle of bluish underskin at the ball of his instep.

"Well, what in hell's it look like, eh? Speak up, blast you! That sick stupid smirk on your face is bloody well worse than anything you can tell me, you know! Ouch!"

Seth had begun removing the wet socks.

"Good God, are you trying to get me frostbitten?"

"Afraid you've beat me to it, Pete."

"I have, eh?" He asked it very quietly. "Looks *that* bad, does it?"

"Maybe not," Seth said, relenting at the bluntness of his verdict, though from what he saw the only question was how far the frostbite had advanced, not whether or not it had started. "Hard to tell with the socks on, Pete. I better cut them away. We'll get something warm and dry around your foot — otherwise —"

"Right! No pictures, old boy! Go to it. Just hurry it up, eh?"

"Want some morphine first?"

"No, no, I'm set! Get on with it, you blackguard."

He had no scissors in his pack. Seth worked with the blade of his jackknife, removing his gloves to manipulate it best, yet unable to keep his hands from trembling. The knife kept digging into Peter's leg, and as he got lower on the foot the frozen socks peeled off with pieces of pasty white skin. He was forced to bite his own lips and swallow often to keep from gagging as he worked, and could only marvel at Peter's stamina in not uttering one cry of anguish.

278

"Don't be ashamed to scream, Pete. It might help."

"But I don't feel any bloody pain, you know."

"Oh — well, that's good," he said, knowing it was in fact the opposite. From the color of the toes and the pasty quality of the skin torn off he saw it was really too late, even if they could have reached some medical aid station within a day. But that would take closer to a week from here!

Hastily Seth removed his jacket and pullover sweater.

"What the devil are you trying to do — get 'frostbelly'?"

"Shut up and lie still — I'm the doctor, remember!"

He stripped off the fleece-lined sweater he wore closest to his torso, and swathed Peter's leg in it, then quickly redressed.

"Thanks, old boy — that's bloody well Christian of you!"

"You're not the first one to accuse me of that!" He was reminded of Rena's taunts, the first time he'd followed her to her room. When was that? Surely not in this lifetime, he thought. Not on this planet!

"Better have a look at the other foot too, old boy! I'm afraid I got them both a bit wet when those blackguard Sherpas sighted the Yeti! Good God, you'd think I'd have brains enough to realize something like this would happen, wouldn't you?"

"You'll be all right, Pete. I've got a dry pair of socks in my pack. We'll get the other one cleaned up and start back just as soon —"

"But I can't feel a thing in those toes, you know? I can't bloody well move them!"

"That's just temporary, Pete. As soon as we get back to camp, and a decent fire —"

"You're humoring me now, aren't you?"

"No! Honest, Pete, I've heard of lots of cases of frostbite much worse than yours. They have all sorts of new medical techniques —"

"That's rot, and you know it! You don't believe a word of that, any more than I do! Good God, am I going to lose my toes?"

"Hold still, Pete, so I can —"

"Why bother? It's too late to do any good!" He jerked his leg free, and tried to get up, though the fleece sweater was only loosely wrapped about the bootless foot, which could take none of his weight, leaving him to fall back, flaying his limbs on the ice like a helpless flounder dropped onto the deck of a fishing vessel. "I'm a bloody cripple! I can't even stand!"

"Pete, please control yourself! We've got a long walk back —"

"Walk? How the hell am I supposed to walk, tell me?"

"I'll help you! But unless you calm down and let me, we won't get back —"

"It's *his* fault," Peter said, staring wild-eyed toward the toothy top of the mountain. "You've done this to me, you blackguard! The least you can do is let us get a look at your ugly face! You damned bastard! Come down here!" In helpless rage he shook his fist at the shadowy whiteness.

"Pete, save your energy, will you."

"Ah-h-h-h," he sighed, like a balloon deflated, slumping round and sitting crestfallen and contrite, his legs lying limp on the snow. "What a God-awful senseless way to end!"

"Hey, come on, none of that talk, Pete! Even if you have to lose a toe or two, that's not going to —"

"I'll lose the bloodless lot," he whispered, no longer offering any resistance as Seth carefully put on the dry sock, slitting its side first, then using adhesive strips to keep it in place as he worked at replacing the boot. "Do you enjoy dancing, Seth?"

"Me? Christ no — Stella used to try to teach me — I am too clumsy — no rhythm," he lied.

"I used to love it, you know! Folk, ballroom, the blasted lot! Damned well good at it too —"

"Listen, brother, you and Jane are going to do more dancing after we get back to Delhi —"

"You've got a Christian heart, Seth."

"Peter, to me that is not necessarily a compliment."

"Coming from this anti-Semite it is!" Then he smiled, as boyish and bright a grin as Seth ever saw on Peter's face, and he removed his right glove to offer his bare hand. "Thanks, Seth — for everything! Now go on — get the hell out of here, before it's too late for you!"

"What are you talking about? I'm not going anyplace without you! Look — just shut up! You listen, I'll talk!"

"It's no use, Seth. You won't go anyplace *with* me — not in this bloody shape, old boy. I'm a cripple! As it is you might not make that damn crevasse back there alone, but at least you'll have a fighting chance."

"Negative! We go back the way we came — *together*. Now come on, Pete, on your feet — hold my neck! Tighter!"

Seth dragged him to his feet, all but carrying him for several lung-bursting paces, but no sooner did they reach the first narrow fault in the icefall than he sensed that Peter's appraisal of their plight was far sounder than his own. He could not possibly make the jump with Peter on his back, and by now Peter had lost all feeling in both feet, was unable to command them to act independently.

"Never mind," Seth insisted. "We'll use the damn ladder over every crack." He extracted the separate parts from his gear and fitted them firmly together, laying the ladder as a bridge across the flaw, jumping to the far side first, then shouting back, "Come on, Pete! You can make it — crawl —"

"Leave me alone, old boy — I've had it —"

"Crawl!" He tugged anxiously at the rope that linked them, fearing depression and lassitude would tempt Peter to lie down on the ice, to succumb entirely. A few hours at this temperature, without motion or shelter, would be enough to kill him!

"Go on alone, Seth. Be a good chap, eh — bring that bloody Sherpa back for me tomorrow — I'll wait right here."

"I can't make it without you, Pete! I'll get lost!"

"You're a bloody liar!"

"Please, Peter — try!" He kept pulling steadily at the line, holding his breath as he watched Peter start across the ladder. It was like the first time Ethan had pushed to his knees in the playpen and started slowly, precariously toward the bars — as weak, as tortured and tenuous as that. At this rate, he knew, it would take all night for them to get back as far as the Yeti's cave. "Atta boy, Pete, you're doing great!"

Peter dragged his lame legs off the ladder and collapsed panting on the ice. Seth pulled the ladder across and broke it down again. He too gasped for air, and saw pinwheels of color whirling before his eyes. He had to rest for a moment on his haunches.

"Any smokes left, old boy?"

"Sure."

"Thanks. Look here, I'll make a bargain with you, Seth. You

leave me these weeds, eh, and I'll keep warm puffing them, while you go back for the dragoons! Is it a deal, eh?"

"It's too cold here, Pete. We won't be able to return fast enough — you could freeze —"

"Good God, not Partridge! With all the bloody alcohol that's been in my veins? I'm frost-proof by now!" Then he took a long drag, and the bluster left his voice as he added, "All but my stupid toes, eh? — the deserters."

"You've got to make the effort to keep moving, Pete —"

"But I just have, you know." He said it with a quiet finality that chilled Seth more than the frost of the glacial night air.

"Pete, please —"

"It's no use, old boy. Out of petrol. Anyway, this isn't so bad a spot. Wasn't really cut out for marriage, you know — not my cup of tea —"

"We can make it, Pete. Just a few hours back to that cave at least —"

"Good God, the bloody stench would kill me sooner than this air! Look at those stars, eh? Can almost reach them from here — Go ahead, Seth. The sooner you start the faster you'll make it back. I'll wait. Don't worry —"

His throat was too choked for Seth to continue the argument. Why was there never anything to say or do when it seemed most desperately urgent to speak and act?

"The blackguard — all this time I felt so sure I'd get him — and now he's got me — serves me right, I suppose. The bloody ape just wants his freedom, doesn't he? All I ever really wanted myself, you know — Jane's a good girl though, I won't deny that. Tell her I said so, will you?"

"You'll tell her yourself, Pete." He unrolled his own bedroll, easing Peter's feet and legs into it, dragging the rest over his backside, then using Peter's roll as well, so that he would be doubly protected. "Keep under wraps, you hear. I'm going to give you a shot of morphine — to help you sleep. We'll get back as fast as possible —"

"No rush, old boy. I feel fine."

I'll bet, Seth thought, injecting the needle into Peter's arm.

"Hang on, Pete."

"Right! Good luck, friend. Cheers!"

"Cheers," Seth replied, but he had to say it with his face turned.

CHAPTER 35

ALL that night Seth walked, climbed, and clawed his way back toward camp. A gale wind followed him off the icefall providentially seeming to hasten his journey, though more than once he slipped and almost disappeared into a crevasse yawning before him as he dug in his ice pick and clung to its shaft. Then shortly after dawn he saw traces of the camp he had left — was it a day, a month, or a year ago? Time had lost the ordinary dimensions of its interludes here. They seemed irrelevant. He thought only of Peter, and each plodding step became half an eternity. He fired distress flares, hoping the Sherpa would see them, and come up to meet him halfway! But either he was not watching, or chose to ignore the call. Seth shouted with all his strength, but only the mountains answered.

Then instead of becoming brighter with dawn, the world darkened, and turning Seth saw the sky behind him leaden with storm clouds. It started to snow. Softly at first, unforeboding. But soon the flakes thickened, the snow turned to hail, angry pellets of ice falling stonelike, obscuring everything, cutting visibility to barely one hundred feet.

He reached camp to find his Sherpa sleeping inside the tent. He kicked angrily at the man's boots.

"Get up — we've got to — go back!"

The lashless Mongoloid eyes blinked, and the flat hairless face smiled in innocence, asking, "Tea, sahib?"

"No time," he said. "Hurry — Peter's back there — frostbite —"

The porter scrambled to his feet and peered out of the tent, tugging a knitted cap over his ears, blinking into the snow.

"Bad weather, sahib — no use for climb."

"Never mind the weather! He's dying up there — don't you understand? He can't move! His toes!"

"Must wait for snow to stop, sahib — maybe one hour, maybe two."

"Too late," Seth shouted. *"Now!* We've got to go right now! This minute! *Now* —"

The man looked at him as if he were stark raving mad, calmly grinning, shaking his head, tolerantly smiling. He would not move!

"Right now, damn you!" Seth shouted, clenching his fists, lurching at him, but the Sherpa simply stepped aside, and his fists hammered futilely against the unyielding ground. He lay there too exhausted to utter another sound. He closed his eyes. . . .

The snow and hail kept falling, till it covered his body entirely, inching up slowly like bath water trickling into an empty tub, lighter than water though, colder, marrow-freezing cold, seeping its frosty flakes into the core of his bones, the hail pellets like clots of blood in his arteries, filling his lungs . . .

Peter, he tried to shout, but his throat was too full of snow to resonate. *Peter!* He kicked his legs, pushed at the icy ground with his arms, shouting, "Peter!"

The sound of his own voice woke him, and opening his eyes, Seth found himself seated erect inside the tent, staring at Hodge.

"Where is he?" Hodge asked.

"Oh, my God — what time is it?"

"Almost noon. We just got here. Where's the Yeti?"

"What?"

"The Yeti," Hodge repeated. "What's happened to him? Did you bastards let him get away?"

"Peter's on the icefall! He's frostbit. *Hurry!"* Still bleary-eyed, Seth rushed out of the tent. The snow was falling, though lighter. "Hurry, we've got to save him!"

"Will you stop blabbering long enough to tell me what in hell's happened to that Yeti? I've been on forced march for more than a day — and instead of finding you on the trail, you're flat on your ass, fast asleep! Now you tell *me* to hurry! Where did you see him? How close did you get? Why aren't you still up there, after him?"

"I told you — Pete's toes — they're frostbit! I had to leave him. He's alone up there. I came back for help —"

"You let the Yeti escape to come back for help?"

"Of course," Seth replied, more shocked than Hodge was by the fact that he seemed to find that so shocking. "Pete was unable to move —"

"But what about *you?* Couldn't you track him alone. Are you such an idiot that you don't realize we may never pick up his trail now — especially after this snowfall? Boy, that is using your head, Professor!"

"Didn't you hear what I said about Peter?"

"Don't worry about Partridge, buddy. He can take care of himself! This is the first time we've —"

"I told you he *can't!* He can't *move!* Don't you understand what that means — up there, at those temperatures!"

"Stop getting yourself in an uproar! If you were so damned worried about him, why the hell didn't you start back before now?"

"I would have, if he —" He glared at the Sherpa, who quickly busied himself, turning away. It was as senseless blaming him as a yak! "I was too exhausted — I fell asleep."

"Well, good for you, buddy! Now that you've had your beauty nap, let's get cracking! Maybe we can still pick up some part of his trail —"

"Is that all you care about, that stupid Yeti?"

"Right now, you're damn right it is," Hodge shouted, his eyes as cold as the icefall itself. "I know you don't, buster! You don't have to tell me — I've watched you try to sabotage this expedition from the day you joined it! But I've sweat my life's blood organizing this hunt, and now that a Yeti's finally been sighted, if you think you're going to fuck me out of finding him — the way you've tried fucking me out of everything —"

"You are a lunatic," Seth whispered.

"We'll see who's crazy around here, Professor! Get moving. You take us to where you found that Yeti — right now!"

"I'll take you to Peter, God help him, if he's still alive!"

Starting up the slope again required the mustering of very special energy by Seth, a distinct and conscious exertion of will on his part, for his blood and muscle cells, all his reflexes, every pore of his being, craved sleep. He understood well how Peter must have felt last night, and knew he had done the kindest thing by letting him remain where he did, but only prayed he had not waited too long to return. Pasang and Hodge accompanied him. Together they would be able to bring Peter down, and after that Seth knew he could sleep! The other Sherpas refused to join the rescue mission, terrified of probing too close to the Yeti's domain. Yadev said he was too tired to leave the tent.

The fresh snow covered last night's tracks entirely, and reaching the icefall, Seth was startled to see how remarkably different it looked! He paused and removed his goggles. Like a rotating stage, it had been transformed entirely after the briefest lowering of the intermission curtain.

"Here? Was it here?" Hodge asked.

"Good God," he muttered, feeling sick. If only he'd left some markers on the trail, cloth strips tied to pitons driven into the boulders — three or four would have sufficed to lead them directly back to Peter's resting place! He'd never imagined it would snow so hard so soon, obliterating his tracks entirely.

"Well, where *did* you see the Yeti?"

"Nowhere, damn you! We found his cave! We followed his tracks!"

"Where's the cave?"

"I don't know." Every cluster of leaning seracs looked identical to him now! Anyway, the entrance would be covered by snow. The crucial problem was finding the swiftest passage to Peter!

"Maybe this will help you remember, Professor!"

Seth turned to find Hodge's drawn pistol aimed at his midsection.

"What the hell are you trying to prove, Hodge?"

"There it is — outraged innocence! Always the virgin, aren't you, Goodman? Pure as the driven snow! My ass! I'm on to your tricks! I know what you're up to! You think you're going to steal *him* away from me too, don't you? Just the way you stole her —"

No, I've never known him, Seth realized, feeling as though a steel band locked around his head as he stared at Hodge's hate-filled, terror-filled eyes — one of those thick forehead bands worn by ophthalmologists, only it was inside his skull. He would waste no time arguing now, not one second, not one syllable for self-vindication. He glanced contemptuously at the small gun in the hand

286

of his erstwhile friend, the great Pacifier, the great Civilizer, unique to modern man! It was so subtle and sophisticated a weapon that people like Pasang, Seth knew, looking now at the startled and confused expression of the gentle sirdar's face, didn't even understand how to use it. No savage, no barbarian, or tribal had ever learned to arm himself with so mighty a portable machine of total destruction. That took a special sort of mentality, a peculiar kind of talent, a very modern kind of restless craving for control, for power, uniquely avaricious hunger, above and beyond all the natural instincts for self-preservation and self-protection that drove even the tiger to stalk his prey and kill. It was the eloquently silent last word that ended all arguments about the relative merits of Civilized and Uncivilized ways of life, the uncomplicated Might that made Right, the final Court of Individual or International Appeals — when all else fails to win you what you want, Shoot!

Seth shook his head numbly, and trudged on, probing at the ice under the fresh snow in front of him, walking like a blind man using his cane to feel the ground ahead of his feet.

"That's it, buddy — just keep moving! Don't get any wise ideas, understand? Don't try and reach for anything in your pockets or I'll blow your balls off, you sneak! I know your kind! I'm on to you, lover!"

He did not reply. He did not look around at Hodge, who kept taunting him, trying to provoke him just enough to be able to work up the courage, the righteous indignation, the beautiful justification of self-defense, to allow him to shoot with that clarity of conscience which vouchsafed the bliss of sleep to killers the world over. Unwittingly, he had allowed himself to fall prey to Hodge's lust for blood. Seth sensed now that that was the real motivating force behind this expedition, not all the high-flown talk about science and contributions-to-knowledge, the socially acceptable rationalizations that had even sufficed to lure him into this madman's trap of blood-and-power lust, of craving for command, for self-assertion over any and all things that came within the ambience of his reach. He felt more like the Yeti now than he had last night when emerging from the lair. Somehow in the twisted dark recesses, the tortured convolutions of Hodge's brain, Seth suspected that this fantasy transmutation had actually occurred, that for Hodge he was now what the Yeti had been all these years of waiting and planning — the beast to be captured and subdued, otherwise killed. He understood better now why Hodge had been so diligent about seeking him out, seducing him to join the hunt, convincing him to come this far! His own vanity, his own curiosity, his own stupidity, had deceived Seth into believing that it was actually his talent, his special knowledge of the area, his climbing ability, which Hodge wanted, for which he'd pursued him so avidly. He knew better now. It was the challenge his independence posed to Hodge, the repudiation of Hodge's superiority implicit in Seth's refusal to continue to follow his lead, accept his direction, after the war had ended, the rebuff to Hodge's ego, which his personal and professional successes, meager and mixed though they were, came to represent. For what, after all, had Hodge of the Great Plans, the pompous pretense, and incredible promise, really accomplished since the war? Nothing he tried ever quite reached the mark he set for himself — no enterprise, no human relationship. In five years he would be fifty, and fifty was too late to begin all over, to start once again to prove himself.

"Sure you're leading us right, lover? Better not try any phony dodges, kid! I've got your number! I know what you want, you jealous bastard!"

"What's that, Hodge?" He asked it very softly, feeling no hatred for the man whose brilliance and strength he admired so much once, the pilot he would have followed unhesitatingly to a flaming tailspin grave when he was twenty-one, his twin brother in love and war! What wild joy, what terrible trial hadn't they shared at one time, Hodge the Mac and Seth the Man? He felt only pain now, hearing his erstwhile alter ego sinking deeper into the quicksand of madness.

"You want all the glory of catching him for yourself! I know you, Goodman! I know you a lot better than you think, buddy! You're trying to screw me out of this victory — now that you've seen him! Now that you realize it's true, and the name Hodge McNeill will be immortalized — you'd like that for yourself, wouldn't you? And not just the fame either — I know you Jews — you want the money, too! Well, think again, kid! I'm onto you!"

"You're wrong, Hodge," he said.

"Don't turn around! I warn you — I'll pump every one of these bullets into your balls!"

Seth bit his lip and turned back to the jungle of ice boulders over which they had tortuously started. If only there were some rational argument, some way of convincing Hodge still of how insane a delusion it was! He felt the band tightening around his brain, as though it were crushing the cortex itself. He had to pause for breath, rubbing his hand across his forehead, closing his eyes from the pain of sheer exhaustion, the strain of chopping ice steps, while trying so desperately to think of some words that might save them both —

"Why should I want to screw you out, Hodge? I never did before —"

"You did with Rena! I told you I was marrying her! You knew that before you laid her, you prick! You did it to spite me! You were so jealous, you even lied yourself blue in the nuts to her, didn't you? You told her you were in love with her —"

"I am."

Hodge roared with laughter. Seth grimaced, controlling his impulse to turn then, to try to grab the gun, for perhaps the laugh meant he was starting to reach him — to bring him back with a lifeline of words. He did not want to risk breaking that now by lunging for the pistol.

"Bullshit! You're not ready to marry her, and you know it! You never will be, you sneak thief! You just did it to screw me out, because you knew I was!"

"No, I didn't, Hodge!" But it burst from him so suddenly, so furiously, with such loud insistence, that Seth felt himself trembling, and for the moment he was not so sure which of them was mad. It was as if, with the blinding lucidity of madness, Hodge had indeed revealed more to Seth about himself, and the ambivalence, the paradox of his own motivations, than Seth was willing to admit. He felt as he had when, poised before his third dive, the curtain was torn from his consciousness to show him a room he preferred to keep darkly hidden. The pain he experienced now was no longer commiseration for Hodge alone. He thought of Rena as well. Of Stella. Of Ethan. Consciously, willfully, since their trek from Kathmandu had begun, Seth had managed to defer thinking further of all three at once. He carefully separated his thoughts about each, the way he had of Anita all these years — they existed on different planes of cognition for him, discreet entities, whose coexistence thus became possible. But now again they were locked in irresoluble conflict, and the challenge of Hodge's assertion that he was not ready to marry Rena and never would be echoed in Seth's mind less as the invective of a lunatic than a question posed by his own soul.

Seth climbed another boulder of ice in silence. The more he repeated that question of intention to himself the more troubled he became at the realization that his mere attempt to ignore it, and his ability to defer its resolution till now were alone testimony pointing to the accuracy of Hodge's conclusion! How could he abandon Stella and Ethan, after all? On what grounds, by what code of moral justice, would he ever be able to defend such action? On grounds of love, he replied, by the code of selfishness! For he loved Ethan surely as much as her, but that was hardly as gratifying a love. And he loved Stella too, but that was more painful with all the mutual tragedy and frustrations it embraced, all the guilt and irreparable loss. Rena's love was pure delight to him, pure beauty, pure joy. What could be more selfish? Nothing, he thought. She is the one luxury you can never afford! No more than you can be twenty again, he told himself. No more than you can marry Anita now! Hodge was right! Amazingly enough, the madman had pierced all the impenetrable fog of Seth's deepest self-deception, and his prophesy was revealed as true!

Hacking his way over the last of the seracs, tumbled like giant lies across his path, left behind him now, Seth emerged onto the open platform of glacial ice that stretched straight and clean as truth itself on toward the peak of Ama Dablam. His arms were limp from the exertion of using his axe, his legs numb, his mind sick with weariness, his body bent with fatigue — or is it age? he wondered. He felt beaten, spent, defeated. Hodge wasn't the only one who could not begin all over again! He'd made his contract with life — with Stella for life — long ago. He could no more break that, than he could stop the earth, or his own pulse —

Yet just then, thinking that, the very ground beneath him collapsed, and Seth fell into a crevasse, whose treacherous gaping scar had been concealed from his sight by a fresh layer of thin ice! His reflexes were so slow from fatigue that he did not even attempt to belay his fall with the axe pick, and before he could so much as shout for help he was swallowed up, falling into the nothingness of oblivion below!

I love you, Rena, he thought. It was the one thought to cross his mind as he plummeted, a free-falling body, destined for instantaneous death!

He was, in fact, so certain that his end had come, that he did not try in any way to brace himself, to hunch up, to bury his axe on the inner walls of ice in front and back of him. He often had thought of death before, of when, of how, it might come — but never this way! The utter meaninglessness, the bizarre stupidity and waste of it all! First the Sherpa, then Peter, now himself, and for what? To teach the Yeti how to become Seth Goodman, or Hodge McNeill — to civilize the beast, and make him just like the rest of us! For the vainglorious dream of a madman! He became so infuriated at the flash of that realization that instinctively he hunched over, drawing up his legs, curling in upon himself as if preparing for a somersault —

An instant later he was wedged firm against the fissured walls of narrowing ice, feeling the frost of its viselike grip against his back and knees. He had broken his fall. He was motionless, suspended like a fetus in a womb of ice. He opened his eyes, and peered up at the fluted veins of green stalactites ringing the sky hole through which he had fallen, feeling much as a fish in the Arctic, he thought, as Pasang's face appeared above the wriggling worm of a lowered line. He managed to clutch at the line with three fingers, but could not bring his other hand into play to help thread it through his waist loop for fear of losing his wedge and sliding lower. He thought his back and shin bones would freeze solid before his single hand secured the line, but finally shouting, *"Tug,"* he hung on for dear life, and felt himself inching out.

Only then, rising to safety, did fears of death fill his mind, the full consciousness of its nearness reminding him of the unique gift of life, which instinctively he had treasured in his youth, but came of late to hold so cheaply that often he thought of tossing it aside, like a rubber ball found amidst a heap of fallen leaves near a curb-stone. Time had mutilated its surface polish, and routine mishaps had added their nicks and scratches, and use had lessened the bounce — so heave it away, Seth! Over the treetops, into the bushes, down the sewer drain — one furious fling! Watch it go! God, what an ingrate he'd become! Filled with despair for the lack of a visa! Filled with anxiety waiting for tenure! Filled with apprehension waiting for his book to be reviewed! Filled with boredom waiting for the semester to end — waiting — while life raced its course and ran dribbling with him toward the final hole hidden in a glacial icefall!

He clung with both fists to the flimsy strand of nylon that dragged him with umbilical tenacity from the womb of death, till his head emerged reborn to see a shaft of light renting the snow clouds, refracted through the mist of moisture vapor not as one rainbow alone, but dazzlingly enough as a raft of rainbows painting the sky's palette so miraculously bright that all but forgetting his still precarious perch, Seth said to Pasang, while the Sherpa struggled to drag him free,

"Hey, look at that sky!"

"Never mind the sky, Professor — keep your eyes on the trail!"

"But *look,* will you — there must be a hundred rainbows! I never saw anything so beautiful!"

"Leave that rope on him, sirdar! I think he's in shock."

"No," Seth insisted, tapping snow off his parka, stomping about smiling. "No, it was a lucky fall! I'm fine. Thank you, Pasang — you saved my life!" He embraced the smiling Sherpa warmly with both arms.

"Me glad, sahib."

"Me too — brother." Then he turned to Hodge. "Listen, Mac, you're wrong! Put away that stupid gun, will you, I've got to tell you something —" *important,* he wanted to say, because everything seemed clear and beautiful now, and it was important for him to tell it to Hodge so that he too could understand —

"Not a step closer," Hodge shouted, raising the pistol to the level of Seth's eyes.

"I do love her, Mac, and I will marry her, and I'm not jealous of you. I never have been." He said it all without advancing a step closer. Then he turned back to search for Peter.

He was not tired any longer. His head was clear. His stride was strong. He tested the ice ahead of him expertly as he moved, jumping the narrow crevasses, waiting for Pasang to rig their ladder for the broader ones. He had a premonition now that Peter was all right. Miracles happened, he saw. Peter would be saved, just as he had been. He would be sitting up, smoking a cigarette, waiting for them to come through, and when they found him — they would all return together! It had to be that way, he sensed. From now on everything was right. He would never be afraid of the truth again. He would explain it to Stella. She was a strong, good woman. She had survived a harsher blow. She would survive this one as well. Someday, when Ethan was old enough, he would explain it to him also, and maybe by then Ethan would understand it himself — the power of love, and its beauty, the unique gift of life, and how it must never be held cheaply, but cherished each moment as the greatest of treasures. He felt younger than twenty now. He was reborn.

Till he saw the axe, rising like a cross in front of the humble tumulus of snow.

"Oh, God," he whispered, stopping stone still.

"You see him?" Hodge asked.

"What's left of him."

The drift had covered Peter entirely with its white shroud. Seth ran to it and removed the crust of ice. Then taking off his gloves and getting down on his knees, he carefully brushed the snow from Peter's head with his bare hands. His face was purple, hard as granite. Mercifully, his eyes were closed.

He was not ashamed of his tears. He felt his entire body shake, heaving with sobs that all but choked him. He wished that he knew the proper prayer to say over Peter's body.

"Take care of this blackguard, Lord," Seth whispered, bowing his head, clasping his almost frozen hands tightly before him. "Bless Peter Partridge, good God, as he blessed You every day of his life. He loved You, Lord — take care of him now."

"Come on," Hodge said. "There's no more we can do for him. Let's get after that Yeti. Which way was he headed?"

Seth could not answer. He could not stop crying long enough to speak. He put his gloves back on, and started using his pickaxe to dig a shallow grave in the ice.

"Damn you, buster, did you hear me?"

He nodded, without looking up. Pasang had begun helping him dig the grave.

"Who the hell told *you* to do that, sirdar?"

Pasang smiled good-naturedly at Hodge, but said nothing.

"What is *this,* mutiny? I'm leader of this expedition! I'll give the fuckin' orders here! We've wasted enough time, you hear me? We're going after that Yeti! We're going to catch him today — God damn you, Goodman — I said stop! *Stop digging!* Or I'll blow out your idiot brains!"

"No you won't," Seth said, looking into the crazed eyes of Hodge the Mac, who sounded, or acted (Hodge had always been a good actor) more crazy than he actually was, Seth decided. Perhaps it was just the cold reality of death so close at hand that toughened him, for he felt not the slightest fear, no tremor of anxiety or apprehension, no hair of his body cringed before the ugly steel shape of that small gun. "You won't shoot up here, Hodge. The report of that pistol could start a landslide of ice that would crush us all, and you know it. Or it might open a crevasse like that one back there, the one I fell into, Hodge! I've been down there — it's a long way to the bottom, Hodge." Then he went back to his digging.

"You think you're pretty smart, don't you, Professor? Well, you're not smarter than me, boy —" He continued to rant, to shout, to assert how great he was, and all the while Seth and Pasang dug silently, till the shallow grave was done. They eased Peter's body into the hole. They covered it with a mound of ice and snow, placing his axe on top, tying a white marker to the silver head.

"Rest in peace, Pete," Seth said. Then he turned to go.

"Where do you think you're going? That's the wrong direction, damn you!" Hodge screamed. His voice was quite hoarse by now.

"No it's not, Hodge. I'm going home. The expedition's over." He turned and started to trudge off.

"Stop! That's an order!"

Seth almost laughed, the words sounded so ludicrous, so preposterous — here. But he could not bring himself to laugh so close to Peter's grave. He turned and said quietly,

"Fuck you and your orders, Mac! I've taken the last of them."

This time he walked away faster.

The cry he heard was so astonishingly inhuman that Seth believed for a split second it must have been a Yeti, till swinging on his heel, he saw it was Hodge, racing down at him mouth distended, eyes red and bulging, the butt end of his pistol raised in one fist, aimed at his skull. He caught the blow of the gun on his lower arm. It felt so sharp he suspected it must have cracked the bone, but it took the wind out of Hodge's momentum. Seth landed a blow square against his jaw. They went down together, clutching at each other, kicking, flailing out wildly with their fists, rolling over and over in the snow, panting, cursing, fighting as they had not ever fought in all the war years.

"You can't quit!" Hodge gasped. "Can't give up!" He had gotten the upper hand, and pushed his stiffened fingers into Seth's neck, trying, it felt, to push them through his windpipe. Saliva drooled from his mouth as he spoke, gasping for breath.

Then Seth brought his good arm off the ice, using what energy he could muster from lying still those few moments, to deliver a haymaker to Hodge's head, full against his ear. It sent him toppling to one side, crying out in pain, covering the ear with his own hand. Seth was on of top of him now. He pinned Hodge firmly against the ice with his greater weight.

"It's all over, Hodge," he said. "We're going home!"

"I'll kill you first!"

"No. You've done all your killing, Mac! You've killed too much!" But even as he spoke, Seth saw that Hodge had managed to grab hold of his pistol again, and was trying to raise it to firing position. Then he lost control of the rage he had tried to keep in close rein, as he gripped that wrist and started pounding it against the ice, till the fingers went limp and the pistol fell free, but he kept on pounding it hard, panting, fuming, tears burning like molten lava from his eyes, shouting, "Killer — Killer — Killer!"

Till he saw that Hodge had fainted, and could not even hear

what he said, and shaking his head dumbly he staggered to his feet.

"Help me, Pasang," Seth gasped. He felt dizzy, faint. "Help me carry him back — We're going home."

CHAPTER **36**

FOR three days they walked, back to Namche. At Tyangboche they stopped for fresh provisions, but they did not stay long. Seth was anxious to reach Namche, to find Niels and Bruno, and hire porters for the trip to Kathmandu. Hodge did not try to stop him. Since their fight on the icefall, Hodge had kept to himself, keeping his own counsel as well, saying nothing to Seth, who made no attempt to draw him out. He suspected that Hodge was biding his time, waiting for Bruno to reinforce him, hoping perhaps that together they could overpower the Jewish usurper and get back to the hunt. But at Namche they learned Bruno was dead.

"He can't be," Hodge said.

"Yes, he has died," Niels assured him.

"But — how? Where?"

Then Niels told of it, of the call of the Yeti, and Bruno's effort to reach him from the cornice.

"But, you heard *him?*" Hodge asked. "You say you heard a Yeti! How far from here? Take me — ?"

"I never go back there," Niels whispered. His hand was still swathed in bandages. He was sallow from loss of blood.

"We'll go together, Niels," Hodge insisted eagerly, his eyes burning.

"We're leaving tomorrow," Seth said, "for Kathmandu." He had been welcomed at Namche by all the relatives of the Sherpa who died. They offered their services if he wanted help returning home. Pasang's task this time was more one of weeding out the applicants than searching for help.

"You'll regret this, Goodman," Hodge swore. "You're going to pay — for doing this to me! Not just to me — to Tony! It's his money you've robbed —"

"That's enough, Mac!"

"Oh, no! Buddy, I haven't started on you yet — you'll pay for this the rest of your life! Your grand-kids will still be paying, Goodman, if you don't bug out — but right *now!* Today! I mean it, buddy! I'm warning you! I'll sue you in every court in America! You're not going to rob McNeill blind and get away with it! You can't steal all this property, and ruin our chances of catching him just when we're ready —"

"Stay by yourself, Hodge, if that's what you want!"

"Oh, no! You're not getting rid of me *that* easily, wise guy! I'm leader of this expedition, and if you come to your senses and admit that —"

"Hodge, I've come to my senses! You're not leading anything anymore, but your own crazy life as far as I'm concerned! Get that through your head and keep it there!"

"Judson'll put a lien on your salary the day we reach Delhi! You won't have a red cent to your name —"

"Shut up, Mac! Shut up before I make you — because if I have to again, so help me God —" He wished now that he had left McNeill to find his own way back from the icefall, to die there as poor Peter had on that barren plain of frost. It was a cowardly wish, he knew, but Seth felt more afraid of Hodge's threats of judicial retribution than he'd been of his drawn pistol. Relatively sane as he was now, McNeill seemed far more formidable an adversary, and in the dim recesses of his mind Seth suspected that what he said about T.J.'s reactions to his usurpation of leadership and of the expedition's property was probably more accurate than anything he could possibly hope for. Not that he had paused to consider such mundane matters till now. He had done the only thing he could have done, without worrying over consequences, but he knew very well that after the smoke settled, from the distance and tranquillity of Delhi, nothing would seem quite as simple as it did up here! All the parasites of civilized society would come to plague him there, after they got back, the Lawyers, the Accountants, the Officials, the Keepers of the Records! Whenever this much money was wasted there were bound to be many people waiting to pounce, seeking to find the culprit, someone to pay the piper, someone to take the blame! And with Mac to point his finger in one direction only, what would be more logical, more probable, more sensibly sound, than to pick Seth Goodman as their fall guy? He felt a shudder of apprehension, a foreboding sense of harassment, law suits, financial ruin, professional and personal disgrace. Even if no court of law would believe Hodge's testimony in preference to his own, and he was not really afraid of that, the mere process of trial, the legal expenses, the time and wearying months of wasted effort involved, would all but ruin him. His sabbatical, what remained of it, would be eaten up entirely by precisely the sort of trivia and civilized ritual Seth hated most. The publicity of any major suit would embarrass his university, undermine his effectiveness as a teacher. The foundation, which sponsored his research project this year, would want to know what on earth he'd been doing in Nepal on the money they had granted him to embark upon a study in Orissa. He would, of course, be obliged to return that grant — but how? He tried, almost frantically, to remember how much money they had in their savings account. Stella kept all the financial records, the bills and checks, the bank books. He suspected there was about fifteen hundred dollars stashed away — or was that their balance *before* the refrigerator? The plane tickets alone cost more than twice that amount! Thinking about money always depressed Seth. Now it frightened him too.

Hodge seemed to detect his enemy's anxiety. He looked and sounded much stronger. "I'm going to ruin you, Goodman! Hand over the keys to that strongbox, kid, and give me back my pistol — it's your last chance! I won't press any charges if you do as I say — right now!"

It all seemed so clear and simple up there, when his life hung by a single rope in the crevasse, it all seemed perfectly obvious and beautiful! How had it become such a sordid mess again?

"I said *now!*"

"Go to hell, Mac," he whispered. "Come on, Niels, let's see how Pasang's doing with the provisions. I'll need your good hand, friend! Think you're up to the walk back?"

"Yes, yes, I will manage all right. I am also eager now to get home. We should leave before it starts to snow again.'

"We will, pal. But we won't rush it this time. I figure we'll take about three weeks to Kathmandu. That should bring us out of the rugged weather zone after a week, and then it's just a matter of endurance."

"You would make a good Dane, Seth," Niels told him, grinning.

"And with that beard, man, you make a great one!" He felt better already — dismissing the bleak prospects of the future from his mind. He was busy enough worrying about the present. They left Hodge alone.

The trek back took longer, but it was a more leisurely journey, and the good weather held. Each day they woke at dawn, climbing and descending for two hours, pausing for breakfast, then climbing several hours more, till early afternoon, when they stopped to swim, or to fish, or simply to lie in the sun, to regain their strength, to mend their bodies and minds, to forget the tragic waste of their futile search, to relearn the values of life, the simple satisfactions of everyday living. Seth and Niels were like children at play outdoors, studying natural life together, catching small game, photographing birds more rare and beautiful than any creatures they had ever seen. They became closer comrades with each passing day, the bonds of shared tragedy forming a solid base for the friendship built upon their mutual interests in nature, in climbing, in the wildlife so profligate all around them. Niels talked quite freely to Seth about his years at sea, about ports he remembered in Africa, about his illness there, and the life he lived in Copenhagen. He even spoke without too much remorse about Ulla. He was not afraid to go back now, he vowed, to try in some way to pick up the threads of his life again, to carry on. Seth told him all sorts of things about Nepal, about village and tribal mores, about the peoples they met, whose hospitality was so gracious, so generous, though they had almost nothing themselves. It was like a story he remembered his father telling, one of those old Yiddish tales from Sholom Aleichem, about the poor Jew who slept on a bed of straw in a tiny hovel but always welcomed strangers to share his room for the night, explaining, "When there's room in the heart, there is room in the home for one more." He told about his parents, too, of their struggle for survival through the Depression years, of his mother's love and arduous devotion to her children, of all the sweetness, all the tender attention she lavished on them, through nights of illness, in days of carefree health — till her own strength was drained entirely, and her heart gave out before she was forty. He told of his father's patient sacrifice then, of the years when the old man seemed eternally alone, unable to speak to anyone of the troubles that often clouded his gentle eyes with tears, of how he stared so mournfully from the window for hours, and how if asked he would sigh and shake his head, saying in a choked voice, "Boys, I just was thinking now about Momma." He could tell Niels anything. Only he did not talk of Rena.

Hodge did not talk at all. He ate alone. He walked alone. He kept supremely to himself, like a monarch dethroned, but still regal in his proud isolation. He stood always apart from the rest of them, Sherpas and sahibs alike, as though it were the only way left for him to assert his primacy, his true command, like a bull elephant, a tusker, standing aloof, standing guard, while his herd of cows and children huddled against one another at the sign of approaching danger. Watching him so haughty and proud, Seth often wished there were some bridge left by which he could reach him, some magic formula, some word, something he could do or say to erase all that had happened this past month, to transport them miraculously back to those halcyon days of their youthful friendship. Hodge the Mac, he wanted to call, get over here, you bastard, I'll tell you a good joke I just heard! It was no more possible than wishing that Peter were alive would bring him back to their decimated ranks. The expedition had taken its toll, and part of it, Seth knew, was all Hodge had been to his life. It was really what made him join in the first place, hoping to recapture that untamed and deathless *joie de vivre,* that Damon and Pythias brotherhood they had known. He felt like a Siamese twin eternally separated from his brother now, who had been destroyed by the operation. There could be no going back again, ever, to Seth the Man and Hodge the Mac.

Yadev brought them to Mandeva the day they reached Kathmandu. The General seemed distracted, preoccupied with weightier problems. He listened impatiently to Hodge's protests, his requests that Goodman be detained in a Nepalese prison till there was time to decide in Delhi what might best be done about his illegal actions — he rose from his cluttered desk, and spoke with control.

"This is not in my hands, McNeill. What you say may well be true, but I have no jurisdiction over such matters. You will have to settle your dispute after returning to Delhi. There is a plane leaving in two hours. I can see to it that you are all accommodated on that — if you wish?"

"The sooner the better," Hodge replied, saving his thunder for ears that were more keenly attuned to the nuances of American law.

"Very well — Yadev, you will escort them to the airport."

"Thank you, Excellency."

They started to leave.

"Did you see anything specially — *peculiar* — up there?" Mandeva asked, almost as an afterthought it seemed.

"Damn right," Hodge said. "Some of our Sherpas saw the Yeti, and we all heard him — several times."

Mandeva smiled indulgently, as though he were by now quite inured to such reports.

"Anything else?" he asked. "Any large-scale operations of any sort — any Chinese?"

"What?" Hodge looked stunned. Seth turned mutely to see that Niels was equally surprised by this question.

"No, Excellency, much-much snow, but nothing unusual," Yadev reported.

"I see." He sounded relieved. "I didn't think there was, but — we can never be sure of anything in this world anymore — can we? No, there are many mysteries," he muttered, talking now to himself. "Well, gentlemen, have a good trip home. I'm sorry you failed."

"I'll be back, General," Hodge said. "Next year!"

Mandeva's smile was as tolerant as his soft reply.

"Perhaps so, McNeill. I wish I could say with as much certainty that I would be here then. But time will decide that for us — won't it?"

Leaving the palace, Seth wondered why he had asked about Chinese operations. There was no time now, however, to unravel that mystery, for Pasang was waiting to be paid, and their last hours in Kathmandu were almost as hectic as their first had been.

The heat haze of Delhi airport welcomed them home without luster. There had not been time for more than a cabled message to

T.J., which Hodge insisted on sending, alerting him to their time of arrival. Seth could not speak to Stella or Rena by long-distance phone at this point. He had waited this long. He could wait another few hours. They touched down at Delhi shortly after two P.M., and were surprised to find Sinha waiting with Tony to greet them inside the customs barrier.

"Welcome home, chaps," said the Air Marshal. "Let's go into this lounge here, shall we? We can talk without being disturbed there, Judson."

"Lead on, Marshal. This is your home base, not mine. Sorry to hear about Peter and Bruno, Hodge, but the rest of you boys look fine. That's quite a beard you've grown, Larsen!"

T.J. sounded different, Seth thought. He even looked different, more dignified, more official somehow.

"What about our provisions and things, Tony?" Hodge asked, looking a bit apprehensively at the luggage.

T.J. smiled reassuringly, and Sinha laughed. "Don't worry about a thing, old chap. We've got you cleared. The baggage will be waiting in my car, you see — it's all been — arranged."

They entered a room furnished with a long table and many soft armchairs, like the boardroom of a modern corporation. There were several decanters of clear water on a tray filled with sparkling glasses. There were even some modern paintings by Indian artists to brighten the walls. None of them had imagined so elegantly furnished a room existed at this airport. None of them had seen any sign of it during the frustrating, heat-and-sickness infested hours of waiting for clearance here the first time they'd arrived. The room was actually air-conditioned!

"Well now," said Sinha, taking the seat at one end of the table, while Tony made himself comfortable at the other. "Do sit, won't you, chaps. Any place you wish will do. Would any of you care for some refreshment? Some whiskey perhaps?"

"Don't mind if I do, Marshal," Tony replied. "Scotch and soda, if they have it."

"I should think that can be arranged easily enough." Sinha pressed a button under the tabletop, and the door behind him opened, a uniformed Sikh appearing as swiftly as the genie at the rub of Aladdin's wonderful lamp. He saluted, took their orders, saluted again, and disappeared.

Seth had ordered nothing, but poured himself a glass of water, to be certain he was not dreaming all this. The water tasted real enough.

"I expect you chaps are wondering what this is all about, eh? Judson, perhaps you should explain —"

"Fair enough," Tony said, placing his arms firmly on the table-top, looking from one set of eyes to another as he spoke, his voice quite deep, more richly resonant than it used to sound. "This is a debriefing for you men. I realize this will come as something of a surprise to you, Hodge, but I happen to be employed — well, let's just say I work for our government — in intelligence. And the Marshal here is coordinating this operation for us as India's official liaison. I might just say, Marshal, you've done a damn good job for us at this. We hadn't anticipated the snag presented by Indian Airways, of course —"

Seth felt his jaw dropping as he listened, looking to see if Hodge was equally shocked by this monologue, finding his expression, if anything, more amazed, more stunned.

"The purpose of your mission, men, was naturally exploratory. We've had soft data for almost six months now indicating that the commies have been planning to set off a thermonuclear blast in Nepal — somewhere around the locale you've been reconnoitering. Damn hard, as you boys know, to get any firm data from up there under ideal conditions. Trouble is, of course, that since Mandeva's palace coup last year he's blocked all our attempts to get in there and find out just what the hell those Chinese Reds are up to. Don't know if you had a chance to see the old bird himself, did you, Hodge?"

"Mandeva?" Hodge's voice was barely audible. He looks, Seth thought, the way I feel.

"Mmm — General Mandeva. He's number two man to the King in theory, but actually he runs the whole show. Got the damned army sewed up. Pretty shrewd old bird, except for his fool blind spot about us and India. Doesn't have sense enough to understand the Reds have been using him as their puppet, keeping him all riled up about how we're trying to subvert his power, how India's trying to take over his miserable country, and all the while they're sneaking up behind his back door, getting ready to blow the whole damn kit-and-keboodle sky high!"

"I don't understand," Seth said, not that he understood anything else T.J. had said more clearly as yet, but this seemed the first point of logical contradiction which he could question. "If they're trying to use him — to use Nepal as their puppet — why would they want to blow it sky high?"

"Mmm. I can see how you got to be a professor, boy. Had us confused for a while ourselves, that point. But it's not good enough to use our sort of logic when you're dealing with Mao and his crew. They've got pretty twisted motives in Peking, I can tell you that much — could tell you a few more things would set your teeth chattering, but no, that's classified. The point here is, what they're trying to do, the Chinese Commies, is get themselves a site rigged in Nepal, relying on Mandeva to prevent us from stopping them, and touch off their blast, which the Russians will think was set by India, since Nepal has always been under Indian protection, get it? Then the Chinese shout for help, charge Indian aggression, and move their damn troops down from Tibet, smack through Nepal and India to knock out India's iron-and-steel focus in southern Bihar! Then when we threaten to retaliate with our nuclear payload, the damn Russians join Mao, instead of warning him to keep hands off neutral India, and — hell, boys, after that you've got me! Then it becomes anyone's ball game."

The logic of his involuted reasoning, the simplicity of his statement, which was so farfetched, so incredibly Machiavellian in its triple deciphering of someone else's double-twist thinking, the awful conclusion he drew from the remarkable premise he posited, left Seth too dumbfounded to speak. He felt an involuntary shudder pass through him as T.J. continued.

"But that's where you boys come in. Naturally, we can't let the Chinese escalate us up to a stand-off confront with the Russians on this business. We've got to make damn sure we know what in hell's going on up there, because if those Reds have started building that pad we sure as shootin' don't intend leaving them finish it. Hodge, did you see anything looks like a launch site?"

"No, nothing," Hodge whispered. He still sounded like a person in a trance, in deep shock.

"Any sign of sizable numbers of Chinese moving about, old chap?" injected Sinha. Hodge looked at him blankly, shaking his head in a negative direction. "What about you others? Larsen? Did you see or hear of anything suspicious?"

"Nothing of what you speak now."

"That's good. Professor?" Seth shook his head mutely. "Well, Judson, I must say — this *is* rather encouraging, you know?"

"Sounds damn good to me, Marshal, but let's have a look-see at your big maps. I want these boys to show us just what terrain they've covered."

"Naturally," Sinha said, and pressing his button again, he ordered the maps. The Sikh brought in their tray of mixed drinks, saluted, and left, promising to bring the map portfolio immediately. "Ah! Well, chaps, I think we can drink heartily now, don't you? Cheers!"

"But why didn't you tell me — any of this before, Tony?" Hodge asked, leaving his drink untouched.

"Dammit, boy I would'uv liked to, but the problem there, you see, was — well, as I said before, the Marshal and me — well, we've tried sending our own people in there for about four or five months now, you see, and damned if we've had any luck with Mandeva. He must have a sixth sense or something, that character. I don't know how in hell he's done it, but he's smelled every one of them out! Even used a lie detector on one team we thought sure would get past him! Anyway we decided — Mmm, this here's good Scotch! Try yours, Hodge, you look as if you can use a drink —"

"You decided — ?" Hodge said, waiting for Tony to continue his suddenly long-winded explanation.

"Oh, yeah! Well we decided to send in a team of — well, amateurs —"

Idiots, not amateurs, Seth thought, biting his knuckle hard. Idiots was a better word for them.

"— people like you boys, of course, who wanted to go up around that Khumbu region, to explore around there, if possible, for *something*. I'll admit to you now, when the Chief suggested that one, I sure as hell never thought we'd be lucky enough to find anyone like you, smack on our target! You know what I mean, Marshal — they're usually headed for one particular mountain peak, and that's all."

"Oh, quite! Yes, it was rather jolly good luck, that you chaps happened along when you did! I must say, McNeill, I suppose if you hadn't thought about going after that fool Yeti, we should have been obliged to get someone to offer a prize for searching him out —"

"Right," Tony chortled. "We'd'uv had to get some of our Madison Avenue people to work up a campaign on that one!"

Hodge backed away from the table as they digressed to talk about what alternatives they would have found to his expedition. His face had gone white as the snow of Ama Dablam.

"You dirty son-of-a-bitch," he said, rising and staring at Tony as he stared once before, Seth remembered, up there on the icefall. "You fat, miserable —"

Sinha had pressed his button. The Sikh was already headed for Hodge, coming swiftly around the table.

"Calm down, boy," T.J. warned.

"You used me like a fuckin' bathmat, like — like a piece of shit you'd find in the gutter! And you tell me to calm down?"

"I must warn you, McNeill," Sinha said, rising, "if you don't get hold of yourself, old chap, and sit quietly, I will have no alternative but to place you under arrest!"

"Oh, *Christ,*" Hodge groaned, his face blazing crimson as he trembled with suppressed hatred, fury, futile frustration, and shame. How he managed to keep himself together, to hold himself down, when every pore of his body seemed ready to blow up higher than a nuclear mushroom, was something which Seth found almost as hard to understand as the story he'd just heard Tony Judson tell. If he doesn't crack now, Seth thought, he may live to be a hundred!

But Hodge did not explode further. He simmered, he boiled, he cursed, mostly under his breath to himself, and then he covered his face with both hands, and cried. He cried like an infant constrained to lie in his crib, hungry, waiting for food, unable to rise from his back, unable to sit, stand, or crawl even — unable to speak one intelligible word. It was painful to watch. It was nerve-racking to hear. Poor bastard, Seth thought, now they've even taken his dream away. Hodge would not go back to Kathmandu for a Yeti hunt next year. Even for him now, Seth knew, the expedition was over.

"But didn't — didn't it ever occur to you," Seth asked, surprised to hear himself talking so clearly, in so unstrained a voice, to Tony, "that some of us — maybe *all* of us, if you really believed that the Chinese were doing what you sent us to see if they were — maybe every one of us would have been blown up, or — or killed?"

"I'm afraid it did, yes."

"*And?* Is that all you've got to say, Mr. Judson? That you were afraid it did?"

"I told you, Professor Goodman, the risk involved in this particular operation was total. We couldn't let personalities — personal factors — enter the equation. In balance —"

"You make it sound like a mathematical formula," Seth said, shaking his head incredulously.

"In a certain sense, if you like, it is. We've got to weigh the total equation. Our risks in the operation are your negative. But there are other risks too, much greater — potential thermonuclear war in this instance — that go with inaction. Balance the loss of life incurred in this instance — two — against a possible two million lives, or potential two hundred million — and there's your equation. I'd say we've come out of this one on the plus side."

"Good God," Seth whispered, feeling almost as cold as he had in the crevasse of solid ice. "Good God, mister, you are as heartless, as ruthless a man as anyone I have ever had the misfortune of meeting." He said it softly, because he felt very much afraid of Tony Judson, far more than he had ever felt of Hodge McNeill.

"I'm sorry you feel that, Goodman," T.J. replied, absorbing the insult as he absorbed everything, like an enormous mountain of solid granite and ice, impervious to rebuke, to challenge of any kind, invulnerable to threat, without feelings, it appeared, even vaguely resembling those associated with the run-of-the-mill human species. Seth could not help but feel a strange sort of fascination, watching Tony Judson now, almost a grudging admiration for this man's remarkable capacity to divorce himself entirely from human sensitivity. He felt as though he were looking at a unique breed of mortal, the sort of man capable of ruling the modern world, thermonuclear civilization's master button-pusher.

"I can only attempt to assure you, Professor," the stone wall continued, "that if the other side *had* begun with the operation we've outlined —"

"You're no better," Seth whispered. He felt himself trembling now. Poor stupid Peter Partridge, that blackguard, didn't even know he died a bloody hero to save mankind from some lunatic's dream of what another lunatic might have been dreaming about!

"I beg your pardon," Tony said. "I didn't hear that." He cupped his ham-sized hand to his pig-sized ear.

"I said," Seth repeated, talking louder, "you're no better, Mr. Judson, than they are! God help the rest of us dumb bastards — someday you intelligence men will blow us all to kingdom come!"

Then he finished his glass of water, because he felt very thirsty.

"Thanks for the drink, Mr. Sinha," he said rising, "but I won't need your ride. I'm going home now — I prefer to go alone."

"Wait, Seth," Niels called. "I come with you."

CHAPTER 37

RENA spread the lotion with her forefinger over the pale skin of her inner thigh. She worked slowly and carefully at perfecting her tan, as a fine cook would in basting a turkey. Most of her body was by now beautifully bronzed, except for the inner thighs, and of course the narrow strips hidden by her bikini. There really was not much hope about tanning the bikini's silhouette, since people were always about, especially whenever she decided to emerge for a sun-bath. But she did want the rest of her skin done to an even shade of brown by the time Seth returned. Soon he will come back to me, she thought, smiling up at the afternoon sun. It was fierce, unrelenting, deliciously hot, like the sun of Tel Aviv and Kinneret. When he comes, we must go there — together, she thought. That helped make the waiting less difficult.

Rena opened her eyes and gazed across the pool. The Indian boy, who had brought out her air mat, was still staring at her. The moment she looked at him, however, he pretended to be busy arranging some beach chairs. He was quite a handsome young man, with sensuously full lips and large sleepy eyes, his naked torso powerfully muscular, but sly as a snake, and obviously stupid. She wished he would leave her alone. All the servants at Maharani's were obnoxious! They followed her every move, strolling around the garden, walking on the veranda, entering and leaving her room — they were always watching, waiting for the faintest signal from her! Bah, she hated them all! The guests were even worse — especially the fat maharaja, who arrived a few days after Seth left, and had made her life miserable ever since, with his importunate proposals of marriage and offers of increasingly lavish gifts! Pig, she thought, closing her eyes, lying back to bask in the sun. Seth has spoiled me for any of them! She smiled secretively, thinking of his warm embrace.

"Miss Gold, I must talk with you."

For a moment she thought it was a nightmare, something she heard in a bad dream — the voice was the one she dreaded hearing most — Stella's. She opened her eyes. She sat erect, blinking anxiously. Yes, it was Stella — standing over her.

"What is it?"

"It's about — my husband."

She said it so portentously that Rena jumped to her feet alarmed, gasping, "What? Has anything happened to Seth?"

"Not yet." Stella kept her hands clasped tightly in front of her. "I haven't much time, Miss Gold. I'm going back to work now, and I've left my son at the school, because I must see you — and talk —"

"Talk," Rena said, so relieved to learn that Hodge had not killed him — it was her constant dread, the nightmare that woke her repeatedly — that she felt much calmer than Stella appeared to be.

"I don't need to beat around the bush, Miss Gold. You know why I'm here."

"What does it mean? Bah! How should I know?" She shrugged, and decided to lie down again.

Stella sat uneasily on the edge of a sunchair at her side, feeling her disadvantage more keenly, Rena sensed, as she eyed jealously the tan body before her. She was so plain, wretched, and haggard, this woman, that Rena could not for the life of her understand why Seth had ever married her.

"Very well, if I must be explicit — I know you've been having an affair with my husband." Stella swallowed so hard after that sentence, Rena thought she would choke. She almost laughed. She is so typical the American woman, Rena thought, wondering how on earth Seth put up with her for one moment.

"Didn't you hear what I said?" Stella asked, as if she had expected Rena to die from her accusation!

"Of course. Does it seem to you I am deaf?"

"I know too well what you are!"

There was no finesse about her, no feminine grace or charm, nothing soft. "What am I?"

Stella locked her fists, and for the moment could not talk, her mouth was clamped so tightly shut, but then she blurted out, "You're a cheap little — slut, who sleeps with other women's husbands!"

She sat up again, shielding the sun from her eyes, looking coldly into Stella's. "How *dramatic!* How romantic a woman you are!"

"I see," Stella sighed, sniffing. She clutched a handkerchief in one fist, touching it to her nose. "So you're going to deny it?"

"What? Deny what?" Rena felt her blood boiling. She was so furious that she practically spit the words into that swollen-eyed, ugly face. "That I am a tramp? A whore? What? What word do you use just now — *slut?* It means the same, not? My English is not so good as you! Of course not, but this much I think I can understand! Yes, I deny that! Completely! It is — *ugly!* Ugly, ugly, ugly, and hateful!" She was trembling uncontrollably.

"But —? You mean — I'm wrong? It wasn't you? I could have sworn —? That's why I kept waiting so long to — to speak? I didn't want to accuse you unjustly, Miss Gold, but after all these weeks when you haven't spoken to me — the way you've been avoiding my eyes even — I felt sure!" She said it with lips quivering, sounding as mawkish as a magpie, looking as though she were ready to get down on her knees, to beg Rena's forgiveness.

"No, I don't mean that at all!" She felt like shouting it at the top of her lungs so that every guest, every servant at Maharani's would hear her, and know once and for all that she could not be had by any of them. But she spoke with tensely lowered voice, her eyes aflame. "Of course, I have slept with him! I love him!"

Stella recoiled as though she'd been bitten by a snake, as though poison or acid had been flung in her face. *"You* — love?"

"Love, that's right! I know it is for you hard to understand! You think it means marriage only — something connected with a piece of paper — a — a certificate! You think it comes from a court, not? You are wrong! You have never known its true meaning, I see that in your eyes. You have never felt it — here — inside! Never in your miserable, ugly life —"

It was a sharp blow, a stinging slap to her cheek, but more startling than painful in its impact. Rena felt herself jolted, stunned to sudden silence. But she did not utter a sound. Not one tear dropped from her eyes. She realized more fully now how superior her strength was to that of this wretched woman. Then she laughed. It was a lusty laugh, her battle cry of victory. And as she laughed harder, Stella cried more bitterly, pressing her eyelids so tight that they wrinkled like scabs of horror over her stained cheeks.

A faint cry of pain trickled through Stella's lips, like the squealing noise of the ram's horn, ending Yom Kippur, the Day of Atonement. Like the whining wail of the widows shrouded in black and hunched double behind the screen in the synagogue, the partition that hid their wretched forms from full view of the Torah. Remembering such abject creatures of womanhood huddled like crows in the narrow stone lanes of Jerusalem, wailing that way as they beat their flat breasts, Rena stopped laughing, and angrily shouted, "Go to hell with your slapping and crying! You have nothing to *say* to me! Leave me alone — let me enjoy the sun!"

"No, please — I must talk to you!"

"You call this talking? Oh-h-h-hch! Go — go back to your work — whatever you do, it needs you more than me!"

"Rena, I beg of you — listen to me! I won't do anything violent again, I promise! I — I couldn't help myself, but please let me speak — hear me. It's as important to your life, Rena, as it is to mine — it's about Seth."

"What about Seth?"

"You don't know him as well as I do, Rena."

"I know all what I need to know about him. I love him, and he loves me!" She watched Stella closely as she spoke the last sentence. Its impact was reflected in a sudden contraction of her adversary's brows, a convulsive tightening of her grip upon her lap, but this time no tears, no violence, no insults. She merely lowered her eyes, gulped, and waited, then looked up again.

"Rena, how old are you?"

"Almost twenty-one. You think it means I cannot love?"

"Certainly not. You may not believe it, but I was also very much in love when I was twenty-one. You know with whom? Seth."

"Och!" Rena turned aside and reached for her cigarettes on the pool deck, extracting and lighting one. "Why should I not believe it? Do you think I would love a man, who is not desired by other women? Yes, of course, you loved him — but I will tell you the difference between us, Stella — *he* did not love you!"

"Did Seth tell you that?" She asked it so softly that Rena was uncertain she heard.

"What?"

"Did Seth tell you he never loved me?"

"What do you mean, tell? In words? No. But a man does not have to tell such things — I know from how he responds to me. I intuit him. I feel how he loves me. He cannot love two women this way. So much I know, even at my age!"

"Yes, I know that too," Stella said, gnawing at her lower lip as if she were determined to bite through it. "I know he's stopped loving me, Rena. I wouldn't be here if I didn't know that. I even know it's as much my fault as yours. Oh, you're a beautiful girl, Rena, I don't deny that. You're much more beautiful than I ever was, and you're much younger now, and —"

"I don't need you to tell me this! Why are you saying it?"

"Rena, I'm not an idiot, and I'm not blind — that's all I'm saying. I've known from the first day I saw Seth look at you that this was going to happen! Even before he knew, long before he would have dared to admit it to himself, I *knew* — because I know him, Rena. God help me, I know him better than I've ever known myself. And still I love him," she gasped, smiling sadly. The tears had started again, but she seemed oblivious to their flow. "Yes, I know that surprises you. You don't believe I'm capable of it, and I un-

312

derstand why, because I'm going to admit something to you, Rena, that I've never admitted to anyone before — until this past week I would have agreed with you. Ever since I lost the baby — "

"Which baby?"

"I had a miscarriage. It was followed by a hysterectomy."

"Oh, I didn't know."

"Ever since then I've thought of myself as a woman no longer capable of love. I felt more dead than alive. Every morning I woke wishing I were dead, and every night I went to sleep praying I would not have to wake again. Can you imagine what it means to feel that way? No, of course you couldn't. Why should you? You're young and beautiful. You have everything to live for — everything. Your whole life is in front of you, Rena, and how wonderful it must seem to you now — how glorious and enchanting and full of dreams — I know how mine seemed when I was your age, and I never had your gifts —" she paused, closing her eyes, as if trying to recapture that spirit of youthful wonder. "For a long time now, everything seemed to be behind me, Rena. It was all past tense. I was dead inside, but I didn't have the strength to take my own empty shell of a life and destroy it. I thought it was only for Ethan's sake that I continued to hang on to life — because he was so young that he still needed his mother. For a while I hated Seth. I blamed him for the — operation. Then I became indifferent to him, and we lived under one roof, but we were strangers — total strangers. I used to think that if only he went away and left me alone I would be able to function better, and feel happier perhaps. I'll even be more honest with you, Rena, and admit that when he left for Nepal, I hoped I would never see him again — I thought it wouldn't matter — that Ethan and I would be much better off alone."

"But now?"

"I told you — I still love him." Stella's eyes were suddenly bright, almost beautiful through the gleam of bitter moisture.

"I don't understand. What has happened?"

"I'm not sure I can explain it. I don't really know. It's — like a miracle. The way blind children suddenly seem to be able to see — have you ever noticed that? I work with them now every day, and at first they appear to be so utterly lost inside themselves, so completely isolated in darkness. You talk to them and they don't respond. You touch them, and they only shrink away from your hand. You try every possible game to draw them out, to tempt them to smile, but nothing works — and then one morning you come and even before you've said hello they look in your direction, and open their arms, and run at you — just as if they could see!"

She brushed the tears from her cheek with the backside of her hand before continuing. Her smile was radiant. "Something like that happened to me, Rena. The second day after he'd gone, Ethan woke before dawn from a nightmare. He was crying for his Daddy when he came to my bed, and I had to tell him Daddy was far away, and wouldn't be back for a long time. And I kissed him, and held him in my arms, and sang him some songs, till he stopped crying, and fell asleep again. Then I thought of what it would mean if Seth really never came back, and *I* started to cry, and — ever since then I've —"

"What do you want of me? Do you think I have missed him any less than you?"

"I won't presume to answer that," Stella replied. She was well controlled now, her temper totally in rein. Only the thin, high pitch of her voice betrayed the effort of will required to maintain that semblance of poise. "Perhaps you do love him —"

"Only *perhaps?*"

"Very well, you do. I'm willing to believe you believe that, Rena. I'm not as old or wicked as you think. I know that physical attractions can be very powerful —"

"Och-h-h, it is not simply physical! You think I can love any man I find handsome? There is much more in Seth — there is — so many things — I don't know to describe them! Why should I have to explain myself to you?"

"Naturally, you don't have to. I'm the one who must try to explain, Rena — myself, and Seth — to you."

"Maybe I know him better than you! You have yourself admitted you lived together as strangers —"

"Only the last few months. For ten years before that we were man and wife — and our marriage was no less successful than most. At times it was the most beautiful — but you're not interested in that. You must be interested in Seth though, in knowing more about him. Rena, he's not an easy man to live with."

314

"You think I only want what is easy? You don't know me, not at all! I am Israeli, not American! For us, life has never been *easy!* It has always been tension, and struggle for mere survival, never knowing when the end must come — maybe now, maybe tomorrow — try to live and work under the sniper's bullet, you will understand what I mean. *Easy!*"

"I'm talking of a man, Rena, not a way of life. He'll tire of you just as he's tired of me. And others. Yes, there have been others — for six months, a year. It's true of his work as well — he's wanted to give that up a dozen times — though no one could have loved it more when he began, and he's still brilliant at it — maybe that's why. No sooner does he seem to master something than he — turns away from it, loses interest — I don't know what to call it, but I've seen it happen often enough now to understand. I suppose that's why he went on this crazy hunt."

"I am not afraid I will lose him," Rena remarked, smiling coquettishly.

"To you he's just another conquest, isn't he?"

"Och!" She glanced at her tanned body, touching her thigh, feeling how silken soft, how warm it was.

"Are you prepared to marry him, Rena?"

"Who cares about marriage? This is all what American women think of! To me it is love that matters —"

"You mean *sex,* don't you? Why keep calling it love?"

"Is it so different?"

"You are a hateful bitch, after all, aren't you? I thought for a few minutes — I almost believed —"

"And what are you, tell me?"

"A mother — a wife," Stella whispered, shaking her head dumbly as she stood up. "I thought I could appeal to you as a human being — to leave me to try as best I could to put the broken pieces of my family's life back together — to make us something wholesome again —"

"So, now do you expect me to cry? First you curse me, then you want me to kiss your hand?"

"No, believe me, Rena, I don't expect anything of you anymore."

"What are you to me that I should sacrifice my love, my own

happiness, for yours? This is what you ask, not? My happiness and Seth's too! All for your selfish, ugly, dried-up —"

"It's wasted, Rena. I won't give you the satisfaction of striking you again. And I won't cry anymore, or beg you. That could only touch someone with a heart — and I no longer think there is one under that bikini!"

"You go to hell!"

"I'm sure I will now. I expect we all will — including Ethan. Oh, my God —"

Then she did cry. She could contain herself no longer. She covered her face with cupped hands, and her body shook like the room in a building next to one that had just taken a direct hit from a bomb. Her voice was like an infant's, as helpless, tortured, and tormented. Watching her Rena could think only of the air raids that had shaken Jerusalem in her childhood, and the nightmare terror that plagued her so many years afterwards, waking to scream in a dark empty room, covering her ears, closing her eyes, yet never exorcising the sounds of death, the vision of her own parents buried under rubble that had taken their lives, while sparing her own, a room, a wall away. She was no older than Ethan then!

"Will you stop it! Stop making that ugly sound! Go! Leave me alone!" Stella ran from her side.

Yet even after she was gone, Rena could not rid her ears of those hideous screams — were they her own, or Stella's? She could not be certain anymore. She felt herself dragged back to that haunted world of eternal emptiness and loss, where nothing would ever look the same again, not the sun, or flowers, or a human smile, and no song would sound sweet. *Aba, where are you? Ema?* Where have they both gone, God? Why them? Why did it have to be *my* parents? Were any two people more loving? More devout? Could any man have praised you, Lord God, more beautifully than my father? Were any of her friends' mothers more loving and kind?

Rena tried to lie back, closing her eyes to the sun. She tried to close out that nightmare as well, yet even Seth's face became somehow confused with her dead father's, and sitting up, terrified, she moaned, "Aba, why won't you come back to me?"

Then blinking her eyes open, with the sun still playing its shadow tricks and the water shimmering green, she thought she saw Seth lying there under the green dust of the rubble, his open eyes flecked with plaster — Seth and Stella beside him. Horrified, Rena jumped up, and raced away from the pool. She ran across the garden as fast as her legs would move. She was panting when she reached her room. She went inside and locked the door. She threw herself onto the bed, and cried, trying to stifle her tears with her pillow, but nothing she did would make them stop. Till at last she fell asleep.

The knocking awoke her. She sat up, startled to find she was still in her suit, the pillow still moist from her tears.

"Who — what is it?" she called.

"Rena, it's me — Seth."

She thought it was still her dream. She ran to the door, opening it with trembling fingers. He was there.

"Oh — is it truly *you?*"

"It's me," he said, holding her now so firmly that she had no more doubts, thought no more thoughts, dreamed no more hideous dreams.

He kissed her — was it once or a million times? Every inch of her body he kissed. And she kissed him with the same hunger, the same all-encompassing passion. They embraced. They loved. As though trying in their first moments, their first hour together, to make up for each second, each day, each week, of eternal separation. They were madly intoxicated with each other's bodies, like the first couple ever to taste the beauty of human romance — they fondled, they relished, they discovered each other anew. They wasted no moment, no breath, in speech. Till both of them lay panting for breath, laughing into each other's eyes, their faces streaming with the sweet sweat of life, of love.

"*Anee ohev otakh,* Rena."

"*Anee ohevet otkha,* Seth *shilee!*"

"What does *shilee* mean, Rena?"

"*Mine!* It means you are mine, darling — always, forever!"

"Yes — it is a good word. How do I say it then?"

"The same way," she said.

"Rena *shilee?*"

"That's right!" She raised her head and now looked at him more soberly. "What happened there, Seth?"

317

"Terrible things," he said. "I will tell you everything, Rena, later."

"Yes, of course, much later," she agreed, smiling.

"No. I mean — now I must do something else." He sat up and started to dress. She felt cold.

"Are you going to see — her?"

"Not Stella," he said. "They told me at the desk that Stella and Ethan are at school — she works at a school nearby —"

"I know."

"I must go to see Jane now. Peter's dead."

"Oh, my God!"

"Yes, and Bruno too."

"And Hodge?"

"Alive, but not very much more — he's broken."

"It sounds awful. Seth, are you — ?"

"Do I seem weak to you?"

She ran to kiss him again, and he lifted her in his arms, swinging with her wildly around the room, till she screamed, "Put me down! I'm so dizzy! I can't breathe! You are strong as iron, darling!"

"I feel strong, Rena. I have to be — for you. Did I tell you how beautiful you look?"

"No! You see how neglectful you are?"

"Past tense," he promised. "No more, Rena — from now on, never again. That much I promise for the moment — will it suffice till I get back from telling Jane what I must?"

"I will hold my breath for you, my darling."

He kissed her again at the door, and hurried out to keep his promise to Peter, to tell Jane of how he had spoken of her with his dying breath.

Rena twirled, arms flung wide, joyously around by herself after he left. She stopped to look at her image in the mirror. Her hair was quite wild, but she had never looked so divinely lovely. It was hardly surprising to her, after all! She had never felt more beautiful, more completely and utterly in love. She laughed at her visage and started to toy with her hair. She put it up, and stood back, appraising herself, then she let it drop, and seductively pulled several strands of hair across her face, under her nose, posing as the femme fatale par excellence. She was irresistibly alluring! She

318

would keep him happy for at least one hundred years — perhaps even more! She sensed inside her, in every vibrating blood cell of her body that she would never grow old, not too old for Seth to love.

Then she heard the knock again, and could hardly believe it — he had gone just five minutes ago, it seemed. He was even more wild to return to her than she was for him to come back!

She flung the door open as wide as her arms, saying, "Seth, come —" but then her heart froze, her tongue went dead in her mouth, her limbs felt ice cold. She backed away from the door, in abject terror, too shocked to scream. "Hodge," she whispered, terrified, "don't —"

He slammed the door, moving toward her.

"Weren't you expecting me to come back to you, Rena?" he asked, lunging at her body. . . .

CHAPTER **38**

LOTTE felt life for the first time that morning. Just when she'd begun to fear the worst, that something had gone dreadfully wrong (for though she'd grown heavier, it was inert unmoving weight, like a tumor silently expanding inside), she felt the motion of life. The faintest quiver at first. The slightest meek ripple of a strange stirring inside. The timid awakening. Like the twitch of a muscle, yet where no muscle had ever moved before. She waited breathless. Then the message came to her again. Like a song sent from a distant, unborn star, its melody still unheard. Only the rhythmic pattern begun, the first fragile step in the dance of life.

Can you feel me, Mother? Here I am, it seemed to say, making the world more beautiful by its mere motion. Yes, I feel you, little one. I *can* feel you! Do not fear. I will protect you with my body. She wished Bruno were here now. She was eager to tell him. She felt very proud and strong, imbued with the miracle of life.

Then she saw Niels approaching her, like an apparition, his face ghostlike, his pace terrifyingly tentative.

"But what has happened to Bruno?" she cried.

"Lotte, I am sorry —"

"What has happened?"

"Please, Lotte, sit down."

"What? Why don't you tell me?"

"He suffered no pain."

"What does it mean?" Though she knew then, but could not keep herself from screaming, "Why don't you answer me? What has become of my Bruno? What — ?"

"Bruno is dead, my dear."

"Ay-e-e-e-e," she cried, stifling the shriek of pain by biting into her finger's flesh. The baby too seemed to know for he did not move now, but lay perfectly still in her womb, locked tight as a closed fist.

"He talked only of you the last days," Niels said. "Of you and the baby, Lotte. He wanted that you will be brave and take good care of yourself and the baby, and I promised him I will do whatever I can —"

"No, but — it has — he has just — just today — come to life!"

"Ah, that is wonderful!"

"But I wanted Bruno — I wanted to — to tell him. And now I will never — he will never — never —" she buried her face in both hands, shaking uncontrollably, violently sobbing.

"Please, my dear, you must now be specially brave, for him as well as yourself."

"But how did it happen, Niels? Why?"

"I can only tell you how, Lotte." He sat then beside her on the porch of the bungalow, while the sun played with shadows of foliage flitting across his face and hands as he spoke, making him look almost like Bruno, scarred and ravaged by the shrapnel, pitted with the plague that was war. And remembering then all the agony he had endured, the shame, the tortured years, she became calm, knowing at last he had found the escape, the release from bondage, he'd sought.

"Yah, so that is what has come of his dream — a grave in the snow?" she whispered, after Niels had finished.

"He was not afraid to die, Lotte."

"This I know."

"Lotte, I would like," he began, reaching out to touch her hand with his trembling fingers, "if you will let me — if it is not too late — for us —"

"Hush," she said, drawing her hand away, not in anger. "No, please, Niels — do not speak so to me — now."

"Forgive me. I — it is just that I want you to know, that if I can ever — if you should ever need me, Lotte. I leave with you my address in Copenhagen, and someday perhaps — after the child is born —"

"Yah, maybe someday I visit Copenhagen."

"Where will you go now, Lotte?"

"To my father's home."

"May I escort you there?"

"No, I — I do not go alone," she said smiling.

"Then here," he said, handing her his card. "Whenever you are ready to visit — I will be there. I wait for you, Lotte. You will see, when you come — it is a most beautiful city."

"Thank you, Niels. You are a good friend to us."

"I have never been a godfather, Lotte. Perhaps, if you will permit me — ?"

"I will write to you when we have settled again."

He rose to leave, but hesitated, staring at his feet, groping for words.

"Have you thought, Lotte, of what you will call him?"

"Of course. Bruno." Then she felt him move again, as though he had heard his name and answered her.

"God keep you both, Lotte, my dear."

"And you — Niels." She closed her eyes after watching him go, and sat very silent, waiting for the next sign, the next stir of life from within.

Jane had returned to her room after breakfast and sat reading the travel guide to Britain, which she'd found at a bookstall in Connaught Circle the day before. She felt by now as though she knew Sussex better than Delhi, and had made lists of all the places of interest within a radius of twenty miles of Partridge Green. There was Brighton, and Beachy Head, and Horsham, and Steyning . . . There was a knock at her door.

"Just a sec! Who is it?" She slipped into her shoes and hearing no answer, thought it was that nuisance of a dhobi coming to ask if she had any clothes to wash. "Sorry, I don't —" she began, opening the door.

"Hi, Jane."

"Seth? My God, Seth, are you —? When in God's name did you —? Where's Peter?"

"May I come in?"

"Oh, gosh, sorry — of course! I feel so — look at me, will you? I'm shaking like a leaf! Good God, did you ever —? Where is that blackguard of mine? I'll murder him for not calling!"

"Jane, I'm — please sit down, will you?"

"*Sit!* Are you mad? I can hardly keep from flying — What's keeping him? Is this one of his stupid ideas of a joke? *Where —?*" She rushed out to look over the veranda, but came back instantly. "Seth, what is it?"

"It's Peter," he whispered, obliged now to sit himself, unable to stand facing her exuberance, the naked glow of her excitement and eager expectation.

"Wh — what about Peter? Why hasn't he called? Where the devil has he — gone? I don't understand, Seth. Didn't he come back with you — on the same plane? Why —?"

"No, he didn't."

"Why in heaven's name not? Don't tell me it's one of those typical Indian bureaucratic goofs again! Where is he? I'll call the embassy —"

"Jane, Peter's dead."

"— or the Ministry —" she said it from the sheer momentum of her words, just as she kept the phone pressed to her ear even after his message registered in her eyes. He had never seen eyes widen so suddenly, gaping tearless at his face in utter disbelief. Nor did they move or blink or become any smaller as she put down the phone slowly, deliberately, and pursed her lips to a thin red line of defiance, and continued to stare at him.

"What did you say?" Her voice was all but inaudible.

"He's dead, Jane."

"You're lying to me."

"I wish to God I were."

"You are lying! You — you must be! You must —"

322

"Jane, try to control —"

"It's a lie! I know it is! I know it! Now tell it to me, Seth — because that's not a joke! That is not in the least bit funny, you bloody idiot! Can't you see, that isn't funny?"

He lit a cigarette and held it out to her.

"Seth, why don't you talk to me? Why don't you tell me where Peter is? Why hasn't he come back to me? Has he found someone else up there? Why are you looking at me that way? What's happened to Peter?"

"He got frostbitten, Jane — we were on an icefall together. He couldn't make it to camp, and by the next day, when we got back to him, he was —"

"Oh, no! No-o-o-o! Not Peter! Not my Peter! No, it can't be true! He was all life! He couldn't possibly — *die.*" Her entire face trembled, as though a hurricane had started inside her body and seemed ready to shake her apart, making her voice vibrate as she twisted her fingers, turning them till he thought they would jump from their sockets, still her eyes remained distended wide, and though they filled with moisture, she would not blink the tears from her lids, but kept staring at him, like someone petrified by a vision that turned her gaze to stone. "I won't let it be true! I won't let it happen, do you hear me? Do you?"

"Jane, you've got to get hold of yourself, or —"

"If he's frostbitten, he'll lose a few toes — is that what you're afraid to tell me? I'm not afraid to hear that, Seth. I'll nurse him! I will. I'll stay with him every instant! Seth, where is he? Is he hospitalized in Kathmandu? Is that where? I'll go to him — right now. I'm ready! Just tell me where I can find him? For God's sake — tell me!"

"Jane, it's no use. Peter is dead."

"Oh, but — but we were going to be married," she cried, and all her defenses collapsed; like a sudden avalanche, the rolling, tumbling race of tears came pouring out, and she staggered, fell in a heap on the floor, shaking, throbbing with anguish.

"Jane, his last words to me were to tell you how much he loved you." He thought she hadn't heard that, or if she heard, that it made no impact, but at last she looked up.

"Did — did he — did he say that — truly?"

"Truly."

"Good God," she whispered, "that bloody blackguard —" She rose and walked unsteadily to the dresser, to open her purse. She took something out of it that looked like a gambling chip. She brought it slowly to her lips, kissing it, crying silently now. "Oh, Peter — Peter Partridge — Peter —"

She was still calling his name, like the soft chanting intonation of a prayer, as he tiptoed out of her room.

CHAPTER **39**

SOMETHING had seized hold of him up there in Jane's room, some dark premonition, some terrible dread feeling of anxiety, *something* — Seth knew not what, but it hastened his steps down the stairway, it gripped him like a chill fist closing around his heart, it shortened his breath, made him start to run, almost knocking over a startled bearer carrying a tray, almost toppling himself as he tripped on the edge of a scatter rug, crossing the lobby, dashing out to the veranda, the wind stirred by his racing body making the bamboo-slatted sun blinds flap furiously in his wake — running back to her room.

"Rena!"

He shouted her name long before he had reached her door.

"Rena!" He called it again, louder, trying the doorknob without waiting for her to answer.

It was locked. He heard her voice from inside, her muted cries. He heard sounds of struggling, shuffling, choking. The blood pounded through his body like a ramrod of stone pounding against plywood. Like a hundred-and-eighty-pound sledgehammer he crashed solid against that door, and it splintered, sprang open, reverberating like all the kettledrums of hell bouncing wildly off that wall, thunder crashing so loud he thought his head would explode from the sound of it alone — and from the sight he now saw!

"I didn't do nothin'," Hodge said, creeping off her prostrate naked body, like an untouchable leper, creeping on all fours like a drooling hyena moving away from his carrion feast. "I — I didn't —" he kept muttering as he crawled away, his eyes no longer able to focus, swimming vacantly, his mouth dripping blood. His pants were open, his shirt torn.

Seth lifted him by the hair of his head. Clutching the hair in one fist, he lifted Hodge to his feet, and holding him stiff-armed, like a dead rooster held up by a butcher, raising his feet clear off the ground, Seth smashed his other fist into that blood-stained mouth and jaw, sending Hodge hurtling against the wall. He sank like a rag doll, sagging, dropping back to the floor.

His heart was pounding blood spots into his eyes as he turned to go to her. His head was spinning like a wheel sprung loose from its axle on a racing car, rolling, wobbling wildly down a steep slope, vibrating with pain, bouncing, crashing like all the dishes clattering out of the pantry on a ship with no gyroscope in a typhoon.

"Rena," he whispered, bending over her, touching her arm gently.

"No, please," she jerked away, as though her entire body were seared with third-degree burns, and the lightest touch was torture.

"I love you, Rena."

"Oh, God." She covered herself, trembling as if she had a high fever, pulling the sheet hastily, ineffectually over but part of her ravaged body, huddling into herself, sobbing like an animal mortally wounded, gulping for air, yet seeming to choke.

"Rena, shall I get — a doctor? Are you all right? Did he hurt you?" *Did he hurt you?* He could have strangled himself for asking her that. He felt himself strangling.

She mutely shook her head, gnawing at her fingers, sucking at them with infantile desperation, seeking solace in some way from the wounds that left so few visible scars.

"Please speak to me, Rena? Just to let me know — that it's going to be all right? It will be all right soon, darling — won't it?"

"No." She trembled as she said that, burying her head under the pillow, shuddering so hard he finally realized she was in physical shock, and hastened to cover her with blankets, with clothes, with anything he could find in that room. It looked like a room gutted by a monster army, a horde of plunderers. He did not recognize it as the room he had left only a few minutes ago. No more than he

325

recognized her. He stared wildly at his reflection in her mirror, and thought he saw the dazed image of a madman. He felt himself going mad, moving his lips without making a sound, piercing the callused flesh of his palm with his tightly pressed fingernails, his ears deafened by the soft groans, the faint cries of animal pain issuing from the tortured mouth of the woman he loved.

"Didn't do — I didn't — nuf — notta —"

Hodge's imbecile grunting reminded Seth of how sane he still was. Looking down at that heap of groveling flesh, rags, and dung, that thing less than human now, which once bore the name of a man, Seth hurried to the phone.

"Desk," he told the operator. "Is Klug there? Yes, I do. This is an emergency! — Klug, this is Goodman. I'm calling from Miss Gold's room. Come with two of your servants at once — there's a body in here — no, it's — it was — just hurry!"

Then he picked up the phone again. "Room service," he ordered. He told them to send hot tea, and sandwiches, and also to hurry.

He went to the bathroom and soaked one of her towels, turning the taps on full in her tub. He went back to her, placing the cold towel gently against the back of her neck.

"Ow-w-w!"

"No, this is good — you'll see, darling. Just trust me, and lie still. This will help."

"But I don't want — help! I want to die!"

"Sh-h-h. No more of that, Rena. Keep covered. You're warmer now, aren't you?" She was coming out of it, he felt, as he was — slowly.

He heard the hurried footsteps on the veranda.

"Gott im Himmel, what has happened here?" Klug asked, looking anxiously at his broken door.

"It's over there," Seth said, pointing to Hodge's incoherently muttering form. "Have your men take it out of here, Klug — better keep a guard over it till you can get a hospital to take it away."

"But, but isn't it — isn't he, Mr. McNeill? Ach!"

"It was," Seth whispered, unable to look at the sack of filth as the servants carted Hodge from the room.

"And — the lady?" Klug inquired, with delicacy. "Is she — ?"

"The lady is fine," Seth said, hurrying him out so that he could close the door — as far as it would close.

Her bath was full. The water soothingly warm. He shut the taps and returned to her bedside.

"Rena? Darling, I've drawn a hot bath for you. It will help — you feel better. Let me put you in —" He stooped to lift her, carefully, gently.

"That's all right," she said, sitting up, but keeping the covers tightly wrapped around her, looking so strangely vacant, so bewildered, soulless, lost, that he thought he would cry out in agony at the mere sight of her once shining eyes. "I will manage — alone — thank you."

"Let me help," he insisted, going with her to the bathroom, bolstering her by the arm, realizing that he was now too terrified to allow her to go anyplace, do anything, without his supervision, treating her as a private nurse might treat a helpless cripple.

"No," she said firmly, not looking at him, but moving out of his reach. "I am able — I must be alone now. I come out soon." Then she closed the bathroom door, and he heard her sobbing louder, for she must have looked at herself in the mirror.

Seth lit a cigarette and almost choked on the first puff. He snuffed it angrily, and paced across the room. He stared through the blinds at the garden beyond the veranda. Incredibly enough, the sun was shining, the plants and flowers, the trees and butterflies, were still there. He could not understand that. He refused to believe it, that the world had not turned into a dung heap covered with bile and blood, blistering, festering, with gaping wounds. How was it possible that nothing outside this room — nothing else had thoroughly, totally changed? He could not assimilate that, the continuity of life outside, the untransmuted state of nature itself, of the universe. It seemed more than incongruous. It seemed monstrously unfair!

He turned his back to the window. He forced himself to stare at her bed. He made himself confront the scene of that crime, the way he had once kept his eyes unblinking as he stared into the coffin of his mother. Look at her, his uncle said, it will be your last look. You should look now, and say good-bye! But the face of death was infinitely calm, composed, at rest. This was a different sort of death

— the death of happiness in life, the death of youthful beauty, the death of love through lust. It made him tremble with hopeless rage. It made him rush to that bed, stripping the torn and pain-wrinkled sheets, stripping the pillow case stained with that maniac's blood and spittle, working himself into a sweat of blind anger, till he found the pillow itself torn to fluttering feathers and roiling dust in his hands, choking him as he breathed in that down, which clung so lightly, yet so tenaciously to the moist-coated skin of his face and arms. He felt himself stop then, staggering back from the chaos and destruction he'd wrought, collapsing exhausted into a chair, staring vacantly at the ceiling.

I am going mad, he thought. I am going out of my mind.

He thought it almost wishfully, but release did not come to him so quickly. Madness did not erase that memory from his consciousness as it had for Hodge. It was the more poignant pain of sane realization Seth felt, the all but unbearable pain which rational cognition of what had happened here made him ponder now, and would leave him to live with till the day he died. And it would return, he knew, this scene, this room, this memory, each time he took her body in his arms, each time. It was burned like a brand of filth in the coils of his consciousness, like the grating, tearing sound of that vile word itself — rape.

I wish I were going mad, he thought. God, help me escape from this into total madness, the oblivion, the joy of insanity!

He closed his eyes and prayed for that release. But it did not come. Instead, he thought of her, visualized her, dressed in her bridal gown, walking toward the altar at which their marriage would be consecrated, and on that gown he saw the stain of Hodge's blood, the drool of his phlegm mixed with blood from his mouth, drawn from his tongue no doubt by her teeth as he forced himself upon her, forced himself into her. Involuntarily, instinctively, as a total reflex action, he started to retch, doubling over, throwing up nothing but green bile, feeling his stomach roiling and churning acid to his throat and lips, tasting the bitter sour acid as he gagged but could not throw up. It lasted more than a minute. He was panting, wrestling, writhing with pain, before it finally stopped, and he was able to light another cigarette. The smoke soothed his lungs. It helped settle his nerves, though watching the hand that held the cigarette, Seth saw it was trembling, like the hand of a dipsomaniac.

Then she emerged from the bathroom, swathed almost entirely in towels, covered by white cloth, like an invalid, whose body wounds had been dressed by a surgeon. Her face was drained, more pallid than the towels, her eyes almost blood red and darkly circled. There was a purple blotch above one cheekbone, an ugly wound that looked as if it had been made by a hammer smashed ruthlessly against the side of her face. Her hair hung limp, soaking wet, dangling like snakes from her forehead. Her lips were bruised and swollen. The transformation of her physiognomy was so radical, so horribly complete, so polar, that its impact, he knew, was immediately reflected in his own startled reaction. He actually gasped, seeing her this way. He blinked his eyes many times, as though trying desperately to make that vision of ugliness disappear, to bring back the image of ineffable beauty, which it had so brutally displaced. He swallowed very hard, but his stomach felt queasy again, and it was only by the strongest exertion of will that he kept himself from throwing up.

"Rena — ?"

"Better go now," she whispered, lowering her eyes, as though it were as painful for her to see his reaction to her transformation as it was for him to bear witness to it.

"Go? Go — where? Rena, I've come — home — to you." He tried to make it sound as convincingly honest as possible, yet hearing his own quavering voice, Seth knew he could hardly convince her of that.

"Please. Please don't speak to me now lies. Not — not now." She moved like an invalid, like a very old woman, bent as though from the scars of bullet wounds in her midsection, as though crushed by buckshot. She sat on the tip edge of a hard chair, and did not look into his eyes, staring down, or was it inward?

There was a faint tap at the door, and she jumped, like a startled, wounded animal. He had to bite his lips hard then to keep from crying at how timid, how terrified, she'd become. It was the bearer, who set down the tray of tea and sandwiches, who took one startled, gaping look at her, and left the room instantly, without uttering a word.

"Have some tea, darling, it will make you feel — better. And look, there are all sorts of little sandwiches —"

"I can't eat," she said.

"Please try, Rena — here. You must build up some strength —"

"Not now. Leave it. I will eat later — alone."

"But darling, stop talking as though I'm a total stranger — look at me, Rena!"

She shook her head mutely.

God, give me strength, he thought, for he needed to build up courage to speak to her now. He knew he would have to speak more convincingly than he'd spoken before. He would have to try to overcome that memory in her mind of his instinctive, immediate reaction to seeing her this way.

"Rena — my darling, beautiful Rena." He spoke very softly, bending on one knee at the side of her chair, whispering the words to her ear. "Rena, I love you. I want to marry you. I want to live with you — always."

She did not move, or utter a sound.

"Darling, did you hear me?"

"Yes."

Her voice alone, dead, flat, cold, was all the answer he needed, more than enough to convince him of the futility, the impossibility of expecting anything from her now, still he had to ask, painful though it was to both of them, he had to persist, saying, "Will you marry me, Rena? I'm sure I can get Stella to agree to a divorce — perhaps it can all be done here, by our Embassy."

"No, Seth," she said, and he winced at the way she said his name now, the first time she had ever uttered it as anything but an invocation of love, the first time since he'd returned to this room that she called him by any name, any reference, at all, for it sounded like the most formal sort of address, the impersonal way she said Seth.

"But why, darling? We love each other —"

"Please, no more. I beg you, no more now. I must go home myself now — to Israel." Then she turned to look at him, and her eyes filled with tears, her lips trembled. "It would not be — the same anymore — for us."

330

He could not speak without crying out, "That's not true, Rena!"

"I would gladly give my life," she said, sounding much older than him, much wiser, much more honest, "if it were not true, Seth, but it is. And you know it is. And I know. And I know that you know."

"Oh, God!" He could not bear to meet her eyes, to stare at her face any longer. He buried his head on her bosom. It seemed to withdraw from the touch, the weight and pressure of his head, yet he kept it there, for he could not look up, and he was crying now uncontrollably, like a child sobbing on his mother's breast, a man-child knowing that he would feel that softness, run to that tender love, that pillow of perfect consolation, no more.

CHAPTER 40

HE took off his shoes, sitting in the unlighted room with blinds and curtains drawn, sitting as his father once sat for seven days after the death of his mother, sitting shivah. He had no prayer book, of course, no tallith or yarmulke to wear, as he stared unseeing in the dusk-filled room to which they had first come upon reaching Maharani's, but he trusted that God would understand his unorthodox call. His heart at least was properly dressed for mourning, cleansed of all gladness, washed of all levity and joy, sanctified by sorrow. His mind also was ready for the penance it would now have to perform. Contrition had banished all pride from his thoughts, sadness filled the pit left by passion. Silently, humbly, reverently, Seth mourned for her. He prayed for Rena's salvation, for her resurrection, for the healing of her spirit with the mending of her body. He prayed with all his heart, all his mind, all his soul.

He asked no favors, no dispensations of any kind, no forgiveness, no pardon, for himself. He was unworthy of that. The pain, the suffering, the mutilation he had caused and inflicted, indirectly if not by his own hand, he could not eradicate or undo. It was too late for that. Too late for him to pay by any coin, any currency, known to earth or in heaven. He could no more escape the justice his conscience would mete out to him now, in daily doses, in portions befitting the crimes of his passion, than he could turn back the clock to that fateful hour when he answered Hodge's cable with a phone call. And though in his foolish eagerness for it to end, he had thought once, and many times after that on the long march home, that the expedition was over, Seth knew now, in a different way, that for him it could never end. Till life itself ended. Or would it darken his trail for all eternity?

He heard the footsteps just a few moments before the door opened. The light flicked on in the room, and it was like a blinding spotlight focused upon a criminal's face by his captors.

"*Daddy's home!*" Ethan shouted, rushing joyously to him, hugging his neck, screaming, "Daddy! Dad! Hurray! Hurray, Daddy's home! Daddy, Daddy!"

He kissed the boy's warm happy face tenderly, gently, trying not to let any tears escape the locked gates of his eyes.

"Seth, when did you come?"

"A few hours ago."

"Hurray, hurray for Daddy! Dad, did you catch him? Did you?"

"No, son."

"Are you all right?" Stella asked.

"I'm all right." He felt himself drowning, choking.

"Are you sure?" She looked at him more closely. "Ethan, stop tugging at your father's neck like that. You're hurting him!"

"No, Stell, it doesn't hurt," he said. Nothing would ever really hurt again.

"Well, *tell us*," she said. "What happened?"

"Everything, nothing."

"You sound — different, Seth."

"I feel different."

She looked puzzled, probing his eyes for the secrets they held enigmatically written, searching his face with that intense concentration and quiet strength of hers, that special power of patience so familiar to his memory. She looked different. Her face looked younger. She wore lipstick now. Her hair was fashionably set. Her eyes were clear and bright. Her dress was a cotton print, close fitting to reveal the fullness and not unattractive shape of her body. She looked almost lovely.

"You look good," he said, quickly adding, "both of you."

"Oh —" She blushed, self-consciously touching the fringe of her bouffant hairdo. "Ethan's been fine, thank God. He hasn't been sick a day since you left — knock wood. And I've been busy at school —"

"I'm glad that's worked out." He said it mechanically, the way most things were said, from habit, verbal inertia. Life goes on, he thought. Conversation goes on. Nature goes on. Still it seemed strangely unnatural to him. He was not quite used to that.

"Well," she said, smiling, trying to add some cheer to the gloom which seemed to exude from his presence, going briskly to the closet, removing a sealed bottle of gin she had bought. She never drank alone. "I suppose we should celebrate your homecoming, Seth, with a drink — shouldn't we? Will you call for some tonic and ice, or should I? You look so tired."

"I don't think I want a drink just now, Stell — thanks."

"Oh." She bit her lip, and deflated swiftly, setting down the bottle with a dull thud on the dresser. "Ethan dear, why don't you go outside now, and play a bit in the garden — till we're all ready to go for dinner?"

"But I didn't ask Dad if he brought me something? Did you, Dad?"

"I'm sorry, son, I didn't really have a chance —"

"Aw — gosh!"

"I'll buy something for you here — later," he promised. It was his stock-in-trade as a father, as a husband, as a son, as a lover — always promises — gifts deferred — credit drawn on tomorrow's bounty. No, he could not ask forgiveness for himself.

"Go ahead now, Ethan — be a good boy."

He went sadly, but did not complain anymore.

"He is a good boy, isn't he," Seth said, almost affirming it in surprise, as if he couldn't believe himself capable of siring anything but a scoundrel.

"What is it, Seth? What have you come to tell me?" She too sounded much older, wiser, and more honest than he. She sat quietly composed on the edge of their bed, her hands pressed into her lap, like a school girl, her unsupported back braced firmly.

"I'm going to take the rest of my sabbatical, Stell — alone." He had not realized it would be so simple to say, but thinking about it now, he sensed that in the future nothing would really be difficult for him to say either.

She kept smoothing out her skirt, moving her lips slightly while she stared at her hands trying to get all the wrinkles out of her skirt. Cotton wrinkled so easily in hot weather — you could never keep a dress well pressed very long.

"Why?" She asked it quite softly, but the faintest tremor betrayed the tension, the precarious quality of her control, poised on the brink edge of tears.

"I have to — I have to think things out, Stell."

"Things?"

"And people — us. Ethan."

"And her?"

"Who?"

"That little — that Miss Gold!"

"So you know." He was hardly surprised. Stella was, in many ways, a wise woman. She had always known him better, he suspected, than he knew her.

"Of course I know! You don't think me a total idiot, do you? Or do you? I suppose you do at that!" Her voice lost its power entirely. She covered her face with both hands, and started to cry, but then quickly regained her composure, rubbing her eyes dry, sniffing away the tears. "No! I've stopped doing that!"

"Sometimes it helps."

"No, I disagree. It's weak. It's weak and vile. It's contemptuous! It's stupid! I — we have nothing to cry about. I work every day with children — most of them orphans — all of them blind. I've come to love every one of them, Seth, as much as I love Ethan. I don't pity them anymore, because they don't want pity. They aren't self-pitying. They don't cry for themselves, and they have better reason for tears than you or I — or any grown-up, who's healthy and strong —"

He admired her spirit. She had not sounded so sure of herself, so proud, so courageous, so devoted to the work she was doing, in all the more than one decade of life they had shared.

"So, you're going off with her," she said, nodding and setting her jaw firm.

"No. I'm going off — alone, Stell."

"And I suppose you expect me to believe that?"

"Yes."

"Why? Why should I? Why should *I* be the one to have to stay here and bear all the ridicule and slander and filth and stares, when everyone else in this hotel will know that you've run off to live with that little bitch of a slut! What makes you think I'm going to stand for that, Seth Goodman?"

"Rena's going home to Israel tomorrow — alone. She was raped by Hodge less than three hours ago."

"What?" She shook her head unbelievingly, but from the tone of his voice, from the look of him as he was forced to say it, she saw it was true, and then, despite her firm resolution, she cried bitterly, with compassion, contriteness, with simple human sensitivity and shocked feeling.

He waited, unmoving, till it was all cried out of her, till she absorbed it as much as one could absorb the unwitnessed tragedy of a stranger. Not exactly a stranger, though her relationship to Rena made it somewhat easier perhaps for Stella to accept this awful news.

"Oh, how horrible," she gasped. "How awful for her — poor girl. Oh, Seth — I'm *sorry."* She went to him then, and buried her head against his breast, hugging his torso, seeking to comfort him with her warmth, her love, her gentle kindness, seeking to solace him. Even as he had sought to solace Rena.

He stroked her hair lightly, touched her trembling back with his hand, gently stroking her, trying to convey by that gesture that he understood, appreciated, her offer of help. She was a good, loving woman. She was a noble, a far better wife, he knew, than he deserved, than he would ever deserve to have.

"Oh, Seth, Seth, darling, don't go — alone. Take us with you. Ethan has missed you so much, Seth, and we — we could try — somehow — someday, Seth — we could try to learn to love again?" She looked into his eyes as she said it, and the question was there as well, in her pleading eyes, her troubled brow. "It's not too late for us, Seth — it doesn't have to be — as far as I'm concerned —"

He understood how hard it must have been for her to say that to him. He had never felt more genuinely grateful, more appreciative, of any gift of love she had ever bestowed upon him. It was almost enough to make him lie, for her sake, for Ethan's as well, to make him tell her she was right, and that he too felt it was not too late, that he did love her, had always and would always love her, that they were more than welcome to come with him. He really was tempted to say it, and he did want to — he even tried —

But the words would not come from his lips. The prison gates of his soul were all locked so tightly still that there was no way for him to reach out, no lifeline had been fashioned as yet to draw him back out of this crevasse of sorrow — how infinitely deeper it was than the crack on the ice through which he had fallen.

"I can't, Stella."

She backed away from him slowly, as though forced to wrench her arms loose from his body, as though he'd been holding her very tight, and it was only by the greatest effort of physical prowess that she could break free. Her expression hardened. Her eyes looked away. She seemed suddenly very tired as she rose.

"What happened to Hodge?" she asked faintly, The inertia of conversation, the habit of curiosity.

"He's been taken away."

"Peter?"

"Dead."

"Bruno?"

"Dead too."

"Did anyone survive this — expedition?" She said it as though it were her most hated word.

"Niels seems all right. No, actually he seems much better now."

"Well, thank God — then it was worth it," she muttered, "for Niels!" It was the only expression of true bitterness to pass from her lips.

"When will you be leaving us again, Seth?"

"Tomorrow."

"Must you go that soon? Ethan's been waiting so long to —"

"I know, but I think it's better as quickly as possible."

"I see." She stood very straight, clasping her hands so tight in front of her that he could see her knuckles go white as bone.

"But you'll sleep here — tonight?"

"Not in this room, Stella. I've asked Klug for another room."

"I see. Do you want a divorce at once?"

"No. I mean — not unless you do. It doesn't — matter to me." Nothing would really matter any more either.

"*I* want? I'm not the one who's running away from our marriage! No, I don't want a divorce, Seth! God help me for being the fool I am," she said, turning and almost smiling. "I still happen to love my husband." She bit into the bone-white knuckles.

"You're a wonderful woman, Stell."

"No, I'm not. I'm a damn fool."

"I disagree," he said, and then he did go to her, holding her shoulders gently, kissing the top of her head, feeling her sobbing, trembling body, wishing he could have said more, done more, to ease the pain of it. "What will you do while I'm in Orissa?"

"Do? Oh — I hadn't thought — I suppose we'll stay here — perhaps we can live at the school. Edwina might find some room for us there — you've never met Edwina Pearson, have you?"

"No."

"*She*'s the remarkable woman, not me. Don't worry about us, Seth — we'll manage — somehow."

Then she broke away and rushed out of the room. He heard her calling to Ethan. He almost went after them. If only he could have rushed out, one impulsive dash, one wild break through those stupid gates, one crazy, fierce leap over that stone wall — *Wait! Wait,* he would have called, *wait for me, gang! Wait for Dad! I'm home, kids! I made it home! Stella, Ethan — wait! It's me, Seth — I'm home!*

He did not think any tears were left, but closing the light, returning to the chair of his mourning, Seth found his eyes burning, his cheeks blazing and moist. He sat, and buried his tired head in both hands.